PRAISE FOR
FOUR AUNTIES AND A WEDDING

"Meddy Chan and her indomitable aunties are back in the hilarious *Four Aunties and a Wedding* by Jesse Q. Sutanto."

—*PopSugar*

"Sutanto deftly blends preposterous humor (British slang, mafia posers) with enduring devotion to prove 'there is no right or wrong way to 'being Asian.'"

—*Booklist*

"Charming, chaotic, and sometimes ridiculous, this tale will appeal to anyone who both adores and is embarrassed by their family, which is just about everyone."

—*Publishers Weekly*

"You can't help but get a kick out of the aunties' outrageous stunts and their even bigger hearts. Keep your friends close and these four aunties closer."

—*Kirkus Reviews*

"Sutanto pushes you to the edge of your seat with this suspenseful rom-com that infuses humor and heritage."

—*USA Today*

"There's a kind of magic to Sutanto's writing. . . . She tackles complicated issues of culture and family ties while also creating convoluted plotlines that'll make you squeal with laughter."

—*The Wellesley News*

"Heart, humor, and the mafia . . . this saga has it all!"

—*Woman's World*

DIAL A FOR AUNTIES

"A hilarious, heartfelt romp of a novel about—what else?—accidental murder and the bond of family. . . . Utterly clever, deeply funny, and altogether charming, this book is sure to be one of the best of the year!"
—Emily Henry, #1 *New York Times* bestselling author of *Book Lovers*

"Sutanto brilliantly infuses comedy and culture into the unpredictable rom-com/murder-mystery mashup as Meddy navigates familial duty, possible arrest, and a groomzilla. I laughed out loud and you will too." —*USA Today* (four-star review)

"I *loved* it. Whip-smart, original, and so funny. I found it impossible to put down and lost count of the number of times I laughed out loud."
—Beth O'Leary, *Sunday Times* bestselling author of *The No-Show*

"It's a high-wire act of comic timing, misunderstandings, romantic foibles, and possibly foiled heists. . . . The glue is Meddeline; endearing, capable, and in full thrall to her elders, who are all absolute hoots to keep company with."
—*The New York Times Book Review*

"If you loved *Crazy Rich Asians* and all the comedic family drama, you'll definitely get a kick out of this story." —PopSugar

"Part thriller, part rom-com, Jesse Q. Sutanto's *Dial A for Aunties* will give you the good laugh we could all use these days."
—*Marie Claire*

TITLES BY JESSE Q. SUTANTO

DIAL A FOR AUNTIES

FOUR AUNTIES AND A WEDDING

VERA WONG'S UNSOLICITED ADVICE FOR MURDERERS

YOUNG ADULT AND MIDDLE GRADE

WELL, THAT WAS UNEXPECTED

THE OBSESSION

THE NEW GIRL

THEO TAN AND THE FOX SPIRIT

VERA WONG'S UNSOLICITED ADVICE for MURDERERS

JESSE Q. SUTANTO

BERKLEY
NEW YORK

BERKLEY
An imprint of Penguin Random House LLC
penguinrandomhouse.com

Library of Congress Cataloging-in-Publication Data

Names: Sutanto, Jesse Q., author.
Title: Vera Wong's unsolicited advice for murderers / Jesse Q. Sutanto.
Description: New York: Berkley, [2023]
Identifiers: LCCN 2022046634 (print) | LCCN 2022046635 (ebook) |
ISBN 9780593549223 (trade paperback) | ISBN 9780593546178 (hardcover) |
ISBN 9780593546185 (ebook)
Classification: LCC PR9500.9.S88 V47 2023 (print) |
LCC PR9500.9.S88 (ebook) | DDC 823/.92—dc23
LC record available at https://lccn.loc.gov/2022046634
LC ebook record available at https://lccn.loc.gov/2022046635

Berkley hardcover edition / March 2023
Berkley trade paperback edition / March 2023

Printed in the United States of America
8th Printing

Book design by Daniel Brount

To Mama, the OG Vera

VERA WONG'S UNSOLICITED ADVICE for MURDERERS

ONE

VERA

Vera Wong Zhuzhu, age sixty, is a pig, but she really should have been born a rooster. We are, of course, referring to Chinese horoscopes. Vera Wong is a human woman, thank you very much, but roosters have nothing on her. Every morning, at exactly four thirty, Vera's eyelids snap open like roller shades shooting up. Then the upper half of her body levitates from the mattress—no lazy rolling out of bed for Vera, though admittedly sitting up in bed now comes with about half a dozen clicks and clacks of her joints. She swings her fuzzy-socked feet out with gusto and immediately finds the slippers she placed next to her bed with military precision the night before. She takes a quick moment to send a text to her son, reminding him that he's sleeping his life away and should have been up and at it before her. He is, after all, a young man with a whole world to conquer. Late mornings, Vera believes, are only for toddlers and Europeans.

After a quick wash, Vera dons her morning gear—a polo shirt with a Ralph Lauren logo so big that it covers her entire left breast (well, okay, thanks to the ravages of time and gravity, it covers the top half of her breast) and sweatpants. Arm sleeves are yanked on and adjusted so that there isn't an exposed sliver of skin between her shirt sleeves and the removable ones. Many years ago, when Vera was a brazen young woman, she never checked her arm sleeves and often walked around with a tanned strip of skin around her upper arms. Those were obviously the wild days, when she lived life on the edge and took unnecessary risks.

Sleeves on, Vera nods at her reflection and marches to the kitchen, where she gulps down a pint of room-temperature water—cold water, Vera believes, would freeze the fats in your arteries and give you heart disease. At the door, Vera dons her orthopedic sneakers and her tortoiseshell sunglasses, and finally, the last and perhaps most vital article of clothing—a visor so enormous that there is no way that a single ray of freckle-causing, wrinkle-making sunlight could snake its way onto her face. Then, without a backward glance, Vera strides out into the world.

And all of this happens without the aid of alarm clocks. Vera should really have been a rooster, but she isn't; she is a pig, and perhaps that is where all the trouble began.

According to the Chinese horoscope, pigs are diligent and compassionate and are the ones to call upon when sincere advice is needed. Unfortunately, very few people call Vera for sincere advice, or even insincere advice. The one person who should be calling her at all times for advice—her son, Tilbert—never does. Vera doesn't quite understand why. When her parents were alive, she often went to them for advice, even when she didn't need to, because unlike her son, Vera was a filial child and knew that asking her parents for advice made them feel needed. Well, no matter. Vera is a diligent mother and goes out of her way to give Tilly all the advice he could ever need anyway. Her previous texts are as follows:

Sent today at 4:31 a.m.:

Tilly, are you awake? It is 4:31 AM, very late. When I was your age, I wake up at 4AM every morning to cook breakfast for Ah Gong and Ah Ma. Qi lai! Seize the day! Carpe diem! Kind regards, Mama.

Sent yesterday at 7:45 p.m.:

Tilly, I notice that this girl @NotChloeBennet has liked TWO of your videos on the TikTok! I think this means she likes you. I look at her profile and she pout a lot, but I think she will make good wife. She went with her mother for manicure last week, this means she is a filial daughter. Perhaps you should slip and slide into her DM. Kind regards, Mama.

Vera had been particularly pleased about using the phrase "slip and slide into her DM." Vera insists on keeping up to date with every trend. She doesn't believe in getting left behind by the younger generations. Every time she comes across a nonsensical-sounding phrase, she looks it up on the Google and jots down its meaning in her little notebook.

Sent yesterday at 5:01 p.m.:

Tilly, it is 5PM, I hope you have eaten your dinner. Your Uncle Lin eat dinner at 7PM every night and he didn't

even live past thirty. You better eat dinner now. Kind
regards, Mama.

This one actually garnered a reply.

TILLY: Uncle Lin died because he was hit by a bus. And
I've told you to stop calling me Tilly. I go by Bert.

VERA: Don't talk back to your elders. I raise you better
than that. And what is wrong with Tilly? It's a good
name, your Baba and I think long and hard about
your name, you should treasure it.

This was followed by more silence from Tilly. But no matter.
There is no time for her wayward son right now, because Vera is
about to start her morning walk, and morning walks are a serious
business. First, there is the stretching. Many people her age com-
plain of stiff joints and unbending limbs, but Vera goes into a low
squat without much difficulty and bends at the waist until the tips
of her fingers touch her sneakers. When he was a teen, Tilly had
been extremely embarrassed about Vera's stretching routine. He'd
begged her to do it in the privacy of their home instead of on the
sidewalk, but one needs fresh air to properly stretch, and anyway,
Tilly should be proud that his mother is setting such a good example for their neighbors.

With her muscles sufficiently warmed up, Vera gets into walking position—chin up, chest out, and elbows perpendicular to her
body. Then she begins to walk, her fists swinging in front of her
chest with the enthusiasm of a North Korean soldier at a national

parade. Vera's morning walk can only be described as vigorous. She is a general on the warpath, eating up the miles with ruthless efficiency. Anyone foolish enough to get in her way is met with a cutting glare (which is invisible behind the sunglasses and the visor), but Vera relishes having to swerve around passersby, as it is a chance for her to put her agility and quick reflexes to the test.

For her last birthday, Tilly gave her a Samsung watch that could measure her steps, but Vera sees no need for it, because she knows exactly how many steps her daily route takes: 3,112 steps, starting on Trenton and Pacific, where her house is, down along Washington, where all the mom-and-pop grocery stores and souvenir shops are preparing to open for the day. Some of the shop owners wave at Vera and call out greetings, but they all know she can't stop for a chat, not when she's on her morning walk. Still, Vera has impeccable manners, so she calls out niceties in Mandarin like, "Wah, the melons look good, Mr. Hong!" or "The weather is finally warming up, Sister Zhao!" as she zips past.

She slows down a little in front of the café that sprouted like a particularly pustulant pimple two years ago on Washington. The owner is a rude millennial who doesn't even live in Chinatown. Vera's mouth twists in a sneer as she walks past, and as she always does every morning, she places a silent curse on the café. Even its name irks her. The Café. She can just imagine the kind of confusion it has caused to its customers. *Where would you like to go? The Café. Right, which one? The Café! WHICH ONE?* You'd think that with a name like that, the Café would have folded long ago. But no, in defiance of all logic, not only did it not go under, it flourished, stealing customers from the older shops in the vicinity. Often, when Vera sits in her quiet tea shop, her mind wanders to the Café and it ruins her perfectly wonderful tea. Truly, the Café and its horribly unhealthy product—coffee, ugh—are a blight on San Franciscans, nay, on humanity.

When she gets down to the Dragon Gate of Chinatown on Bush Street, she turns the corner and walks along Stockton all the way to Woh Hei Yuen, where the Tai Chi Quan group is just starting their routine. Her husband, Jinlong, came here every day up until he had his stroke. He often tried to get Vera to join him, but Vera did not see the point in tai chi. Too slow to do much good, surely. It's about as effective as yoga, which is to say, not very. Each time after Jinlong finished with tai chi, Vera would check his pulse and he never once broke eighty. What is even the point? Still, she walks through Woh Hei Yuen and waves at the tai chi group and ignores the way her heart cracks a little when she sees that Jinlong isn't among the slow-moving people. Silly woman, of course Jinlong isn't here, he is safe in a silver urn in her living room, and that's that.

First thing Vera does at the end of each walk is to press her thumb against the inside of her wrist and measure her heart rate. Satisfied that it's at a respectable ninety-two beats per minute, Vera trudges inside, through her dark tea shop and up the stairs back to her living quarters. After an invigorating cold shower, Vera eats a well-balanced breakfast of congee, preserved duck eggs, and fermented tofu. Finally, she toddles back down and bustles about tidying up and preparing her shop.

As a teenager, Tilly delighted in pointing out the inaccuracies in the name Vera Wang's World-Famous Teahouse.

"First of all, nobody knows about it, so it's really not 'world-famous,'" he said with a roll of his eyes.

Vera tutted, but before she could answer, Jinlong said, "Not true, your mother was very well-known back in China for her teas. Many customer come from faraway places just to taste her tea."

"Mm-hmm," Tilly said, clearly unconvinced. He quickly moved on to his next attack. "And why is it called Vera *Wang*? You're Vera *Wong*."

"Ah," Jinlong said with an admiring glance at Vera. "That's because your mother is very smart lady, very savvy. Vera Wang is very famous person, even white people know her name. So your mother said we might as well name it after her."

"That's called misrepresentation, Baba," Tilly snapped. "You guys could get sued!" Then he added, very spitefully, Vera thought, "If anyone knew about this teahouse, that is. But I guess since nobody knows of its existence, it doesn't matter."

Jinlong only laughed and patted Tilly on the back. "Oh, er zi, you are so full of knowledge about the law. Maybe you go to law school, eh?"

Things were so much easier back then, when Jinlong was around to act as a buffer between Vera and Tilly. After Jinlong's death, the relationship between mother and son had sagged slowly but inevitably into almost nothing. Tilly did indeed go to law school. Tilly is now a junior associate at a fancy law firm near the Embarcadero, with offices so high up that you can see the car lights twinkling on the Bay Bridge at night. Not that Vera would know; it's not like Tilly ever invites her to his office, but she likes to imagine what Tilly sees when he gazes out of his office window.

Stop thinking about Tilly, Vera scolds herself as she lifts the last chair from the table and sets it on the floor. She goes to the front door and flips the sign from CLOSED to OPEN, then she walks behind the counter, perches on her stool, and awaits her customers.

Vera Wang's World-Famous Teahouse is open for business.

TWO

VERA

Truth be told, Tilly wasn't wrong when he pointed out that calling Vera's teahouse "world-famous" was stretching the truth just a tad. It is true that back in Guangzhou, Vera ran a teahouse that enjoyed a steady stream of loyal customers as well as the occasional out-of-towner who had heard of her special concoctions. But here in San Francisco, California, she'd had to start from scratch. In its best years, Vera Wang's World-Famous Teahouse attracted more than its fair share of regulars despite its humble positioning, tucked between Lucky Laundry on one side and Winifred's Patisserie on the other. But the customer base was mostly elderly immigrants, and over the years, the steady stream turned into a trickle, then a drip, and now, the only remaining customer Vera can rely on is Alex.

This morning, as on all other mornings, Vera heaves up her tome-sized ledger from a cabinet and sets it down with a soft thump on the counter. She puts on her reading glasses and peers down at her ledger, her eyebrows going up in an effort to help her read the tiny handwriting.

May 23rd—Prunella vulgaris, dried watermelon peel, goji berries
May 22nd—Luo han guo, premium bird's nest, rock sugar
May 21st—Fragrant toasted barley, chrysanthemum, candied
winter melon peel
May 20th—Osmanthus buds, oolong

A small smile touches the corners of Vera's mouth as she reviews the list of teas she concocted for her best customer. He particularly enjoyed the fragrant toasted barley, and no wonder, as its smoky taste went beautifully with the vanilla scent of the chrysanthemum and the sweetness of the candied winter melon peel. What should she make today? Taking off her glasses, Vera gets up from her stool and reviews the floor-to-ceiling cabinet behind the counter.

Vera's tea cabinet is a thing of wonder. It has exactly 188 little drawers, each one filled with some high-quality ingredient shipped from the dewy hills of China. Okay, so Tilly had once pointed out in his usual disagreeable way that many of those ingredients haven't been used in years and are probably expired. Vera would be the first to admit that perhaps the Tianchi tea might be past its best years and should be thrown out along with at least twenty other ingredients that she hasn't checked on for years, but she'll get round to doing it when she does a huge spring clean of her magical drawers. It's just that with the lack of customers, she hasn't had to even think about these ingredients that nobody has asked for.

Anyway, on to the present matter. Vera taps her chin twice, thinking, then climbs up a little stepladder and opens a drawer. Jujubes, also known as dried red dates. They're subtly sweet and would go well with—oh, what is she thinking? Jujubes are so heaty. Alex has too much yang, which means he is naturally a bit too heaty, so she mustn't give him any jujubes, no matter how wonderful they taste. Vera climbs down the stepladder and turns now to her counter display, which has about two dozen of the more popular ingredients. Right, ah, yes, she'd bought a big pack of mung beans the other day from Mrs. Ong's shop. That would do well. She scoops out the little emerald-colored beans and pours them onto her traditional Chinese weighing scales, narrowing her eyes like Shaina from *Love Is Blind* season two as she works out the perfect proportion for Alex and his poor wife, Lily. Once she has the right amount weighed, she transfers it into a small mesh bag. Then she drops in two pieces of rock sugar and a knot of pandan leaves and pulls the drawstring closed. There. All Alex has to do is plop that into some water and let it boil for fifteen minutes, and he and Lily can enjoy a nice, healthy beverage that has cooling properties.

Like clockwork, the little bell on the front door jangles as Alex pushes it open. The sound always makes Vera smile. She likes Alex, the only true gentleman remaining in this era.

"Ni hao, Alex," she calls out.

"Zao an hao," Alex replies. He's wearing his usual tired smile as he shuffles to his favorite seat in the teahouse, the one right by the window.

"And how are you today? The usual?" Vera says in Mandarin as she fills her potbellied kettle and puts it on the stove. Though Alex is always happy to take her special mixed herbal teas home, he never deviates from his morning tea, which is a pot of Tieguanyin. Tieguanyin, which translates to Iron Goddess of Mercy, is a type of oolong from Fujian, though it tastes nothing like oolong. It's quite bitter when it first hits the tongue, but once swallowed, it leaves behind the most delightful sweetness in the mouth, clean and comforting. It's one of Vera's favorite teas, and she takes care to brew it right.

When the kettle is boiling, Vera takes out a small clay teapot and two teacups half the size of a shot glass. She sets them on a draining rack next to the sink and pours the boiling water all over them, ensuring that the cups and pot are scalding hot. Quickly, she transfers them to a tray and scoops some Tieguanyin into the little pot before filling it up with hot water. She then pours out the first brew, which is meant to scald away any harshness from the leaves, and refills the pot with more hot water before bringing the tray to Alex's table.

Alex smiles as Vera sets the tray down and pours both of them some tea. He lifts his cup delicately, touching only the rim to avoid burning himself, and takes a sip. He inhales deeply, his eyes fluttering shut in an expression of bliss. "Mm, no one can make tea quite like you do. Lily misses this place so."

Poor Lily, Vera thinks for the millionth time. At least a few times a day, when her thoughts go to Alex, Vera utters a small sigh and thinks, *Poor Lily*. She was diagnosed with Alzheimer's a year ago and deteriorated quickly, to the point where she never leaves her house. Alex refuses to let anyone else take care of his beloved wife, choosing to live like a hermit. The only time he allows himself to go out is when he stops by Vera's for ten minutes, while Lily is still sleeping. He actually sets a timer for himself, in case he and Vera get carried away chatting. He doesn't even get his own groceries. One of his sons—the filial one—does the weekly shopping and drops it off at his front door every Sunday. It is this son who Vera chooses to bring up this morning, because Alex looks extra tired and Vera knows the mention of his son will cheer him up.

"Tell me, how is Facai doing?" Facai means "striking wealth," a great name, which has brought Alex's son much fortune. Vera approves of it. She wishes Tilly would go by his Chinese name too.

As expected, the corners of Alex's eyes crinkle as he smiles. "Oh, wonderfully, just wonderfully. He is truly favored by the gods. He's been in such good spirits these days; he says that things are going swimmingly with his business."

"Ah yes, of course." Vera nods sagely as she sips her tea. "Well, there is no chance of him not succeeding with you and Lily as his parents." She's not flattering Alex; like many Chinese elders, Vera truly believes that the bulk of anyone's success is thanks to their parents' hard work and sacrifice.

But it becomes apparent that she's said the wrong thing. Alex's smile loses its vibrance and he lowers his eyes. "I wish I could agree with that sentiment, but for my other son, Jiancheng." Jiancheng means "strength and stability," but from everything Vera knows about Alex's second son, he is anything but strong and stable.

"I'm sorry to hear that, but I empathize with your suffering." Vera has spent many of these conversations complaining about Tilly, and it's over the numerous ways that their sons have disappointed them that a true bond of friendship has been forged between Vera and Alex. "I sent Mingjin a text this morning when I woke up to make sure he's awake too, and until now I have yet to receive a reply. What other mother would be so attentive to text her grown son every morning? But does he appreciate it?"

Alex scoffs and shakes his head. "These young people, they don't understand the many sacrifices we've made for them. When I was young, I would never have let my parents wake up before me. No, I was always awake before they were, polishing my father's shoes. My baba never went to work with dirty shoes, all because of me."

"Yes, exactly!" Vera crows, her chest expanding with righteous energy. "This is precisely what I'm referring to. Every morning, I had a hot breakfast ready for my parents. Hah! This younger generation, they don't know how good they have it."

"Lily always spoiled them, you know." Alex's eyes soften. "She said they're behaving like normal American kids, and isn't that what we wanted?"

Vera sighs. "She has a point."

They both gaze into their teacups wistfully.

"And how is Lily?" She hates asking this question, because there hasn't been a positive response for close to half a year now, but she feels obliged to do so.

Alex's shoulders slump. "She's the same."

Meaning she rarely has a moment of lucidity. When Lily is awake now, she spends most of her time snapping at Alex to stay away and demanding that he let her see her husband. It's taken the life out of Alex. The only source of joy he has now is Facai and these short teatimes with Vera. Altogether too soon, though, his timer goes off, and Alex finishes the last of his tea. Vera hurries to the counter and picks up the bag she prepared for him earlier.

"Here," she says, pressing the mesh bag into his hands. "Mung beans and pandan. Boil for fifteen minutes, maybe twenty if you want it richer in flavor."

"You are too good to us," Alex protests, but by now, he knows it is a losing battle and pockets the bag without too much back-and-forth. When Lily was healthier, Alex used to spend a full five minutes arguing with Vera over paying her for her teas, but time is in short supply these days.

Vera watches him walk down the block to his apartment building, a dilapidated, aging building with ten units, all of them filled with graying tenants. So much of Chinatown is like that, slowly fading away. The kernel of sadness in Vera's heart grows, becoming heavier until it is overwhelming. Because, as much as she would love to tell Tilly that he's wrong, Vera knows deep in her soul that her teahouse is far from world-famous. The opposite, in fact. And watching the first and last customer of the day walk away kills Vera just a little bit every day. She already knows what to expect from the rest of the morning. It will slowly melt into the afternoon, which will stretch on in unbearable silence until five p.m., when Vera will shuffle slowly from her stool to the front door and flip the OPEN sign to CLOSED, and for the dozenth time that day, she will ask herself, *What is the point?*

Let's face it, the shop hasn't been turning a profit for years now. She's only been able to keep it open because she and Jinlong paid it off in full seven years ago, and now she just has to pay off the monthly electricity bills and so on. Even so, without the heavy weight of a mortgage on her back, the shop is still a burden, and every day Vera is aware of her dwindling savings. Soon, no matter how frugally she runs it, Vera will no longer have enough funds to keep it going, and it will be the end of Vera Wang's World-Famous Teahouse.

That day, Vera closes up an hour early, unable to bear the weight of her loneliness as it stretches on. Her steps, trudging up the rickety stairs to her living space, are so heavy. It's not in her nature to be sad, but no matter how vigorous her morning walks, the loneliness catches up, always. Before she goes to bed, she sends Tilly a reminder to go to bed early because going to bed late causes prostate cancer, everyone knows that. She doesn't wait for a reply. She knows there won't be one coming. When she finally falls asleep, she dreams of death and wishes it was finally her turn.

The next morning, her eyes snap open as usual, and thus begins a new day. No use lying around feeling sorry for herself; a whole twenty-four hours is here to be seized in a chokehold. Dressed in her usual morning gear, visor securely on her head, Vera marches down the stairs to her teahouse, where she finds herself, for once, shocked speechless.

For there, lying in the middle of Vera Wang's World-Famous Teahouse, is a dead man.

THREE

JULIA

The problem with having your husband walk out on you isn't that you find yourself missing him the day after, but that you realize just how much you don't know how to do. Bills. Driving a car. Maintaining the house. Julia hates Marshall for walking out on her—on them—but right now, the only person Julia hates more than anyone else is Julia.

Here she is, at eleven o'clock on a beautiful San Franciscan morning, her two-and-a-half-year-old daughter playing next to her, and she can't even decide what to make for lunch. Because for the last ten years of her life, lunch was dictated by Marshall.

I want a tuna melt, babe, he'd say, and she'd prepare a tuna melt.

How about a meatball sub? And she'd get right to making it, with meatballs from scratch.

And on the days when he had to go on business trips, she'd just make his favorites because the truth is, Julia doesn't know what her favorites are anymore. Her favorites are whatever Marshall loved. Over the years, she's learned to love what Marshall loves because seeing him smile and tell her, *This is delicious, babe*, gave her so many endorphins that she decided she loved it too. Isn't that what being married means? Loving what the other person loves?

But last night, after ten married years and fourteen altogether as a couple, Marshall told her unceremoniously that he'd "made it" and was finally leaving her "sorry ass." *Honestly*, Julia thinks as she helps Emma push a particularly stubborn piece of Lego into place, *there is nothing sorry about my ass*. She keeps her ass in very good shape, damn it. And it's this ridiculous thought that smacks into her with sudden ruthlessness and triggers hot tears rushing into her eyes. Who the hell cares about her ass right now? *Although*, a small voice pipes up as she stifles her sobs, *it really is a very good one*.

She checks her phone for the millionth time, but there are no calls, no messages. Julia has been waiting for the phone to ring for so long, checking it every few minutes to make sure that it's still working, still has both Wi-Fi and cellular connection, that when the doorbell rings, she jumps and grabs her phone.

Emma looks up from the elaborate Lego palace she's building. "Mommy, door is ringing."

"Huh?" It takes a second for Julia to recognize the jangle as the doorbell and not her phone, and once she does, hope and dread bloom in equal measure, fighting for space in her tightening chest. She's suddenly finding it challenging to breathe. She stands, forcing herself to take a deep inhale, pushing her constricting rib cage out. *I can breathe. I'm okay. Everything will be okay.*

Maybe life might even be better without Marshall?

Nope, that's impossible. He took care of them. He took care of everything.

By the time she reaches the door, she still has no idea what she's going to say, but it doesn't matter. People seem to know that Julia doesn't have much to say. They either talk over her or ignore her entirely. She's used to it. Anyway, it's probably just Linda from next door pretending to drop by with cookies, wanting to know what the shouting last night was all about. Julia has to walk around the huge trash bags lined up behind the front door. She'll have to take care of them at some point.

But when she opens the door, what she finds is very much not Linda. Two officers stand before her—a Black woman and an Asian man, both of them wearing very strange expressions. They're sort of smiling, but the smiles are heavy and apologetic. Julia's stomach knots painfully; those aren't the kinds of smiles you give when you have good news to share. They're the kinds of smiles that know they're about to ruin someone's life. For a fleeting moment, Julia is tempted to slam the door in their faces and lock the dead bolt. But of course, she does no such thing. Julia is nothing if not agreeable and compliant. Julia is nothing if not helpful and pliant. *Julia is nothing,* Marshall's voice whispers in her head. Marshall's voice in Julia's head is so much meaner than the real version.

"Morning, ma'am," the Asian officer says. "I'm Officer Ha and this is my partner, Officer Gray. Are you Julia Chen?"

Somehow, she manages to nod.

"Is it okay if we come in?" Officer Gray says.

No, she wants to shout. Nothing good is incoming from them, that much is clear. But her head nods again, bypassing her brain.

"Oh," Officer Ha says as they walk inside and notice the trash bags. "Did a bit of spring cleaning?"

Julia's stomach twists so violently that she almost gags. She can see Marshall's PlayStation peeking out of the bag nearest to them. Practically brand-new. Spring cleaning. More like gathering all his things because she knows he's not coming back.

"Something like that," she mumbles. Quickly, she turns and almost knocks Emma over. She hasn't even realized that Emma has attached herself to Julia's right leg, clinging like a little koala. "Sorry, baby." She bends down and scoops Emma up. Julia's always surprised by how heavy her little girl has become. How tall and solid and full of possibilities. "It's okay," she whispers to Emma as she leads the officers into the living room. "It's okay," she repeats, more for her own sake than Emma's, really.

Officer Gray smiles. "Hi, sweetheart. What's your name?"

Julia doesn't bother waiting for a response before answering on her daughter's behalf. "It's Emma." Emma never talks to strangers. She barely even talks to their neighbors, and they've known the people living on this street for as long as she's been alive. It's one of the many things Marshall hated. Well, maybe "hate" is a strong word. Or maybe not, since he hadn't even looked back at his daughter when he walked out last night.

"What a pretty name. It suits you," Officer Gray says. "How old are you?"

Most kids, as Julia has been told over and over by various people, would only be too happy to announce to everyone they come across how old they are. But not Emma. Emma buries her face in Julia's shoulder and refuses to look at the officers, who in turn give awkward smiles to Julia. Marshall's words echo in Julia's head: *It's fucking embarrassing, the way she behaves. Why can't she be a normal kid?*

Julia swallows and gestures at the officers to sit down on the couch. Their couch is much nicer than it has any right to be, its base made of solid wood, the seats covered with real leather. It's one of Marshall's picks, of course. He always goes for the most expensive options, charging everything to his credit cards and assuring her that money will be coming in, so why not invest in their future comfort? He loves this word, "invest," uses it for every frivolous purchase he makes.

She herself sinks onto an armchair next to the sofa and shifts Emma from her hip to her lap. Belatedly, Julia realizes that she should offer the officers a drink, some water at least. But Emma is heavy on her lap, and she doesn't want these officers to stay any longer than they have to. She hardly slept at all last night; how could she, after everything that happened? And she's tired now, so tired.

As though sensing her eagerness to get this done and over with, Officer Ha clears his throat and leans forward a little. "Is your husband Marshall Chen?"

"Is there a playroom we can play in?" Officer Gray cuts in, smiling at Emma, who's peeking at her.

At the thought of being separated from Julia, Emma closes up, smushing her little face into Julia's chest and shaking her head fiercely. Julia holds her tight. "It's okay, she can stay."

"Are you sure? We're here with ah, sensitive information."

Julia nods and clasps her hands tightly behind Emma's back to keep them from trembling. She inhales the scent of Emma's hair, that sweet smell of clean childish sweat and warm sugar. Her breath goes in shaky, rattling all the way to her lungs, and she has to hold back a sob. Here it comes.

Both officers nod, clearly disapproving of her choice. That's okay, Julia's used to disapproval. And just because Officer Gray thinks Emma is cute or whatever doesn't mean she knows Emma. Nobody knows Emma. They use words like "painfully shy" and "very quiet." Julia can't imagine leaving Emma alone in a room with anyone else. She would freak the hell out and then Officer Gray would probably panic and think something's wrong with her child. She's so sick of people thinking there's something wrong with Emma.

"Okay, well." Officer Ha clears his throat again. "Ah, we're sorry to inform you that this morning, your husband was found dead at a teahouse in Chinatown."

The words are so foreign to Julia that her brain fails to compute what he's saying. And when it does start digesting the information, it latches on to the strangest part of the sentence. "A teahouse?"

Officer Ha nods. "Yes." He consults his notepad. "Vera Wang's World-Famous Teahouse."

"Why would a dress designer have a teahouse?" Then again, Eva Longoria owns a bunch of restaurants, so maybe that was a stupid question to ask.

Officer Gray shakes her head. "No, it's owned by someone named Vera *Wong*, actually."

And something about the way she says it reaches deep into the dark coils of Julia's brain and tickles it. Julia does the worst thing she can possibly do in this moment. She laughs. It lasts less than a second, but she sees the officers' eyes sharpening in that instant, and she wants to slap herself. God knows, Marshall wanted to on many occasions, and can anyone blame him? This is just the stupid crap that Julia does that he has to put up with every day.

Had to put up with. Because he's dead now, isn't he? He doesn't have to put up with her anymore. She almost laughs again but manages to wrestle the traitorous sensation down.

"I don't understand," she manages to croak.

Officer Gray's expression is still cold and mistrusting. "He was found by the owner of the teahouse, Ms. Vera Wong, at around five a.m. this morning. It seems he had broken into her teahouse sometime in the night before dying."

It's a struggle to make sense of the words. "How did—uh, what caused the death?"

"We're still waiting for the autopsy results, but he had a bag of MDMA in his bag, so it might have been an overdose," Officer Ha says.

"MDMA?" Is he even still speaking English?

"You might know it as ecstasy, or Molly, or E?"

Julia's brain refuses to process the words.

"Do you know if your husband regularly used MDMA?" Officer Ha says. But from his tone of voice, it's clear that what he means is: *How can you not know that your husband regularly used MDMA?*

"There were also some wounds on his body," Officer Gray says. "A bruise on his cheek and scratches on the other. Would you happen to know anything about that?"

She shakes her head numbly, and her head throbs with the movement. Unbidden, she gets a flash of Marshall shoving her away as he leaves and the back of her head cracking against the wall. She bites her lip, forcing herself to focus in this moment. Do not show them that she's hurting. Do not show them that he wounded her.

Do they believe her? Julia can't tell. Does it matter if they believe her? He's dead. Marshall is dead.

As though the thought seeps into Emma's head through osmosis, the toddler starts fussing in Julia's lap, her little chubby hands pawing at Julia's breasts. "Boop," she demands.

Julia's cheeks burn and she finds it hard to meet the officers' eyes; then she berates herself. How stupid to be concerned about them judging her for having a two-year-old who still nurses. Who the hell cares about breastfeeding when she's just been told that her husband of ten years just died? And yet, here she is, clasping Emma's arms firmly but gently and pulling them away from her chest. "Later," she says softly, even though she knows this is futile.

As expected, Emma gets louder. "Boop!" she demands. "Boop!" Julia's embarrassment sharpens into shame. It's bad enough that Emma still demands the breast, but can't she at least say it in a complete sentence? She's able to; when it's just the two of them, Emma speaks in long, adult sentences. "Can I have milk, please, Mommy?" "Mommy, look at the ladybug, why does it have black spots?" "I love the swings, push me higher, Mommy!" Well-formed sentences that disappear the moment they have company. Then, of course, as usual, Julia feels ashamed that she feels ashamed of her own child. What a terrible mother she is. And what a terrible wife. Look at her, judging her toddler's speech when her husband literally just died.

"Boop!" It's a full-on shout now, right next to Julia's ear, shatteringly loud. Julia jerks physically and the suddenness of the movement shocks Emma. For a second, she blinks up at Julia, wide-eyed; then the corners of her mouth screw down.

"Sorry, sweetie—"

Too late. Emma's mouth opens wide and she emits a piercing wail. The only time Emma isn't quiet or shy is when she cries.

Both officers look like they want nothing more than to run out of the house.

"Sorry, this really isn't a good time," Julia says, which is a strange thing to say, isn't it? It's not the thing to say to officers who are trying to talk to you about your spouse's demise. Is it? Who knows what the proper thing to say is? Julia is sure she looks guilty. She feels guilty, asking herself what an innocent person would say, as though she isn't innocent. But then again, she isn't. She has so much to hide, and part of her is grateful that Emma is shrieking because it gives her an excuse to kick these officers out. She stands, grunting under Emma's weight.

"All right, if you do think of something, give us a call." Officer Gray has to shout to make herself heard over the din. She takes out a business card and places it on the coffee table before she and her partner stand and stride toward the door. Julia notices the striding, so confident, with a definite destination in mind. She can't remember when the last time was that she'd walked with such sureness. Nowadays, she walks with her shoulders rounded, her head perpetually bent to the ground, eyes glued to the top of Emma's head.

At the door, Officer Gray pauses and turns to face Julia. Their eyes meet, and Julia almost sobs because there is so much pity in Officer Gray's eyes. But then Officer Gray's gaze slides down to the trash bags, and Julia goes cold as she watches the officer's expression harden. There is no way that she doesn't spot the PlayStation this time, along with the silk ties. She must know these are bags filled with Marshall's things, lined up by the door as though Julia had foreseen his death. Officer Gray says something, but

Julia can't hear her above Emma's wails. Then she shouts, "We'll be in touch."

Julia doesn't wait for them to turn and walk away before shutting the door and hurrying over to the sofa, where she nurses Emma. She doesn't even realize she's crying until a tear plops on Emma's cheek, and after that there's no use trying to stop the sobs from shuddering through her body.

FOUR

VERA

It is 8:55 p.m., almost a whole half hour past Vera's bedtime. She can't remember the last time she failed to fall asleep at eight thirty p.m.; Vera goes to sleep very promptly every night. She's never understood people who have difficulties sleeping. For Vera, sleep, like most other things in life, is a matter of discipline and willpower. Every night, as she slaps on her numerous moisturizers, she tells her body that it is almost time for it to retire for the night, and it never disappoints.

Except for tonight. Tonight, Vera finds herself lying in the dark, rolling the hem of her blanket between her thumb and index finger restlessly. For the sixth time, she takes a deep, forceful breath and mentally demands that her brain shut down for the night. Like a surly teenager, her brain ignores her, remaining stubbornly awake.

When the red numbers on the clock turn to nine p.m., Vera gives up trying to beat her consciousness into submission and rises. She gives an annoyed huff and shuffles out of the bedroom and into the kitchen. She turns the kitchen light on and winces at the sudden brightness. When her eyes finally adjust to the light, Vera potters about, making herself a nice cup of caffeine-free chrysanthemum tea. As she works, she chides herself for being silly. Why should the mere discovery of a dead body in her little shop make her lose sleep? She's being indulgent, that's what she's being.

But then again, a small voice pipes up, *it's not the dead body, is it? It's the other thing.*

Vera sighs. Sometimes, she hates her own mind for being so astute. The kettle boils then, so she pours the water into her mug and watches as the dried chrysanthemum flower unfurls gently before toddling over to the dining table. She sits down and automatically, her eyes flick to the tissue box in the middle of the table. Unbidden, memories from earlier that day flood her consciousness.

By the time the police arrive, Vera is relatively calm. Well, her heartbeat is a little bit elevated, but since the dead man is lying just two paces away from where she sits, Vera supposes this is acceptable. She's prepared for the cops—she's boiled enough water for three whole teapots and prepped each pot with a pinch of Longjing tea paired with ginkgo leaves, a combination known for sharpening the mind and ensuring that the police officers will do their best investigative work here. Maybe they will be so impressed by how clearly their minds are working after just one sip of Vera's magical tea that the station will become regular customers. Maybe they might even spread the word to other precincts and she'll soon have to fulfill regular bulk orders to all of the police departments in the whole of the Bay Area.

She's also tidied up the shop a little. Well, around the body, of course. Vera has watched enough *CSI* to know that she mustn't touch the body itself in order to preserve any traces of the culprit's DNA, but she's not about to let a whole swarm of police officers into her tea shop without sprucing the place up a little. She's gone upstairs to the apartment and fetched a particularly pretty vase, as well as an ancient framed photo of herself in her twenties, just so they know that she used to be quite the looker in her time. She almost swept up the broken glass from the front door but remembered that it was probably evidence. She's very proud of her crime scene; it must surely be the most pleasant crime scene the cops have ever been to.

When the cops arrive, Vera greets them at the door with a tray of freshly brewed tea, but they actually push her aside—gently, of course, but still—and tell her, "Ma'am, please stand out of the way."

"But—" It takes a second for Vera to gather her mind as three officers tromp into her tiny shop. "I have prepare some tea for you. You better drink it now, before you start investigating. It is Longjing and ginkgo leaves, known for clearing your mind."

The first police officer, the one who pushed her aside like she was a child, barely spares her a glance. "Ma'am, we're not going to eat or drink anything here. Gray? Can you?" He gestures at another officer and cocks his head at Vera.

Officer Gray, a kind-looking Black officer who looks about Tilly's age, walks toward Vera. She's wearing a polite smile. "Ma'am, can you step outside for a moment? I need to take your statement."

"Oh, no, thank you," Vera says quickly. "I need to stay and make sure your friends don't miss anything."

"What the—?" the first officer mutters. "Hey, ma'am, who drew the outline around the deceased?"

"Ah." Vera swells with pride. They have noticed just how helpful and resourceful Vera is. "I do it. I save you some work." Vera knew what was supposed to happen at crime scenes—the police would draw an outline around the body using tape, but unfortunately, Vera was rather short on tape, so she had to make do with a Sharpie. She had been ever so careful as she drew the outline, making sure to leave about a half-inch gap between the Sharpie tip and the body so she didn't come into contact with it. The resulting outline is, if she may say so, excellent—both accurate and clear. She should tell the cops to switch from tape to Sharpie.

But the cops don't seem impressed. In fact, they seem really annoyed. "Get her out of here," the first officer barks.

"Ma'am, come with me," Officer Gray says, and Vera frowns but does as Officer Gray says.

On her way out, Vera turns to the first officer and calls out, "I haven't move anything, Officer. Everything just the way it was before this man is murder."

One of Officer Gray's eyebrows rises. "Murder? What makes you think it's murder?"

Vera sighs at Officer Gray. Why is she asking such an obvious question? "It just . . . I can sense the aura, can't you? Very bad aura. Ah, maybe your generation will know it as 'vibes.'"

"Because the victim has . . . bad vibes?" Officer Gray says.

Vera has the feeling Officer Gray doesn't believe her. Why be a police officer when you can't even count on your instincts? This is why these officers need her tea. She lifts her tray up higher, hoping Officer Gray will be able to smell the delicious tea. "Come, you drink this tea now. You need it. It will clear your mind and improve your memory."

"Ma'am." Officer Gray sighs. "Stop trying to make us drink tea. Put that tray down and come outside with me. Now."

Vera is aghast. She's old enough to be Officer Gray's mother, for god's sakes. Officer Gray should not be talking to her elders like this. Still, they are police officers, so Vera supposes she needs to follow the law or whatever, but as a sign of rebellion, she keeps hold of her tray as she walks out of her teahouse. She can't believe she's being shooed out of her own teahouse. Given that the man died in her teahouse, one would think that she has the right to follow every step of the investigation and offer up her many theories on what might have killed him. (Her current favorite theory is that he and his would-be killer had come to Vera's for a nightcap and, upon finding the shop closed, had been so disappointed that one was driven to kill the other. Hey, if people can kill each other over road rage, why not tea rage?)

Outside, Vera is disappointed and surprised to see that there are no additional cops. Where is the CSI team? Where are the blood-spatter guys with their huge, bulky cameras and hazmat suits, and the bright yellow-and-black police tape, and the curious crowd pressing in, eager to see the murder victim? Where are the young and voracious reporters disguising themselves as detectives so they can steal into a crime scene?

But no, her street is just as quiet as ever, with the exception of—ugh—Winifred, whose head is peeping out of her cake shop. Every time Vera calls Winifred's shop a "cake shop," Winifred is quick to correct her.

"It's a patisserie," Winifred would say primly. "Insisting that I can't call it a patisserie just because I'm not French is racist, Vera."

"It's not because you're not French, Winifred; it's because you don't serve French pastries. Your cake shop serves Chinese pastries."

"Many of them are French-influenced!"

"Just because you call your taro bun *petit pain au taro* does not make it French influenced."

Anyway, now Winifred is watching from her definitely-not-French cake shop and Vera can just imagine what must be going through Winifred's mind. Hah! Well, she can wonder all she wants; it was Vera's teahouse that the man chose to be murdered in and not Winifred's faux patisserie.

"Ma'am?"

It takes Vera a moment to realize that Officer Gray's asked her a question. "Yes?"

"I said, can you tell me exactly what happened, starting from what you were doing before you found the body."

"Yes, of course." Vera is prepared for this. "So, at four thirty this morning, I wake up as usual. No alarm clock, you know. I wake up at four thirty exactly every morning, this is call discipline. What time you wake up every morning?"

Officer Gray closes her eyes for a moment. "Ma'am, this isn't about me. Continue, please."

"Hah." Vera sniffs. "You young people always waking up late, is very bad for your health."

"So you woke up . . ." Officer Gray says, waving her hand with what Vera thinks is more impatience than is called for.

"I wake up, then after I brush my teeth, etcetera, I go to the kitchen and first thing I do is drink a big glass of water. Every morning I do that. It cleanses the kidneys, you know, and—"

"Right, drank a glass of water, and then . . . ?"

"I put on my visor—you know, California sun is so strong, no sunscreen is enough, not even SPF 90 sunscreen is enough. You must wear a hat, you understand? Protect your skin from the sun, otherwise you will get cancer."

"Wear a hat, yes, got it. So as you were saying?"

"Then I go downstair, and that is when I see dead body."

"Do you know the identity of the deceased?" Officer Gray's pen hovers over her notepad.

Vera shakes her head. "Never see him before. But judging from his face, I think he is in early thirties, or maybe he is actually older. Asians have very good skin, you know. Yes, I would say maybe late thirties."

To Vera's immense disappointment, Officer Gray doesn't write any of this down.

"Aren't you going to write that down?"

Officer Gray ignores the question. "So you don't know the deceased." *This* she writes down. Not all of Vera's wisdom, but Vera's lack of knowledge about the victim. "Did anything strike you about the body?"

"Well, yes." By now, Vera is desperate to be of help.

Officer Gray perks up.

"It was dead, for one," Vera says wisely.

Officer Gray deflates. "Yeah, that's . . . yeah, I got that. Anything else?"

"I leave it alone. I don't touch it, because I know you will be wanting to check for DNA and fingerprints and all that," Vera says with a touch of pride. She cranes her neck and looks pointedly around them. "Speaking of DNA, where is your CSI team?"

Officer Gray's mouth thins into a line. "I'm afraid we don't actually work like that, ma'am. God, I hate those shows," she mutters. "Right now, my supervisor's looking for signs of foul play, and forensics will be called in if he finds any signs."

"What?" Once again, Vera is aghast. Everything she watched on TV has prepared her for nothing short of a small army of hazmat-suited professionals. "Well, there is clearly sign of foul play."

"Oh?"

The tray of tea in Vera's hands stops her from pointing, so she jerks her head at her front door. "Look, the killer break the glass!"

Officer Gray nods slowly. "That could be a sign, though I would really urge you to not jump to conclusions. There could be a dozen reasons why the glass was broken. Is there anything else you can think of that might be relevant to this investigation?"

"What about drugs?" she blurts out.

Officer Gray stares at her. "Drugs? What do you mean? Ma'am, did you touch the victim? Did you go through his belongings?"

Only very carefully, Vera wants to snap out, but she manages to hold herself back and say, "Of course no. I just think he look like the kind that have drugs, you know? I can tell, very bad sort."

Officer Gray's eyes narrow and Vera feels like a wayward child being reprimanded by an elder. Oof, she hasn't had that feeling in a looong time, and she is not a fan.

"We'll see about the drugs."

Doubt bubbles up from the pit of Vera's stomach, but she swallows it back down. She peers into her teahouse, where from her dusty window she can see two officers looking around the shop. She's further disappointed to find that neither is brushing the shop carefully to collect prints, nor doing any sort of fancy investigative work. Shouldn't they be radioing it in and calling for backup?

Can't young people do anything right these days? Must she do everything?

The answer to that is, of course, a resounding yes. And that is why Vera sighs and shakes her head. "No," she says to Officer Gray. "There is nothing else."

Later, after the police have left, and much later still, after the medical examiner has retrieved the body and taken it away, Vera stands in the unsettling quiet of her teahouse, looking down at the spot where the body was. Aside from the broken glass, there are no signs of a dead body having been there. Well, there is Vera's very helpful outline, of course, but other than that, nothing. Not even a drop of blood.

The medical examiner hadn't even been that perturbed when he came to take the body away. His team had refused Vera's tea as well, but she'd managed to corner one of the underlings and terrified the poor kid into telling her that they're just going to take the body to the morgue, but right now it looks like a heart attack, no foul play involved.

"No foul play?" Vera barked. "It's clearly murder!"

"Uh, no, I don't think—uh—it doesn't look like it? But we are unable to—uh—confirm until further—uh—investigation," he'd said before scampering away.

Oh, honestly. It seems she must do everything herself, including find the man's killer. Though, Vera admits to herself as she sips the untouched Longjing and ginkgo tea, maybe she isn't being fair. She drinks her mind-sharpening tea every day, after all, so can she blame everyone else for not being as astute as her?

Okay, perhaps the fact that she's taken something out of the dead man's clenched fist has given her a bit of an unfair advantage.

But no, it's likely to be the tea.

....

Now, as Vera sits in her kitchen, she takes out the thing she's hidden in the tissue box. It's a thumb drive, its casing black and shiny. What came over her to take it out of the dead man's hand like that? She should've left it for the cops to find, then maybe they would've taken it more seriously.

But, Vera argues with herself, we all know how useless the cops are. Just look at them today, so casual and dismissive. Vera knows they won't do anything. Well, okay, she doesn't actually know that. But she's sure she would do a better job than they possibly could, because nobody sniffs out wrongdoing quite like a suspicious Chinese mother with time on her hands, and what does Vera have but time, now that Jinlong is gone and Tilly is off doing god knows what?

Yes, she did the right thing by taking the flash drive. And she knows, of course, that the killer will be back for the flash drive. In fact, Vera is going to take out a space in the local paper to put out an obituary ASAP. And she will post about it on the TikTok and the Twitter. No doubt the killer will be watching. They will know that it's strange for an obituary to come out so soon after the death. They will know it's a message. And when they come, Vera will be ready for them.

VERA WONG'S MURDER CASE

Victim: Marshall Chen, 29
Cause of death: Unknown
Suspicious signs:

1. Bruise on left cheek (someone punch him??)
2. Scratches on right cheek (someone scratch him!?)
3. Holding a flash drive (WHAT IS INSIDE?! Maybe nuclear code? Is he spy? KGB?)
4. His fingers swollen. Everything swollen. Like me in third trimester.
5. He has baggie full of DRUGS. You see? Must be a bad person. This is not Hollywood, why is he carrying drugs around?

So ~~scary!~~ EXCITING! I am helpless old lady. What to do? Is my duty to find killer before killer go on rampage. Killer will come back for flash drive. I will identify killer and catch ~~him her~~ them!

FIVE

RIKI

Riki wasn't sure what to expect from a place called Vera Wang's World-Famous Teahouse, but it certainly wasn't this tiny, very sad-looking shop. In fact, it looks so forlorn and so forgotten that he actually walked right past it, going all the way to the little souvenir shop down the block before realizing he'd gone past the little dot on his Google Maps. He doubles back and walks very, very slowly, examining each shop sign as he passes. When he finally spots the teahouse, words like "dilapidated" and "forgotten" and "covered in dust" pop to his mind. He's not quite sure how he feels about Marshall dying in a place like this.

A decent person would think, *Poor Marshall, he didn't deserve to die here in this sad little teahouse,* or at the very least, *Poor Marshall's wife and kid, even though I don't know either of their names, but they must be really sad, so I am sad for them also.*

But Riki isn't a decent person, is he? No, because his first thought is: *Bastard deserved it. I'm glad he died here.*

Then, of course, the startled realization comes. That was a

horrible thought to have. What kind of person has thoughts like this? Then, of course, follows the usual barrage of thoughts, as though Riki's mind is made of two individuals who are arguing with each other. *Let's not pretend you're too good for these thoughts. You know what you did.*

I did what I had to in order to survive. And at the end of the day, it was all for Adi's sake.

Aren't you sick of using your little brother as an excuse for every bad deed, every crime you've committed?

And on and on it goes. In fact, Riki would've probably stayed out there in front of Vera Wang's World-Famous (*boy, that description is taking quite the liberty*) Teahouse for a long while if the rickety door hadn't swung open with a creak. The bell on top of the door jingles, slicing into his heated debate with himself. For a moment, it annoys Riki, because he was sure he was winning against himself, but then he finds himself staring soundlessly at the face peering out of the shop and all thoughts fall silent.

It's an old woman, probably around her sixties, with big permed hair that Riki's familiar with, having grown up in Indonesia; her thin lips were painted bright pink, way too bright for her skin tone, and her eyebrows thickly penciled into a sharp arch.

"Yes?" The woman speaks, and there's something about her tone of voice that makes Riki feel all of five years old, caught with his hand in the *krupuk* jar.

He gives himself a little shake. He's twenty-five, not five, and the top of the old woman's head doesn't even reach up to his nipples. Oh god, why is he thinking about nipples right now, at this very moment? What the hell is wrong with him? Of course, as soon as he thinks that, all he can think about are nipples, like some pervert. "Ah . . ."

The old woman steps fully out of her shop and lifts her chin up, up so she can stare at Riki directly in the face. "You been standing there for exactly four minutes. I think this unusual behavior, even for a millennial."

"Oh, uh . . ." Riki scrambles to find something to respond with and his brain burps out, "I'm not a millennial?"

The woman's eyes narrow with suspicion and move up and down, making his skin prickle. "Hmm, you don't look young enough to be Gen Z. You need to take better care of your skin."

Back in Indonesia, Riki's mother had always nagged at him and his brother, Adi, to reapply sunscreen every two hours, but nobody ever followed that advice. And now he's paying for it. He feels oddly guilty about it now, and suddenly self-conscious about his skin, and why in the world is he thinking of that right now?

"I think you better come in," the woman says, and retreats into the teahouse without bothering to see if Riki has agreed.

With quite a bit more trepidation than he was prepared to experience this fine morning, Riki takes a deep breath and follows the little old woman into the dark teahouse.

It's like stepping into another world entirely, one that seems stuck in the 1950s. Not that Riki would know what a teahouse in the 1950s looked like. This one, anyway, is small and dark despite the two large bay windows beside the door. Maybe it's the layer of grime on the windows, or the numerous yellowing posters plastered across them, but it has the effect of transforming the teahouse into a slightly dank cave. Riki finds himself bunching up, his shoulders narrowing so he won't accidentally touch anything.

The walls are yellowing too, and one side is completely covered by an ancient floor-to-ceiling cupboard that has hundreds of little drawers. Riki almost shudders to think of what might be in those drawers. Spiders, most likely. They look like they haven't been opened in centuries. The other walls are covered with Chinese posters and cheap Chinese paintings of lotus blossoms and birds and cherry blossoms. They're all crumbling, bits of paper peeling so the birds look monstrous, the flowers a grayish peach instead of a soft pink. There are four tables with two chairs each, all of them in that cheap, tacky Asian style that Riki finds familiar—elaborately carved backs and legs, probably machine cut in China, outdated and uncomfortable as hell to sit on. The whole place smells of old people and makes Riki incredibly sad. Then he takes another step forward and almost jumps out of his skin, because there, on the linoleum floor before him, is the outline of a man.

The old woman, already behind the counter, catches Riki looking. "Oh, that is dead man. I assume you are here because of dead man?"

Riki can't quite tear his eyes away from the outline. It looks macabre, with one arm stretched up above the head. *Astaga*, he thinks. He knew that Marshall died, of course he did, that's the whole reason he's here, but to see the actual position Marshall was in . . .

"Good outline, yes?" the old woman says with what sounds suspiciously like pride in her voice. When Riki finally drags his gaze from the outline to her, he finds her smiling triumphantly.

"Uh, yes?"

"I draw it myself, you know." She practically thumps her chest as she pours some water into a kettle and sets it on the stove.

"What? Wouldn't the police have done that?"

She snorts. "Hah! The police. What good are they? They come in, they take couple of photos, they take body and go. Did they even take fingerprints?"

The pause stretches on for a couple of seconds before Riki realizes she's expecting him to answer. "Oh! Uh, did they take any fingerprints?"

"No!" she says loudly, and slams a wrinkly fist on the counter hard enough to make Riki jump.

Riki's not quite sure what to say, but it seems polite to share in her indignation, so he ventures, "Why not?"

That's apparently what she wanted him to say, because she raises an accusatory index finger and points at the ceiling. "Exactly! Why not? I say to them, why you not taking fingerprints? Take my fingerprints! Take fingerprints all over the shop! Do your job. And you know what they say?"

Riki's prepared for this by now. "What?"

Her voice lowers conspiratorially. "They say, 'Ma'am, we are doing our jobs. Please stand aside. And stop trying to make the team drink tea.'" She leans back and huffs before taking out a teapot and sprinkling a pinch of tea leaves into it. "I make them my best oolong, but none of them even took a sip. None!"

She's so obviously offended by this slight that Riki feels compelled to nod with empathy.

"Well, one nice officer took one sip. She said is nice. I say, 'This is best oolong, a Gaoshan oolong, very expensive, you know.' She said is the best tea she ever had. Hah, of course is best tea! I going to brew her a different oolong, because she obviously appreciate tea, but another officer tell me stop making tea for team. Can you imagine? How rude!" She pauses for a breath and gasps a little. "Oh dear, speaking of rude, I been very rude myself, haven't I? I'm Vera, Vera Wong. Owner of this establishment." She says this as grandly as though she were the queen of England, showing off Buckingham Palace to him.

"Er, yes, very nice," Riki says. "I'm Riki. Riki Herwanto."

"And why you loitering in front of my teahouse, Riki Herwanto?"

"Um—" Why indeed? He looks down at the outline of Marshall's dead body, flushing with guilt. He could swear his cheeks must be burning. The tips of his ears feel like flames are slowly licking them. He should've thought this out, but then again, that was just what he'd been doing out there on the sidewalk before Vera ambushed him. Quick, think of something! He fishes into thin air and plucks something out. "I read about his death in the obituary and thought it sounded strange because of . . . well, him dying in a teahouse and everything." Then his brain burps out, "I'm a reporter."

"Oh!" Vera's eyes glitter like diamonds. "From which newspaper? *SF Chronicle? Bay Area Times?*"

"Uh . . . you wouldn't know it, it's online."

"Aha, online! Yes, I follow many online news." Vera waggles her index finger. "I always say, if you want stay young, you must think like youth. So youth follows news online, I follow news online. Which one you from?"

"I . . . from . . . uh. *The Bay . . . the Buzz.*"

The gasp that comes out of Vera is so high-pitched that Riki barely catches it. "You mean the Buzzfeed? Wow! Fabulous, wonderful job, child."

"Um." He's about to say no, but then it strikes Riki, *Why not?* Buzzfeed is such a huge company it must have hundreds of employees. Less chance of Vera finding out he's a fraud. "Yep, that's the one."

Stars are glittering in Vera's eyes. "Ooh! I think to myself this morning, I think: Vera, no doubt the newspapers going to come in here with many questions. So you must look presentable." She primps her hair gently and smiles at Riki, who belatedly realizes that she's waiting for a compliment.

She must've put on that awful pink lipstick and penciled in her eyebrows especially for today. Quickly, Riki nods and says, "Yes, you look very . . . ah, presentable."

"Make sure you take my photo in good lighting. And maybe you can do that thing—that Photoshut thing to make my wrinkles disappear?"

"Photoshop? Uh, sure. But first, can I ask you a few questions about Marsh—uh, about Mr. Chen? The guy—the man who died here?"

"Oh yes, ask away." Vera pours hot water from the kettle into the little teapot. Riki's never seen a teapot so tiny; it's about half the size of a small Starbucks cup. It hardly seems worth the bother.

"Well, um . . ." What would a reporter ask? "Tell me everything. You were the one who found the body?"

"Yes, yesterday morning, I come downstair, it was around four forty-five a.m.—I like to rise early, you know, early to bed, early to life, that's what I always say. I come downstair, about to go out on my morning walk—every morning I go for long walk, that's how I stay so slim, yes?" Vera puts the tiny teapot and two teeny teacups onto a tray.

"Yeah, very slim. So anyway, you came downstairs and that was when you saw him?"

"Yes. At first I think maybe a trick of the shadow, but then I go closer and aiya! Dead body right there." She nods toward the outline of the body as she brings the tray over to one of the tables. "Come, sit. You drink this. Jin Xuan, very good for health."

Reluctantly, Riki settles into one of the chairs, which is just as uncomfortable as he had expected. "So what did you do then?"

"I call police, of course!"

That's it? He doesn't know whether to be disappointed or relieved. "Did the police find anything of interest?"

"Hah! I tell you, they useless, absolutely useless. I tell them, I say, this man murdered. And they say we cannot jump to conclusions. Look at my door, I tell you, look at it!"

Riki obliges. The window of the front door is missing, jagged pieces of glass remaining in the frame.

"Does that look like accident?" Vera says, placing a teacup in front of Riki. "Who would break my glass like that? Break in the door and die in my shop? Tch, such bad luck. Is obvious, it's murder."

Riki nods, trying to keep himself from looking too bothered by the fact that this old woman is so convinced that Marshall was murdered. When he reaches for his teacup, he finds to his horror that his hand is trembling ever so slightly. He quickly picks up the tiny teacup, wincing at the scalding heat of the china—why don't these things have handles?—and slurps up the whole thing in one go.

"Aiya! You must take your time. Chinese tea is delicate, not meant to gulp down like that. Is not coffee." She says "coffee" like the word itself is repulsive on her tongue. Before Riki can refuse, Vera pours him another cup of tea. "Drink like this." She picks up her own teacup deftly, thumb and index finger nimbly touching the rim, and takes a small slurp. Then she inhales, her eyes closing, a small smile touching her lips. "Ah, Jin Xuan, one of the best type of tea. Is also called 'milk tea' because the taste is so creamy and sweet, almost like milk."

Riki mimics Vera and picks up his second cup of tea gingerly, slurping it the way she does. And this time, he does actually taste the creaminess she described. It really does taste like milk. He looks down at the tea, which is clear and light and definitely doesn't look milky. How strange, for something to taste so different from the way it looks. But then again, Riki thinks with a shot of guilt, that's exactly what he is. Someone pretending to be something he's not. Someone who's here with a far darker ulterior motive. When he looks up, he finds Vera studying him so intently that shock bolts down into his very core and he nearly spills the remaining tea. He's known Vera for all of ten minutes, but already he can tell she's not to be messed around with. Her eyes are shrewd, her expression calculating. Does she know? Did she serve him this particular tea because she knows he's trying to be someone else? Is she testing him with all of her statements about Marshall being murdered?

And the last question, searing through his chest: Does she know of his ties to Marshall?

SIX

SANA

Sana has never had her mother's grace. Nor her mother's any-thing, come to think about it, but on this particular morning, what she resents in particular is not having her mother's grace, because here she is in front of Vera Wang's World-Famous Teahouse, trying to make a good first impression, and of course, what she does instead is bump into a customer leaving the teahouse so hard that she makes him drop his bag.

"I'm sorry! I'm so sorry." That's the other thing Sana does that annoys her mother. *Don't start your sentences with an apology. Stop apologizing so much. It's not sincere, it's irritating.* She knows all of this, and yet she can't seem to stop herself. She bends over to help the guy pick up his bag and only ends up bumping heads. "I'm sorry!" the apology darts out of her mouth without any thought.

"Don't worry about it." They both stand up and Sana gets a glance of him before he ducks out. Warm brown skin, just like hers, but he's not Indian like her. Maybe Southeast Asian? Very attractive. Not that she's here for that. It's just kind of hard to not notice those huge eyes and that jawline.

Sana gives herself a little shake. She needs to focus. But focus on what, exactly? She's not even sure why she's here. Killers often come back to the scene of the crime. The thought is a toxic one, floating up and releasing poison all over. Sana winces. *I'm not a killer. It's not my fault he's dead. He deserved it. Probably.* She winces again. God, these are awful thoughts to have, aren't they?

Thankfully, with a tinkle of bells, the door to Vera Wang's World-Famous Teahouse swings open once more, jerking Sana from her mental spiral. An old woman peers up at her. The woman's eyebrows are statement brows, and the statement is: *I am fucking fabulous and don't you forget it.* "Yes?" the woman says. "Can I help you?"

"Oh, um, yes! I—is this Vera Wang's World-Famous Teahouse?" The moment Sana says these words, she wants to kick herself. Because it literally says VERA WANG'S WORLD-FAMOUS TEAHOUSE right there, above her head, in huge, bright red letters. *Don't be repetitive, dear,* her mother's voice echoes in her mind. *It's better to say too little than too much.* Her mother should know; her books are notoriously short, leaving her legions of fans starving for more.

The old woman smiles proudly. "Yes, it is. Oh my, very busy day for me. So many new customers!" She ushers Sana in. There's no one else inside the small, dark teahouse.

Sana stands there, uncertain. So many new customers? As in . . . her and that one guy she ran into? The thought fills her with sudden sadness as she takes in her surroundings. It's obvious that Vera Wang's World-Famous Teahouse is past its best years.

"Sit, sit! I make you some tea. What's your name?" The old woman, presumably Vera Wang herself, waves at the tables before bustling behind the counter.

Sana goes to the nearest table and perches gingerly on one of the chairs. "Um, it's Sana. Sana Singh. I'm here because—"

"Let me guess, because of dead man?"

That startles Sana a bit. "Yes. I—I read about it in the obituary, and—"

Vera nods and gestures at the floor. "He's there."

"What?" Sana jumps up. When she looks to where Vera is pointing, she realizes with a mixture of horror and relief that there's an outline of a man's body drawn on the floor. Okay, so he—as in the dead body itself—isn't actually there. She wills her heart to stop thumping quite so hard. The outline seems to have been drawn using a Sharpie. "Did you—did the police do this? I would've thought that they'd use tape."

"Ah, the police. Useless, the lot of them." Vera snorts as she sprinkles some tea leaves into a teapot. "No, of course they didn't. I do myself. Good job, eh? I stay very close to body. Sometimes the Sharpie touched the body a little."

Sana gapes at her. "The cops were okay with you doing that?"

"Oh, I do it while waiting for them to arrive. I even make some tea for them, all before they arrive. But are they grateful?"

There's a beat of silence, then Sana rushes to fill it. "No?"

"Very ungrateful." Vera pours hot water into the teapot and carries it on a tray to the table. "Sit, we have some tea. This is Qimen Hongcha from Anhui Province in China. Try," she orders, serving Sana the drink in a teacup so small it looks almost like a doll's teacup.

Sana does so, and it's nothing like she's ever tasted before, but at the same time it's also somehow familiar. It's smoky and smells of spring flowers. "So soothing," she murmurs, taking a longer sip. Before she knows it, the tiny teacup is empty and Vera plucks it from her hand and pours her another.

"Now, what can I do for you, Sana?"

"Oh, right." It takes a second for Sana to gather her thoughts after the beautiful tea. "Um, I'm . . . I have a podcast," she says finally.

Vera's eyebrows wrinkle together. "Oh dear. I'm sure I have some cream for that."

"Um, no, it's a sort of . . . Internet radio show?"

"Ah." Vera's face brightens. "Wonderful, you're radio host?"

"Sort of, but it's not like a real radio station or anything. It's just me talking into a mic." Her mother's voice whispers: *Never minimize your work, dear. If you don't take it seriously, no one will.* But the last time Sana took herself seriously, it led to her dropping out of school, so maybe her mother doesn't actually know shit. "About true crime," she adds quickly.

"Ah, and you want to talk about the man who die here." Vera nods and takes a sip of her tea. "But why?"

"Why do I want to do an episode on it? Because, I mean, a man died in a tea shop, that's gotta be suspicious, right?" Is it? Sana has no idea aside from that if it's Marshall, then it must be suspicious.

Vera shrugs. "The police don't think so. They say they don't think there is foul play."

No foul play. Sana nods, careful to keep her face neutral. "Um, can I ask you what you know about the case?"

"There is no case, I telling you, the police, they say is open-and-shut. He probably overdose on drugs, stumble into my shop, and die."

"Right." Had Marshall been using drugs? Sana isn't sure about this, though at this point, nothing about Marshall should surprise her. "Well, just humor me. I don't often get the chance to interview the sole witness to something like this. I need content. I mean, uh, not to sound crass. Sorry, that sounded terrible."

"So you think something suspicious about his death?"

Is it just Sana's imagination or is there a cunning glint in Vera's eyes? She's getting the sense that there's something very much unsaid behind Vera's words, but Sana isn't quite sure what it is. Whatever it is, she needs to tread carefully. "I don't . . . know one way or another," she says, picking every word with care, "but I do think that there might be a story there."

Vera leans back, her eyebrows arched at an alarming angle. "Mm," she says, stroking her chin. It seems to Sana that Vera is greatly enjoying this, though she doesn't quite understand why. "The boy that's in here before you, he is from the Buzzfeed. He also thinks there is good story here."

Buzzfeed? Why would Buzzfeed be interested in Marshall's death? Do they have a true crime section? No, that's so far off from their brand.

"I wonder why so many people are thinking this is good story," Vera muses.

"Can you tell me everything you know about the man who died here?" Sana urges. The more Vera goes off track and starts musing out loud, the more on edge Sana becomes, convinced that the old woman knows something. Knows that Sana is hiding something. But she also senses that Vera herself is unwilling to part with some vital information.

"Well, I find him in the morning, on my way out."

"How long had he been here by the time you found him? What time was it that you found him?"

"Before five a.m. I wake up early every morning. What time you wake up every morning?" Vera's eyes narrow in anticipation of Sana's answer.

"Um, early. So he came in here between . . . what time and five a.m.?"

"Well, I go up to my apartment early, maybe at four p.m. I am awake until eight p.m., maybe nine. He must have come in here sometime after that, otherwise I would have heard."

Heat courses through Sana's veins. Eight or nine p.m. That would be only a few short hours since she last saw him. The fear becomes so sickening that she nearly throws up then and there. She forces herself to take another sip of the hot tea. "And was he—what was the body like? Did you see his expression?"

Vera's face turns somber. "Oh yes. Very unhappy. Very shock, so much horror in it."

The fear becomes nearly overwhelming. He'd been in shock, horrified. Can she blame him? A huge tidal wave of self-hatred washes over Sana. Marshall had been a fucking asshole, there can be no denying that, but she hadn't meant to—

"That is why," Vera says, leaning forward conspiratorially, "I myself believe he is murdered."

She says this so simply that it takes a while for the words to sink in. And when they do, Sana suddenly finds it hard to breathe. She knows. Vera knows.

Vera's eyes travel from Sana's face to Sana's hands, and her expression morphs into a frown. "Oh my dear, your nails are so bad."

"What?" Sana glances down and spots her nails, chewed down to the quick. Horrified, she balls her hands into fists, but why bother? It's too late. Vera's seen her nails. Is she putting two and two together, even now? Vera strikes Sana as someone who doesn't miss much.

But then Vera suddenly says, "Who's that?" and stands up so quickly that the wooden chair she's been sitting in clatters to the floor, making them both jump in fright.

Heart halfway up her throat, Sana turns around and sees a Caucasian woman, carrying a small child, peering in through the cloudy shop windows. Vera is already striding toward the door, but before she gets there, the woman turns and walks swiftly away.

"Hey!" Vera calls out. "Come back! I see you!"

Sana runs to the doorway and looks at the woman's hastily retreating back. Even with the toddler in her arms, the woman is surprisingly fast. Already she's almost at the end of the block. Sana wants to run after her, but that would look suspicious, and she can't afford to raise anyone's suspicions. Not after what happened between her and Marshall.

Vera, who has no such compunctions, is already trotting after the woman. *This is my chance,* Sana thinks, and steps back inside the teahouse. She looks around, first at the gruesome outline of the dead body, then at the numerous drawers and cabinets. She's not even sure what she'll find here, not sure what in the world she's even looking for, just that maybe Marshall might have left something that could vindicate her. She walks to the impressive wall of drawers behind the counter and takes a deep breath before opening one of them. A plume of dust puffs out, making her cough. Inside is some strange-looking root, all gray and shriveled.

"It's cordyceps."

Sana jumps and slams the drawer shut. Vera is back, slightly out of breath after chasing the woman. Her eyes are sharp, but her expression is one of open curiosity instead of disapproval, despite catching Sana snooping.

"Sorry!" Sana says. "I was just so curious."

"Nothing wrong with a little curiosity," Vera says. Then she adds, with that little glint in her eyes, "Although you know what they say about curiosity and cat."

After that, Sana can't leave quite fast enough. She hastily gives Vera her number in case Vera thinks of something, then hurries out of the shop, walking down the block and turning a corner before she bursts into tears.

SEVEN

VERA

No one can say that Vera is boastful. No, Vera is many things, but boastful is not one of them. And yet, even she has to admit that her first day of investigating has exceeded all expectations. And as a Chinese mother, Vera has had years of practice at harboring unrealistic expectations. Truly, even the police would be forced to admit that she's very nearly solved their case for them. It's not even time for her afternoon tea yet, and already she has three whole suspects. *Superb work, Vera, simply marvelous,* she tells herself, as she brews a pot of jujubes and goji berries tea.

When the tea is done, Vera settles on her chair with a satisfied sigh and takes out her notebook. She picks up her 0.5-millimeter ballpoint pen with a flourish and smooths out the notebook and begins writing in painstakingly uniform letters.

VERA WONG'S MURDER CASE

Suspect 1: Riki Herwanto
—Too handsome to be real reporter

—Claims to be Gen Z but looks more like millennial. Murder ages you, maybe he look older because the guilt make him stress?

Suspect 2: Sana Singh
—Has a pot catch but claims it's not a rash
—Nails are bitten very badly, WHY? Is it to get rid of evidence of her scratch Marshall??

Suspect 3: White Lady with Child
—Runs very fast while carrying child, must be very strong, strong enough to kill Marshall
—And why run away from my shop? Very suspicious!

Clues: flash drive → what is inside?

Vera picks up her things and totters upstairs, where she settles at her kitchen table before ringing Tilly. Uncharacteristically, he actually answers the phone.

"Ma, I'm working," he grumbles.

In the background, Vera can hear noises of people talking in very clipped, businessy tones of voices. She nods to herself with satisfaction. She's raised Tilly well, just listen to him, among all these businessy people. She will respect his time and cut right to the chase. "Tilly, I have very important business. If you come across dead body, and the dead body is holding flash drive, how do you unlock the flash drive?"

"What? I— What? Ma, what is this—is this because I didn't come home for dinner last Sunday?"

"And Sunday before that, and Sunday before that, but no, it is not. Although I cook your favorite braised sea cucumber, take me three hours, but never mind. Now tell me, how do you unlock flash drive?"

"Wh—" Tilly stops, gives an exasperated sigh. "A flash drive from a dead body? I don't even— Why do you need to know that?"

"Oh, I just find a dead body in the teahouse yesterday, isn't that curious?"

There's a long silence. "Like, a real dead body?"

"Yes, it is a man, his name is Marshall Chen. Quite silly name, if you ask me, not regal like Tilbert, don't you think? Why can anyone name their son Marshall, like he is policeman?"

"Ma—" Tilly takes a deep breath. "Did you call the cops?"

"Yes, of course! I do it straightaway, after I draw outline around dead body. The cops all think I am very helpful." Okay, that part is an exaggeration, but Tilly doesn't need to know every detail.

"Did you—but—why are you asking me how to unlock the dead guy's flash drive?"

"Oh, no reason, just curious." Did that come out sounding very casual and innocent?

"Ma," Tilly's voice has turned low and serious. "Tell me you didn't take a flash drive from a dead body."

Vera stays quiet.

"And tell me," Tilly says, more urgency coloring his voice now, "you haven't plugged the drive into your computer."

Vera glances at her laptop screen, which is asking for a password to unlock the flash drive.

"Because," Tilly continues in the ominous tone of voice, "there could be a ton of bad stuff on the flash drive, like viruses and spyware and—"

Vera quickly yanks the flash drive out of her computer. "Aiya, of course I don't connect to my computer, do you think I'm so stupid?"

"Okay . . . but you shouldn't even have the flash drive in the first place, Ma." Tilly sighs again. "Look, you need to hand that over to the police, you understand?"

"They don't even take case seriously. They say it looks like just innocent death!"

"Maybe because you took evidence from the—oh my god, I can't do this. I can't be talking to you about this while I'm at work. Look, Ma, don't do anything. I'll call you later, okay?"

"Okay, drink more water and—"

Tilly hangs up before Vera can remind him to look for a girlfriend at his office. She stares at the phone for a bit, then sends him a text.

Don't forget to look for girlfriend at office.

Text sent, Vera turns her attention back to the flash drive. *Who would think that big secrets might be hidden in such a small item?* she muses, poking the flash drive. Technology, what a wonderful and terrible thing. Getting up, Vera fetches her fanny pack and tucks the flash drive into the inside pocket before zipping it shut. There, that's a good hiding place. She tromps back downstairs in case there is a line of customers clamoring to have some world-famous tea, but the shop is empty, as usual.

With a guilty start, Vera recalls how Alex had stopped by earlier that morning, but she'd quickly shooed him away because she'd been waiting for the killer to come and she couldn't risk them getting scared away by Alex's presence. Well, she'd better make up for her rudeness now.

She decides to bring over some of her specially made tea and maybe buy a couple of Singo pears on the way to his apartment.

On the way home, she will buy some more groceries to cook for him and she'll drop those off later in the afternoon. Yes, that is a good plan.

Less than ten minutes later, Vera locks up her shop, jams her visor firmly on her head, and heads up Washington with a basket slung over one arm. Inside are: one (1) packet of luo han guo and chrysanthemum tea, one (1) packet of goji berries, dried orange peel, and dried winter melon peel tea, and one (1) packet of butterfly pea flowers and lavender tea. At Mrs. Gao's grocery store, Vera stops to buy two Singo pears, two dragon fruits, and one large bitter melon. Satisfied with the amount of nutrients and vitamins in her basket, she continues the hilly walk to Alex's apartment building.

At the front door of Alex's building, Vera is about to press the buzzer when someone comes out, so she lets herself in and climbs the staircase to the third floor. None of the apartment units have a bell or a knocker. Vera raps on the door to Alex's apartment.

"Who is it?" Alex's voice calls out in Mandarin.

"Alex-ah, it's me, Vera. From the teahouse," she adds.

"Oh!" Footsteps hurry toward the door, a chain is unlocked, and the door opens to reveal Vera's favorite customer.

"Oh dear," Vera blurts out. "Alex-ah, you look terrible." She's not one for false courtesy. Honesty is the best policy and so on, after all. "It must be because you haven't had my teas for a while now. I'm so sorry about this morning. I know you must be dying to have some good tea, but oh, you won't believe what happened!"

Alex nods. "Yes, Winifred told me that there was a death in your shop. I am so sorry, Vera," he says with so much feeling that Vera can't help but be touched. Here is a true gentleman, she thinks. "It must be horrifying. I came by earlier to check on you, but you seemed quite eager for me to be on my way—"

"Oh, that's my fault! I was so rude to hurry you along like that. You see, I'm convinced that the dead man I found in my shop was, in fact, murdered, and I have a plan to flush out the killer, so I didn't want you hanging around my teahouse as it is simply too dangerous," Vera says dramatically.

Alex stares at her, seemingly taken aback by this proclamation. "What makes you think it was murder?"

"Never you mind, dear Alex, you have so much on your plate already. I won't bother you, I know you must be tired looking after Lily. Right, I can't stay long because there is a murder to be solved. You better stay away for the next few days until I catch the culprit. No use putting yourself in danger. But don't you worry, I'll stop by every once in a while to drop off more tea."

She hands Alex the basket of fruit and tea and tells him to take good care of himself before taking her leave.

"Thank you, Vera."

She could've sworn he teared up a bit then. She's going to have to tell Tilly about it, that a customer was so grateful to get her tea that he actually teared up. Not that Tilly would believe it. Her heart feels twice as big as before when she walks out of Alex's dank apartment building. It feels good to do good deeds. Imagine just how amazing she'll feel once she solves the murder case.

There is a bounce in Vera's step as she makes her way back to the teahouse. She's so busy admiring the sights around her that it takes a moment for her to notice the man standing outside her shop, and when she finally does, Vera's heart stops beating for a moment. It really does skip a beat, her blood freezing in her veins, her feet stopping short, her limbs turning into granite. It is fair to say that this is the most shock that Vera has ever experienced, even worse than when she found the dead body in her teahouse. Dead bodies rarely, in Vera's vast life experience, appear in teahouses, but it's not physically impossible for one to pop up occasionally. But what she is now seeing is utterly impossible. Because the man standing outside of Vera Wang's World-Famous Teahouse is the very same man who turned up dead inside just one day ago.

EIGHT

OLIVER

The first thought that zips through Oliver's mind is: *Oh no. My brother just died very recently and now I'm about to kill this poor woman.*

Indeed, the old woman standing a few paces away from him looks like she's this close to having a heart attack, or a brain aneurysm, or whatever it is that happens when someone old gets a good shock. Or a bad one, depending on how you look at it.

Oliver quickly raises his hands in what he hopes is a nonthreatening manner. "Don't worry, I'm not him! I'm his brother! His twin brother."

Understanding melts across the old woman's face. Her gaping mouth closes before opening again and going, "Oh . . ." She steps forward and scrutinizes his face unabashedly. "Wah, you look exactly like him."

"Well, yes. It's an unfortunate side effect of being twins." Actually, the unfortunate side effect of being twins is that there are minute differences, and Oliver got the short end of the stick with every minute difference. He's an inch shorter than Marshall, his eyes are just a tad less intense than Marshall's, his chin a touch weaker. Back in high school, people used to call Oliver "Discount Marshall."

"Aiya." The old woman stabs a finger at Oliver. "You almost give me heart attack!"

"I'm very sorry." He really is. Despite the accusatory finger in his face, the old woman seems nice, and Oliver would've been very sorry if she had died.

"I'm Vera. Owner of Vera Wang's World-Famous Teahouse." She says this with a flourish, as though she's saying, *I'm the queen of England.*

Oliver gets the feeling that he's supposed to be impressed, so he nods, raising his eyebrows. "Cool. I heard that was where my brother . . . uh . . ."

"Oh yes, it is. You want to see the outline of his body? Hmm, but maybe that too upsetting? Well, never mind, if you get upset, I have just right tea for you. Come in. What's your name again? Let me guess, something starting with *M* also? Michael? Mark? Morris?"

She seems to be having such a good time coming up with names starting with *M* that Oliver almost wishes he were named Michael or Morris. But that's always been Oliver's problem, hasn't it? Always a people pleaser, or as Marshall had called him back in high school, "suck-up" or "loser" or "pathetic embarrassment." There had been many other names Marshall had come up with for Oliver, most of them involving private parts, but Oliver doesn't like to think of them. Everything is okay as long as he doesn't think too much about Marshall.

But then why is he here if he doesn't want to think about Marshall? Oliver is surprised to find, when Vera unlocks the front door of the teahouse and beckons him to follow, that his knees have turned all loose and jellylike. He has to focus on taking one step after another, inhale, exhale, as he walks inside. And there it is.

He'd seen the outline from outside, of course, but the windows are so cloudy he could easily pretend that the outline was just an oddly shaped shadow. But now he's seeing it in stark lines and it suddenly hits him that Marshall is dead. This is where Marshall lay down to die. What was going through his head in the last moments of his life? Did he think about Oliver? Did he blame Oliver? He should, it's all Oliver's fault, everything has always been Oliver's fault.

It had been that way ever since their mother had died while making Oliver's favorite dessert when Oliver was six. Oliver had loved shaved ice and begged her to make some, and he was her favorite, everyone knew it, so she said yes, of course. Oliver and Marshall had been in the living room playing Who Can Make the Loudest Fart Noises, when they heard the thud from the kitchen. They'd rushed to the kitchen and found their mother on the floor, a pool of blood spreading like a halo around her head. There were puddles of water everywhere, spat out by the shaved-ice machine. She'd slipped on one and hit her head on the corner of the kitchen counter, and that had been that. Marshall and Dad had blamed him for her death. He had blamed himself for her death. But they also got into the habit of blaming him for everything else, and Oliver wasn't quite sure how to handle that on top of his own grief and guilt, so he did the only thing he could. He shouldered the rest of the blame, trying to make himself as small and unobtrusive as he could. It had worked with their dad, who, for the most part, pretended that Oliver did not exist, but nothing went unnoticed by Marshall. Marshall would pinch him, then when that garnered no response, he would punch him, on the arm at first, then the torso, then the head, as Oliver curled up into a ball and wished he would die too.

Except now it's him looking down at an outline of Marshall's body and not the other way around. There's nothing right about that. What's Dad going to say? He'll know, first of all, that it was Oliver's fault, because this is the way it has always been in their family. Except this time, he would be right. It is Oliver's fault.

"Sit," Vera says so loudly and so suddenly that Oliver jumps. His legs bypass his brain and he sits before realizing what he's doing.

A wooden tray is set before him, and Vera pours him some tea. It smells like sweet flowers and milk, and tears prick Oliver's eyes. He can barely remember what his mom had smelled of, of course, but somehow this scent is bringing her back to life in front of him.

"This is Huangshan Maofeng," Vera says, handing him a fragile-looking teacup. "Try."

He does so, and it takes him straight back to his mother, and Oliver can't hold back the tears anymore. Vera, for her part, seems unperturbed that a complete stranger is sitting there crying in front of her. In fact, Oliver thinks as he accepts a handkerchief from her, she looks rather pleased about it.

"That is the correct reaction to this tea," Vera says, taking a sip. "It is very rare, all my teas are rare, you know, and when it is picked, the farmers sob because the fragrance is so beautiful it reminds them of the celestial gardens in heaven."

"Really?" Oliver sniffles, fighting to get his emotions under control.

Vera shrugs. "I don't know, I make it up. Americans like it

when I tell them stories about each type of tea." Her accent becomes stronger, more exaggerated. "Oh, this tea, from Fujian Province in China, is guarded by a golden dragon that fly above the fields." She cocks an eyebrow at him. "See? Convincing, eh?"

Oliver nods and gives a weak smile.

"Now, tell me why you are here."

This is said in such an authoritative voice that Oliver is sure he can't refuse even if he tries. Not that he wants to refuse; something about Vera is strangely inviting. Maybe it's the fact that she oozes with a motherly aura. "I wanted to see the place where my brother was last alive," he croaks.

She pours another cup and hands it to him. "Your brother, what is he like?"

Oliver takes a deep breath. He should say the right things. You never speak ill of the dead, everyone knows that. He should tell her that Marshall was a good person, someone who always made everyone around him happy. He should tell her that Marshall's death is a horrible loss for everyone who's ever known him. The words are already forming in his mind, but when Oliver opens his mouth, what comes out is, "My brother was maybe the most charismatic person I've ever come across, but he was also the most cruel. He took pleasure in humiliating others, in making sure everyone knew he was better than they were. And his favorite target was me. He made sure that I knew, and everyone knew, that I was the bad twin. I hated him." Oliver's voice shakes. What the hell is he doing, telling her all this? He might as well tell her he's guilty and hold out his wrists for her to handcuff. Not that she has handcuffs, she's a little old lady who owns a tea shop, for goodness' sake.

He expected Vera to be horrified at all the toxic things he's spewing, but instead, she nods sagely and slurps at her tea. "Ah yes, I figure, this man is not good man. Is why he is murdered."

Tiny pinpricks shiver down the back of Oliver's neck. "M-murdered?" He finds, to his horror, that his hand starts to shake, and he hurriedly puts down his teacup before the tremors become too obvious. "Wha— The police didn't mention foul play to me."

Vera releases a surprisingly powerful snort and flaps a hand at him. "The police. What do they know? They don't even take fingerprint. They are not at all like on TV, you know, with all that fancy CSI stuff, oh no, they come in, they look around, they take my statement, then they call medical examiner. I thought, aha, this medical examiner will know what he is talking about, but he come, he look at the body, he take the body away. End of story." She leans forward, her eyes on Oliver. "No, if you want to solve the mystery of your brother's death, we must do it ourselves."

"Uh . . . I don't . . . I'm sure there's protocol in cases like these, and the police I'm sure are doing their best to look into it and make sure everything looks kosher." Actually, he hopes they're as incompetent as Vera described.

"And what is it you think happened?" Vera narrows her eyes at him. Suspicion rolls out of her in thick waves. She's not even bothering to hide that she thinks he's one of the main suspects.

Oliver can practically feel his pores expanding and releasing sweat. "There's nothing determined yet, we're still waiting for the medical examiner to confirm it, but they think it might have been an allergic reaction."

Vera's eyes narrow even further. They're so narrowed they're practically closed by now. Oliver half wonders how she's still able to see. "An allergic reaction to what?"

Oliver shakes his head. "Marshall was allergic to quite a few things. Beestings, peanuts, almonds, feathers—one time, our mom got this secondhand goose-down duvet, and I remember she was so pleased because they're usually so expensive—"

Vera nods. "Ah yes, what a good find. Good woman, your mother."

"The best," Oliver says with a wan smile. "Anyway, Marshall and I still shared a bed at the time and that night, I remember hearing this awful noise. It was like he was trying to breathe through a thin straw. It was horrible. I woke up and tried to shake him awake, but all he did was continue doing that whistling breath, and I started screaming and crying, and our parents barged into our room and got him his inhaler, and then they had to rush him to the hospital; his face was all swollen and his hands—" Oliver shudders. "His fingers were like sausages, all red and swollen, the skin was so tightly stretched. I thought they would burst. He had a rash for days afterward, even after the swelling went away."

"Hmm." Vera scratches her chin. "Interesting. Well, this is all very helpful, Oliver. Thank you, I have a good list of suspects."

"What?"

"Nothing concrete enough to show you, but—" She shifts in her seat and takes out her phone. "You put your number in there, and I will call you once I find killer."

"Uh . . ." He tries to think of a million reasons to say no, but when he glances at Vera's kind but also razor-sharp expression, he knows anything he comes up with would be futile. So Oliver keys in his number, all the while wondering just what the hell he's gotten himself into. He gets the feeling he's going to regret stepping inside Vera Wang's World-Famous Teahouse for a long time to come.

NINE

RIKI

After the second consecutive missed call, Riki's phone gives up on silent mode and starts wailing. The noise slices through his nightmare-filled sleep in which little Adi is shouting, "Kakak, when can I come to America too? Why have you left me behind?" and Riki wakes up in a pool of sweat, heart thudding and mouth dry. He paws his bedside table for his phone, unplugs it, and goes, "Adi? What's wrong?"

But instead of Adi's, a woman's voice comes out. "Riki? Are you still asleep?"

Riki blinks blearily, trying to clear his sleep-fogged mind. "Who's this?"

"It's Vera."

Nope, the name isn't—

Oh. Right, Vera. The little old lady from the tea shop. Why the hell is she calling him at—Riki glances at his watch—what the hell? It's only 7:32 a.m. That can't be right. His heart suddenly revs up again, before his mind catches up. She must be calling because something is very, very wrong. "Vera, what happened?"

"Well, I have been checking the Buzzfeed, you know, and I don't see your article anywhere! And I think to myself, ah, since it's not up yet, maybe I still have time to give you some important detail to put in your article."

It takes a moment for Riki to figure out just what in the world Vera is talking about. The Buzzfeed? Oh, right. He stupidly told her he's from Buzzfeed when he met her yesterday. Oh god. He massages his forehead. Why had he said that? "Uh, right," he mumbles.

"For example, make sure you mention my shop address. It's important that people know where to find me, yes? And also, you didn't take pictures of my shop yesterday. Do you forget to? I have put on more makeup today, and my hair is looking very nice, so come by and take photos of me and my teas, okay? You know, I read that articles that have plenty of pictures are the ones that do best. You reporters, you're given a bonus if your article goes viral, right?"

Are reporters given bonuses based on how many clicks their articles get? Riki has no idea, but he could conceivably see that happening. He nods, then realizes Vera can't see him, and says, "Yeah . . . ?"

"Ah, well, there you go. Come here, take many photos of me, take photos of the body outline too, that'll be good for the article."

"Um, now? It's not even eight o'clock yet." Riki had gone to bed at two in the morning and he feels like he could use another five hours of sleep.

"Aiya, the early morning light is best for photographs, how do you not know that? No wonder none of your article has gone viral yet. Get up, young people should not be sleeping their youth away. Take a shower and come here for breakfast, there's a good boy." With that, she hangs up, leaving Riki blinking at his phone, half wondering if the call actually happened or if it had been a dream.

He lies back down, and as soon as his head hits the pillow, the flashback attacks.

You listen to me, you slimy piece of shit. Pay me, Marshall, or I will fucking kill you.

The animal rage in his own voice is so palpable it turns the words almost physical. *I will fucking kill you.*

Riki shoots straight up in bed, breathing hard. He rubs his face several times, trying to shake away the flashback. He's never lost his temper like that before. Never, not once in his lifetime, not even when he was a hormonal teen and Adi was annoying the shit out of him. Not even when he found his college roommate in bed with Riki's then girlfriend. But Marshall had reached deep into Riki's subconscious and triggered some kind of fight-or-flight response and Riki's fury had been so strong he had scared himself. And now Marshall is dead. Why in the world did Riki even go to Vera's tea shop? If anything, he should go to Marshall's house, or maybe Marshall's office, to find what he's been looking for this whole time. But no, he'd gone to Vera Wang's World-Famous Teahouse, and now here he is, having to go round to her shop and pretend to be a reporter.

The thought of keeping Vera waiting is somehow terrifying, so against all his survival instincts, Riki gets up and takes a cold shower in the hope of sharpening his mind. When he gets dressed, he notices that his fingers are trembling slightly, fumbling a little with the buttons of his shirt. *There's nothing to be nervous about*, he reminds himself. *You did nothing wrong. Nothing at all.*

Problem is, he's never been any good at lying to himself.

B ack in Indonesia, Riki's parents had taught him to never show up at someone's house without bringing a gift, so before arriving at Vera's, Riki stops by at the French bakery next door. He has no idea what Vera would like, so just to be safe, he gets an assortment of pastries, both sweet and savory. He tells the nice old lady manning the store that he loves French food, which seems to please her greatly.

When Riki walks into Vera's tea shop, she doesn't even look up from behind the counter, where she's got jars of herbs and dried fruits out. "Ah, finally you are here. I am making a special brew for you." Then she looks up, and to Riki's bewilderment, when she catches sight of the bag he's holding, she actually glowers. "Is that—"

"Um, I brought some pastries from the French bakery next door? I thought you might like—"

"Hah!" she snorts. "*French* bakery? That is a *Chinese* bakery."

"Oh, um . . ." Riki looks at the paper bag, which clearly says: WINIFRED'S FRENCH PATISSERIE, DÉLICIEUX TOUS LES JOURS. "I don't speak Chinese," he admits, "but this looks French to me?"

"*Hah!*" Vera says again. She seems to be getting louder and angrier, and Riki has no idea why. She strides toward him from behind the counter, and he has to resist the urge to throw the bag down and run away. It's like watching a shockingly fierce Jack Russell terrier come charging at you, baring its little fangs. She snatches the bag from him—Riki doesn't even bother resisting—

and takes out a pastry at random. The pastry is wrapped in plastic and on the plastic is a sticker that says: PETIT PAIN À LA CRÈME. "*Hah!*"

Are the "hahs" supposed to mean something? Riki wonders but keeps his mouth sealed. He gets the feeling that he's stumbled upon some long-lasting grudge, and back home in Indonesia, he has enough aunties and uncles to know that the best thing to do when they get like this is to shut up and hope you magically learn how to turn yourself invisible.

"Petit pain à la crème!" Vera snorts. "This is custard bun!"

"Yes . . . I think that's what it says in French as well?" Riki ventures.

"I bet it does. I bet that silly woman just look on Google Translate and change everything into French." She reaches into the bag and pulls out yet another offending pastry. "Brioche aux oeufs salés." She snorts but takes the time to unwrap the bun and rip it into two halves before announcing, "Just as I think. This is salted egg yolk custard bun." She seems like she's about to launch into another tirade, then she sniffs at the bun before taking a small bite. "Hmm." She chews thoughtfully. "Not enough salted egg yolk. Skimping, such a cheapskate. Still, now that you buy it already we might as well eat it, mustn't waste food, you know. Sit."

Riki obeys, taking out the rest of the pastries with no small amount of trepidation. Vera takes out a few plates and Riki meekly places the buns on them. He chooses to place them upside down so that the French names aren't visible.

"So," Vera says as she settles down across from him and pours out tea for both of them, "what is the holdup? Young people should be moving fast, take the world by its male genitalia, and so on."

"Um . . ." He shouldn't be taken aback by the use of the term "male genitalia." Vera strikes him as the kind of person who says whatever the hell she wants at any given time. But since the current given time is barely past eight thirty in the morning, Riki is only half-awake and very much not ready for words like "male genitalia" being lobbed at him by a savage old lady. He sips at his tea slowly, trying to buy more time, then is distracted because, gosh, this tea is really good. It's bitter but in a surprisingly refreshing way, like it's cleansing his insides and leaving nothing but pure sweetness behind. He picks a pastry at random and bites into it, and savory-sweet salted egg yolk custard fills his mouth. Eaten with the bitter tea, the bun is so comforting he feels his muscles relaxing after just one bite.

"Is it really that good?" Vera says, biting into the other half of the bun. She sniffs and answers her own question. "It's not half-bad, I suppose. Anyway, so why is my article taking such long time?"

"Oh, um. Well, I have to polish it, and after that I'll have to send it to my editor and, uh, wait for her to, you know, edit it? And then, um . . ." He has no idea what other steps are involved in the process of publishing Buzzfeed articles, but he prays hard for there to be a multitude of obstacles along the way.

Vera is shaking her head. "Oh, this is more inefficient than I think. Dear me, you young people want everything fast, but when it comes to your work, you do everything so slow."

The mention of work weighs on Riki's shoulders. Because Vera's wrong. As far as Riki knows, every "young person," including him, wants to be productive, to be the most efficient in the workplace. To rush up the career ladder. And Riki most of all, because it's not just his future he's been struggling for, but Adi's as well. Adi, who is only twelve and yet knows so much more than Riki does.

His thoughts are interrupted when the little bell above Vera's door chimes. Vera's face lights up. "Ah," she says, "just in time. Let me introduce you to my other suspect."

TEN

SANA

Sana has had enough of pushy older Asian women, she really has. Every morning, she tells herself that today will be the day she stands up to her mother. She already has a whole speech written, and rewritten, and scrapped, and rewritten, etcetera. She's practiced it several times in the mirror, making sure she hits that perfect tone between confident and respectful. At night, before she sleeps, she lies in bed and imagines what it might be like when she finally recites the speech to her mom. But every other day, her mother calls, and every other day, Sana's speech refuses to come out of her mouth. It lodges in her throat like a stray cough drop and ends up choking her.

And now, here is Vera, a complete stranger, maybe ten years older than Sana's mom, and Vera is exactly the kind of pushy Asian mother figure that Sana's had to put up with her whole life. Well, Sana is going to use Vera as practice fodder. Yes, that's a good plan. If she can stand up to Vera, she can stand up to her mother, no problem. The whole way to Vera's teahouse, Sana's rehearsed what she's going to say.

Look, Vera, you can't just call me at seven in the morning and tell me to make myself "presentable." You can't do that. I'm not your kid, and even if I were, you need to treat me like an adult. Because that's what I am.

No, too long-winded.

Vera, I'm blocking your number because clearly you do not understand boundaries.

Yes, perfect. Vera will ask what boundaries are, and Sana will explain everything to her patiently.

Except when Sana walks into Vera Wang's World-Famous Teahouse, the first thing she sees is the unreasonably attractive guy she ran into the day before. Then, before Sana can gather herself, Vera is already on her.

"Ah, Sana! Come in, come in! Sit, you sit here, right next to Riki." Already she's grabbed hold of Sana's wrist in a surprisingly strong grip and led her to a chair adjacent to Riki.

Riki, for his part, is wearing an expression that a frightened, kidnapped boy might have. His eyes are wide, his mouth slightly open like he's dying to ask a question but is scared of what the answer might be. Their eyes meet and Sana widens hers in a *Do you know what the hell is happening?* gesture, and he gives a minute shake of the head. The small exchange loosens her up a little. At least Riki seems as lost as she feels.

"Riki, this is Sana," Vera says, as she sinks into her own seat. "Sana, this is Riki, my other suspect."

Sana's skin suddenly feels two sizes too small for her body. Suspect? She balls her hands into fists and puts them behind her back, wondering how long DNA lasts under one's fingernails.

There's a moment of silence, then Riki clears his throat. "Um, you keep saying this word 'suspect' . . . uh . . . is there something we should be aware of?"

"Oh yes," Vera says cheerfully, pouring a cup of tea for Sana, "you are two of my suspects, of course. Suspects in Marshall's murder," she adds, in case they hadn't quite got that.

"Wh—" The question lodges in Sana's throat, and while she struggles to speak, Vera hands her the tea, and years of teachings about how to treat your elders kick in and Sana automatically says, "Thank you, Auntie." Then, of course, she wants to kick herself because, first of all, Vera is *not* her auntie, and second of all, even if she were, she's an auntie who is accusing Sana of literal murder.

"Oh, such a polite girl you are!" Vera smiles at her, but the smile wanes when she spots Sana's hands. "Wah, your hands are spattered with paint. You should wash them, paint is no good for your skin, that's why your hands are so dry."

Sana removes her hands from the table, her cheeks burning with embarrassment. "Yeah, it's—I was just, uh, painting my room." *Hah*, a little voice says in her head. *You wish you were painting your room.* In truth, she'd just mixed the paints before standing in front of the blank canvas for a whole hour, holding up her brush until the paint trickled down the bristles and the handle and her hand, all the way to her elbow, before she threw down the brush and stormed out of the room. Same old story.

"How old are you again, Sana? What year are you born in?"

Sana tells her, and Vera scrunches her face up in deep thought. A moment later, Vera shakes her head with a tut. "Ah, you are a dragon. Not compatible with my son. I been thinking, *if* you are not killer, of course, that I should introduce you to my son, but he

is an ox, you know, so it's not compatible. Dragon will eat the ox."
Vera turns to Riki. "And you? What is your zodiac sign?"

"Uh. I'm a rat?" Riki says apologetically.

"Oh!" Vera claps, a huge smile swallowing her face. "Wonderful! Perfect match, you two! I just know it. I know you will make a good couple. If neither of you is Marshall's killer, then this is match make in heaven. Such good luck."

Sana and Riki look at each other and the only thing that makes Sana feel less mortified is seeing how embarrassed Riki is. At least it's not just her. Also, who cares about feeling mortified? She should be panicking at the whole murder-suspect thing. But there is just so much going on, and oh, now Vera's placed a bun right in Sana's face and is ordering Sana to eat it. Sana complies without thinking, and before she knows it, she's got a mouthful of taro bun and is listening to Vera talk about how the bun is actually Chinese, not French, despite what Sana might think. Bold of Vera to assume that Sana is thinking of French pastries when her mind is basically just going, *Waaaaaah?!*

"So Sana here," Vera is saying to Riki, "has a potcut—now, I know you might think it is sounding like very bad skin condition, but is actually like a radio show, but on the Internet. Very good, right? It's like your job, Riki, but on the radio! Well, not on the radio, but on the Internet." She nods to herself, satisfied with her explanation, then says to Sana, "Riki here is a reporter from the Buzzfeed!"

"Wow," Sana says through a mouthful of not-French taro bun. "That's really impressive," she says to Riki, who scratches his cheek and looks down at his teacup. Aww, he's humble too. Her insides are writhing at the thought of Riki and Vera finding out the truth about her, that she has neither a podcast, nor a potcut, and that she's in fact not doing much with her life aside from failing to do the very thing she's wanted to do ever since she dipped her chubby hands in a paint pot at age one.

"Um." Riki clears his throat. "You mentioned that we're both suspects? Can I ask why?"

"Oh yes." Vera sets down her teacup. "You mustn't take it personal, okay? Oh, you young people take everything so personal nowadays. So what if I think you might be a killer? That doesn't mean I think you are a bad person."

"Uh . . ." Sana licks her lips. "I mean, I think it kind of does?"

Vera tuts at her. "What nonsense. Of course not."

"But why do you think we're suspects in the first place?" Riki says, tugging at the collar of his shirt.

"So many reasons." Vera holds up her left thumb. "One, everyone knows that killers always come back to scene of the crime. Yes? They like to admire their handiwork. So I know, all I have to do is wait and see who turns up. Both of you turn up yesterday, so you automatically go on my list. See? Nothing personal."

"You said there are many reasons?" Sana says, though she's unsure that she wants to know the other reasons.

"Yes, of course. Okay, ladies first. Sana, where were you on night that Marshall was killed?"

Sana's mind implodes, filling her head with nothing but bright white light and a high-pitched squeal. *Say something*, she screams silently at herself. *Anything!* But nothing comes out.

"This is silly," Riki says.

Sana looks at him, her heart sprinting like a hunted rabbit.

"We don't know Marshall, Vera. We certainly don't have to tell you where we were on the night he died." He seems so sure of himself when he says this. Is this what it's like to be able to stand

up to an elderly Asian auntie? Sana is both impressed and horrified at the same time. "Let's focus on why you think Marshall was
killed to begin with."

Vera shrugs, though her expression stays sharp and alert. "Okay,
you don't have to tell me for now. I will figure out later. Let's see,
why else do I think Marshall is killed? Well, this Marshall guy
sounds like very bad person, the kind that would get killed, you
know?"

Sana could swear her intestines have morphed into snakes and
are slithering around inside her belly. She feels like throwing up.
Because yes, Vera is exactly right. Marshall was a very bad person,
the kind that would very much get killed. Then she reminds herself that she's not supposed to have known Marshall personally, so
she forces her features into what she thinks is an expression of
bland interest. "Oh? What have you found out about Marshall?"
She belatedly adds, "I'm asking because of my true crime podcast,
obviously."

Vera leans closer to them and says in a conspiratorial voice, "I
think that this Marshall guy has something people want. Something that he keep himself, very safe."

When Sana was six, her parents took her and her sister up to
Tahoe and Sana saw snow for the very first time. She and her sister
had flung themselves into the soft snowbanks and threw snowballs
at each other, laughing and shrieking. She remembers her sister
grabbing the back of Sana's jacket from behind and dumping a fist-
ful of snow down her collar and the shock of the cold freezing the
back of her neck before slithering down her back. This moment
feels exactly like someone dumped a handful of snow down her
neck. Something that Marshall kept safe? How does Vera know?

But before Sana can say anything, Vera claps once and stands up. "Okay, you all done drinking tea? Come upstair and help me carry something down. You young people are much stronger than me. Come!" she barks when both Sana and Riki remain sitting, looking stunned.

Sana and Riki stand at the same time and exchange another helpless glance before following Vera up the narrow, rickety stairs. Faded pictures hang on the wall, many of them crumbling inside their old-fashioned, chipped frames. The second floor turns out to be Vera's living quarters, a small, dark space filled to the gills with what looks like broken, ancient junk. Sana eyes the towering piles of old newspapers and magazines, the cobwebbed sewing machine, an old typewriter missing half its keys, and boxes probably filled with similarly unusable items. It's a familiar sight to her. Her parents' house is pristine because her mother is ruthless about keeping her house immaculate for the many interviews and videos she shoots for her fans, but as a kid, whenever Sana visited her friends' homes, especially the first-generation kids, she'd often find houses filled with crumbling boxes full of stuff. Mementos from their parents' homeland, too old to use, too precious to throw away, too painful to look at. So they are left to age gently, a reminder of everyone who was left behind.

"Come," Vera calls out from the small kitchen, and Sana tears her eyes from the mountains of memories in the living room and heads toward the kitchen.

Vera is unloading container after container from the fridge and piling them on the kitchen counter. "Put them inside those bags." She points at a couple of reusable shopping bags.

Sana and Riki each take a bag. "What's in these?" Sana says as she picks up a Tupperware container and peers through the plastic. She spies something brown swimming in thick gravy.

"Food. That one has pepper beef, very tender. I marinade the beef chunk in rice wine, make the meat so soft, like biting into marshmallow."

"I don't know that beef should have the consistency of marsh-mallow," Sana says, sliding the container into the bag.

Vera frowns at her. "Obviously it's just a saying. You will see later, it is the perfect tenderness. Ah, that one has braised tofu and mushroom. Children will love that. It was my Tilly's favorite."

Before long, both bags are stuffed full of containers.

"Okay, carry them downstair," Vera says cheerfully. "Be care-ful! I spend all morning cooking!"

"It's literally only ten in the morning," Riki says. "You couldn't have cooked all this food this morning."

Vera gives him a savage side-eye. "You can if you wake up early enough." She marches past them and starts heading down the stairs.

"But—" Sana heaves the bag up with a grunt. "Wait, what's all this food for?"

Vera doesn't miss a beat. "My fourth suspect, of course." Just then, the downstairs bell chimes. "Ah, that'll be my third suspect. Come, we don't have all day!"

Sana will learn to stand up to pushy Asian aunties one day. It seems, however, that today is not that day.

ELEVEN

VERA

Vera's murder investigation is going so well that she wonders why more people don't just decide to leave their boring desk jobs and go into detective work. She's started daydreaming of having the huge VERA WANG'S WORLD-FAMOUS TEAHOUSE sign taken down and replaced with VERA WANG: PRIVATE INVESTIGATOR. Maybe she should, just to see the expression on Winifred's face. Then again, maybe the reason why her investigation is going so well is because no one expects a tea expert to also be an expert at solving murder mysteries. Vera is basically undercover. Yes, better to hide the fact that she is a sleuth as well as a tea doctor, as she sometimes likes to refer to herself. Tilly, of course, would say, "What's a tea doctor? Do you treat teas when they have indigestion? When they break a limb?" But that's Tilly for you. He's going to be very annoyed when he finds out that his mother has only gone and solved a murder.

Just this morning, Vera woke up to a text from Tilly. A text! From Tilly! Without any prompting on her behalf! It said:

Ma, call me back when you get this. We need to talk
about the flash drive. You could get in serious trouble for
doing that. We need to discuss how to properly handle
this. I still can't believe you did that.

A *bit naggy, if you ask me*, Vera thinks. She'd replied with:

Of course I don't have flash drive, what you think I am
so stupid? I was just asking hippotechnically.

Tilly had replied with more questions, which Vera conveniently forgot to reply to.

The thought of telling Tilly and Winifred about her newfound
sleuthing skills puts an extra bounce in Vera's step and she practically prances down the stairs. As expected, Oliver's standing
there, looking wary and hesitant, his shoulders rounded. If he'd
been wearing a hat, he'd be clutching it in two sweaty palms,
wringing it in front of his chest. As it is, hats have gone the way of
yore, so Oliver merely stands there, one hand in his pocket, the
other clutching his phone. When he sees Vera, both relief and
panic war on his face, if that is possible. Vera can practically hear
his thoughts: *Oh good, she's here.* And *Oh no, she's here.*

"Oliver! Good boy, you're just in time. Sana, Riki, this is
Oliver."

Behind her, Sana emits a loud, horrified gasp, and Riki freezes
midway down the steps. They both stare at Oliver like—well, like
they're staring at a dead guy.

"I'm his twin," Oliver says quickly, before either of these poor
kids gets a heart attack.

They both visibly sag. Sana recovers first, giving what Vera thinks sounds like the world's fakest laugh. "Oh man, you guys really do look alike."

"How did you know my brother?"

There's a split second of a pause, then Sana laughs again and says, "I didn't know him personally, I actually have a true crime podcast and I'm here to do a story on him. I know what he looked like, of course, because I googled him."

"Yeah, same here," Riki says, offering Oliver his hand. "I'm Riki, I'm a reporter covering a story about your brother. I'm so sorry for your loss."

Inwardly, Vera shakes her head. Young people really need to learn how to lie better. All she needs to do is get them alone in a room with a bright light she can shine directly in their faces and the investigation would be over in five minutes, but where would the fun be in that?

"Thanks," Oliver says, then almost apologetically, he adds, "We weren't close."

The three of them nod at one another, then stand there looking extremely awkward before Oliver raises his eyebrows at Vera. "Um, is there a reason why you asked me to bring my car here?"

"Oh yes. Are introductions over, then? Good, good. Let's go. No dillydallying! Like I always tell my Tilly, you young people should move fast. Grab life by the you know what!" Like a mother goose, Vera herds her three suspects out of her shop. She locks up the door and catches sight of the top of Winifred's head bobbing behind the door of her fake bakery. Vera smirks and waves at Winifred. Hah, she'd bet money that Winifred is writhing with curiosity to know what's going on. Outside of Vera's teahouse is a shiny new Benz. Impressive. She hadn't pegged Oliver to be the type to drive a Benz, but, she supposes, this is why one should never judge a book by its cover. She strides to the Benz and pulls the passenger door open. Or tries to, anyway. It's locked.

"Uh, that's not my car," Oliver mumbles. "That one is." He jerks a thumb at a sad, clunky-looking Volvo parked behind the Benz.

Vera doesn't allow herself to even turn her head in the direction of Winifred's bakery. She can just imagine Winifred snickering to herself. Gah! She marches to the Volvo and yanks open the passenger door.

"Where are we going?" Sana says, standing on the curb and hugging the bag of food to her chest. Her eyes are wide with concern.

Vera sighs. "Are you wanting to investigate for your potcut or not? Get in. I told you already, we are going to see my fourth suspect."

Sana and Riki exchange another glance—they probably think they're being very subtle with their glances, but Vera's counted seven already. It only reaffirms her belief that these two are meant for each other. Then they climb into the back seat. Vera climbs in as well, and sinks into the front passenger seat with a small sigh. She will never admit it to anyone, but she is rather tired. Four hours of nonstop cooking will do that to you. But it'll all be worth it when she can finally gather all her suspects in a single place and do a Sherlock Holmesian reveal of who the killer is. Not that she knows right this very moment, but she will once they're all in the same room, she's sure of it.

As she settles in her seat, she spots a thick, bound stack of papers next to her feet. "What is this?"

Oliver stiffens. "Oh, that's just—that's my old manuscript. I'd forgotten it was there. Could you just put it back where you found it, please?"

Vera does so, making a mental note to take it with her when she gets out of the car. In her experience, it's best to nod and agree with what people say before doing exactly what you wanted from the very beginning.

"So where to?" Oliver says.

Vera rummages in her handbag and locates a piece of paper on which she'd scribbled an address a few nights before. "Here."

Oliver looks at the piece of paper, then his head jerks up. "What the hell?"

Sana and Riki lean forward. "What's wrong?"

"This is—" Oliver sighs with open exasperation. "It's Marshall's home address. How did you even—"

"I use the Google, of course," Vera says primly.

"You can't just look up people's home addresses online," Oliver says, aghast.

"Oh yes, you can." In truth, Vera had dug out Marshall's wallet from his pants pocket and found his driver's license and taken down his home address before tucking it back into his pants pocket. All this while wearing her thick yellow dishwashing gloves, of course, because Vera would never be so careless as to tamper with potential evidence. Somehow, she doesn't think that these youngsters in the car with her would approve of her doing this, even if she had been wearing gloves.

"How?" Sana says from the back seat.

"It's easy," Vera says. "Now, drive."

"What? No! I'm not just going to show up unannounced at

Marshall's house, my god, Vera. His wife and kid are probably home, they'd be grieving, and—"

"So they'd need company. And food, probably. This is why I cook all morning. Now, be a good boy and drive, don't make me waste all this home-cooked food."

"No, uh-uh."

Vera sighs. "You are so dramatic. Fine, I will call Uber. It will be so expensive in the city, you know. Daylight robbery. But I have no choice."

"Are you seriously going to do this?" Oliver cries. "It's so—I don't know—so inappropriate!"

"His poor wife is probably wondering what happen to Marshall."

"Wha—but—wait—"

Vera gives him a withering look. "Oliver, don't waste my time. Time is precious. Just because you young people have a lot of it, you think you can waste it? Is obvious he has wife. She come by to my teahouse yesterday with a toddler, but then she run away when I see her. Who else can it be but his wife and daughter? Now we have to check on them, make sure they are okay. His poor wife. Her husband suddenly turn up dead, you don't think she needs company? Unless, of course, she is the one who kill him. Either way, I have to pay her a visit." Vera takes out her phone and makes a big show of tapping on the Uber app. "Oh my, twenty-five dollars one way. Ridiculous! Still, I have no choice." She gives Oliver a pointed look.

"Oh my god," he groans. "Fine! Jesus." He pinches the bridge of his nose. "Look, we can't just show up there out of the blue, okay? Let me give her a call first, for god's sake."

Vera nods happily. "Good idea, yes. Put her on speaker, there's a good boy."

Oliver gives her a look. "I'm not putting her on speaker."

Young people nowadays. Vera tuts but decides to let him have his way on this one. She's lived long enough to know the importance of picking your battles. She waits patiently as Oliver calls Marshall's wife, pricking her ears when the call is answered. In the silence in the car, she can hear the woman's voice on the other end ever so faintly. Marshall's wife sounds lovely, she thinks. Not at all like a murderer (or murderess?), but then again, you never know nowadays, do you?

"Hey, Julia. It's me. How're you holding up?" Oliver grimaces to himself.

Vera notes with interest that Oliver's voice has turned soft and tender. Well, well. She makes a mental note of this obvious show of affection. Perhaps a motivation for killing Marshall?

"Yeah, uh, listen, this is going to sound really weird, but, uh, is it okay if I drop by? Just for a bit. There are some people with me who want to meet you. I know it's probably the worst time . . ."

"Tell her I cook lots of food," Vera hisses, nudging Oliver brutally with her elbow.

Oliver winces and tries to move away from her, but there's not much room inside the car, and Vera is able to get another vicious elbow nudge in before he bats her arm away. "We have food. Lots of it."

"Chinese barbecued pork, when Tilly is a toddler, oh, he can eat a whole one himself. Her child will love it."

Oliver pauses as Julia says something, then sighs, closing his eyes. "It's a long story." A moment later, his eyes fly open and he sits up straight. "Really? Okay. We'll be right over." He hangs up with a look of disbelief.

Vera doesn't even bother trying to hide her smug smile. "See? What I tell you? Nobody can resist Chinese barbecued pork."

Yes, her investigation is going very well indeed. She should have known she would be a natural at this.

TWELVE

JULIA

They never tell you these things about motherhood. Things like your toddler having the ability to literally wrap herself around your leg and cling on like a little octopus as you hobble around the house, grabbing trash bags stuffed full of your dead husband's things and shoving them in the home office. Okay, maybe that last part has more to do with marriage than it does with toddlers.

"Sweetie, can you let go of Mommy, please?" Julia says for the fourth time as she lifts an excruciatingly heavy bag. It has a pair of dumbbells inside, she realizes, and a part of her knows that she should take out the dumbbells, but it's also the same part of her brain that's currently preoccupied with (1) Emma's limbs resolutely suctioned around her left leg; (2) Oliver dropping by with a couple of friends; and (3) one of his friends having mentioned Chinese barbecued pork, and despite everything, Julia could really do with a slice of the sticky-sweet, savory pork. So she doesn't take out the dumbbells and instead gives the bag a hard yank, after which, of course, the bottom rips and out fall dumbbells and adult Lego sets and ski jackets and all sorts of other stuff. "Shit," she cries, and immediately feels terrible for swearing in front of Emma. "I mean shoot."

"You said 'shit,'" Emma says into Julia's leg.

"No, no. I said 'shoot,' you just heard wrong because you've got an ear pressed into my leg." Oh god, now she's gaslighting her daughter, and she hates herself even more. "No, you're right. Mommy did say 'shit.'"

"Shit! Shit!" Emma shouts, laughing.

Maybe she should've continued gaslighting Emma? What's the right thing to do here? Well, the right thing is obviously to not say "shit" in the first place. And now Julia wants to cry, because she isn't just a terrible wife whose husband left her right before dying, she's also a shitty mom who, whenever Emma nurses, scrolls through Instagram nonstop and wonders how the other moms have everything so put together. How do they have the time and energy and brain space to dress their kids up in color-coordinated outfits when Julia can barely find a single pair of matching socks for Emma? How do they have the time to braid their daughters' hair into such intricate hairstyles when Julia can barely even brush Emma's hair?

And what about the fact that Emma seems so very unaffected by Marshall's absence? Julia hasn't told her that Marshall is dead because she has no idea how to explain the concept of death, and Emma only asked once where Daddy was, and when Julia said Daddy wouldn't be coming home, Emma only nodded and went back to playing with her Duplo. Is that a normal reaction to have to the news that your dad wouldn't be coming home? Maybe it's normal for her because even when he was alive, Marshall was hardly ever around anyway, and when he was, he was always criticizing Emma. Or maybe Marshall was right and there's something wrong with Emma. Julia can't remember a time when her life did not revolve around worrying about Emma, or worrying about what Marshall might think.

The doorbell rings then, and Julia freezes. She's nowhere near ready. Emma is still shouting "Shit!" and now there's a pile of Marshall's stuff right here behind the front door and—Julia glances down at her clothes—yep, she's still in her pajamas. Well, they're not technically pajamas—she's wearing sweatpants and a T-shirt stained with egg yolk and mushed-up broccoli—but she did sleep in these clothes, so maybe they count as pajamas? The point is, she's a mess, and she's about to see Oliver for the first time in years. And his friends. She can't possibly let them see her like this, she—

"Hello?" someone calls out. It sounds like an elderly woman. "Julia, is it? It's Oliver here, with Vera!"

Who's Vera?

"I bring lots of food! Braised pork belly, chili garlic chicken popcorn, Chinese barbecued pork . . ."

It's the mention of food that bypasses all Julia's insecurities. She's been having nothing but canned tuna ever since Marshall left (Emma has been fed cereal and steamed veggies, which she largely refuses) and her stomach goes: *Screw you, brain, I'm telling right arm to open the door.* The door is opened, and Julia catches a glimpse of Oliver before a graying Asian woman pops in between them, wearing a huge smile.

"Ah, Julia! So nice to finally meet you. I'm Vera, of course, but you know that. I see you outside my teahouse the other day."

"Oh." Julia has no idea what to say to that. Why had she run away when Vera had spotted her outside the teahouse? That must have looked so strange. Something only a guilty person would do.

"Anyway, I have so much food for you!" Still beaming, Vera slides past Julia into the house.

Julia takes a step back, stunned. Did she invite Vera inside already? Maybe she did and she forgot because my god, there are a million things running through her mind, like: *Where's the food? I can smell really delicious food*, and *Who are all of these people?* and *Wow, it's been a long time since I saw Oliver*. Even though to most people, Oliver and Marshall look alike, Julia has always found numerous differences in their faces. Marshall was perhaps objectively the more good-looking of the two, with that sharp smile and excitingly wicked glint in his eyes, but Julia had always been more drawn to the kindness in Oliver's face. Though right now, she's too self-conscious to be drawn to anything. She's so ashamed of how different she is now, no longer the girl he knew in high school. She looks away, unable to meet Oliver's eyes.

"Come inside!" Vera calls out, as though this were her house. She flaps at Oliver and the other two people behind him. "Bring the food inside, I will heat them up." She turns to Vera. "You have oven, right? And saucepans? The food have to be heat up properly, cannot microwave."

"Uh . . ." Julia struggles to keep up. "Yeah. I have those things, but—"

Vera bends down, propping her hands on her knees. "Oh, hello, little girl. I'm Grandma Vera. Come help me in kitchen." Without waiting for Emma to reply, Vera toddles off deeper into the house, humming to herself. "Where is kitch—ah, never mind, I find it!"

To Julia's surprise, Emma unwraps herself from Julia's leg. But she doesn't follow Vera. She stands there, twirling her hair, staring with uncertainty.

Julia starts to say, "You don't have to—"

Vera's head pops out from behind a corner. "Oops, that is bathroom, not kitchen. Oh, I am lost. Where is my helper?"

One corner of Emma's mouth twitches up into a small smile, and she totters after Vera. Julia stands there, mouth agape. *What just happened?*

"Sorry," someone says. It's a pretty South Asian girl who looks like she's in her early twenties. "We didn't mean to barge into your house."

"Vera kind of took charge," the guy next to her says, grimacing apologetically. Like the girl, he looks like he's in his twenties. He looks like he's mixed-race.

"That's okay," Julia says. "I'm Julia."

"I'm Sana."

"I'm Riki."

They smile awkwardly at one other, then jump when Vera shouts, "Eh! Where is all the food? I am waiting!"

"Uh—" Sana lifts up a huge bag. "Is it okay if we—"

"Yeah, of course." Julia steps out of their way and watches as Sana and Riki hurry toward the kitchen.

Oliver clears his throat and steps inside the house, both hands in his pockets. He gives her a bashful smile that takes her right back to their high school days. "Hey. It's been a while."

She nods, her throat all choked up. She doesn't trust herself to speak, because now that she's seeing Oliver in the flesh and hearing his voice, she's reminded of what she'd been like as a teen, so full of confidence, her world a beautiful fireworks of possibilities. He must be so disappointed in how she's turned out. After a while, she manages to say, "Yeah."

"So, this is your house." Oliver looks around. "It's nice."

"It's a mess," she says automatically, because present-day Julia can't take a compliment, feels like a fraud whenever she's given one. "Sorry," she mumbles, because present-day Julia has to punctuate every sentence with an apology, as though she were sorry for existing at all. Marshall had hated that about her. *Stop apologizing! God, you're so pathetic,* he'd snap, and she'd say, *Sorry, I'm sorry, I'll stop!*

Oliver's gaze snaps toward her and Julia freezes. She has no idea what he's about to say, but it'll probably be something along the lines of how gross she's become, how slovenly, how disappointing. But the look in his eyes is sad and lost, and for a second, Julia feels some strange emotion welling up in her chest, then he breaks eye contact and the moment is gone. He turns his head instead and pauses when he sees the pile behind the door. Of bags full of things that are unmistakably Marshall's. For the hundredth time, Julia gives herself an inward kick. Why hadn't she done something with Marshall's things after the cops came? But she hadn't known what to do with them. She couldn't really throw them out, not now that Marshall is dead. She also didn't want to unpack them all and return them to their old spaces in the house because, well, why bother? He's dead. And so she'd left them there, and now Oliver is staring at them with, quite rightly, confusion.

"Um, that's—uh." She struggles for an explanation and fails. Should she tell him that she'd packed them up before she heard about Marshall's death? Or after? Definitely not after, right? Because then that would make her look so ruthless, a wife who couldn't wait to get rid of her husband's things as soon as she learned of his passing.

"Is this Marshall's ski jacket?" Oliver bends over and picks up a black jacket.

"Yes." Her insides churn.

"Oh, and that's his old Star Wars Lego set." Oliver gently folds up the ski jacket and places it on top of the pile of things.

He must think she's the world's worst person. Her insides are screaming at her to give him an explanation.

But when he looks at her, there's nothing but that quiet sadness in his eyes. "Do you . . . need help taking these anywhere?"

Julia's throat closes up again, so she just shakes her head silently. Oliver nods, seemingly understanding that there's nothing she can say right now that would make things better.

"I'm sorry for your loss, Lia," he says softly.

That stops the mess of self-hating thoughts in her head, just for one moment. The way he's using the nickname he gave her in high school. The sincere emotion in his voice. Julia feels tears drowning her eyes. "I'm sorry for your loss too, Ollie." And they find themselves in each other's arms. Julia closes her eyes and breathes in his familiar scent. They used to be best friends. They used to be each other's touchstones. And she can't understand why they drifted so far apart over the years.

Just for a moment, held tightly in Oliver's arms, Julia lets herself pretend that everything will be okay.

A shriek shatters the moment, and before Julia realizes it, she's already running toward the kitchen. This is something that will never cease to amaze her, the way that ever since Emma was born, her instincts have become razor-sharp when it comes to anything involving Emma. Julia used to be a deep sleeper until Emma came along; then the slightest noise would propel Julia from the depths of her sleep and shoot her out of bed in under a second. And now she's hurtling toward the kitchen because Emma has shrieked, and Julia should have known better than to leave Emma alone in the kitchen with strangers—what idiot mother does that? She has never hated herself quite as much as this. Every day is another chance for her to practice yet more self-hatred. Poor Emma, what—

"Mommy, look!" Emma is shouting, and there are no tears, just Emma holding up a bun in the shape of a pig. Julia stops short, her heart still thumping wildly, and as she watches, Emma lifts the bun and squeezes. Thick yellow cream squirts out of the bun pig's butt, and Emma screams with laughter. "The pig poops!"

Julia is torn between being grossed out and laughing. From where she's standing at the stove, stirring a pot, Vera looks at them and smirks. "Very good, eh? I say to myself, ah, what will her daughter like? And I make these buns, they filled with salted egg yolk custard. Lick it off your arm, Emma, don't just waste the custard, there are children starving in—well, everywhere, I would think. Even here in San Francisco."

Emma lifts her chubby arm and licks the golden liquid from her wrist. Her eyes light up. "Lick, Mommy," she orders, lifting her sticky hands.

"No, honey," Julia immediately says, "that's . . ." *That's disgusting*, Marshall's voice slices through her mind. Already she can see him, his upper lip curled up in disgust. *Why're you letting her get away with that kind of behavior? You need to do better at disciplining her.* For a moment, Julia freezes, unsure what to say to her own daughter. She's so used to nodding along with whatever Marshall says, but Marshall isn't here now. Marshall won't be here for good. And would these strangers in her house judge her?

But then Vera comes out of the kitchen, wiping her hands on a washcloth, and says, "Has your mommy try the custard?" Emma reaches up higher, her eyes shining with excitement, and Julia's heart cracks open. She wants to try the custard, would happily lick things off her daughter's sticky hands any time she gets the chance to. And so she does. And it does, indeed, taste very good. She hugs Emma tight and whispers, "Thanks, baby girl." And just for a fragile moment, as fleeting as a butterfly's fluttering wings, Julia feels that maybe she's not the world's worst mother after all.

THIRTEEN

OLIVER

It's hard to believe that he's finally here, after all these years, inside Marshall and Julia's house. He'd stayed away for so long, unable to bear the weight of their marriage, the weight of his bitterness and festering resentment toward Marshall. He's in Julia's space, after all this time, and he doesn't quite know how to handle himself. When they were teens, he was the one who spent the most time at Julia's, hanging out in her bedroom, listening to music and eating sour gummy worms, and doing homework or chatting or whatever. Her parents had trusted him so much that they were okay with her keeping the door closed when he was over.

"It's because they know you don't have the balls to do anything," Marshall had said.

Maybe that was true. Oliver certainly wanted to do all sorts of things, but he never did, never even tried, because . . . why? He never understood why he didn't. Maybe because he always worshiped Julia, always saw her as someone so far beyond his reach. Marshall didn't have any such qualms, of course. Marshall didn't even seem to realize that Julia existed, not until the night she wore a low-cut top to Bobby Cullen's party and Marshall couldn't keep his eyes off her chest. Oliver had a sick feeling in his stomach the whole night, but, of course, he didn't do anything, not even when Marshall snuck up to Julia with a red cup stinking of cheap booze and that smirk that no girl could ever resist. Oliver had thought it would be just another one of Marshall's many short-lived flings. But weeks went by and they kept going strong. And when high school was over, they didn't split up for college. Instead, Julia decided to defer her enrollment at Columbia and instead followed Marshall to Santa Cruz. Oliver lost it then. He told her she was throwing her future away for his asshole of a twin who'd cheat on her the first week of college, and she told him that his jealousy was an ugly thing to see, and that was that. They didn't talk again for years afterward. When he found out that they'd gotten married right out of college at city hall, he sent a congratulatory card but received no reply. When Emma was born, Oliver popped by at the hospital with flowers and a onesie set, but Marshall told him that Julia was too out of it to see any visitors. He got to catch a glimpse of Emma, so tiny, swaddled in a pink blanket, and then the tears attacked his eyes and he stumbled out of the hospital before he broke down completely.

Over the next few years, Oliver tried to be a good uncle to his only niece, sending her gifts every birthday and Christmas, but received no thank-yous from them. He liked their photos on Facebook and Instagram, smiling quietly as he watched Emma grow from a tiny infant into a chubby toddler. Most of the photos that Julia posted had captions like: "Best daddy ever!" and "I'm so lucky to have such an amazing husband!" so Oliver figured that they were happy and accepted that he'd been very wrong about

Julia and Marshall as a couple and that it was best for everyone involved if he kept his distance.

But now, he's here in their space, and he feels like he's violating their privacy, like he's somehow broken their happy bubble. He has no business being here in his brother's house, standing a few paces away from his wife, watching as she licks custard off her daughter's arm. He turns away, wanting to give Julia as much privacy as he can, and his eyes rest once more on the pile of trash bags filled, strangely enough, with Marshall's things. Oliver doesn't understand, can't come up with a good enough explanation for the bags. It feels very soon for Julia to have packed up all of Marshall's things. Just two days after Marshall's death. Or maybe she'd packed them up before Marshall died? But why? According to Instagram, they were deliriously happy with each other.

Then Emma catches sight of him and freezes in mid-laugh. *Oh shit*, Oliver thinks. He tries for a smile, but it comes out all wobbly.

"Daddy?" she says, and Oliver could swear that it's not a happy question but a fearful one, and his heart aches for this little kid.

He watches helplessly as she clings tighter to Julia, cringing away from him. What had Marshall done to this little girl?

"I'm not your dad," Oliver croaks finally. "I'm your uncle. Uncle Ollie. I know I look like your dad, but . . . uh. We were brothers. Twins."

"You remember that story we read, sweetie?" Julia says to Emma. "The one with the twin girls and how people always confused the two of them? But they were really different people, weren't they?"

Emma nods hesitantly before regarding Oliver with suspicion.

At least there's a little bit less fear in her eyes now. "Not Daddy," she says.

"Nope," he says firmly.

"Okay, lunch is ready," Vera calls out. "Hurry up, everybody sit."

And with that, the awkward moment is past. Oliver lets out his breath, and Julia pats him on the shoulder as they walk to the dining room. His palms are still sweaty at the way Emma reacted to his face. He hasn't spent much time with kids, but he's pretty sure that they shouldn't be reacting like that to someone looking like their parent. Hatred flares in his belly, white-hot, as he realizes just what a shit father Marshall must have been to her. He tries to shake it off, focusing instead on the moment.

Part of Oliver marvels at how easily Vera has claimed this space even though it's the first time she's set foot here. He catches Julia's eye, and she widens those sapphire blue eyes of hers and gives him a helpless smile, and somehow, just with that one look alone, they're suddenly back in high school, conveying entire messages with a single glance. He smiles back, and they gather round the dining table, where Vera has somehow produced an entire feast worthy of a Thanksgiving celebration, except of course they're nowhere near Thanksgiving. Oliver counts at least a dozen different dishes, all of them steaming and looking as delicious as though they came straight out of a cookbook.

"Sit!" Vera barks. "Don't just stand there gaping, later the food get cold." She turns to Emma, who's clinging to Julia's neck. "You," she orders Emma, "are my assistant, so you must sit next to me."

"Oh, she's—" Julia begins, but stops in surprise when Emma unwraps herself from around Julia's neck and nods.

"I sit there," Emma says, pointing to the baby chair that's been set next to Vera's seat.

"Okay," Julia says hesitantly, but Oliver can read her expression, even after all these years, and she doesn't look unhappy about it. More like pleasantly surprised. She places Emma gently in the high chair and clicks the buckles into place, then hovers uncertainly behind her.

"Sit," Vera demands, pointing to a chair two places away from Emma with a wooden spoon. Julia meekly does as she is told, and Vera turns her laser gaze to Oliver. He feels his pores open up and start to sweat under that stare. "You, sit there." Between Julia and Emma.

"Um . . . okay." He does as he's told and wedges himself in the seat between his niece and her mother, who he's very much trying to not have feelings for.

Sana and Riki are told to sit next to Julia, and when Vera is satisfied with the arrangement, she harrumphs. "Okay, now eat." She stands, grabbing a serving spoon, and starts doling out food onto everyone's plates. "This one is black pepper beef, you eat more of this, Julia, you look very pale, very anemic, you must have more beef. And you, Riki, you look very constipated, so I cook this one for you, steamed cod with black fungus."

Poor Riki turns red and sputters, "I'm not—um, I'm not constipated."

Vera simply tuts as she serves up an extra-large portion of fish and black fungus on Riki's plate. "I can always tell just from looking, you very constipated." She turns her attention to Sana, who visibly shrinks back in her seat. "And you, you seem very chilly, too much yin. You should have more heaty foods, that will increase your yang. Here, spicy garlic tofu, will warm you up." Sana sighs, probably relieved that Vera isn't talking about her bowel movements. Vera side-eyes Oliver, and the back of his neck prickles. "And for you, Oliver, I make rice wine chicken with glutinous rice. Very comforting. I think you are needing some comfort food, yes?"

His stupid throat closes up at that, because, yes, Oliver does need comfort food, and a Chinese version of chicken soup sounds like something he would kill for right now. He nods as she spoons fat chunks of chicken, so tender that it's falling off the bone, and rich broth into a bowl. It smells heavenly. Like coming home, Oliver thinks, inhaling its rich, complex scent.

For little Emma, Vera serves up a bowl of stewed beef noodles, and from somewhere in her pocket, Vera produces a pair of child's chopsticks. The chopsticks are attached to each other at the top, so they're easier to use. She places them in Emma's hand and says, "Now you eat like a big girl, because you are my assistant, okay?" Emma nods and spears the chopsticks into her bowl, using them to shovel the thick noodles into her mouth.

Everyone digs in, and for a minute, the only sounds around the table are of cutlery clanging against bowls and plates. Vera is busy serving up more food onto people's plates. Oliver has just taken two bites of his chicken stew when a pile of braised pork belly appears on his plate, alongside a mound of garlic-fried bok choy. He can't remember the last time he gathered with other people and ate together like this. He can't remember the last time he had food this good, food that doesn't just fill you up, but also nourishes you, body and soul. With every bite, Oliver can feel the love and care that have gone into the preparation, and both his stomach and his heart are being fed right now.

"This is so good, Vera," Sana says. She spears a chunk of tender pork belly and inhales its scent, closing her eyes. "Oh my god, this is amazing. It's just got that home-cooked taste that you know you'll never find at any restaurant. I feel like a kid again."

"Mm." Riki nods, his mouth full of cod. He swallows and says, "To be fair, I've never had black fungus before, but I know what you mean. This food tastes familiar somehow. It's kind of addictive, actually."

"I know exactly what you mean," Julia says. "It tastes like food your grandma would make you."

Vera smiles a quiet, knowing smile, then turns to Emma. "How is my sous chef doing? Wah, you almost finish it already!"

Emma grins and opens her mouth, showing a mouthful of half-chewed noodles. "I eat the yummy noodles."

"Close your m—" Julia starts to say, but Vera says, "Oh yes, very good. You eat the yummy noodles," and Julia's mouth snaps shut. She stares at Vera. For a second, Oliver wonders if Julia is annoyed at Vera for the interruption, but she doesn't seem irritated. She seems more . . . curious, looking at Vera in what Oliver can only describe as wonderment.

When Vera stands to give Emma a second helping of noodles, Julia mutters, "I've never seen her eat so well before. Usually I have to spoon-feed her, and she'll be screaming and throwing the food everywhere."

Oliver raises his eyebrows at her. "I guess not even two-year-olds can say no to Vera," he says under his breath.

She laughs, and it's a familiar laugh. For a moment, she looks just like the teen he was best friends with so many years ago. "I can't imagine anyone saying no to Vera," she whispers.

Oliver's about to answer when he feels something wet tap his forearm. He turns to see that Emma has placed a noodle across his arm.

"Eat," Emma says in that very serious way that only two-year-olds can muster. "'S good for you."

"Oh my god, Emms," Julia says, wiping her mouth. "I'm so sorry."

"No, it's fine." And it really, truly is. It's the first time Oliver's received a gift from his niece, and he does not intend to refuse it. He pinches the noodle between his thumb and index finger and says, "Hey, thanks, Emma." Then he slurps it up with exaggerated noise and goes, "Mm-mm. You're right, that was really good."

Emma nods solemnly, and Oliver feels a fierce wave of love for this little kid who looks so much like Julia. It tears him up that he's already missed out on so much of her life. Then Emma grabs another noodle with her bare hand and places it on Oliver's open palm. "Eat more. 'S good for you."

Maybe he should've thought twice about slurping up that first noodle.

Oliver can't remember the last time he's felt so stuffed. Happy too. Full and satisfied and warm. Emma went into a food coma after her third bowl of noodles, and Julia picked her up and put her in her bedroom, so now there's just the four adults plus Vera, gathered around the coffee table. They're all wearing slightly glazed expressions, their brains only half functioning after the feast.

And that's when Vera goes, "Okay, so now we talk real business. Which one of you here kill Marshall?"

It seems as though everyone not only stops talking but stops breathing as well. The air in the room freezes and it's dead silent. Then someone coughs. Riki. He gives a choked laugh before clearing his throat. "Vera, come on."

Vera deadpans him. "You think I'm not being serious? Why?"

"Wha—" Riki gestures helplessly. "Because—I don't know, it's ridiculous. And it's kind of disrespectful of you to go to his widow's house and accuse someone of murder?"

"Disrespectful?" Vera blinks, as though she's just been slapped, and Oliver gets it. In Chinese culture, respect only flows in one direction, from the younger to the older, like a river. The older generation doesn't owe the younger ones respect; if any is given, it is done so out of kindness and generosity, not necessity. So for someone as young as Riki to tell Vera that she's crossed a line is inconceivable. Oliver is so torn. Part of him, of course, agrees that Vera has indeed crossed a line, coming into Julia's house and openly accusing one of them of killing Marshall. But the other part of him, the one that's been raised by two very traditional Chinese parents, is squirming with discomfort.

Before he can respond, Vera turns to Julia and takes her hand. "My dear," Vera says, "I am sorry. I don't disrespect you. I just want to solve your husband's murder, is okay?"

"Uh . . ." Julia's mouth opens and closes, and no words come out.

"Maybe you should leave it up to the police," Oliver suggests.

Vera shoots him such a withering look that he feels his soul shrivel up and hide. "Oliver, I already tell you, the police are useless. Now," she says, turning back to Julia, "you don't have to worry, okay? I will do everything." She squeezes Julia's hand before letting go. Then she stands, chin raised high and chest expanding. Her aura fills the room. "One of you," she intones, her glare sweeping across the group, "is Marshall killer."

White-hot fear surges through Oliver's entire body.

"What makes you say that?" Sana says. Oliver can't help but

notice that Sana's hands are clasped together so tightly that her knuckles are white.

Vera starts walking around the living room. "I have deduce that the killer will come back to my teahouse to look for something."

It feels as though ants are crawling down Oliver's back. "What?"

"Doesn't matter what," Vera says. "All four of you have never been to my teahouse, but after Marshall die, you all pop up, one by one." Her sharp gaze stabs into each one of them, and they all shrink back. "Now, we all know that Marshall is not good person. No offense, Julia."

Julia, who's been staring slack-jawed, manages a small shrug. Oliver isn't quite sure what the shrug is meant to convey.

"That means you all probably have reason to kill him. So now, I am going to ask you, where are you on the night that Marshall is murder?"

They're all gaping at Vera now, torn between shock and anger. "We don't have to tell her anything," Riki says. He looks at the others desperately. "We don't."

Sana nods slowly. Oliver wills his heart to stop thumping. Wills his brain not to go there. To the night that Marshall died. But, of course, it hurtles there with lightning speed. He sees what he did. The drugs in his hand. The way they rattled. All their lives, Marshall got away with everything. He just wanted to make sure Marshall wouldn't get away this time. Payback for all the times throughout their lives that Marshall slithered away, snake-like, out of trouble. He almost throws up then and there.

"It was a weird day," someone says.

Oliver's head snaps up. It takes a moment for his mind to catch up and register that Julia is speaking. Everyone is staring, wide-eyed, at Julia, sweet, fierce Julia who was always so full of wild ideas about traveling everywhere and taking in as much of the world as she could. And Oliver wants to tell her to stop talking, to protect herself, but as usual, he stays quiet.

"Marshall and I had split up the day before," Julia continues in a shaky voice. Her eyes are bright with unshed tears. When she finally looks up from her lap, her eyes land immediately on Oliver's, and it's as though she's talking to him alone, just like the old times. "That's why all of his things were packed up. He'd found an apartment, he said, and it was—it was amicable." Julia blinks hard, like she's trying to keep herself from crying.

"Hmm," Vera says, massaging her chin. "He just walk out?"

Julia nods.

They're all probably thinking the same thing: *What about Emma? How could anyone walk out just like that, leaving behind his wife and kid?*

Something must be missing from the picture here. Oliver wants nothing more than to believe Julia, because it's Julia, for god's sake, his best friend and biggest heartbreak. But because she was his best friend, because at one point, he was sure that their hearts had beaten as one and their thoughts had flown seamlessly back and forth from one to the other, as though their minds had been connected, because of all this, Oliver knows that Julia is lying about the night that her husband—his twin brother—died. He looks at her, and for the first time he wonders if perhaps he doesn't know Julia that well after all.

FOURTEEN

VERA

Vera can't remember the last time she had so much fun. People always say that your wedding day is the happiest day of your life, but honestly, people should try solving murders more often. Okay, well, "solving" is a bit of a stretch since she hasn't quite yet figured out who the killer is, but she's close. She can feel it. Generations of Chinese mothers have perfected the art of sniffing out guilt, and Vera can practically see waves of guilt churning out of the young people gathered before her. Each and every single person in this room reeks of it, which is understandable; when Vera was young, she had plenty to be guilty about as well. But, ah, which one is specifically guilty about killing Marshall? Though even as she thinks that, Vera also finds herself wondering what everyone is feeling so much guilt over. Despite their possible involvement, she has to admit that so far, she really likes everybody here. She has brought them together against their will but they've all been so agreeable. Well, that's mostly thanks to her good social skills; Jinlong used to say that Vera could convince anyone to do anything. But there is something about this group of youngsters that makes Vera feel particularly protective. Still, needs must. She is here to solve a murder, after all, not make friends.

She whips out a slim notebook, one of those cheap lined ones that schoolkids use, and takes her time smoothing it out on the coffee table. "Okay, number one: Julia—split up with Marshall." Vera nods to herself, and when she looks up, she finds all of them staring at her.

"Did you have that notebook on you this whole time?" Oliver says. There is a bit of awe in his voice.

"Tch," Vera tuts, "every detective knows that taking notes is very important. Now, what about you? Where are you on the night that Marshall is kill?"

Oliver looks away from her so quickly it's as though her gaze has just burned him. "Um, I was at my dad's place. I was dropping off some things."

Vera narrows her eyes for a second. She knows a lot of things, like, for example, how people often add details as they go along when they lie. Oliver squirms under her gaze, like a trapped insect writhing under a needle. Then she decides she's had her fun with him and, with a sniff, jots down his answer in her notebook before turning to Riki. "You?"

Riki shakes his head. To the casual observer it might come off as a flippant shake, but Vera is no casual observer. She's seen this headshake plenty of times before, usually from Tilly when she asks him why he still doesn't have a girlfriend. It's a shake to distract and make Vera think she's asking a silly, irrelevant question. That's how she knows she's on the right track. She keeps staring at Riki until his defenses fold underneath the weight of her unwavering gaze and he mumbles, "I was hanging out at my place, playing computer games."

"What game?"

Riki's mouth parts like he wasn't expecting her to ask that, because of course he wasn't expecting it. "Ah, *Warfront Heroes*?"

Vera makes a note of that. "Is that online game? Like *Clash of Clans*?"

"You know *Clash of Clans*?"

"Of course I know *Clash of Clans*. So is this *Warfront Heroes* thing online?"

Riki nods slowly. "Ye-es?"

"Ah, so you play with your online friends," Vera says, writing furiously. "So they can vouch where you are at the time Marshall is kill."

"I don't—I haven't joined a guild or anything. I usually play on my own."

"Hmm, okay." Vera nods before turning to Sana, who's—oh, okay—Sana is openly glaring at her. "Yes? You ready for your turn?"

Sana raises her chin, no longer the meek girl Vera knew. "You're not my mom, Vera. You don't get to pry into everyone's business. I'm not telling you anything. I don't have to."

Vera diligently jots this down in her notebook.

"What—" Sana sputters. "Don't write that down. What are you even writing?"

"Well, refusing to give information is in itself information," Vera says simply.

"But! It doesn't mean I'm guilty!"

"I don't say anything about you being guilty." Vera closes her notebook and smiles at them. They stare back open-mouthed, like guppies.

"You mean we could've just refused to tell her?" Riki whispers to Julia, who shrugs helplessly.

"Missed a trick there," Oliver mutters to himself.

"Well, this has been very—" Vera is already in the process of standing up and making her dramatic exit when the doorbell rings. They all freeze, then as one they look at Julia, who looks about as calm as a rabbit that's just heard the victorious screech of a hunting eagle.

"Were you expecting anyone?" Oliver says.

Julia shakes her head; then she seems to take hold of herself and walks toward the door. Vera hears the sharp intake of breath and smiles to herself. She can guess who's at the door, and my, my, things are truly about to get interesting, aren't they? Her grin widens as Julia says, "Um, hi, Officer. Can I help you with something?" and Vera has to stop herself from rubbing her palms together. Won't the police be impressed when they find her here and realize that she's been helping them out with their investigation?

But when Officer Gray steps inside the house and sees everyone else in the living room, even Vera would be hard-pressed to describe Officer Gray's expression as impressed. It's not even close to "pleasantly surprised." If Vera were to be honest with herself, she might describe it as "annoyed" or "vexed." Maybe Officer Gray is hurt that Vera failed to invite her over to partake in the feast?

"Officer Gray," Vera calls out, "so very nice to see you."

"Vera." Officer Gray's eyebrows are still raised in an expression of WTF-ness. "What brings you here?" She looks around at everyone else pointedly. "I wasn't expecting such a crowd."

"Oh, I come here to cook for widow, of course," Vera says. "Come, there is still a lot of food left over, although little Emma has finish all of the beef noodles, I'm afraid. She's a growing girl, you know. Don't hold it against her."

"I'm not—" Officer Gray stops herself, takes a deep breath, and says, "Mrs. Chen, I'm actually here to see you. Can we talk in private?"

Well, this just won't do, Vera thinks, as Julia hurries forward, nodding, and leads Officer Gray into a side room. The door clicks shut behind them. The silence the two of them leave behind is thick and heavy. Vera glances at Oliver and Riki and Sana before scurrying over to the closed door.

"What are you doing?" Oliver hisses. "You can't do that."

Vera ignores him. She's gotten very good at ignoring people over the years, especially when they say things like "You can't do that" or "You're not supposed to do that." At her age, Vera reckons that she's gained the right to do whatever the hell she pleases. She leans closer to the door, then presses her ear against it gently. She can hear muffled voices but no discernible words. She clicks her fingers at the other three.

"Get me a glass," she whispers at them. They just continue gaping at her. *Tch, young people nowadays. Hopeless.* She presses her ear closer to the door, and that's when it swings open, making Vera stumble and almost fall. Luckily, thanks to all of her brisk-walking sessions, Vera is very strong and coordinated for her age and she manages to right herself. Unluckily, she's also just been caught red-handed. Or red-eared, as the case may be. Still, she recovers quickly, standing straight and smiling innocently at Julia and Officer Gray. Julia looks a thousand miles away, which Vera is quickly learning is sort of Julia's thing, and Officer Gray looks both amused and annoyed, which Vera is also quickly learning is sort of Officer Gray's thing.

"Were you trying to listen to a private conversation, Vera?" Officer Gray says.

"Yes."

Officer Gray's mouth is already open, about to say something, when she pauses. *Hah*, Vera thinks. The officer probably was expecting a denial from Vera. Officer Gray narrows her eyes before sighing. "Look, I might as well tell you as well, because I'm actually about to go to your shop."

"Oh? Aha, I know it. I been waiting for you to change your mind about having some of my tea. Is very good, you know, just ask them." Vera nods at the others.

Officer Gray sighs again. "No, Vera. I'm not going over for tea. I'm—" She pauses, glancing at Riki and Sana, who are staring at her from one side of the room. "Who did you two say you were again? What's this . . . gathering about?"

"Oh, these are my—"

Before Vera can say "suspects," Riki says, "Hi! I'm Riki, I'm a reporter. I was here to—well, interview the people involved in this case, but I'll get out of your way now."

"Yep, same here," Sana pipes up. She grabs her purse from the back of one of the dining chairs and hurries toward the door, where Riki is already slipping on his sneakers. "Bye! Thanks for the meal." They open the door without hesitation and hurry out. And with that, they're gone.

Vera makes a mental note to add their hasty departure to her notebook. That will go under their "I Am a Murderer" column.

"Okay . . ." Officer Gray mutters. She glances at Oliver. "You might as well listen too, Mr. Chen. We've identified the cause of Marshall Chen's death."

A small gasp escapes Vera's mouth and she quickly clamps it

shut. Ooh, but this is exciting, isn't it? She could get used to this, she really could. Nothing quite so dramatic ever happens in the tea business. In the single moment that Officer Gray pauses, a thousand and one causes of death fly through Vera's head.

Strangulation!

Poison! Ooh, what kind of poison? Maybe the kind that melts your insides? But no, that would make the most dreadful mess.

Radiation! Oh yes, a radioactive agent slipped into his drink. Wait, that would make her teahouse radioactive, maybe. Okay, let's hope it's not that.

Sneaky acupuncture! Like the one that Jet Li did in that awful Hollywood movie where he inserted an acupuncture needle just so and it blocked the blood flow and caused internal hemorrhage. Yes, that one. That's Vera's favorite. Dramatic, but clean, so she won't have to close down her teahouse for fear of radioactive contamination.

By the time Officer Gray speaks again, Vera's practically rubbing her hands together.

"He had an anaphylactic shock, otherwise known as a severe allergic reaction—"

Vera deflates. Allergic reaction? That is by far the least exciting option available.

"—to bird dander."

Vera feels as though she's just been smacked upside the head. Bird dander? Dimly, she registers Oliver telling Officer Gray that yes, when they were kids, Marshall had a severe allergic reaction to a goose-down duvet. She remembers Oliver mentioning that. But then this means—

"So this is not murder?" she wonders out loud. Because how could anyone murder using bird dander, of all things? Gah! Already, Vera is mentally shredding her little notebook. She feels herself deflating. Bird dander, of all things, really, now.

"We're still looking into it," Officer Gray says, "but it doesn't look like foul play was involved."

But what about the flash drive? Vera wants to shout. *What about the scratch on his cheek, and that bruise on his eye?* Something else prods at her mind. "You say you want to come by my shop to tell me this? Why?"

"Well, we thought it prudent to see if there's anything in your shop that might have bird dander. Do you have any pet birds, or—"

Vera harrumphs. "Of course not. Don't be silly. I run a teahouse, not a bird shop."

"Okay," Officer Gray says. She turns to Julia. "Well, thank you for your time, and again, I'm sorry for your loss."

Vera's head is boiling with shouts of *No! You must've gotten it wrong somehow! Did you even check his body for radiation?*

But all she can do is stand there quietly as Julia leads the officer to the door. Then Officer Gray is gone and Vera can find no other reason to hang around, now that there is no murder to solve, and so, with a heavy heart, Vera takes her leave.

VERA'S NOTEBOOK

Cause of death: Bird dander
Suspects:

1. The city of San Francisco, because letting all these pigeons roam free
2. Maybe he kick pigeon and it kill him
3. Big Bird
4. Oliver because he is only one who knows about bird allergy!?

But why he die in my shop??

Maybe he know he is having allergy reaction, and he think, Ah, tea will help because tea is good for health.

Poor Marshall. Why he don't call out to me to make him tea?

Oh yes, he cannot talk because throat closing up.

OH, STUPID CASE!

FIFTEEN

RIKI

Riki can't remember the last time his body has been this tense, all his instincts shouting at him to run. Well, okay, he can. Unfortunately, that was also the day that Marshall died, so maybe it's best not to recall that particular memory.

For a while, he and Sana walk down Julia's street without talking. Sana seems to be deep in thought. He notices that she chews her lower lip when she's deep in thought, which is kind of cute.

Kind of cute? What the hell, brain? Just—god, just keep it together, will you?

"Are you calling an Uber?" Sana says.

"Huh?" Right, they'd come here in Oliver's car. Riki looks around him, trying to get his bearings. He's somewhere in Laurel Heights. Getting an Uber all the way from here to Twenty-third Street is going to cost him. "No, I'll probably just take the bus. You?"

She nods. "Same. Where are you headed?"

He tells her, and her face lights up. "Oh hey, that's where I live too. I'm actually not too far from Castro."

"Cool, that's just a few blocks away from me." He can only afford his place because it's an old studio right above a nightclub. He wonders how Sana can afford her place. Prices there are notoriously high.

As though reading his thoughts, she says, "My mom is rich. She helps me out with my rent. I have a roommate, though."

"Oh, cool." Riki often gets tongue-tied when he's nervous, and he's finding that he's increasingly nervous around Sana. Back home, his mother teased him about not being able to talk to pretty girls, but he'd been so sure he'd managed to shake off that shyness. Maybe it's the whole "one of them is Marshall's killer" thing? That's definitely a mood killer. As they walk, he searches for something to say. "Is your mom a techbro?"

Sana snorts. "Hah! You know, maybe that would make her less obnoxious, actually. But no, my mom's an author. You might have heard of her. Priya M. Singh?"

"I'm not a big reader," Riki says apologetically. Saying this to the daughter of an author feels wrong. His insides are burning with embarrassment.

"Ah. You heard of the HBO series *The Spice Ladies*?"

"I don't watch it, but yes, I've heard about it."

"My mom wrote that."

"Wow." He's honestly impressed. The show isn't a blockbuster like *Game of Thrones*, but it's successful enough to trend on Twitter every time a new season comes out. "That's amazing."

"Eh." Sana shrugs and blows a stray lock of hair off her face. "It's honestly not that great. I mean, the money is fantastic, and I'm grateful for it, don't get me wrong," she says hurriedly. "But . . .

my mom's this ridiculously driven person. She publishes like four books a year and is super productive and she's always like, 'There's no such thing as a writer's block, darling. It's all in your mind. If you want to create art, go ahead and do it.'"

Riki nods, mulling her words over quietly. He'd never once considered the challenges that someone raised in an affluent family might face. He'd assumed that if you had money, then surely all your problems were very easily fixed. If not by throwing money at them, then by the sheer privilege of having all the time in the world to spend on tackling said problems.

"I never thought of how tough it might be, growing up with such an accomplished parent," he admits. "Do you think Stephen King's kids feel the same way?"

Sana snorts out loud, the pleasant surprise evident in her laugh. When she glances up at Riki, her eyes look more lively than he's seen them before. "Probably? But his son is actually a very successful writer too. Also, everything I've heard about Stephen King makes him sound so down-to-earth. Not at all like my mom. She's just so obnoxious about it, you know? She's like, 'Sana, it's all mind over matter. Artists and their mental blocks, I swear! It's all just in your mind.'"

Riki cocks his head to one side. "Do you get a lot of blocks when you're writing material for your podcast?"

"Oh," Sana says, seemingly a bit taken aback. "Yeah. Yes, I guess so. Yeah, like the words are hard to come by sometimes." She looks down at her hands for a while. "I can feel it inside me. I want to create something—something wonderful, but . . ." She sighs. "There's a block. I can't explain it, but I know my mom's wrong. Blocks definitely happen to writers and artists and all other creatives."

"Yeah, I mean, just because she doesn't experience them doesn't mean they don't exist. That would be like saying just because you've never had a migraine, they can't happen to other people," Riki says.

"Yes!" Sana cries. "Exactly."

Their eyes meet, and Riki swears it's like their minds are connecting. He feels warm and—dare he say it—happy. He can't remember the last time he felt this way. It's been months, ever since . . . well, ever since everything went down with Marshall. The thought of Marshall sours his mind, weighing on his shoulders like a deadweight.

As though sensing the shift in Riki's mood, Sana says, "What—what do you think that cop found out? It has to be pretty important for her to show up in person, right?"

Riki isn't sure what to say. What would a real journalist who is completely uninvolved with the case say? It hits him that that's basically what Sana is—she's not suspicious of him, of course not, she's only asking for her podcast. He needs to start thinking of himself as her counterpart and nothing else. Right. He can do that.

"Yeah, we should've stuck around," he says with false confidence. "You know, to ask questions and such."

"We should've," Sana agrees. "I guess I just didn't want to be disrespectful, like in case whatever the cop had to say was sensitive and really affected Julia . . . I thought she might have needed some privacy."

Riki steals another glance at Sana, surprised. He doesn't know much about investigative reporting or true crime podcasting, but what he does know is that they tend to get a bad rep for poking around sensitive spaces and brashly ignoring the need for privacy.

He's impressed that despite Sana's need for information, she's so respectful of Julia's privacy. Surely that's very rare.

Unless . . .

The little voice in his head whispers, *Unless Sana is hiding something too, just like you.*

Riki almost snorts out loud at that. Ridiculous. His stupid mind is grasping at straws, clutching at anything or anyone that might take the spotlight away from himself. And yet.

And yet he can't stop his mind from barreling backward and studying everything that Sana has said. He thinks back to that first morning he went to Vera's teahouse, just mere days after Marshall's death. With a start, he recalls now that he bumped into a girl on his way out. He was so spooked by Vera at the time that he didn't give the girl a second thought. But now, walking down the street with Sana, he looks at her, and the sunlight, streaming at just the right angle, low against the steep San Franciscan hills, hits her just so, turning the edges of her skin and hair golden, making her deep brown eyes a honey shade. She looks so beautiful. And also undoubtedly like the girl he bumped into outside of Vera's teahouse that morning.

Something turns inside Riki's chest, something sharp and ugly and full of fear. Who is Sana? What does she know? He thinks back to how Vera insisted that one of them is Marshall's killer. He dismissed Vera's ridiculous accusations because that seems to be the sensible thing to do when it comes to Vera, but now he has no idea what to think. He goes over what to say to Sana, and now he's no longer nervous because she's so attractive, but nervous because he has no idea what her connection is to Marshall, but there must be a connection there, and when it comes to Marshall, chances are, it's not going to be anything good. *Careful, Riki.*

"So, ah," he begins, taking painstaking care to keep his voice casual, "what did you say the name of your podcast was?"

Sana glances up at him, and he realizes he's completely failed to sound relaxed. It's clearly not an innocent, throwaway question, but a loaded one. Oh crap, what does he do now? He needs to think of something quick.

But even as Riki quietly panics, his phone buzzes with a text message. He grabs it, practically yelping out loud with relief. "It's Vera!"

Sana raises her eyebrows, her eyes still wary. "What did she say?"

Riki swallows before reading the message out loud. "She says 'Stupid case is over. Marshall die from allergy attack to duck. You are no longer suspect, but you should still come by for tea.'"

Sana's phone beeps and she takes it out of her bag. She reads the message and laughs. "I got the same exact message from Vera. I think she just copied and pasted."

Relief and confusion surge through Riki's entire being. Wait, what just happened? Marshall died from an allergic reaction? To a duck? What?

"So that was weird, huh?" Sana says. Her voice is slightly shaky. "A duck. Huh."

Riki nods slowly, his head spinning. So he was worried about Sana for no reason? But when he looks down at her again and their eyes meet once more, he can see the walls clapping back into place behind her eyes. Her chin lifts, her jaw squaring, and she says, "Oh yeah, my podcast. I'll tell you if you tell me where your office is. Was it Buzzfeed you said you work at?"

Cold crawls down Riki's spine. No, despite the strange but seemingly innocent way Marshall died, there is something that Sana is definitely hiding. And maybe, worse than that, she knows about him and Marshall. Riki's throat is so dry that he coughs a little before he speaks. "It's cool," he says, trying to emphasize with each word that he's on the retreat, that she doesn't have to worry about him, "I just remembered that my friend recommended another podcast to me, so I won't have a chance to listen to yours for a while yet."

Sana's chest expands as she inhales deeply, her eyes softening. Message received. As long as Riki minds his own business, Sana will mind hers. He can just about live with that.

SIXTEEN

SANA

Sana knows the bitter taste of unfulfilled expectations very well. After all, it's basically what she is, isn't it? She sees it in the mirror every morning, smells it in her hair, her natural musk, sees it on her skin like a stain that refuses to be scrubbed away. She wears it on her entire body; it's become such a huge part of her identity she doesn't quite know who she is without it.

Now, as she stares at the big and overwhelmingly huge blank canvas in front of her, the heaviness of all that unfulfilled expectation smothers her. It crushes her under its weight and fills her throat and her nostrils and chokes her entire body. She looks down, paint palette in one hand and brush in the other, both hands frozen, the brush hovering just inches from the pristine canvas.

"Just fucking draw, damn it," Sana hisses at her hand, but still it won't move. Her teeth are gritted. She feels a trail of sweat rolling down her temple, past her cheekbone, tickling like an ant, and she shudders, wipes it off with her arm. *Just one brushstroke*, she tells herself, *if you do just one, the rest will come easily.*

It has always been this way from as early as she can remember. Her parents told everyone who would listen that Sana learned to paint before she could walk, or even stand. There are countless photos and videos of chubby little baby Sana on her hands and knees, dipping her hands into puddles of paint and smearing them across drawing paper, an expression of intense concentration on her face. At every family gathering, her mom would brandish these photos on her phone at their relatives and do that deep-throated laugh of hers that goes: *Oh ho ho*, but like a middle-aged woman in a Japanese anime instead of Santa Claus.

"*Oh ho ho!*" she'd say. "Oh, my Sana has taken after me. So creative, isn't she? She'll be an artist, you'll see. No, not a writer, oh, publishing is so volatile, no, I wouldn't want her to be a writer. She can follow her own path, of course, but just look at her, she's got that je ne sais quoi, doesn't she? An artist from birth." She'd give a pointed pause and say, "Of course, if she wants to be a doctor or a lawyer I shan't stop her, but let's face it, art runs in our family." This latter part would be said very meaningfully, with a little sweep of her long-lashed eyes, to drive home what a uniquely open-minded mother she is, especially within the Asian community, which is well-known for driving their children to study medicine or law or business. Who's ever heard of an Asian parent wanting their offspring to pursue art? She'd remind Sana of this every chance she got.

"You're so fortunate, my dear. You can do anything you want, anything at all! I'm not stuck in the old ways. If you don't like science? Who cares? Not good at math? Why, I myself failed elementary math, and look where I am now." A multimillionaire whose books are basically a household name. She was so proud of not having the stereotypical Asian expectations of Sana, of telling everyone that Sana is a natural artist and that she's so proud of her artist daughter. When Sana got into CalArts, her mother threw her a huge bash at the Fairmont, renting out the ballroom to fit three hundred of her relatives and friends.

"To the next creative force in our family," Mom said, raising her champagne flute, and Sana could practically feel envy seeping from her cousins, most of whom were enrolled in premed or pre-law or some kind of engineering program. She's so lucky, they all said, so fortunate that her mom is so understanding and supportive. That her mom is world-renowned author Priya M. Singh, who understood and respected the creative arts. So lucky she was allowed to pursue her dreams. So lucky her mom was paying for her to go to CalArts.

Except here she is now, no longer at CalArts. Living in SF instead of Pasadena, not drawing, not painting, not creating anything. With a furious cry, Sana flings the paintbrush at the floor. Lucky Sana. Blessed Sana. Fraudulent Sana.

The phone rings then, and Sana glances at the screen. "MOM" is flashing on it. With a sigh, Sana wipes her paint-smeared hands on her apron and answers.

"How is my little art genius doing?"

Sana closes her eyes and counts to three before replying. Her mom is just proud of her. She knows that. But there's just something infuriating about her mom calling her "my little art genius." Somehow, in ways that Sana can't quite explain, it manages to come off as both condescending and yet full of heavy expectations. "I'm good," she manages to bite out.

"Are you busy creating?"

"Um, the usual. You know," Sana mumbles.

"Oh, sweetie. Don't tell me you're still blocked. Remember, there's no such thing as a creative block. God, the number of writers I've come across who insist they're blocked . . ." Sana's mom sighs, and Sana can practically hear her eyes rolling through the phone. "You know, it's like I always tell you: It's mind over matter. I just tell myself: Nope, writer's block doesn't exist. I don't have time for writer's block. And it's that simple! Just tell yourself that."

Sana squeezes her eyes shut. *Shut up, Mom*, she wants to yell. *You don't understand what I'm going through. I am blocked, damn it.*

And it's all because of Marshall.

"Thanks, Mom, you're right," she says, because what's the point in saying anything else? "Sorry, I actually have to go because I was in the middle of painting . . ."

"Ah! Yes, of course. You should put your phone on silent when you're creating. Respect your art, Sana."

It takes a lot of effort not to fling the phone at the wall. "Yep, thanks, Mom. Respect my art. Got it. Talk to you later." She hangs up with an exhausted sigh, then trudges to the small kitchenette and begins to clean her paint palette. It's clear there will be no painting done today either. As she wipes off the globs of paint, jagged pieces of memories flash through her mind. Of Marshall, always of Marshall. He's haunted her for so long now. She foolishly thought that the news of his death would set her free, the asshole got what was coming to him, but why is she still blocked? Why does her hand refuse to move the brush across the canvas? Why, why, why?

Her teeth grind loudly, painfully. What the hell kind of death is that? An allergic reaction. How completely anticlimactic. In her mother's books, bad guys are knifed, drugged, strangled. Deaths that are intentional, premeditated, and dramatic. Nothing like an accidental allergic reaction. It feels wrong somehow, like even though Marshall died, he also got away. Which, Sana tells herself, is an incredibly stupid thought to have. The guy's dead, for god's sake. What more could she ask for?

Her love for painting back, her body screams. His death should've set her free, so why is she still stuck here?

Mind over matter, her mom whispers. *It's all in your mind.*

She knows it's all in her mind, obviously everything is in her mind, but that doesn't mean she knows how to make it unstuck.

Right. Sana takes a deep breath. So in the end, what she needed wasn't revenge. It's something else. Closure. That's it. She needs to . . . what? She needs to regain ownership of what Marshall stole from her. Yes, that's it!

The thought alone revives Sana. It makes sense now, why she still can't paint. So what if Marshall is dead? It doesn't erase what he did to her, what he ripped from her trusting hands. The naïveté he destroyed, her belief that people are basically good. What Sana needs to do is to reclaim what is rightfully hers.

And to do that, she's going to have to go back to Marshall's house. Days ago, the thought of it would've made her balk, but just this morning, she was driven there and ended up having a whole feast there. She met his widow and played with his daughter. Could she really do it? Lie to get back in there?

She thinks of Riki then. *Buzzfeed reporter my ass,* she thinks. *He's so clearly hiding something.* Sana's not sure how she missed it before. Probably because she was so distracted by her own guilt. But she's not the only one hiding something here, she's sure of it.

And if the others have their own secret motivations for hanging around, then why can't she? She's supposedly doing a podcast about this, so why not capitalize on that cover story?

An opportunity has been handed to her. She would be a fool not to take it. Sana places the clean paint palette down, her resolve strengthened. She goes back into the living room and locates her phone. She texts Vera, asking her for Julia's number, and Vera sends it right away, accompanied by a message that says:

You better tell me why this all about!

Sana swallows and dials Julia's number.

"Julia? It's Sana, from earlier today with Vera Wong. I'm so sorry to bother you, but I was wondering if I could drop by at some point to ask you a few questions about Marshall? It's for my podcast."

She couldn't possibly sink any lower. She thought that when she attacked Marshall that had been the lowest point of her life, but apparently there are levels even beyond that. Like tricking a grieving widow into letting her inside the house so she can steal her dead husband's possessions.

SEVENTEEN

VERA

Vera has never been one to give up after just one setback. Oh no. So what if Marshall had very inconsiderately died from an allergic reaction instead of graciously dying from something more exciting and violent? It's all mind over matter, and Vera has been so convinced from the very beginning that Marshall's death was a murder that she is going to will it into reality, despite what everyone else believes. After all, there's the flash drive to think about, and the scratch mark, and the bruise on his cheek, and the fact that he wasn't a very nice person when he was alive.

So she takes a day to quietly seethe and give herself multiple pep talks about not giving up when the going gets tough. The only good thing about this is that she is able to tell Tilly that the man was killed by an allergic reaction, which seemed to relieve him greatly. On the second day, Vera decides she has had enough moping about and it is time to get cracking and chase down her destiny of solving Marshall's murder. Destiny, Vera thinks, is something to be hunted down and grabbed tightly with both hands and shaken until it gives her exactly what she wants.

After her daily walk, complete with the usual stink eye for the Café, Vera shoves her sleeves up and gets to work, chopping and steaming and frying and boiling. There are a lot of components to be julienned and pureed and turned into crispy, juicy things, and at the end of all that hard work, Vera gazes down with all the pride and love that a mother might have for her newborn baby. In front of her is a tower of four tiffin containers stacked neatly one on top of the other. It stands at almost two feet tall and looks very impressive. Vera harrumphs with satisfaction, takes off her apron, and carefully applies some makeup. She then jams her visor on her head and picks up the heavy tiffin tower and marches down the stairs and out of the teahouse.

The San Francisco Police Department Central Station is on Vallejo, only a few blocks away from Vera's teahouse, a straight line down Stockton. Normally, the walk would be nothing to Vera, but the tiffin tower makes it somewhat more difficult, and Vera finds to her horror that by the time she arrives, she is out of breath. She takes a few minutes to recover and dab at her damp forehead before lifting her chin once more and straightening up.

Being an upstanding citizen and a pillar of her community, Vera has never had reason to walk into the police station. But she has a very good idea of what to expect, because she has educated herself with *CSI* and *Law & Order*. She knows there will be Bad Guys probably shouting very exciting threats at anyone who dares look their way. There will also be Bad Cops who are doing very shady things and will look around very shadily once in a while. This is quite the adventure, and Vera wonders why she hasn't thought of venturing into the police station for fun. Then she strides into the gray building, her eyes wide with expectation, and . . .

Like so much in life, the SFPD Central Station is a disappointment. No one is threatening her life. No one is shouting. No one is even looking her way. People are just typing into computers like this is a regular office instead of a police station. Vera sniffs. Honestly, what is the point of having a police station without some *~drama~*? She goes to the main reception desk, which is being manned by a young officer who looks like he's barely out of high school, and says, "I need to see Officer Gray."

"Which department?" the young officer says.

Vera considers this before saying regally, "Homicide." She knows this is the most revered department of all the departments.

The officer narrows his eyes. He looks like a schoolboy struggling to see the blackboard. "Do you have an appointment?"

Technically no, but surely coming in here armed with a delicious feast would be enough to grant her an appointment. "Yes."

"Name?"

"Vera Wong."

He looks at his computer, then makes an apologetic face and says, "Hmm, sorry, I'm not seeing your name here."

"Tch, is this police station or is this—" Fortunately for the young officer, Vera's tirade is interrupted by the arrival of Officer Gray, who walks in carrying a takeaway latte from—unfortunately—the Café. Vera calls out in a friendly shout that can be heard all the way to the top floor, "Officer Gray! Eh, Officer Gray!"

Officer Gray glances up from her phone, and when she spots Vera, her face visibly falls. Vera doesn't notice, or maybe she chooses not to notice. Either way, Vera heaves the tiffin tower from the reception desk and hurries over to Officer Gray, beaming. "Good morning, Officer."

"It was," Officer Gray says meaningfully. If her hands hadn't been full with her latte and her phone, she would be pinching the bridge of her nose. "What brings you here, Vera?"

"Ah, I cook too much food for myself and I think, hmm, who can use a good meal? And I think, oh yes, of course, Officer Gray!" Vera's smile widens. Then she sees the coffee cup with that hateful logo and those hateful two words, "The Café," and her smile falters. "You shouldn't drink such rubbish," she scolds Officer Gray, plucking the cup from the officer's hand. "Will give you liver cancer, everybody knows. Come, I show you what I cook." She marches down the hallway, dumping the full cup of coffee in a nearby trash can as she does so.

"Wait, that's my—" Officer Gray stares forlornly at the trash can, looking like she's considering whether she should fish the cup out. With a sigh, she trudges after Vera. "That latte cost seven dollars and I only had the one sip," she hisses at Vera.

"Seven dollars? Tomorrow I will bring you tea for free."

"No, that's okay," Officer Gray says quickly. She follows Vera as she turns a corner and keeps marching. After a few minutes of this, Officer Gray clears her throat. "Um, just out of curiosity, where is it that you're headed, Vera?"

Vera stops and turns around with a frown. "Your office, of course."

"Right. Silly me. Except you seem to be leading the way?"

Vera sniffs. "I keep expecting you to catch up and lead, but you young people nowadays, always walking so slow. This is because you are always staring at your phone, all day, every day, just hunch over your phone, later you will have hunchback."

"Right . . ." Officer Gray nods. "Would you like me to show you where my office is?"

"Yes, and take this, it's so heavy. I been waiting for you to offer to carry it, but you young people don't have many manners."

With a sigh of defeat, Officer Gray takes the tiffin tower, which is indeed surprisingly heavy, and beckons to Vera to follow her. They walk up the stairs to the third floor, and Vera says, "Ah, this is where the excitement happens." But all Vera finds is yet another office setting with a marked lack of violent criminals.

The office is open plan, and Officer Gray leads Vera to her desk near the windows. Nobody takes much notice of them, but as soon as they get to Officer Gray's desk, Vera clicks the tiffin tower open and all sorts of wonderful smells waft out. Before Vera is even done arranging the containers neatly on Officer Gray's desk, two other officers have wandered close, following their noses.

"Braised lion's head," Vera says, pointing to a container filled with fist-sized meatballs drowning in glistening gravy. "Spicy sesame noodles, roast pepper chicken, garlic-fried broccoli, and tomato-egg stir-fry. Come, eat." She opens her shoulder bag and takes out a bunch of disposable bowls and chopsticks.

Officer Gray wants to protest, she really should, but maybe she'll do so after one meatball. They look amazing, and when Vera places a bowl in Officer Gray's hands, she just nods and spears a meatball. The other officers shamelessly help themselves to the spread and lavish praise on Vera for the delicious food. Vera nods, obviously pleased, and heaps more food into everyone's bowls as she urges them to eat more. Before long, the tiffin containers are empty, at which point Vera says to the other officers, "Okay, go away now, I need to talk to Officer Gray."

One of them, a burly sergeant, calls out, "Do you think you

can make more of those lion heads, ma'am?" to which Vera says, "Yes, of course, but now I need privacy."

Officer Gray shakes her head at Vera, and Vera stares back impassively. "I've never seen these guys take orders so well, not even from our captain."

Vera shrugs. "If they want good food, they need to listen to me."

"Can't argue with you there. So, Vera, what can I do for you?"

Vera squares her shoulders, and Officer Gray leans back a little, as though she's expecting Vera to pounce. "Well, I want to know what else you doing to investigate Marshall Chen's murder."

Officer Gray sighs. "Vera—"

"No, don't tell me is not murder. Is very clearly murder."

"Really? Why?"

Vera holds out a thumb. "Number one, he has scratch on his cheek." She holds out her index finger. "Number two, he has bruise on cheek also, like someone punch him. And number three, there are no ducks in San Francisco!" She says the third thing with gusto. It's her trump card. Vera almost places her knuckles on her hips and goes, "Hah!" but she manages to hold herself back. Just barely.

But Officer Gray doesn't look impressed. Actually, she looks more confused than anything. "I'm sorry, come again? There are no . . . ducks? In San Francisco?"

"Yes, you say he die from duck allergy."

"No . . ." Officer Gray says slowly, drawing out the syllable. "I said he had an allergic reaction to bird dander. It could've been any bird."

Vera frowns. "Not any bird. For example, if he allergic to pigeon, then he would die a lot sooner, because this city is infested with pigeon."

"Not necessarily. The bird dander was found in his stomach, so unless he ate a pigeon feather and all—"

"His stomach? So he eat it?" Vera's frown deepens. "So he is allergic to chicken too?"

Officer Gray shakes her head. "Not according to Mrs. Chen."

Well, now, this is getting interesting. Or maybe it's going nowhere, but Vera blithely refuses to consider that possibility. "Okay, so what about the scratch and the bruise?"

"They could've been caused by him stumbling around when he started to feel unwell. He might've bashed his head into a wall—I mean, he broke into your shop, for god's sake. His knuckles were injured from breaking in. It's most likely that he sustained other injuries too."

Vera can't quite believe what she's hearing. All those suspicious signs just being batted away. All wasted. "Have you done DNA test?"

"DNA tests? What for?"

"For—" Vera gestures vaguely. "I don't know, to find if he has murderer's DNA on him! They always do in *CSI*. You should watch *CSI*, you will learn a lot from it."

Officer Gray closes her eyes. "God, I hate that bloody show," she mutters.

Vera nods. "Yes, it can be bloody sometimes."

"No, I didn't mean— Never mind. Look, I assure you we know all about *CSI* and all the other shows, and yes, sometimes we check for DNA samples, but in this case, it wasn't an appropriate avenue . . ."

As Officer Gray continues explaining why they're not spending any of the city's funding on pursuing Marshall's death, frustration boils in Vera's veins. *And what about the flash drive?* she wants to shout. Though to be fair, she's mostly angry at herself about the flash drive, because if she hadn't taken it, then maybe they would've taken the case more seriously.

Guilt is not a feeling Vera is familiar with. As soon as it rears up, Vera squishes it firmly. She did what she had to do in order to ensure that the case fell into the most capable hands, which are hers, obviously. Just look at these cops, sitting at their desks, typing into computers. They've gotten too complacent. No, Vera did the right thing. She chose to take on Marshall's case, and now she will see it through to the bitter end.

EIGHTEEN

OLIVER

It has only been a couple of weeks since Oliver received word that Marshall died, but it feels like an entire lifetime has passed. It also, strangely, feels like not much has changed, which is ridiculous. But then again, he'd never been close to Marshall, not since their mother died. He and Marshall would meet up once or twice a year, tops. The last time they'd met up, well, that was the day before Marshall died, and that hadn't gone well at all.

You've always been jealous of me. The knockoff twin. That's what they all called you.

"Eh, what are you doing? Don't daydream when you are on the ladder," Vera calls up to him.

"I'm not daydreaming." He was most definitely daydreaming. He clears his throat and screws a new lightbulb into the light fixture before climbing back down the ladder. "I've changed the bulb for you, but I think your electrics need rewiring. I don't think the power is running as efficiently as it should."

"Oh, I can't afford new electrics," Vera says. She picks up a tray from the counter and gestures at Oliver to join her at the table.

"Don't worry about it, I'll do it for you one of these weekends." Oliver can't quite explain it, but when Vera called him this morning, asking if he could help her change a couple of lightbulbs, he hadn't minded at all. In fact, he found himself looking forward to coming back to Vera's little shop and spending time there. Especially now that it's clear that Marshall's death was an accident.

"I make tang yuan." Vera pushes a bowl filled with five large glutinous rice balls swimming in lightly sweetened broth toward him.

"Gosh, I can't remember the last time I had this." He sips at the broth, which is steaming hot and spicy-sweet with a strong kick of ginger. The warmth slides straight down his throat and into his belly like a comforting flame. He bites into one of the tang yuan and finds it chewy and soft in the best possible way and filled with a sandy-sweet black sesame paste. His mother used to make tang yuan, and he remembers it being just as comforting as it is now. Maybe it's not so strange to like Vera's company; something about her soothes his soul.

"Is it good?" Vera is watching him like a hawk, practically unblinking.

"Yes." Oliver bites into another tang yuan and finds this one filled with sweet peanut paste. "It's so good. I love tang yuan."

Vera nods, satisfied. "So I am thinking maybe one of these nights you all come for dinner here—"

The ringing of Oliver's phone interrupts her, and with a quick apology, Oliver answers. It's the tenant from 3B, telling him that they can't get any hot water. Oliver promises to look into it and hangs up. "I can't stay long. I'm supposed to be on the job."

"Speaking of job," Vera says, "I have start reading your manuscript . . ."

"My manuscript?" It takes a beat for him to recall Vera finding it in his car. He narrows his eyes at her. "Vera, I thought I told you to put it back where you found it."

Vera looks entirely unapologetic. "Why? So you can forget it exist for another ten years? No, I take it home and I have been reading it. It's not so bad. Maybe a bit slow to begin with; I keep falling asleep when I read it."

"Thanks a lot, Vera." Actually, Oliver can barely remember what he wrote in that manuscript. He vaguely remembers that, like the stereotypical amateur writer, he'd based it loosely on his own life story. He really should tell Vera to give it back to him, but he doesn't have the time right now. Finishing up his tang yuan, Oliver takes his leave and drives back to his place.

His steps are leaden as he makes his way to the basement to check on the water heater. Working as a building manager had seemed like the perfect job all those years ago. Quiet, low-key, with plenty of downtime to work on his writing. And Oliver has been working all this time on his writing, he hasn't just been sitting on his ass, waiting for various things in the building to break so he can be useful. It's just that this job was meant to be a temporary one, one that he would quit once his writing took off, and now it's been more than ten years and Oliver is still in the same place, literally, same chair, same little apartment, same everything. And nothing but rejections on his writing.

As Oliver works on the water heater, his phone rings again. He sighs, putting his tool in his pocket and retrieving the phone; 3B has always been impatient. He taps on the green phone icon and turns his attention back to the water heater.

"I'm working on it," he says by way of greeting.

"Oliver?" The voice stops him in mid-crank. That's not 3B. It's the voice he's dreamt about ever since high school.

"Julia?" Oliver straightens up, wiping off his sweat with his forearm, as though she could see him. "Hey, what's up?"

A shaky sigh. "Sorry to bother you, is this a bad time?" She sounds so apologetic that his chest tightens.

"No," Oliver says quickly. *Never a bad time for you*, he wants to say, but that would be very inappropriate, so he leaves it at no.

"Okay, um, this is going to sound weird, but . . ." She sighs again, and this time he catches the tone of frustration and pain behind the sigh. "I just got a call from some guy who says that Marshall was renting an apartment downtown. Marshall had mentioned it before he left, but I guess I must have forgotten about it after he died. I thought he'd just gotten it, but it turns out I was wrong. I can't even—he had a secret apartment, Ollie!" Her voice shakes then, almost breaking, and Oliver is filled with the familiar sense of anger toward Marshall. God, why did Marshall have to be such a raging dick? "God knows what he was doing in it for how long, I mean . . . gah!" She takes a deep breath. "Anyway, the landlord said he's going to empty out the apartment tomorrow, but he asked if we wanted to go over to retrieve Marshall's stuff. I can't go because of Emma. Do you have time to go? I'm sorry, I know it's such an imposition, but I just don't—"

"I'll go," Oliver says simply. He'll go, because it's Julia asking, and he'll do anything for her. Always did everything for her, back in school, when she let him. And seeing her again last week after so many years had been one of the most incredible moments. He desperately wishes they could go back to how they were before. "I'll grab everything that looks useful."

Julia snorts bitterly. "I don't know if I want to know what's even in that apartment." She pauses, and Oliver finds himself holding his breath. When she does speak again, her voice is tight with pain. "Um, if you do find . . . you know, something, uh, you know—if he was, uh, betraying our marriage vows—I'd rather not know."

"Of course." He's about to add that Marshall was loyal to her and he's sure he won't find anything that would say otherwise, but then he stops himself. Because why bother lying? The only person Marshall was ever loyal to was himself. But still, Oliver hates that Julia now knows this about Marshall. Despite everything, despite his own feelings for her, he'd always hoped that Marshall would prove him wrong, that Marshall would treat her right.

"Thanks, Ollie." There's another pause, so long this time that Oliver half wonders if she's hung up. But as he lowers the phone to check that the call is still ongoing, she says, "It was really nice seeing you the other day. After all this time."

His heart swells and he finds it hard to draw breath. "It really was," he replies with so much unspoken emotion. "And so good to see little Emma too. I hope—uh—I hope we see more of each other now."

Oh god, that came out all wrong. That was so fucking creepy, oh my goddd.

Like he's hitting on her now that her husband has passed. Argh! That was not at all his intention. He scrambles to save it. "I just meant—uh, I hope we don't lose touch again?"

A small laugh, more sad than happy. "Yeah. D'you know, I never quite figured out why we stopped hanging out."

The thought of Julia wondering why they stopped being friends is so acutely excruciating that Oliver can't quite find the words to reply to her.

"See you around, Ollie," she says, and hangs up before he can say anything.

Oliver stares at the phone for a long time, his thoughts and emotions warring in the cool darkness of the basement. When the phone rings again, it is apartment 3B, asking why they still don't have any hot water.

The next morning, Oliver finds himself standing in front of Marshall's secret apartment, key in his hand, licking his dry lips with increasing nervousness. He has no clue whatsoever what he might find inside. Hard-core porn? Illegal firearms? Who the hell knows what Marshall wanted to hide from Julia? But certainly it would be something shady, because otherwise Marshall wouldn't have had to hide it.

Well, whatever. It's not Oliver's job to keep Marshall out of trouble anymore. He stabs the key into the keyhole and turns it. The lock clicks open and Oliver turns the handle.

The stale smell of old cigarette smoke hits him full in the face. That's right, Marshall was a smoker. Had been ever since he was a sophomore in high school. One time, Baba discovered Marshall's pack of cigarettes and without missing a beat, Marshall blamed it on Oliver. The few startled, silent seconds that Oliver took to respond were all that was required for Baba to believe Marshall. He'd been so disgusted, his upper lip curling into a sneer as he looked at Oliver.

The apartment is your typical overpriced San Franciscan fare.

Oliver looked it up last night and saw that the rent starts at twenty-five hundred for a studio, which this one is. That's a lot of money to spend on a secret apartment that looks like it was primarily used as . . . storage? There's a floor mattress, the sight of which triggers a whole-body shudder running through Oliver, because he can just about imagine what Marshall was using it for, but aside from that there are no other pieces of furniture, merely boxes stacked on top of one another. It doesn't look at all like a place that anyone lived in.

Oliver goes to the far end of the studio and opens a window to let some of the stink of stale smoke out. He looks at the boxes, dreading to find out what's inside them. Taking a deep breath, he reaches out for the nearest cardboard box and opens the top.

Huh.

O-kaaay.

Inside is not a stash of wrapped bricks of cocaine or stacks of counterfeit money or anything that he'd expected but a sculpture about four feet tall. It's a model of a U-shaped spaceship, its surface carved with extremely elaborate minute detail. Oliver lifts it very, very carefully, because it's obvious even to him, someone who knows nothing about sculptures, that this is a true work of art. The amount of detail that has gone into this spaceship is staggering; you can even see people inside the tiny carved windows. He places it on the floor before stepping back and staring at it, dumbfounded.

A piece of art, a beautiful one at that. Why does Marshall have it? Oliver feels like he shouldn't be handling this delicate piece of art with bare hands, but he hadn't thought of bringing gloves here, and he needs answers, so he lifts the piece gingerly and peers at the bottom of its base.

Sure enough, there are words carved into it.

F. Martinez. *Failure to Launch.*

Oliver sets the piece back down, his mind racing. *Failure to Launch* is obviously the title of the piece, and F. Martinez presumably the sculptor. Fleetingly, he wonders about the possibility of it being filled with drugs—maybe Marshall was smuggling drugs? But no, he dismisses the thought as soon as it surfaces. This is true artwork, not a front for some drug-running business.

He opens the next box. This one is filled with prints of beautiful photographs of waterfalls and forests, each one so vivid that Oliver can practically hear the rush of the rivers in the pictures. In the lower left-hand corner is a signature he can't make out. By now, Oliver has no freaking clue what is happening, so he opens more boxes, and the more he finds, the less he understands.

Before long, the studio looks like a tiny art gallery, albeit one owned by the most eclectic collector. There are oil paintings, and jumbled yarn pieces strung together with bits of broken glass and feathers, and cartoon drawings, and more sculptures. Some of the pieces are lone ones; others come in a set. They've all been made by different artists.

Oliver is absorbed by the bizarre discovery, his mind racing ahead—or rather, backward, into the past, digging frantically to figure out just what the hell Marshall was up to, but still he can't make any sense out of it.

"Oh, Marshall," he says, his voice heavy with sorrow and regret. "What have you done?"

NINETEEN

JULIA

Cooking has never been one of Julia's strong suits. Marshall confirmed that many times over, but over the course of their married life, she tried very hard to improve, first consulting cooking websites and blogs, then moving on to YouTube videos, and finally learning through TikTok. Unfortunately, despite all the hard work, Julia still never quite got the hang of it. At best, her food is passable, but it can never be accused of being anything that might cause cravings, unless the craving is for the meal to be over. Yet another thing marking her down as an incompetent housewife and human in general.

But one thing she does excel at is charcuterie boards. Well, she used to call them cheeseboards, up until the term "charcuterie board" took over the Internet. Her charcuterie boards absolutely slay. It's too bad that Marshall never liked cheese or cured meats or any of her boards, even the dessert ones; otherwise it would have been charcuterie boards every day.

It feels weird having thoughts like these when Marshall is

dead. They seem so petty, to be remembering him this way. Shouldn't she be mourning him more? This morning, she received a call from the medical examiner telling her that the examination is over and that she can now make funeral arrangements. In a daze, she'd opted to have him cremated because that was the cheaper option, and no service because—well, she just wasn't sure if anyone would turn up. It had made her feel like the world's worst wife. But now she's trying to focus on anything but that. Focus on the charcuterie board, she tells herself.

She's having a good time making one with Emma, which feels wrong; she probably shouldn't be having fun putting together a charcuterie board so soon after Marshall's death. But Emma is having a great time smearing her little fingers with fig jam and then licking them off and then dipping the fingers back into the jam pot, and Julia is telling her off but also laughing, and maybe everything will be okay? There is no way that their savings can last beyond next month's mortgage payment, so Julia has no idea what she's going to do then, but for now, she's making a charcuterie board with her daughter and she doesn't have to worry about Marshall telling her that it's shit. Things could be worse.

Emma's just fussing over the charcuterie board, putting grapes down here and there with fierce concentration, the tip of her tongue sticking out of her mouth, when the doorbell goes off.

"That'll be Uncle Ollie," Julia says, and for a second, Emma looks scared. "Are you gonna be okay?" It's strange, asking Emma this, when in the past, they didn't have a choice but to be okay with any visitors, because Marshall thought asking Emma stuff like this is "pandering" to her and encouraging her to be difficult.

Emma looks at her, then down at the charcuterie board, which admittedly isn't one of Julia's best because a lot of the deli meats and cheese have splodges of little jam fingerprints on them. "Will Uncle Ollie like this?"

Julia doesn't even think twice before saying, "Of course." Only after she says those words does it hit her how true they are, because Ollie has always liked what she liked.

Emma nods solemnly. "Then Emma is okay." Her little jam-smeared face looks so brave that Julia crouches down and gives her a tight hug. How did she end up with such a special girl?

Emma chooses to stay in the living room while Julia opens the door; she's still not a fan of greeting people at the door.

"Hey," Oliver says with a smile and hands her a paper bag. "I got you some cookies. They're whole-grain?"

Julia laughs at the uncertainty in his voice. "You didn't have to. Come on in."

They walk inside the house and find Emma hiding behind the sofa. Anxiety churns in Julia's belly. This is one of the many things Emma does that irritated Marshall to no end. *It's so embarrassing,* he'd say. *Can't she just be fucking normal? Other kids her age are always running up to people and saying hi, but she's gotta hide like some creepy kid. You're just enabling her, Jules.*

"Hey, you wanna come out of there and say hi to Uncle Ollie?" Julia can hear the tiny note of embarrassment in her voice, and she hates it, hates herself for it. The top of Emma's head shakes to and fro, and Julia gives Oliver an apologetic smile.

"Sorry, she's . . ." She doesn't know what to say. *She's shy?* Yes, but apparently you shouldn't say such things in front of the child, lest it become their identity.

"No worries, I totally relate." Oliver lowers his voice. "I wish I could hide behind furniture when people come over too."

Julia laughs. "Take a seat, Emma and I made you something."

Oliver sits down on the sofa, pointedly ignoring the set of eyes peering at him from the other end, and Julia hurries to the kitchen. When she comes back with the charcuterie board, Oliver's eyes actually light up.

"Oh wow, this looks fancy," he says. Then he spots the little jam fingerprints on the deli meats and his smile wavers a little.

"Emma helped make the board," Julia says, again with that note of apology in her voice.

Oliver laughs. "Awesome job, Emma." And with that, he picks up one of the smudged pieces of meat and pops it in his mouth. "Yum. Oh, sorry, I don't think I'm supposed to just eat the deli meat on its own, am I? I'm a beginner at this. Can anyone tell me how to put everything together?" He raises his eyebrows at Julia and the two of them hold their breaths, waiting for a response. "Okay, I guess I'm just gonna fumble through somehow."

There's a dramatic sigh from behind the sofa, and Emma's head pops up. "No," she announces in her somber voice. "You'll ruin it." She marches out from her hiding spot and leans over the board, inspecting it solemnly before pointing at a cracker. "Take that."

"Okay." Oliver does so, then follows her further instructions, spreading fig jam on the cracker before placing a slice of brie on it and layering that with some turkey. He pops the whole thing in his mouth and goes, "Mm." After swallowing, he says, "Wow, that was the perfect bite. Thanks, Emma."

Emma nods and proceeds to put together a perfect bite for herself, except she doesn't bother using any tools, choosing to smear the jam on with her fingers.

"I made sure to wash her hands before you arrived," Julia whispers.

Oliver smiles, then clears his throat. "Uh, so I went to . . . the apartment."

Julia stiffens. Right, of course, this is the main reason Oliver's here. He's not here for a chat; it's not a casual, friendly visit. He's here to update her on what shady thing Marshall was involved in when he was alive. She feels panic begin to rise, churning hot and acidic in her belly, burning its way up to her chest, constricting it. He shouldn't talk to her about this now, in front of Emma.

Maybe Oliver reads the quiet panic in Julia's face, because he glances at Emma before nodding. "Don't worry, there wasn't anything . . . bad."

"Really?" It's less a question, more a plea.

"Yeah." Oliver's eyes soften. He's noticed the desperation in her voice. "Really. It was strange, actually, because it was just filled with a lot of artwork. There were sculptures, paintings, photographs . . . and it seemed like a totally random collection. I couldn't find any connection throughout all of them. Although, mind you, I'm not exactly an art connoisseur, so even if there had been a cohesive thread between all of them, I probably wouldn't have noticed."

"Artwork?" What the hell? It's so far off from what Julia had been expecting—clear signs of adultery—that she has no idea how to react, or even how to think. Her late husband was never particularly artistic that she knows of. But maybe that goes to show just how little she ever knew about him. Maybe that proves that Marshall was right when he told her that she's dumb, that she's ignorant, that it's a waste of time telling her anything, and that's why everyone is so sick of her. "Was he— I mean, you were brothers—" she says haltingly. "Was he into art?"

Oliver shakes his head. "Nope, never was. I mean, I wasn't particularly artistic myself, but I'd say I was more into creative endeavors than he ever was. Don't, like . . ." Oliver takes a deep breath. "Don't beat yourself up over not knowing this about him, because I—well, my dad and I—are as confused as you are."

The burning shame, that familiar feeling that's accompanied her for years and years, recedes, just a little. It's not just her that Marshall has hidden his interest in art from. It's his own twin brother, and his father, which means she's in good company. She can just about deal with that.

"All that stuff's in my car, by the way. I don't really know what to do with them. There's not much space in my apartment, so . . ."

"I'll take them." She has no idea what she's going to do with them, but it's not like she can trash all this stuff her late husband obviously cared about. She swings Emma up onto one hip and together, she and Oliver make their way out to his car. When Oliver opens the trunk and shows her the stash, Julia is even more taken aback. The artwork is, as Oliver said, eclectic, but more than that, it looks like serious art. She feels guilty once more, because what kind of wife would underestimate her husband like that? Why wouldn't Marshall have been into actual good art? Didn't he say that night he left that he'd made it rich? It's probably because he had an eye for high art, a talent he'd kept hidden from her, and for good reason. She's quiet as she helps Oliver take the pieces into the house, deep in her thoughts, Emma heavy on her hip.

The pieces of artwork are placed just inside the doorway, leaning against the wall. They look obscene inside her house, so wrong and so out of place. Then Julia spots the photographs, and they give her pause because they're so achingly beautiful. They're all landscape photography, mostly of waterfalls, very different from what Julia was interested in back in high school, but she retains enough knowledge of photography to know that she's looking at the work of a competent photographer. She admires the way they captured the light and how vivid some unexpected parts of the scenery have been manipulated to look. Julia's throat closes and she puts down the prints with reverence before turning away with a slight sniffle.

It's at this time that Emma decides she's had enough excitement and starts fussing, burying her face in Julia's chest and going, "Boop."

Julia wants to die with embarrassment. God, what's Oliver going to think?

Oliver glances down at Emma as he wipes the sheen off his forehead. "Do you guys want me to go? It's no problem."

"No, stay." There's no reason for him to stay here, Julia reminds herself, but the thing is, she hasn't even begun to process this strange new discovery about Marshall, and there's no one else she'd rather talk about it with than Oliver. "I just—I just need to nurse her for a bit." She hates how pathetic she sounds, how sorry. Marshall was so disgusted by the breastfeeding the longer it went on.

But Oliver doesn't bat an eye. "Oh, sure. Yeah, of course."

As Julia heads toward her bedroom, Oliver calls out, "Hey, this is gonna sound weird, but do you mind if I check out Emma's room for a bit?"

It's so far from what Julia expects that she laughs a little. "Sure, knock yourself out."

The whole time Julia nurses Emma, she wonders what in the world Oliver could want in Emma's room. How utterly strange this day has been, and yet it's not completely awful. She strokes Emma's soft head of hair. When they're done, she swings Emma up onto her hip again and walks out of the room quietly. Julia's used to moving quietly because noise bothered Marshall. She startles when Oliver pops out of Emma's room.

"There you are," he says. "All done?"

Julia nods, unsure what to say, and Oliver clears his throat and looks at Emma. "So I got a few things for you that I really, really wanted when I was a kid. Do you wanna take a look?"

Emma hides her face in Julia's armpit, and Julia shrugs. "It's not a no." She makes her way into the room and gasps.

Somehow, in the space of twenty minutes, Oliver has managed to put up a small white tent in a corner of Emma's room. Above the tent is a colorful sign that says: EMMA'S QUIET CORNER. Inside the tent, Julia spots mounds of pastel-colored cushions and a couple of soft toys. The entire corner looks magical.

Oliver hands Julia a board book. "This is a sensory book. It's got all sorts of different materials in it that she can play with." He nods at Emma. "When I was a little boy, I was always really scared of unfamiliar things. Strangers, or situations, it didn't matter, I was scared of them, and I always wished that I could have my own little corner to hide in whenever it got too much for me. So I thought maybe you'd like this."

Emma is staring at the tent with mouth and eyes wide open, wonderment written all over her face. "Mine?" she croaks.

"Yes, baby." Julia is surprised to find that her voice is wavering. She lets Emma down gently and tears rush into her eyes when the little girl toddles over into the tent and cries out, "*Wow!*" It's the exact sort of thing that Marshall would've hated, because he didn't want to "pander" and "make her soft." But it's also the exact thing Julia knew, deep down inside, that her daughter needed. And yet it had taken Oliver, someone who's only met Emma the one time, to provide it. "Thank you," she whispers to Oliver, who smiles back. They gaze at Emma's chubby feet sticking out of the tent flap.

The bell rings then. "Oh, I forgot to let you know," Julia says, "Sana asked if she could come over to ask more questions for her podcast."

They go to the front door, leaving Emma in her bedroom, chattering happily to herself. Julia only agreed to being interviewed because she thought it would look suspicious if she said no, but now, after seeing Emma so happy, Julia is in such high spirits that she doesn't mind having to answer questions about her late husband. The feeling lasts up until Sana steps inside and sees all the artwork in the hallway. Sana's face tightens with what Julia swears is not just anger, but white-hot fury, and it is then that Julia realizes that maybe she's not the only person hiding some dark secrets about Marshall.

TWENTY

SANA

The entire way to Marshall and Julia's house, Sana wasn't sure what to expect. It's different, coming here again without Vera striding ahead of her, conveniently giving her a legit excuse for coming by. Now she's here on her own, and, well, she definitely was not expecting to see the pile of artwork just left in the hallway like that. The entire pile looks so pathetic somehow, a little grave-yard of stolen art, and hers probably hidden inside it.

She hadn't ever thought of the possibility that she hadn't been Marshall's only victim. In hindsight, she realizes of course she's not his only victim. Why the hell would she be? Of course he was preying on multiple artists, selling them hope before betraying them and then ghosting them. The discovery that there seem to be dozens of artists in the same position as Sana should comfort her. She's not alone. She's not the world's most gullible idiot for falling for Marshall's ruse. But it doesn't make her feel comforted at all. In fact, she feels even worse. The knowledge that she's noth-ing special, that her art wasn't even that unique, as it turns out.

That she was caught up in nothing more than one of Marshall's many, many scams. It makes her pain feel ridiculous.

Stop that, Sana scolds herself as she follows Julia into the house. *Just freaking let it go already. Enough moping around, feeling sorry for yourself. I bet none of these artists are still hung up on their precious stolen art.*

Still, Sana can't quite shake it off, that heaviness settling on her shoulders like a weighted blanket. Part of her wants to sift through the canvases and find her paintings. She wants to grab them and run away. But she can't. If she did that, Julia would know that Sana had a connection to Marshall, that Sana isn't just a random true crime podcaster here to research a story. That Sana very much had motive to kill Marshall. And worse, that Sana had been tracking him down for months—some might say she was stalking him. He was certainly horrified when she'd shown up that day and confronted him. *Crazy bitch*, he'd spat at her. *Get the fuck away from me before I report you for harassment and stalking.* And now here she is, in his freaking house, under some ridiculous, flimsy guise that would fall to pieces as soon as anyone even breathed on it.

When they get to the living room, Sana is surprised to see Oliver there. She doesn't like Oliver, although it doesn't have much to do with his personality, which for the record seems decent. But he looks so much like Marshall that Sana can't quite bury her hatred deep enough.

"Hey, Sana," Oliver says, and Sana has to stop herself from shuddering. Even his voice is like Marshall's.

"Hey." *What the hell are you doing here?* she wants to say to him.

As though reading her mind, Oliver clears his throat. "I was just here dropping off some of Marshall's stuff. I think you might have seen some of it in the hallway?"

It feels as though her skin has shrunk two sizes too small for her body. She can see Julia and Oliver looking at her, so she forces herself to nod in what she thinks is a casual way. "Cool." Belatedly, Sana realizes that as a podcaster looking into Marshall's death, she can actually be a bit nosier. It's only natural for her to be curious. God, this whole pretending to be someone you're not is so hard. How the hell did Marshall do it so effortlessly? Sana quickly sifts through what she's about to ask, looking for anything that might give her away; then she says cautiously, "It looks like there's a lot of artwork? Was Marshall an art collector?" The questions fight her, every word struggling not to come out, because hah! An art collector? More like an art thief.

Julia and Oliver exchange a glance that sends another electric tingle down Sana's spine. Something's off here. The two of them look shifty as hell. Were they in on it too? Was Marshall working together with his wife and twin brother to steal art from starry-eyed college students? The thought sits in Sana's stomach like a lump of burning coal.

Julia gestures at them to take a seat, probably to buy herself some time to consider her answer. She takes a deep breath and sighs. "Honestly, I don't know—I didn't know anything about the artwork until . . ." She checks her watch. "About an hour ago, when Oliver brought them over."

"I found them in an apartment he was renting downtown," Oliver says.

"Marshall hid the artwork from you?" Sana says. She has no idea what to make of this. As much as she hates to admit it, she likes Julia. Something about the woman feels sad. Even the way

Julia stands is somehow sad, like a flower that's drooping gently. Sana doesn't want to suspect Julia, and yet. And yet, how could Julia possibly not know all the shady shit Marshall had been up to? At best, maybe she had an inkling that he'd been up to no good and had decided to turn a blind eye to it.

Julia shakes her head. "I know it sounds pathetic." Her voice wobbles. "But I'm just a stay-at-home mom. My world revolves around cooking and cleaning and looking after Emma."

There is so much apology in Julia's voice that Sana almost reaches out to hold her hand. *Focus*, she scolds herself. "So . . . you guys probably don't know what Marshall was doing with the artwork?" *Where's the money?* her mind screams. *The money from all the stolen art, where the fuck is it?*

Again, that shifty look between Julia and Oliver. What are they hiding? They know something, Sana is sure of it.

"I have no idea," Oliver says.

Julia nods. "Yeah, I'm the same. I had no idea he was even venturing into art. Marshall was . . . he was always having one bright idea after another. He was into apps for a while, you know, back when apps just started being a thing, then he went into crypto . . . he never quite caught the trends in time to make it big, but he made enough for us to get by." Again, her voice wobbles, almost breaking this time. "Sorry, I just—I have no idea how I'm going to make the mortgage payments now that he's gone."

Oliver reaches out and pats Julia's shoulder. "What about your parents?" he says gently.

Julia sniffles, shakes her head. "I haven't talked to them in years. Marshall never got along with them, and over time it just became easier not to deal with all that stuff . . ."

Red flags aren't just going up in Sana's mind, they're waving and flapping madly, her gut churning at every little detail that Julia is revealing. She knows firsthand what a manipulative person Marshall was, and now she's imagining all too easily Marshall slowly, subtly isolating Julia from her family, making sure that at the end of the day, she only had Marshall to lean on.

It. Does. Not. Matter.

Right. It's not her business. She's not here to fix Julia's problems. She can't even fix her own. She's here for closure.

But what would it take to bring her closure? Well, first of all, she would like her paintings back. But she knows that isn't enough, because having the physical paintings themselves is only one part of the equation. She needs their digital rights back too. Well, or something similar. Sana's not quite sure how the whole thing works, but she knows that owning the physical object doesn't necessarily mean she owns the virtual part of it. Which sounds so freaking ridiculous it's hard for her to wrap her head around the whole concept. That she, the artist, might not even own the rights to her own work. If it had been an IP project, that would've made some sense, at least, and is the sole reason why Sana's mother had always advised her against doing IP work.

IP work is only ever worth it if they are going to pay you oodles of money, my darling, her mom would say. *Money up front. Because you don't own the IP, so always demand money up front. Know your worth.*

It's her own fault. She'd been so eager to make a name for herself. This is the problem with creative people; their self-image is divided into two parts—one thinks that they're a genius who will one day create a masterpiece of such breathtaking brilliance that it will still be discussed with reverence hundreds of years later; the other part thinks they are trash raccoons rooting around in the dark and coming up with nothing but more trash. There is no in-between. It's either "super genius" or "trash raccoon," and somehow these parts coexist within the head of one very tortured artist.

So when Marshall approached her and told her that her art would make the perfect NFTs, Sana had been both wildly grateful and also smug. She'd thought: *Yes, someone is finally recognizing my talent and is about to make me rich!* Simultaneously, she'd also thought: *I'd better agree real fast before he finds out I'm a talentless hack!* And of course she'd jumped at the chance without really researching what the hell NFTs even are, and how she should protect her own work. Although, to be honest, even if someone had sat Sana down and told her how to protect her work, Sana would've cringed and refused to take the steps to protect herself, because it would've made her feel ridiculous and arrogant when she should just be grateful that Marshall had picked her out of all the other hopeful artists in her year.

Okay, focus. Sana knows she needs to set aside every distraction—god, there are so many of them—and concentrate on why she came here. "It's funny that you mentioned crypto, because—" Lord, is she making any sense? Does she sound casual enough? "—I recently read about this stuff called NFTs?"

Julia and Oliver stare at Sana, confused.

"It stands for non-fungible tokens, and it's basically like . . . something you can own and trade online?" She really needs to stop ending everything with a question mark. "I wonder if maybe . . ." Tread carefully. "Maybe that was what Marshall was doing with the artwork? Selling them as NFTs online."

"How does that work?" Julia says. "So it's like online rights? But what about the actual physical art? Does that matter?"

"Yes and no," Sana says. "The physical art itself could come with it, or it could be a separate entity, but there is virtual ownership as well. NFTs can sell for up to hundreds of millions of dollars."

"Wow," Oliver says. "I'm kind of having a difficult time wrapping my head around it, but . . . it does sound like the kind of thing Marshall would've been into, yeah."

"Yes," Julia agrees. "Like I said, he was always into these kinds of things."

The tip of Sana's tongue darts out and licks her dry lips. "If he was doing that, then he'd probably have all the information on his computer, maybe on a cloud, or in a physical drive, or . . ."

Julia frowns. "I wouldn't know. And I don't think I'd be comfortable looking through his computer. It's just so much."

"Oh yeah, of course," Sana says quickly. *Shit, shit!* She scrambles to find a way around it. She needs to get into Marshall's computer. She must. "Could I . . ."

But already, Julia is shaking her head. "I don't think so, I don't like the thought of it. It's kind of violating."

Oliver, looking more wary than ever before, leans forward in his seat, resting his elbows on his knees. "What did you say the name of your podcast was again?"

"Oh, it's . . ." Oh god, she's blanking out now, of all times? *"Murder or Accident?"* Sana's insides shrivel up with a painful squeak. *Murder or Accident?* What the hell kind of a name is that?

Julia is nodding with a highly skeptical expression, and Sana can't blame her. "I'm going to check it out now; it sounds so interesting."

Oh god. Entire star systems are exploding inside Sana. She needs to come up with an excuse to stop Julia, but she can't, her mind is a complete blank, she's not a writer like her mother, who by now would've come up with at least five different legit excuses as to why Julia won't find her nonexistent podcast online. Powerless, Sana watches as Julia takes out her phone and swipes to unlock it. Here it comes, she's going to be exposed as a complete fraud, and then the suspicion will come, and maybe then they'll even find out how she's been following Marshall for weeks.

All these thoughts bubble inside her until they surge out of her with too much urgency. "Wait—"

There's too much panic in Sana's voice. She hears it even as she says it, and she catches the surprise in both Oliver's and Julia's eyes, but she can't stop it, it's too late, she's going to reveal everything—

And that's when Julia's phone rings.

The words that are already halfway out of Sana's mouth die and she forces herself to sit back down.

"It's Vera," Julia says, obviously surprised.

Anxiety leaps up in Sana's chest once again. She has no idea how to feel about Vera. She likes Vera, despite everything, but she is also terrifying. But everything's fine, Sana reminds herself, because Vera told everyone that Marshall's death isn't murder after all, it's an allergic reaction to a duck, right? Right. She's probably calling to ask about Emma or something.

Julia stands up and walks to the far side of the room as she answers the phone. "Hi, Vera, how's it— Oh, Vera, are you okay?" She glances behind her shoulder, and she looks so worried that Sana's panic spikes and she wonders if she's about to throw up right here in Julia's living room. Her hands are gripping her knees so tightly that they've gone numb. "Oh, Vera," Julia cries. "That's awful. Have you called the police? Okay, you just sit tight, Vera.

We'll be right over. Yes. I'll see you in a bit." By the time Julia hangs up, both Sana and Oliver are on their feet.

"What happened?" Oliver says.

Julia's face is pale, her eyes wide with fear. "Vera's shop has been broken into."

None of them says it, but Sana knows they're all thinking the same thing: first, Marshall's death, and now a break-in? What are the chances that the two are unrelated?

TWENTY-ONE

RIKI

Riki knew coming in that something bad had happened to Vera's teahouse, but seeing the destruction in person is still a big enough shock that for a while, he's unable to find the right words, if indeed there are right words to be said at such a time.

Vera Wang's World-Famous Teahouse wasn't a fancy place to begin with, but it had been neat. Now it looks like someone went through it and methodically broke every jar of tea and herbs, covering the floor with broken glass and tea leaves and dried herbs everywhere, like a horrible trash heap. It looks so awfully wrong that part of Riki wishes he could not be here. But then again, maybe that's been the problem all along. He'd rather run away from problems than face them. Well, no longer.

Which sounds more impressive than it really is, because honestly, Riki wouldn't know how to run away from this problem even if he wanted to. Because it's not just that a teahouse has been broken into. A teahouse where Marshall Chen died just a week ago has been broken into, and now Riki is standing in the middle of a literal mess while Vera strides up and down, flapping her arms and ranting loud enough to be heard above the crunching of broken glass under her shoes.

"Look at this!" she cries for the seventh time.

Riki wonders when the others will arrive. Don't they know that a strapping young lad like him is no match for the utter force that is Vera Wong in a rage?

"They break everything! How can? They don't think of how wasteful it is, oh no, they just smash everything!"

Riki can only nod in agreement. He should probably say something, but he has no idea what, and it seems a shame to spoil Vera's tirade. He could swear she's enjoying the uninterrupted rant. The little bell above the door tinkles as the door swings open to reveal Sana. Riki could cry with relief at the sight of her, he really could. Also, he can't help but notice how pretty she looks today. Not that she doesn't look pretty other days. Gah, even in his own head he's hopeless at this stuff.

Sana's eyes light up when she sees him, and Riki can't help but smile. Then Sana takes in the destruction before her and her mouth drops open in horror, and now Riki feels extremely stupid for smiling in the middle of a little old lady's robbed store. Of all the highly inappropriate times to be smiling! He wants to apologize and explain that he's smiling not because he finds anything funny, but because . . . uh, he thought Sana had smiled at him fir— Nope, never mind, that sounds even worse.

"Oh, Vera," Sana says, going directly to the old woman and hugging her tight. "Are you okay? Oh, this is terrible!"

Hugs. Why didn't Riki think of hugging Vera? He watches, dumbly, as Oliver walks in, followed by Julia, who's carrying little Emma. They all gasp at the mess, then Emma walks over to Vera and grasps Vera's hand in her tiny one, patting it and saying, "Don't cry, Grandma. It'll be okay." Yep, this is definitely how normal people react at a time like this. Riki himself only stood there gaping like a stunned fish after stammering, "What happened?" as though it wasn't obvious what had happened.

Vera smiles as she accepts all the hugs being given her way. Then she straightens up and brushes off her pants. "I come down this morning and the shop is like this." She gestures around the small space. "All my rare teas destroyed, just like that!"

"Did you hear anything?" Riki says.

"Oh no, I always put in earplugs when I sleep because San Francisco so noisy, you know. At night can hear sirens, people shouting, laughing, that kind of thing."

"You've called the cops, right?" Julia says.

Vera blinks. "No, I don't want to. What good have they do? Nothing! I even go to the station, asking them to investigate more, and they tell me to stay away."

"But, Vera," Julia says, "this is serious. Someone broke in! Look at the place. I think you need to report this."

"They will just say is drunk kids from SF State or Berkeley. Anyway, is okay, I will do my investigation myself."

Riki wants to push her into reporting it too, but then he thinks of what that would entail. The fact that he'd have to talk to the police himself, that they would come round and dig, and dig, and no doubt they'd put the break-in and the murder together and tie all these strings together, and who knows what it'll lead to?

"I think Vera is right," Sana says. Riki glances at her in surprise. "I don't think it's a good idea to call the cops." She licks her lips, looking at them with wide eyes. "I just—I don't know, I haven't been impressed with how they've handled everything."

That makes no sense, Riki thinks, but a larger part of him is sagging with relief. *Yes, don't call the cops*, it squeaks. He looks around at the others, and they too are looking hesitant and uneasy, as though they are torn about what to do. Surely they're all hiding something too, because normal people would definitely want to call the cops, right? He has no idea what to think. His mind is as much a mess as the shop is.

He steps farther into the shop and peers over the counter before turning to Vera. "Did they take anything? Is money missing?"

Vera shakes her head. "No, I check my safe and nothing is taken."

"Where's your safe located?" Oliver says.

"Upstair in my house."

"Hmm." Oliver frowns, glancing around. "So that doesn't rule out the possibility that they might have been looking for money and didn't want to risk going upstairs."

"Aiya, you think they might have come upstair and murder me?" Vera cries. Beside her, Julia wraps an arm around Vera's narrow shoulders and squeezes while little Emma clings to Vera's leg.

"No," Riki says quickly, before he even realizes what he's about to say. Everyone looks at him, and he wants to sink into the ground. "I—uh, it's unlikely. I think that's exactly what they didn't want to do. They didn't want to hurt anyone, they only wanted to look for . . . something." It's only after the words are out that Riki realizes just how shady they sound, because uh, how the hell would Riki know what the burglars were after?

"There can only be one person," Vera says. "It is the killer."

Riki freezes. He can't even muster up the brain cells to remind himself to blink, or breathe.

"It is, right? The killer come back because there is some evidence that they are looking for." The more Vera says, the more certain she looks, her eyes glowing with a righteous flame. "Marshall must have leave behind some clue about who kill him. You see? If we call the police, they will just bungle it all up. They will tell me to stop meddling in investigation. No, it's clear, I have to do this myself. I am on the right track, I must be doing something right, that's why the killer break in."

I might throw up, Riki thinks. *I might actually hurl right now, this very minute, standing here with this old lady and these suspicious strangers in this broken shop.*

Vera isn't done with her speech. "Now we know that even though Marshall die from allergy reaction, it is in fact *murderrr*." She stretches out the word with so much drama that Riki is somehow surprised that there isn't an accompanying thunderclap.

His faux pas in mentioning that whoever it was must have been looking for something, paired with the shattered remains of Vera's jars everywhere around them, somehow increases in intensity until it reaches a crescendo, overwhelming all his senses. All Riki can hear is the roar of his blood as every drop of it seems to rush into his head, a deafening sound that drowns out everything, even his thoughts. He can see it in his mind's eye, the force that it took for someone to smash these thick jars, dashing them across the floor, their innards scattering everywhere like brains spattering out of a smashed skull. And there, on the floor, staring up at him accusingly, is the outline of Marshall's body, looking particularly gruesome with the mess all over it. It's almost as though Marshall has just died all over again. There is so much violence around him. And suddenly, as though a jagged piece of glass has just been stabbed into Riki's head, the memory slices into his mind.

His fist, as though an entirely separate entity from his body, swinging so fast he could feel the wind whistling past it. Making that horrible, delightful, satisfying wet crunch against Marshall's cheek. The way Riki's knuckles had felt every single layer of Marshall's face then—his cheek moist with slight perspiration, then the surprising soft yield of Marshall's cheek, followed by the painful shock of his cheekbone crunching against Riki's hand. The way the pain had seared all the way up Riki's wrist and forearm and elbow.

And, above all, how good it had felt. How the monster inside him had wanted to hit Marshall again, and again, until nothing was left.

It's too much. Riki can't bear it. He stumbles outside, glass crunching under his sneakers, stares following his back. He knows he must seem guilty as hell, and he is. Vera mentioned the nasty bruise on Marshall's cheek, and no doubt the police would be looking into that, and all this while, here's Riki, the very cause of the bruise, hiding in plain sight. Why is he even here? Why didn't he just stay the hell away?

Because guilty people can't stay away from the crime scene.

Riki's never hit anyone in his entire life, until that night, but that's not going to matter. No one will believe him, not when the first person he hits turns up dead the very next morning. All this time, he'd thought that he was doing everything he could for Adi, but all he's done is fucked everything up beyond measure. Tears rush into his eyes.

"You okay?"

The voice jerks Riki out of his spiral and he looks up to see Sana next to him, looking at him with wide, concerned eyes. He turns his head so she won't see the way he's this close to bawling. "Sorry, it's just—it's a lot to take in."

Sana nods sympathetically. "Yeah, god, someone really wanted to smash up her shop. Poor Vera."

Poor Vera indeed. Riki's insides twist painfully. He actually feels physically ill. He's familiar with this feeling, especially ever since meeting Marshall. God, what a cursed day that was. He wishes he could turn back time and grab his past self and shriek at him to run the hell away.

"I think we should offer to help her clean everything up." It takes a moment for Riki to realize what he's just said. Help clean everything up? All he wants to do is run away and never come back. But, selfishly, he also knows that cleaning everything well would hopefully make the place less suspicious to the police. Vera did say she wouldn't contact the police, but it's best to be extra safe. Sweep away any evidence that might remain here.

Sana's face lights up and she says, "Ah! What a great idea!" And before Riki knows what's happening, Sana grabs his sleeve and pulls him back inside. Every part of him is wailing, *Nooo!* But there is no timeline in this reality where Riki would pull his arm away from a pretty girl, even if said pretty girl is leading him back inside a claustrophobic shop filled with ghastly debris.

"Vera," Sana calls out, "don't worry." Inside, she lets go of Riki's arm and goes directly to Vera, putting her hands on the old woman's shoulders. "I know this is terrible," Sana says gently, "but don't worry, Vera, we're going to fix up your shop for you, okay? All of us here are going to help you with it." She glances up at the others, and for a second, Sana looks almost as fierce as Vera. Riki finds himself nodding almost automatically. Julia and Oliver nod as well, and Emma says, "Emma helps too."

"Oh," Vera chokes out. "You don't have to. I hate to be bother."

To Riki's surprise, Vera's cheeks are red. In fact, even the tips of her ears are red. The sight of it makes him feel suddenly protective of her. She might be formidable in some—well, okay, most—situations, but at the end of the day, Vera is a frail old lady who doesn't deserve to have her shop smashed up.

"We want to do it," he says with a firmness that takes even himself aback.

Vera moans. "I don't know, I think maybe is better if I stay with my son. I don't feel safe here, you know? What if whoever break in come back to finish off the job? Oh, but I also don't want to be a bother to Tilly. He is so busy . . ." She trails off meaningfully, and for a second, they're all quiet as frantic eye contact is made among all of them, silent messages flying back and forth.

Finally, with a sigh, Julia says, "You can stay with us."

"What?" they all say.

"Oh, I can't bother you like that—" Vera sputters.

But Julia points at the broken lock on Vera's rickety front door. "At least until we get your lock fixed. It won't take any time at all. And, Vera, I really think you need to pause on this investigation. I don't want you to endanger yourself. Come stay with me and Emma for a couple days. Keep us company." She smiles, looking a bit uncertain herself.

Emma, sensing her cue, nods and says solemnly, "You come sleep with Emma."

Vera hesitates, looking very torn. Then she releases a long breath and says, "If you insisting, then okay."

Riki stares in amazement as Julia nods and smiles. He never would've seen this offer coming from Julia. When he first met her, she came across as weak-willed and very lost, but now here she is, opening up her home to an almost complete stranger. And Sana, insisting that they clean up Vera's shop. He feels his affection and respect for them growing, and surely that is a mistake, a bad omen, when the thing that has brought them all together is an unsolved murder.

TWENTY-TWO

VERA

Well, isn't that a turnup for the books? Somehow, Vera has gone from a murder to a break-in and now to the house of the aforementioned murder victim. And his lovely wife and daughter, of course.

Vera is never one to be presumptuous or to trouble others, and so she is determined to be the very picture of courtesy, the ideal houseguest. This is why, when she gets to Julia's house, she marches right in, stopping at the hallway to take off her shoes. Emma walks in behind her, and Vera says, "Take off your shoes, Emma, we are not animals."

Emma does so, and after a moment's pause, so does Julia, who is wearing a little smile as she follows Emma and Vera inside, lugging Vera's giant suitcase. Once in the living room, Vera sighs loudly before plopping down on the sofa with more drama than she intended. Though of course, she always intends maximum drama, all the time, so is more drama actually possible?

"Shall I put your things in the bedroom?" Julia says, heaving as she tugs the suitcase behind her. "Gosh, Vera, what do you have in here?"

"When you get to my age, you will need so many things just to keep everything where they belong," Vera says cryptically, with a vague gesture at her own body.

Emma's eyes widen. "Why? What might fall out?" She turns to Julia, wide-eyed. "What might fall out, Mommy?"

"Oh, this and that," Vera says. "After you breastfeed, no bra will be able to control all the flopping."

"Honey, why don't you go play in your new tent?" Julia says quickly.

"Come," Emma says, pulling Vera's hand. "I show you my new tent."

Vera can't help smiling as she follows the little girl down the hall. Is there anything sweeter than having your hand held firmly by tiny fingers? Behind her, Julia pants as she yanks the suitcase down the hallway. Vera considers telling her that it's a fancy new design with hidden wheels that pop out with the push of a button, but Julia seems so happy to be helpful. Anyway, it's probably empowering to be able to lug such a huge and heavy burden without any help.

Emma's room is small and humble, but very neat. In one corner is an impressively decked-out tent, complete with soft toys and cushions. Emma crawls in and beckons Vera to come in after her, but Vera says, "At my age, even with all the extreme stretching I do, if I kneel down, there is chance I don't get back up."

She lowers herself carefully and sits down on the edge of Emma's bed. Emma's head pops out from the tent flaps.

"You see dead body?" Emma says.

Vera, who has watched *Sixth Sense*, knows enough to keep an open mind. "Do you mean did I see dead body last week, or do you mean am I seeing dead body right now?"

"Both."

"I see a dead body last week, yes. But there are no dead bodies right now."

"What dead body look like?"

Vera mulls this over carefully. She believes that honesty is the best policy, but when the truth involves telling a two-year-old about her father's dead body, maybe a little fudging is in order. "Hmm, it looks like normal body, but dead."

Emma seems satisfied by this answer, and her head retreats back inside the tent and she starts singing to herself. It's a tuneless song sung in her raspy voice. Shame, but it seems that Emma does not have a future as a singer. Which is fine, as being a singer is definitely not one of Vera's preapproved careers. In Vera's opinion, Emma is better suited to be an architect. Vera sits there for a while, half listening to the very not-gifted voice, and looking around the room to get a better idea of Emma's life.

Although the room itself is small and the furniture obviously secondhand, on the walls hang breathtakingly beautiful photos. Vera stands and peers closer at them. She's never seen such fairy-tale-esque colors in photographs before. They're all of Emma throughout the infancy stages of her life, and in each one, the photographer managed to capture some magical quality so that Vera can practically hear baby Emma's coos and gurgles just by looking at these images. And the colors! *My god*, Vera thinks. They are beautiful sun-kissed pastel hues, and something about them transports Vera to when Tilly was a little kid who sat on her lap as she read fairy tales to him. The greenery in these photos is lush, with a gentle teal and emerald shade, making the leaves and grass look as soft as blankets. And everything is tinged with golden sunlight. The entire effect is ethereal, like Emma is a little baby stolen by elves.

As a Chinese mother, Vera has often prided herself on being immune to the seduction of art. She does have some calligraphy hung up in her shop and her house, but they're less art and more reminders to BE FORTUNATE. But now, standing here in front of these photos, even Vera has to admit that there's something here. Something very, very special.

When she's done admiring the photos, Vera realizes that the little tent is quiet. She creeps over and takes a peek to find that Emma has fallen asleep. After checking to make sure there are no choking hazards around Emma, Vera creeps out of the room and closes the door gently behind her. Then she makes her way to the kitchen, where she finds Julia doing the dishes.

"Did Emma fall asleep?" Julia says over her shoulder.

"Yes." Vera stands next to Julia and starts drying the dishes.

"Oh, you don't have to do that."

Vera ignores Julia, because just look at the state of this kitchen. "What you do all day?"

Julia glances at her before turning her focus firmly back onto the plate she's scrubbing. "I look after Emma."

"Hmm. Do you work?"

Julia sighs, shaking her head and scrubbing the plate with what Vera thinks is excessive force. "No, Vera. I'm a stay-at-home mom."

"Ah." Vera wisely chooses not to say anything more, letting the silence stretch on and on, knowing from years of experience that she won't be the first one to fold.

And, of course, she turns out to be right. "I don't need your judgment, you know," Julia says.

"Oh, I'm not judging. My mother was stay-at-home mother too. But she had nine children, so maybe is not the same. But," Vera adds quickly, "no judgment."

Julia rolls her eyes. "Right. I know it's not trendy to be a stay-at-home mom, but it's not like I had a choice, you know? Not many places would take a college dropout. Hell, not many places would take even people with college degrees. Nowadays, you need to have a master's or something to even get an entry-level job."

"Oh, I'm sure," Vera says. Gently, she takes the plate before Julia can scrub it to the thinness of a piece of paper. "Julia, I not saying being a stay-at-home mom is bad. When my Tilly is little, I stay at home with him until he go to kindergarten. But . . . I wonder, is it your choice to be stay-at-home mom?"

Julia gapes at her. "Wha— Yes, of course it is," she insists.

"Hmm." Vera peers at her, unconvinced. She's had years of worming the truth out of Tilly. Her interrogation skills would humble most CIA agents. "I just asking, because I see the photos in Emma's room, and I find it hard to believe that a photographer with your talent doesn't want to pursue a job in photography."

"I—" Julia's mouth drops open before closing. "How do you know I took those pictures?"

Vera leans across Julia and turns off the tap. "Come, you go sit down and I make some tea."

"But—"

Silly girl, probably about to protest and insist on making the tea herself. Vera has no time for that. She shoos Julia out of the kitchen and bustles about, filling a saucepan and putting it on the stove before opening one cupboard after another until she finds the tea cabinet. Of course, Julia is in dire need of some proper Chinese tea, but Vera is knowledgeable enough to not turn her nose up at Lipton. She knows that teas like Lipton aren't necessarily bad, as long as they're prepared properly. Lipton, like many other Western brands of black tea, uses inferior tea leaves that are then roasted at a higher temperature, killing all traces of subtle flavoring. The result is a strong black tea that can stand up to aggressive boiling and generous amounts of sugar and milk. Vera cuts open three tea bags and pours the leaves into the pot of water, letting it boil for at least five minutes to make sure that every bit of flavor seeps into the water. By the time she's done, the tea is midnight black. She strains it before adding a splash of fresh milk and—ah, what luck—a spoonful of condensed milk.

The smell that wafts from the tea is so comforting it's like a hug. Vera notices Julia's shoulders tensing when Vera walks out into the dining room, but after a sip of the milk tea, Julia releases her breath, the tension leaving her face. Vera smiles inwardly. Good tea always has that effect on people. It's a comforting drink, which is why Vera has chosen to dedicate her whole life to bringing it to more people. The last thing that these youngsters need is coffee, which only serves to make them more stressed-out and unhappy, why can't they see that?

"So," Julia says after taking another sip, "how did you know I took those photos?"

"Well, at first I think they are so good you must have hire a professional. But then I look closer, and I see something in it. I think to myself, this photographer capture the essence of this baby. You can sense the love behind the camera. I can sense these things, you know," Vera says with a touch of smugness. "I am a mother, I can sense mother's love."

Julia smiles, but it looks so sad it's almost wrong to call it a smile. She looks down at her mug. "You're right, I took those photos. Sometimes I'm tempted to take them down because seeing them is almost painful."

"Why painful?" Vera can venture a guess as to why it might be painful, but it's polite to ask questions. Tilly says it always pays to play dumb. Or something.

"Because you're right, Vera. I wanted to be a photographer. I wanted to study photography. That was what I majored in, and I loved every single class I took. It was the best time of my life." The last sentence comes out in a pained whisper, and as soon as she says it, Julia covers her mouth like she's let slip something dirty. "I didn't mean—god, that's such a shitty thing for a mom to say, isn't it? I love being Emma's mother, but . . ."

Vera places a hand on top of Julia's. With their hands so close together, she can't help noticing how wrinkly and age-spotted hers looks compared to Julia's youthful skin. She hurriedly removes her hand. Vera may be sixty, but that doesn't mean she is immune to vanity. "I know what you are saying," she says. "I love being Tilly's mother, but if you ask me what is the best time of my life, I will say is when I am twenty, still going to school, the world is still full of possibilities." For a moment, Vera stares off into space wistfully, remembering that invincible way she'd felt back then, before she graduated college and was spat out into the unforgiving real world.

Julia nods. "Yes, exactly. Anyway, even though I dropped out, I'd accrued a lot of debt, so I had to take whatever job I could find to start paying it off. Marshall too."

"Why do you drop out? You fail your classes?"

"No." Julia laughs. But the laugh is short-lived. "Well, Marshall said college is overpriced. I mean, he's not wrong," she adds a tad defensively. "Especially to study something like photography. He said I could just pick the skill up myself rather than waste tens of thousands of dollars on it. I thought he had a point. So I dropped out, found a job at a department store. He also wanted to start trying for a family, and that took a lot longer than we expected." Her voice fills with pain at the memory, but then she forces a smile. "Anyway, he proposed sometime after he graduated and we kept trying for a baby, and finally after years of trying, I had Emma, and that was that. I never had a chance to do much photography. I had all these plans, all these dreams for it, but . . . I guess that was all they were. Just dreams."

"Unrealized dreams are one of saddest things in life," Vera says. "Well, after serious illness and death and all that."

"Yes, it's kind of a first-world problem." Julia snorts. "I feel like an asshole complaining to you about it when your shop was broken into."

Vera waves her off. "Oh, you don't worry about that." Then she claps, once. "So! What is stopping you from doing photography now?"

Julia stiffens. "What do you mean?"

"You go online and look, I'm sure there are many people looking for photographer. You do portraits?"

"Well, yes, but—"

"Then start there. Charge very little, you are only starting out. Maybe even do it for free until you are more comfortable."

"But there's Emma, and—"

"I look after Emma," Vera says.

"Wh—" Julia's mouth drops open. "Uh . . ."

"I am mother too. Actually, I am Chinese mother. You can't get better than that. We raise the best children in the world, you just look at any hospital, all the surgeon are Chinese." Vera beams with pride, as though she has personally been responsible for all the surgeons in every hospital.

"Um . . . but . . . she's very—" Julia gestures helplessly. "She's not very good with being left behind with other people. Believe me, I've tried. I found this affordable childcare place right down the street—it's actually a neighbor who runs a little nursery from her house—but oh god, when I tried leaving Emma there, the screaming . . ." Julia grimaces from the memory. "My neighbor basically refused to take her in."

"Tch, then your neighbor is not a good caretaker," Vera tuts. "You see how Emma is with me. She knows I am safe."

She can see that despite everything, Julia agrees with her. It's true; Emma has taken to Vera like a baby duck recognizing a mother duck.

"You don't have to leave the house if you don't want," Vera continues. "Just work in bedroom, or maybe in backyard. Don't worry about Emma, okay? Good. I am glad we agree."

Without giving Julia any time to answer, Vera pats Julia on the shoulder and stands. She stretches dramatically and says, "Okay, now you go on computer, look for photograph job. I will make healthy snack for Emma and then wake her up."

Julia looks slightly dazed, something Vera has become familiar with over the years. Vera is pleased to see, however, that after a few moments of stunned silence, Julia gets up, fetches her laptop from the dining table, and carries it into the bedroom.

TWENTY-THREE

VERA

It takes a surprisingly short time for Vera, Julia, and little Emma to settle into a new rhythm. The first day, Julia foolishly tries to prevent Vera from taking over the running of the household—telling Vera not to bother cooking dinner for them, telling Vera not to bother cleaning up afterward, telling Vera not to try to teach Emma mathematics. She soon learns, however, that "telling Vera not to" is a futile act and before the second day is over has surrendered completely to Vera's machinations.

When Vera moved into Julia's house, she'd naïvely thought that she would only stay for a day, two max, before returning to her quiet life atop her deserted tea shop. But the shop is now closed for the time being, something she thought would've absolutely devastated her in the past but is in fact a bit of a relief now. Yes, she does miss it, but it's also freeing to not have to worry so much about not having any customers and wondering how much longer she can keep it open. She's sent a text to Alex, letting him know that she is staying at a friend's and apologizing for the lack of teas, and sweet, kind Alex replied immediately, telling her not to worry.

Last night, Tilly called, asking why she hasn't texted him for days. Hah, what a turnup for the books that was.

"Oh, you know," she said, "the shop had break-in, so my friend say come stay at her house."

He sputtered for quite a long time at that. "*What?* Ma, what do you mean the shop was broken into? Did you report it to the police?"

"Tch, the police, what good are they? They can't even solve murder, you think they can bother to solve a burglary? No problem, I solve myself."

"Jesus, Ma! And where are you staying right now? What friend?"

"I have many friend now, Tilly." She hadn't quite been able to keep the smugness out of her voice.

"Where? I'll come pick you up. You can—" He'd sighed then and said, "You can stay with me."

"Oh, silly, I don't want to bother you." To think! Turning down an offer like that! An offer she would've killed for in the past. But here she is, a changed woman, no longer a burden on her son.

"Oh my god, Ma. Just—okay, fine, you're a grown woman, you can handle yourself. But I'm going to transfer you some money, okay? And let me know if you need anything, you hear me?"

"Yes, yes. So naggy." She'd hung up with a smirk on her face, and who can blame her? She was so sad about Tilly being a neglectful child, and here he is, insisting on sending her some money. He's not so unfilial after all.

She never imagined that she would slip so easily into Julia's life, much like a puzzle piece slotting neatly into place. It seems to Vera sometimes that this has been where she belonged all along, living in a house with two girls, one she is coming to think of as her daughter and the other she has from the very beginning adopted as her granddaughter. Oh, Emma, how Vera adores this tiny, somber girl.

In the mornings, Julia wakes up to find that Emma is already dressed, her hair tied in intricate pigtails, sitting in her high chair and slurping congee all on her own. Vera sits next to her, reading the newspaper. When Vera spots Julia, she'll say, quite simply, "Sit." And Julia will sit, and a steaming bowl of freshly cooked congee will appear before her, along with a plate of condiments— fried egg, spicy tofu, and crispy fried youtiao. There will also be a cup of green tea as well as a glass of rich soy milk. And Julia will eat and marvel at the way that Emma is feeding herself with a spoon instead of flinging everything around and screaming for French fries and chicken nuggets. When they are done, Vera will whisk everything away and wipe Emma's sticky face down before lifting her from the high chair and taking her to the park down the block.

The first time Vera does this, Julia follows, worry clawing at her. What if Vera is, in fact, a bad person with bad intentions toward Emma? So Julia follows, and Vera huffs and rolls her eyes, and at the playground, Julia watches, astounded, as Vera plops Emma right next to another little girl, and the two girls begin to—well, not play with each other as much as play next to each other. Still, it has always been such a struggle for Julia to get Emma within five steps of another child before Emma shouts, "No, I'm shy!" that this is a shock to see. How does Vera do it?

This question becomes an anthem for the whole day, and the next, and the next. How does Vera do it? How does Vera clean the house so tidily, how does Vera cook so quickly, how does Vera do anything? If someone told Julia that Vera is half-magic, she would believe them.

In the evenings, Vera retires to the master bedroom, where Julia has graciously put her after Vera lamented on the first day she arrived how in Chinese culture, the elders will always get the best room in the house. There, Vera snuggles in the king-sized bed and reads Oliver's manuscript. Vera has never been a big reader, but she knows enough to gauge that Oliver's manuscript is far from polished. It's too raw, the pacing rushed in some parts, then slowing down to a crawl in others. But the thing that makes Vera keep reading is the story, which is about two brothers, one of whom is the perfect kid, or so everyone else thinks, and the other is the disappointment who skulks in his brother's shadow, watching silently as his brother cheats his way through life. The shy brother falls in love with a girl who ends up marrying the golden brother. Vera is wondering if it will end with the shy brother poisoning the golden boy, maybe by smothering him with a down pillow? Part of her wants to skip to the end, but she hates spoilers, so here she is, patiently reading it page by page, and despite the erratic pacing, she's sort of enjoying it.

It is on the fourth day of Vera's stay, as she and Emma make pulled noodles in the kitchen, that there is a shout from the bedroom. Moments later, Julia comes thundering down the hallway and arrives all out of breath, her blond hair falling wildly around her face. She takes in the sight before her, of Emma covered in floury handprints, with strands of noodle dough in her brown curls, mid-laugh, and pauses. Vera can tell that Julia's instinctive reaction is one of horror. The old Julia, Vera guesses, would've scooped Emma up and hurried away to clean her off. Probably before Marshall gets home. But then Vera sees the dawning in

Julia's eyes. The realization that Marshall isn't coming home. Marshall isn't going to be around to bitch about the mess, or inappropriateness, or whatever the hell Marshall would get angry about. And then Julia opens her mouth and laughs, and god, Vera thinks, what a sound it is.

It comes straight out of Julia's belly, an unfettered laugh that is both joyful and unashamed of its rawness. Emma stares for a moment, then she joins in, giggling and smushing more noodle dough on her cheeks, throwing her head back and laughing some more. Vera herself can't help but join in, and she can't remember the last time she's enjoyed herself so much. They all laugh until their sides hurt, until they're gasping for breath; then, still breathing hard, Vera asks Julia what's just happened.

"Oh!" Julia says, as though she's forgotten what made her rush over here in the first place. "I got it! A photography job!" She looks half-stunned when she says this, her expression a cross between fear and excitement.

Vera doesn't give any time for the fear to take over. She whoops and envelopes Julia in a hug. "Oh, good job, you!" She beckons to Emma to join the hug. "Come, your mama going to be photographer."

"Wow! Wow!" Emma shouts. She probably doesn't even really know what a photographer is, but she's more than happy to jump in and wrap her short arms around the two of them.

"Now, you tell me all about it," Vera says, stepping back.

"It's a small job," Julia begins apologetically, and Vera's hand immediately shoots up and smacks her lightly on the side of the head. "Ow, what the—! What the . . . heck, Vera?"

"You don't describe your job like that," Vera scolds. "Is a 'small job,' hah! Can you see men saying that? No, men will talk it up with bullshit, that is why they get even bigger job next time. There is no such thing as 'small job.' And don't say in that silly tone, oh so apologetic, I am just silly woman having a small job. No!" Her index finger shoots up and points at Julia's face like a sword. "You go and do this job proudly."

"Uh . . . okay." Julia gingerly pushes Vera's formidable index finger down. "So it's a sm—it's a portrait photography session for an influencer. Well, she's not quite an influencer yet, but she's getting there and she needs headshots, so." Julia pauses and Vera can tell she's about to apologize again, or say something else to minimize the job, but she manages to stop herself. Vera nods and harrumphs.

"Sound good to me."

"The pay isn't much," Julia blurts out.

Vera sighs. She supposes it's too much to expect for Julia to embrace this new empowered side of herself in a single day. "The first time I open a teahouse, each pot of tea only cost two cents. Now I charge three dollars."

"And that's inflaaation," Emma sings.

Both Julia and Vera stare at her for a while, but Emma just continues playing with the noodle dough. Finally Vera says, "Yes, that is not wrong. Maybe you shouldn't be an architect, maybe an economist. Or a hedge fund manager, yes. Anyway," she says, turning her attention back on Julia. "You will go and do this job and you will be very confident, none of this"—she gestures at Julia—"sorry look. You will be good. Very good. More than very good."

"Very gooder," Emma says.

"Yes," Vera says. "Very gooder. Now you go away, Emma and I making dinner."

Julia walks out of the kitchen in a daze, and Vera looks down at Emma, who looks up at her and smiles. "We make something out of your mama, eh?"

Emma gives a solemn nod, and the two of them resume pulling noodles for dinner.

The next morning, Julia is insufferable. From the moment she gets up, she is so jittery and nervous that Vera finally sets her to cleaning the bathroom. The bathroom doesn't need cleaning, of course, because Vera has cleaned it to within an inch of its life, but it's clear that Julia needs to do something with all that nervous energy. Julia's nerves have affected Emma as well, and now Emma is having a hard time going through her new morning routine. As Vera struggles to keep Emma from wriggling away while she tries to tie up the little girl's hair, she wonders if perhaps this used to be the norm in the before times. When Marshall was alive, maybe Julia always carried this nervous energy with her, and maybe that's why Emma was so insecure. Vera sighs. So many maybes.

But scrubbing the toilet seems to work; when Julia finally comes out, she's less jittery.

"Thanks," she says to Vera. Then she laughs. "I don't know why I just thanked you for ordering me to clean the bathroom."

"Because you know is for your own good." Vera hands her a Tupperware container. "I make lunch for you and client. Spring rolls, plenty of veg, very good for you. Give you energy to work. Now you go away."

"It's not really time yet—"

"Better to be early is what I always say."

Julia opens her mouth, probably to argue, then seems to think twice. *Good*, Vera thinks. *She's learned that it's useless to try and argue with me.* Julia goes and gets her camera bag, which she packed very carefully last night. At the door, she pauses, dawdling, oozing with uncertainty. "Are you sure you'll be okay with her?"

Vera has no idea if Julia is asking her or Emma. Either way, what a silly question. Why would anyone not be okay with Vera? "Go," she scolds, shooing Julia away. And with one last glance over her shoulder, Julia walks out the door. Vera and Emma go to the bay window to watch Julia's car leave the driveway, then Vera turns to Emma and says, "Okay, now we get to work."

Emma nods. Vera puts a cardigan on the little girl, making sure the buttons are all done up, and the two of them walk out of the house hand in hand. First, they take the bus to Chinatown, where Vera buys fresh, cheap groceries. She shows Emma how to pick out the freshest fish ("You poke them in the eyes, like this"; Emma is surprisingly enthusiastic about poking fish in the eyes) and how to haggle with the shop owners for the best price. By the time they're done, the shopping trolley that Vera has brought is loaded to the brim. They stop by for a quick snack at the fortune cookie bakery, where Emma eats three cookies, then they make their way back to the house. After unloading everything into the fridge, Vera slices up an enormous Korean pear and shares it with Emma while reading her a story.

The reading goes like this: "'The king says, "You are a beautiful girl, but if you can't turn this roomful of hay into gold by sunrise, I will have you kill—"' What? What is this silly story? Rumpy—Rum—Rumpapum? Even its name is stupid. Emma, you listen to Grandma Vera, this king is a very bad man. You hear me? Right, so . . . where are we? Yes, so . . . 'With the help of Rumpy—Rumpapum, she manages to turn three whole rooms of hay into gold, upon which the king says, "Amazing! You shall be my wife!" And Anne is overjoyed—' *What?* Emma, you listen to Grandma Vera. Are you listening? This Anne is very stupid. Very! Stupid! You hear me? Why is she happy that crazy king wants to marry her? She should be horrified. She should carry a dagger with her on wedding night. That's what Chinese maidens used to do, you know. In old days, Chinese maidens don't get to choose who they marry. They don't even get to meet their husbands until the wedding day. So part of the traditional wedding outfit is a little dagger, just in case their husband turn out to be bad man. Emma, are you liste— Oh, you are asleep. Harrumph. Just as well, then. I will have talk with your mother about giving you stupid books."

Vera gets up gently, placing the little girl down on the sofa. From Emma's room, Vera fetches a woolen blanket and drapes it over her before giving her an affectionate pat on the head. She smiles at Emma, marveling at the way the little child has wormed her way into Vera's heart in such a short time. She loves the way Emma's eyelashes curl up ever so slightly. It reminds her of when Tilly was little and how soft and warm he had been then. She creeps away, careful to avoid the creaky parts of the floor, and starts tidying up Emma's bedroom, picking up various toys and clothes that have been strewn about and putting them in various cubbies. When the floor is free of toys and other debris, Vera turns her attention to the rest of the house.

Because the truth is, even though Vera has been feeling at home here, she hasn't quite forgotten about her true purpose for being here. She is here to find out the truth about Marshall. And so, squashing any traces of guilt way, way down inside her, Vera creeps out of Emma's room. Right, she has of course searched the master bedroom top to bottom. She has also gone through the kitchen, the dining room, and the living room. Which leaves the garage.

She marches out to the garage and looks around the space. It's filled with quite a bit of junk, most of which looks like it hasn't been touched in years. There are also racks on one side of the wall, with detergent and various tools sitting on them. Vera narrows her eyes and opens one of the cardboard boxes at random. It's filled with what looks like old baby clothes. Hmm. She opens another box, then another. Tennis rackets, old shoes. Gah. This is going to take forever. And the worst part is, Vera isn't even sure what she's looking for. She has a vague idea that there might be a ledger of some sort? But there's no guarantee of that, is there?

In one last-ditch effort, Vera grabs a fold-up chair resting against the garage wall and places it under the racks. She steps onto the chair carefully and peers at the upper shelves. And her heart stops, just for a moment. Because there, right in front of her, is something smooth and silver. Something that's clearly out of place in the gloom of the garage. She reaches over and slides it off the shelf.

It's a laptop.

Vera's heart bursts into a gallop. Who would hide a laptop away in the garage? Someone who was doing something nefarious. Someone who was doing something so shady that it might have gotten him killed. Someone like Marshall.

With an agility that she didn't know she had, Vera hops off the chair, clutching the laptop to her thumping chest, and hurries back inside the house. She checks on Emma, who's still fast asleep on the couch, and scurries into the master bedroom. Swallowing, Vera opens the laptop. It asks for a PIN. Vera groans out loud. Nooo! Not when she's this close to solving the puzzle!

But then Vera looks again at the screen, and it isn't, in fact, asking for a PIN. The actual words are: "Please insert key to unlock."

These newfangled machines! Vera lifts the laptop and checks underneath it, half expecting to find a keyhole. Nope. None of the sides either. Just to be safe, she even checks the top. No keyhole. The only holes it has are those for USB drives.

Vera's mouth drops open, her breath hitching. A USB drive! Of course!

Quickly, she lifts the hem of her shirt to reveal the fanny pack she's been wearing since she found Marshall's body. She unzips it, takes out the flash drive, and uncaps it with a trembling hand. *Here we go.* She inserts the flash drive into the laptop and waits, breath held.

The laptop screen blinks, then two words appear: "Shaking hands . . ."

Then: "Key accepted."

The screen changes, showing a folder named: "Assets."

Vera clicks on it, and it opens up to show dozens of folders. Eyes narrowed, Vera scrolls down, unsure what she's looking at. Until one of the folders' names catches her eye. She opens it. And gasps.

TWENTY-FOUR

OLIVER

The last thing that Oliver thinks he'd be doing two weeks after his brother's death/possible murder is spending his Sunday morning going to Chinatown to tidy up a teahouse, specifically, the very same one that his twin brother was found dead in. *But here we are*, he thinks, as he parks up and finds Riki and Sana outside Vera's teahouse. The sight of them is strangely nice, as though they've been friends for a while instead of strangers thrown together by tragic circumstances. He waves at them and they wave back, and when he walks out, Sana hands him a takeaway cup.

"Figured we could all use some coffee," she says.

"Ooh, better not let Vera see this," Oliver says, and Riki and Sana grin, which makes Oliver feel sort of . . . happy. It's an unfamiliar feeling, but he likes it. He fishes out a key from his pocket and unlocks the door. He came by yesterday on his own to fit a new lock.

The inside of Vera Wang's World-Famous Teahouse is just as gloomy as Oliver remembers from the last time he was here. All that smashed glass, the overturned chairs. The three of them pause at the doorway, and Oliver senses their uneasiness at the sight of all that destruction. Then Oliver says, "Come on. I brought supplies."

And he has. For the first time ever, Oliver is thankful for his position as a super. He only needed to buy stuff like trash bags and cleaning liquid, but everything else reusable he borrowed from the supplies closet. Cleaning gloves, brooms, and mops. Together, the three of them unload the things from Oliver's trunk and get to work, lifting the furniture out of the shop before sweeping away the broken glass and herbs from the floor. Then Oliver starts mopping while Sana cleans the bay windows. Unfortunately, the gruesome outline of Marshall's body doesn't come off, which creeps him out.

"You'll need to use some isopropyl alcohol on that," Sana says. "And maybe toothpaste and baking soda."

Oliver nods, shuddering as he turns away from the outline of his dead twin's body. If only every bad thing in life could be removed just by mopping it away.

Riki returns after disposing of the trash bags, wipes his brow, and inspects the furniture they have removed from the shop.

"These are pretty good pieces, actually," Riki muses, tilting one of the chairs this way and that.

"Oh?" Oliver doesn't much care about furniture, but the way Riki is studying the chair is interesting. There's a deftness to Riki's movements, like he's utterly comfortable working with furniture. "Are you into carpentry?"

"A little bit. Back in Jakarta my dad is a handyman." There's a note of sadness in Riki's voice, but then he continues. "I think I could take out this part right here"—he points at the back of the chair, which is half falling apart with age—"and replace it with something more modern, add a cushion to it, give it a new coat of paint . . . it'll look great, actually."

Oliver can't really picture it, but he nods along encouragingly. "Sounds good."

Sana steps back from the bay window and looks around the shop. "Huh, whaddaya know? Now that the windows don't have an inch-thick layer of grime, the shop actually looks bigger." She hesitates. "Not to sound ridiculous, but before I cleaned the windows, the dirt seemed almost shadowy, like someone was watching."

"Maybe the pastry lady next door?" Riki says.

"Maybe."

The three of them look around. Oliver is surprised to find that Sana is right. The shop really does look bigger and brighter. He frowns at the lights in the shop. Even after changing the bulbs, the shop could do with better lighting. "I'll get her more lights. A couple of those cheap IKEA light stands would do the shop a world of good." Just saying it out loud makes Oliver feel better. He's doing something, producing instead of staying inert and helpless.

Riki brings in three chairs and they sit down for a break, sipping their coffees in companionable silence.

"Do you know how Vera's doing at Julia's?" Riki says.

"I can't imagine having Vera staying at my place," Sana says. They all laugh.

"Surprisingly, Julia told me she kind of loves having Vera there," Oliver says.

Sana and Riki gape at him. "Seriously?" Riki says.

"Yep, seriously." Oliver takes another slurp of his coffee, savoring its smoky flavor. "She said Emma's really opened up, thanks to Vera. And apparently Vera cooks a feast for pretty much every meal. I've been invited once or twice and those meals are to die for."

"Oh man, that does sound good," Sana says.

"I miss my mom's cooking so much," Riki says. "Back home, she used to cook all these huge meals for us too. Every Sunday, she'd make at least seven or eight dishes for us, and each one was amazing."

Oliver smiles and nods. "What's Indonesian food like?"

"Spicy," Riki says with a laugh. "Everything smothered in different sambals—that's chili paste. My favorite is terong balado, which is eggplant fried with the most gorgeous red chili and tomatoes."

"Ooh, I love eggplant," Sana says. "My dad is the cook in our family, and he makes this spinach and eggplant curry that is sooo comforting. It's creamy and rich and to die for."

Oliver thinks back to his mom's garlic eggplant dish. It seems very weirdly specific to be talking about eggplant dishes right now, but somehow, it makes sense. There's just something about eggplant that's so comforting.

"So Julia's eating well, huh?" Sana says.

"Yeah. The only downside is that Julia's sleeping on the couch because she gave Vera her room."

Sana laughs. "Of course she did. Poor Julia. I can just see Vera guilting her into giving up the master bedroom to Vera."

"Oh, like you wouldn't?" Riki says, nudging her with his elbow.

Sana widens her eyes. "Are you kidding? I am terrified of Vera; of course I would. And don't even try to tell me you guys are not scared of Vera. You should see the way you two behave around her."

"No, whaaat?" Oliver says amid laughter. "How do we behave?"

"Like schoolkids who know that they've done something really, really bad."

Oliver's laughter catches in his throat. Riki looks uneasy. Just for a moment—then they both force out their laughter. Oliver glances at Riki. What's going on there? Oliver knows exactly what he did, but what does Riki have to feel guilty about? But the last thing Oliver wants to do is to start being suspicious of Riki or Sana, because he genuinely likes them. So he shakes off that uneasy feeling and tries to come up with an easygoing response that won't ruin the moment.

But whatever Oliver is about to say is interrupted by the tinkling of the bell as the door is pushed open. Abruptly, they all fall silent and stare as Officer Gray walks into the shop. Officer Gray is so far from who Oliver expects to see that for a split second, his brain short-circuits and goes, *Wait, am I at the police station again, waiting to identify my brother's body?*

"What the hell is going on here?" Officer Gray demands. She definitely does not look pleased to see the three of them.

Oliver scrambles to his feet. Something about Officer Gray makes him feel like he needs to stay on his feet. It's probably the uniform. Or the gaze that kind of reminds him of Vera. Or maybe the fact that he can very much see the gun that she carries in her holster. Or maybe all of the above. Being the oldest of the three of them, Oliver feels like he needs to be the one who answers her question. "Uh, hi, Officer." He tries to come up with something better. "How're you doing?" Oh god, that came out so wrong, like Joey from *Friends'* sleazy come-on line.

Officer Gray narrows her eyes. "I said, what is going on here?"

"Uh . . ." Oliver looks around helpless at Sana and Riki, both of whom are wide-eyed with obvious fear. "Well, we were cleaning up Vera's shop?" he squeaks.

"Why?"

Oliver grasps the first answer that comes to mind. "Uh . . . because . . . we're nice?" He cringes inwardly. That was quite possibly the stupidest answer anyone could have come up with.

Officer Gray nods at Sana, then at Riki. "You two, aren't you the reporters I saw at Julia Chen's house the other day?"

Riki's face pales. "Uh, yes?"

"I'm not a reporter," Sana says quickly. Then, quietly, she mumbles, "I just have a podcast."

"Right," Officer Gray says, "and now here you two are, together with Marshall Chen's brother, in Vera's teahouse."

The mention of "Marshall Chen's brother" turns something in Oliver's stomach. How pathetic that even after Marshall's death, Oliver would still be known as just his brother.

"Anyone care to explain to me why the three of you are together? Is it a book club? A coffee club?"

The thing is, Oliver isn't even sure why he feels like Officer Gray has just caught them doing something illegal. Surely cleaning up an old woman's shop that was burglarized counts as an actual good deed? The realization makes him stand a bit straighter. He looks Officer Gray in the eye and says, "You see, Officer, Vera's shop was broken into a few days ago, and so we thought we'd help her out a bit by tidying it up. There was a huge mess, and—"

"Back up," Officer Gray says, and Oliver's mouth snaps shut. "You said her shop was 'broken into'?"

Oliver nods hesitantly.

"And nobody thought to report this to us?"

Oliver's mouth drops open. "Uh, well—"

The answer, of course, is no. Nobody thought to report it to the police. And why the hell not? My god, now that Officer Gray is pointing it out, it seems like the most obvious thing in the world, and yet only Julia suggested it, and when it was shot down, no one insisted that going to the cops was the right thing to do. *Whyyy?* Oliver's mind wails.

Because Oliver doesn't want anything more to do with the cops, that's why. He has enough to hide from them. The less he has to do with them, the better. But what about the others? They'd all been there that day, when Vera had called them over to show them the catastrophic destruction of her store. And out of all of them, only Julia suggested calling the cops.

Maybe it's because they, too, have something to hide.

The skin on the back of Oliver's neck prickles, and he looks at Sana and Riki in a new light. A light he really doesn't want to see them in, because he's growing to like them, to see them as friends, almost. And now he can't shake off the feeling that they know something. What could they be hiding?

TWENTY-FIVE

SANA

Sana has never been so nervous in her entire life. She feels light-headed. She's never felt light-headed before. She didn't even understand what it means to "feel light-headed," couldn't even imagine it, and now here she is. It feels a lot less pleasant than it sounds. She'd thought that maybe it would feel like her head was weightless, but no, actually, it feels like the insides of her head have been replaced by nothing but water and everything is now sloshing around and she feels like she might either faint or puke or both.

Officer Gray is going on and on about how irresponsible they all are for not reporting the break-in to the police, especially since a death occurred in the shop not long ago.

"But you guys said Marshall's death was an accident," Sana hears someone say. To her horror, she realizes a moment too late that the someone was her. *Stop talking, mouth.* But her mouth has grown a mind of its own and continues blathering. "Vera said so."

"Oh, Vera said so, did she?" Officer Gray throws her hands up. "And is Vera a cop?"

The three of them are silent.

"Is Vera a private detective, maybe?"

Riki raises a tentative hand. "I think she counts as an amateur sleuth?"

"Oh, for fuck's sake." Officer Gray turns her back on them for a second, taking in a deep, frustrated breath. Then she turns back around to face them. "Let me make this very clear. Vera does not have any authority to do or proclaim anything about Marshall Chen's death, you hear me?"

Sana feels her head nodding mechanically.

"So when something like this happens," Officer Gray continues, "I don't want to hear about it from her neighbor."

"Her neighbor?" Oliver says.

"Probably the owner of the bakery next door," Riki says.

"Oof, Vera's not going to be happy about that," Sana mutters, recalling Vera's vitriol about the French bakery next door.

"Are you three musketeers done? Yes, Winifred next door was the one who called us to let us know that it seems like everything inside Vera's shop has been smashed up."

"Winifred must've been peeping through the window," Riki says.

"She would've had to press her face right up against it," Sana says. "It was so grimy before I cleaned it, there was no way she would've been able to look inside unless she was, like, this close to the glass." It's starting to dawn on Sana why Vera might not like Winifred, even though Winifred's French pastries are decent.

"Well, thank goodness she did," Officer Gray says, "because otherwise, we wouldn't have known about it. And now thanks to you three, it seems like all the evidence has been swept up and . . ."

"Thrown into the recycling bin," Oliver says helpfully. "The bins are right outside. I can show them to you if you want."

Officer Gray takes a breath through her teeth. "I'll let the team know." She looks around the shop and closes her eyes for a moment. "Did any of you see anything suspicious?"

"Aside from the whole shop being smashed up?" Sana feels like she's being disrespectful somehow, but she swears she's not trying to be. She's honestly, sincerely—okay, maybe not sincerely—trying to be as truthful as she can. But she can't deny that everything about this does seem a bit shady, and that's when it hits her that it's not just her acting shady. Oliver and Riki are obfuscating too, and why? She's already guessed, deep down, that Riki is very much not a Buzzfeed reporter, or any reporter, really. But what about Oliver? What's he hiding?

She can only watch quietly as Officer Gray walks around, inspecting the teahouse and grumbling to herself about having to call "the team" in and how much she hates "those nerds." Finally, Officer Gray tells them to not touch anything else in the teahouse, then she's off, leaving behind her a vacuum. Sana, Riki, and Oliver stand there, not quite knowing what to say. The air between them is thick with suspicion. Sana takes out her phone, coming up with an excuse to leave, when she sees that there's a text from Vera. It says:

Meet me now. I know truth between you and M!!! 😠

By the time Sana gets to the meeting place Vera suggested, down one of the less popular piers at the wharf, she is so out of breath she thinks she might die. Or maybe she might die because she's panicking, not because she's out of shape? Either way, it's not a great feeling. The old woman is already there, probably having chosen the most ideal position to look more mysterious and wise. A few paces away, Emma is drawing on the pavement with colored chalk.

"Vera—" Then her breath hitches, and to Sana's horror, she finds herself bursting into tears. Oh no, no, this isn't supposed to happen. The whole tram ride here, Sana has gone over what she will say to Vera. First of all, she will obviously tell Vera that she's mistaken. Then Sana will take a page from all the gaslighting assholes she's known in her life and insist that Vera imagined everything. Hey, if there's ever a silver lining to dating college frat boys, it's learning how to gaslight with the best of them. But then she sees Vera's slight frame against the vast ocean, and the way Vera's Asian perm blows in the sea breeze, and something about it cracks her apart. She can't lie to Vera, not like this. Not ever.

As Sana weeps, hands envelope her. Vera hugs her tight. "Aiya, why you cry?" Vera mutters, patting Sana's back. "So dramatic, you young people."

"But you—your message—" She's gasping too hard to form a coherent sentence.

Vera pulls away so she can look Sana in the eye. "Just tell me, you kill Marshall? Is it you? You give him pigeon?"

"What—no!" Sana cries. Thank god the pier is deserted at this hour, because that came out a lot louder than she intended. But even if there were people about, she wouldn't care anyway, because it is imperative that she make Vera understand this. "No," she says again, in a stronger, more level voice. "I did not kill Marshall. I wished him dead, so many times, but no."

Eons pass as Vera regards Sana silently, her sharp eyes cutting through Sana's skin and flesh and bone, straight into the depths of her heart. Then Vera sniffs. "Okay. I believe you. For now."

Sana sags with relief. Emma toddles over to them and Vera hugs her before taking out a bottle of warm milk from her bag. Emma accepts the offering with a solemn nod and goes back to drawing on the pavement.

Vera turns her attention back to Sana. "But now tell me, why Marshall has a folder with your name as title?"

Immediately, Sana's entire body is abuzz with electricity. "A folder? What folder? Where did you find it?"

"In Marshall's laptop, of course."

"How did you have access to— You know what? Never mind. What's inside?"

Vera raises her eyebrows. "You tell me."

"Was it—" Sana swallows thickly. The hope is too much, turning and turning inside her, surely it will kill her. Her voice comes out thick with it. "My paintings?"

Vera nods. "They are quite good. Maybe not amazing, but not bad."

A part of Sana wants to laugh because this is such an Asian mom way of giving a compliment—never give too big of a compliment, always remind the child that there is room for improvement. But most of Sana is awash with relief, a plethora of it. Maybe now that she can get her art back, she'll finally be able to get over her block. But the thought of the block is still very real. The part of her that Marshall damaged isn't going to be repaired magically.

"Come, you sit down."

Sana lets Vera lead her to a bench. Vera reaches into her bag and pulls out a thermos and two cups. She pours steaming-hot tea into one and hands it to Sana. Sana wraps her hands around the cup, warming her fingers. The tea's fragrance envelopes her as she raises it to her lips, as comforting as a warm blanket. It tastes faintly sweet and seems mild at first sip, but its fragrance lingers in her mouth long after.

"Chrysanthemum with dates," Vera says. "I don't think you need caffeine."

"Oh Vera." Sana half laughs, half sobs.

"Now you tell me what happen."

And she does, going way back, because somehow, Sana knows that Vera is here to listen to everything, not just the thing that happened with Marshall, but everything. And she wants to tell someone. She's been hungry for it ever since she was a kid.

"When my mom was growing up, my grandparents—they're your stereotypical Asian parents—"

Vera's eyes narrow, and Sana hurries to add, "Which isn't necessarily bad. But it really didn't do any good for my mom. They pushed her hard to study engineering. She hated it; she wasn't very good at math or science, and she was always disappointing them. Anyway, she dropped out of college, and they basically disowned her. She was homeless for a while, sleeping on friends' couches, but that whole time, she was writing a book. And when she finished, the book found an agent, and then a publisher. It didn't sell for much, but my mom wrote another book, and another, and now she basically has an empire built on books, and my grandparents couldn't be prouder."

"Oh, well, good job to her!" Vera seems genuinely delighted.

Sana sighs. "Yeah, good job, Mom. I'm happy for her, I really am, and I think she's amazing. But because she went through such a hard time, her motto is now: 'If I could do all that while I was *literally homeless*, then everyone can do anything they set their mind to.' From when I was little, she'd always tell me how lucky I was to have a mom who isn't a stereotypical Asian mom. To have a mom who understands and values the importance of the pursuit of creativity, who doesn't just expect me to be a doctor or lawyer or engineer. Actually, given my mom's background, I think she would've been disappointed if I'd told her I wanted to do any of those things." Sana gives a bitter laugh. "But luckily for both of us, like my mother, I gravitate more toward being creative rather than analytical. I chose art. She was *so* happy. I think—" It's a struggle to find the right words.

"Sometimes, I feel like the fact that I chose art is my mom's achievement, not mine. Anyway, it doesn't matter. Whatever the roots, I chose art. I was good at it. I got accepted to CalArts. My mom was always boasting about it to our family, always telling the aunties and uncles, 'See what happens when you don't keep trying to squeeze your kids into such narrow lanes?' It was kind of annoying, but whatever. I was happy at CalArts. I had good friends, I was doing well in my classes. My teachers liked me. But my mom's voice was always at the back of my mind. Her expectations that I couldn't just do 'well'; I had to be like her. The top one percent of people in her career. She releases like four books a year because she has to be the best at publishing. And she wanted me to be like that, to be the best artist at CalArts."

Vera nods thoughtfully, her eyes looking sad. A few times, Vera sucks in a breath like she's about to interrupt, but then she manages to stop herself and sip some more tea instead. At some point, Emma totters over, rubbing her eyes, and Vera scoops her into her lap. Within minutes, Emma has settled her head on Vera's shoulder and fallen asleep. Sana can't help feeling a stab of jealousy at the simplicity of the kid's world. Draw on pavement, drink warm milk, take a nap. She gives herself a little shake. How pathetic to be jealous of a toddler.

"Anyway, there was so much pressure, and I knew—I just knew I wasn't ever going to be the best. I'd have classes and in every class there's always that one person who's just so ridiculously talented, you know? And that person was never me. And the pressure kept building, and I was starting to panic—I was one semester away from graduating and I still hadn't made a name for myself, and there was my mom with all her expectations and hopes, and then . . . I met Marshall."

At this, Sana has to pause, because the memory is so painful. So raw. "We'd just had our spring show, and I was watching my top classmates getting approached by gallery owners who walked right past me and my paintings. Like, they'd just glance at my paintings and their eyes would slide away. Hundreds of hours I'd poured into them and it took less than a second for the pros to tell that they were worthless. But then Marshall came up to me and said, 'Are you the artist of these paintings?' I said yes, and his eyes shone like he'd just hit the jackpot, and he said, 'Wow. These are exactly what I was looking for.'"

Sana glances at Vera, embarrassed. "You probably think I'm stupid, don't you?"

Vera frowns. "I think this Marshall is very cunning, and I think you were under lot of pressure."

Sana's mouth twitches into a sad smile. "Thanks, Vera. Yeah, I was. Anyway, he told me he's an NFT collector." Sana snorts at the memory. "I didn't even know what an NFT was. Then I thought it was only for virtual art, but Marshall told me that it could be anything, even art in the physical world. Even sculptures. He said that the NFT world was a lot more diverse than these stuffy art galleries, and he could tell that there was something special about my paintings." Her voice wobbles then. "I guess I wanted to believe in him so badly. More than anything. He explained more of the technical details to me, but by then, I was so desperate, so eager to believe him, that I would've agreed to practically anything. I didn't understand most of the technical details; I didn't really bother to. He had me sign all these agreements that I didn't really—I tried reading them, I did, I swear, but it was all in legalese and there wasn't a chance in hell that an arts student like me would've understood them."

"What is this 'legalese'? You mean like Chinese?" Vera says.

Sana laughs despite herself. "No, Vera. It's not like Chinese. Well, it might as well have been Chinese for all that I understood, but it just means, like, really complicated language that you often find in legal documents that only those who've had training in legal terms would understand."

"Hmm, yes, I see. Legalese."

Sana half wonders if by this time next year Vera will have taught herself to be well-versed in legalese. She wouldn't put it past Vera. "Anyway, long story short, it turns out that in signing those documents, I signed away all of my rights to my own art. It all belonged to Marshall. As soon as the papers were signed, he basically fuc—uh, sorry, he basically ghosted me."

"Oh, I know this 'ghosted,'" Vera says proudly. "I often hear it on the TikTok. It means when someone disappears very suddenly, like a ghost."

"Um. Yeah, that's right. So he ghosted me, and meanwhile, I was watching my paintings on the marketplace and I saw that one of them had sold for a few hundred dollars. It wasn't much, not compared to some of my classmates' stuff, but it was something! I mean, I created that out of nothing. I poured everything inside me into the paintings; the whole time I was working on those pieces, I ate and breathed and slept in this fog because I was so consumed by them. And to have them stolen from me like that . . ."

"Hmm, yes. I can see how that must be very painful."

"It felt like he had stolen a part of me and left me with this gaping hole. And the worst part is, when I told my mom about it, she just laughed and said, 'Oh, sweetie. Move on. Do you think I haven't had my work stolen before? The literary world is just as full of thieves. Plagiarism everywhere. I once told a friend about a book idea I had, and next thing I knew, she'd written a book with exactly that same idea. You know what I did? I moved on. You are more than just one idea.'"

"Well," Vera says, "I agree, we are all more than just one idea. But having our very first idea stolen, before we have even plunge into the water, is devastating."

"Yes, exactly!" Sana cries, so loudly that Emma twitches a little. Sana winces, hoping she hasn't just woken the poor kid up, but after a few moments, Emma settles back down. "Sorry, I'll be a bit quieter. Anyway, when I couldn't move on, my mom started getting frustrated. I got the sense that she was angrier at me for not being able to just shake it off like she would've than at Marshall for actually thieving it in the first place. She kept telling me it's a good lesson to learn early, and to stop moping, and to 'just keep swimming,' and the more she said that stuff, the worse I felt. I became blocked. I couldn't even bear to pick up my paintbrush for a while. And even after the hurt stopped being so raw, I picked up my brush and I stood in front of that blank canvas, and there was . . . nothing. My mom told me that she often wrote her pain into her books, especially when she was homeless. She told me to use this pain as fuel for my art. But I couldn't. I just felt numb. I felt blocked." Sana laughs bitterly. "Blocked. My mom doesn't believe in blocks. She says that's just us being indulgent."

Vera pats Sana's arm. "I see. It's a terrible thing that has happen to you. But why do you come to my teahouse? Pretending to have a pot catch?"

Sana's breath releases in a long, exhausted sigh. "It all built up after a while, my resentment, my anger. I tracked Marshall down to the Bay Area. I rented a small studio and I was following him. I didn't even know what I wanted to do. I just felt like I needed to be close to my art, and that meant being close to Marshall. Does that sound ridiculous?"

"Yes. But it's okay, I do a lot of crazy things too."

"Ha. Well, one night, he spotted me and called me out. Told me to get over myself, that most of my pieces hadn't even sold. They were worthless. That I didn't have any talent. All the stuff I'd always been so scared of about myself. It was too much. I lost control." Sana's voice breaks. "And I—I attacked him. I scratched him." She looks down at her hands, shuddering at the memory of Marshall's skin being raked under her nails. Nails that should have paint under them, not blood.

"But you don't kill him?"

Sana shakes her head. "No, I told you, I didn't. He shoved me away, told me he was going to call the cops. I was so horrified by what I did—I've never attacked anyone like that before—I turned and ran away. I was so scared. For the next couple of days, I kept waiting for the cops to—I don't know—break down my door and storm my apartment. But they never did. Then I read about Marshall dying. He died later that same night I'd scratched him." Sana's eyes are haunted. "I had to come to your teahouse to—I don't know—I just—you won't believe how awful I've felt ever since that night. I don't even know why I went to your place. And—this is going to make me sound like the worst human ever—I'm still not over my stolen art! God, you must think I'm horrible, but even after Marshall died, I'm still hung up on the art. I still want to find it and reclaim it."

Vera squeezes Sana's arm, and when Sana finally meets her eyes, there is so much compassion in them that Sana feels the tears coming. "Oh, silly girl. Of course I don't think you are horrible human. No, horrible human are people like Marshall. Come here." And with that, Vera pulls Sana into a hug. The kind of hug that only a mom could give. Sana surrenders to it completely, feeling every wall she'd painstakingly built over the years crumbling. She cries until there is nothing left, then she cries some more, and the whole time, Vera strokes her hair with all the patience in the world. When they're done, the sun is setting and the air is biting cold.

"Well, it's been a long day. Come over to mine," Vera says, grunting as she stands with Emma still dozing in her arms.

Sana wipes at her puffy face. "You mean to Julia's?"

Vera tuts. "Nobody likes a pendant, Sana."

Sana almost tells her it's "pedant," "not pendant," but thinks better of it.

"You come to dinner now, then when I am next free, you are meeting me at the beach."

"The beach?" It's the last thing Sana expected to hear. "Why?"

In answer, Vera just gives a secret smile and walks on ahead, leaving Sana with no choice but to hurry after her.

TWENTY-SIX

JULIA

Julia can't remember the last time she's felt so alive. What a shitty, awful, no-good thing to think as a mother. But it's also unfortunately sort of true? She adores Emma. Emma is everything to her, the air that she breathes. But ever since Emma was born, Emma's also consumed every moment, every thought in Julia's head. So often, Julia would find herself just staring off into space while half watching Emma play, waiting for Emma to call out to her. Because Emma is always needing her for something, every few minutes. Playing with her is somehow both mind-numbing and also demanding, so taxing on her attention that over the years, Julia's intellect has deteriorated so gently and so softly that she hadn't known it was happening at all.

But now, it feels as though an effervescent vitamin has been dropped into the tepid waters of her brain, and all of a sudden, the sparks are back, cool air flowing so clearly through her lungs. She feels as though she's come back to life. She feels the first stirrings when she meets up with Cassie, the TikTok influencer. Immediately upon seeing Cassie, Julia's mind goes into camera mode, studying the angles of Cassie's jawline and cheekbones and the tint of her eyes and hair, and planning how best to highlight those unique features using natural light. She hasn't thought in that way for so long, assessing people's faces as a photographer instead of her eyes just sliding over them in that dead, glazed way she's been doing.

And when the session begins, everything comes flooding back to Julia. She expertly positions Cassie so that the girl is outlined by golden sunlight, then starts telling mom jokes to make Cassie laugh or roll her eyes. With every few clicks, she tells Cassie that she looks wonderful, that the camera loves her, that her aura is amazing, and after a few minutes, Cassie is so relaxed that the two of them start chatting like friends as they work together.

As she works, the little hairs on the back of Julia's neck rise, and she turns and spots someone in the distance—too far away to tell if it's a man or a woman—but something about the figure makes her think she knows them. She hesitates, unsure if she should wave, unsure even if the lone figure is indeed watching her.

"Everything okay?" Cassie says.

Julia snaps back to her client. Her *client*. My god, she has a client. She hurriedly nods, making herself smile. "Yes, just looking for the best lighting." She glances behind her shoulder and finds that the figure is gone. She must be imagining things. She shakes off the weird moment and focuses her attention fully on the shoot once again.

When she's done, she shows some of the photos in the viewfinder to Cassie, and Cassie says, "Holy fucking shitballs, man!" which is somehow the best compliment Julia has ever received.

She practically hops back to her car, one hundred dollars richer. Not the biggest paycheck, but definitely the most rewarding. Vera has sent her two texts, both of them pictures of Emma. Emma at the pier, pointing at the seals, and Emma at home, pretending to paint Vera's toenails. It looks like Emma's also having the time of her life. The entire drive home, Julia sings at the top of her lungs to the latest Taylor Swift song, something she hasn't done since she dated Marshall, because he'd told her that her singing sounded like a wolf in heat. When she gets home, Julia looks up at the house and sees warm yellow light from the front window, and for the first time, she doesn't feel exhausted or depressed to come home. It used to be just her and Emma, most of the time, and she'd be coming home lugging grocery bags while Emma screamed or cried or asked some unanswerable question like: "Do earthworms have butts?" and arriving at the house just meant coming back to a cluttered space devoid of any joy, and she knew that she would have to rush about and try her best to pick up as much of the mess as she could while also cooking a meal and trying to get Emma bathed and fed, all before Marshall came home.

But now, Julia opens the door and what greets her first is the soul-enriching smells of Vera's cooking. Followed by the patter of Emma's little feet as she runs to the door. "Mommy!" And Julia goes to her knees and hugs her baby girl, inhaling the sweet child smell of her, and truly she has never known a moment filled with so much joy. When Julia opens her eyes, she sees that there's someone else in the living room.

"Sana!" she says, straightening back up and lifting Emma as she does. "Hi, I wasn't expecting—"

"Sorry," Sana says, standing up. "I—uh, Vera sort of invited me here? I tried telling her no, but . . ."

Julia snorts. "I'm guessing that didn't go well." She places her camera bag carefully on a side table. She's not quite sure how to feel about having Sana here. The last time Sana came, she'd asked quite a few invasive questions, though maybe that made sense, given she's trying to do a true crime story about Marshall. Still, Julia's not in the mood to talk about Marshall right now, so she half hopes that Sana will leave soon.

"Um, I kind of have something to tell you," Sana says, not quite meeting Julia's eyes. Something in her voice makes the back of Julia's neck prickle. This does not sound good.

Vera's head pops out from behind the kitchen door. "Ah, Julia, you home. Sana is here."

"Yes, I see that, Vera."

"She has something to tell you."

"Yep, she was about to tell me."

"Emma," Vera calls out, "you are supposed to be my sous chef, remember? Come here and help me make dumplings."

Before Julia can react, Emma wriggles out of her arms and dashes off to the kitchen. Great, now Julia's left with Sana, and for whatever reason, the vibes in here are painfully awkward.

"Um . . ." Sana begins.

Vera's head pops out again. "Sana is quite long-winded, so I help to shorten: Sana does not have a pot catch. She is an artist. Marshall steal her work. She did not kill him." She smiles at the two of them, who are standing there with mouths agape, then says, "Okay, now I make dumplings."

Julia turns back to Sana, her mouth opening and closing.

"Wh—" Nope, nothing comes out. She doesn't even know where to begin. Then, sighing, Julia decides to just go with it. She sinks into one of the sofas and leans back. "All right, you'd better tell me from the beginning."

"Maybe not from beginning, it will take too long, the food will get cold. Just tell her from the spring show," Vera calls out.

"Yep, I think we got it from here, Vera," Julia says. She catches Sana's eye, and there is some understanding between them, a spark of laughter.

Sana takes a deep breath. "I was at CalArts . . ."

A bout fifteen minutes later, Julia sits back, her thoughts swimming in circles. She's stunned. No, she's actually not. She feels like she should be stunned, that's the thing, but is she really? Was the revelation that her dead husband was conning college kids really such a shock? No, because when Julia thinks about it, it fits Marshall, the pieces sliding easily into the negative spaces of the image of Marshall. For years, she's learned to only see the good side of Marshall, to believe him when he tells her that he wants nothing but the best for them, and after Emma arrived, he'd say things like it's only the three of them against the whole world. But now it hits her. Why against the whole world? Nobody should be against the entire world. Not unless you're someone like Marshall, who goes through life by cheating and swindling everyone he comes across.

She's so incredibly sad for Sana, this young woman, a kid, really, coming across someone like Marshall so young. It's only then, when she thinks the words "so young," that it hits Julia that in fact, she came across Marshall at an even younger age. She was in high school, for god's sakes. Yes, he had been as well, both of them the same age, but now that Julia thinks about it, she should've seen it then, the way that Marshall had slowly, subtly prized all her support systems away so that by the end of high school, all Julia felt she could count on was Marshall. Her friendships had been peeled away by Marshall's calculated comments about how he didn't like Mindy, or how Oliver had talked bad about Julia behind her back. Her parents, perhaps sensing something rotten in Marshall, had tried to talk her out of dating him, but it only ended up pushing her farther away from them. And then there were Julia's own dreams, her goal of being a photographer, gently discouraged with so much patience on Marshall's part that she hadn't even known he was doing it. Even after having Emma, Marshall had kept Julia from joining any mom groups, telling her that the women would just judge her for not being able to breastfeed properly, then later on, as she kept breastfeeding, he told her that the other moms would find it weird that she was still nursing Emma.

God. Julia isn't sad now; Julia is fucking furious. At Marshall, yes, but most of all, at herself. How could she have been so goddamn stupid? How had she let him tear her down like that, piece by minuscule piece? Such tiny pieces of her that she hadn't realized they were being taken away from her until she is left suddenly hollow. And now she's faced with another one of his victims, a young person whose future had been so bright, who is now staring at Julia with wide, fearful eyes. Eyes that are jaded and bitter and broken.

"Oh, Sana." Julia reaches out and grasps Sana's hand. Sana flinches but doesn't pull away. "I am so sorry that he did that to you. I don't know if your paintings are among the ones that Oliver found at Marshall's apartment, but you are welcome to look for them. And of course, you are welcome to the . . . uh, the NFT part of them? I don't quite understand how it works, but everything is yours, you can have it once I figure out how to give you owner-ship." Julia shakes her head. "Look, it's not that I suspected you, but I guess Vera's been going on about how one of us is the killer, and honestly, I haven't really known what to think. I mean, now we know you and I didn't kill him, so who did? Do you think it really was an accident?"

"I don't know," Sana says. "From what I knew about Marshall, I think he crossed a lot of people."

Julia nods. "Yeah. Any of them could've . . ." Her voice trails away, and for a moment, they both stare into the distance, each one lost in her own thoughts. "And there was the break-in, which seems too coincidental to have been done by someone else. Oh! Is that why you didn't want Vera to report the break-in to the police?"

"I'm sorry," Sana says, her voice cracking. "Yeah, I didn't want to have to talk to the cops and—I don't know, I just wasn't sure what they might say. I mean, at the end of the day, I did attack him. I scratched him, I don't know how long DNA lasts under fingernails, and I just . . . I got scared. I'm so sorry."

"I understand," Julia says, and strangely, she does. Well, maybe she doesn't quite understand, but she can definitely empathize, and at the end of the day, she knows in her gut that Sana isn't guilty of killing Marshall, at least.

Tears shine in Sana's eyes. "And I'm sorry I lied to you about having a podcast. I just—"

"It's fine," Julia says quickly. "I don't hold that against you."

"I do," Vera says, popping back out from the kitchen. "Lying is bad." Her head pops back into the kitchen.

Julia and Sana stare in the direction of the kitchen for a while, then grin at each other. "How long do you think she's been listening?" Sana whispers.

"Oh, the whole time, I'm sure." Julia squeezes Sana's hand. "I'm sorry that my husband traumatized you so much that you haven't been able to follow your passion ever since."

Sana gnaws on her bottom lip. "I should just move on, right?"

"No. I mean, well, yes, that would be ideal, but it sounds like he broke you down." Julia takes a deep breath. "When I was a teen, all I wanted was to be a photographer. And Marshall—god, I don't even quite know how he did it—but over time, he convinced me that it was a useless dream, that it wouldn't pay enough to make a living, that I should just treat it as a hobby. So I did, but then he'd tell me that my hobby was too expensive, too time-consuming, and so on. And finally, I stopped doing it altogether. I haven't done any photography for years aside from those portraits I did of Emma." Julia shakes her head in wonderment. "Actually, today was the first day in years that I took photos of someone other than Emma."

Sana raises her eyebrows. "Oh, cool! Who did you take pictures of?"

"This TikTok influencer. I think her name's Cassie . . . Red?"

"Oh my god, CassieRed!" Sana squeals. "I follow her! She's not yet at that breakout stage, but she's getting there, I can tell. I love her TikToks. I can't believe you got to shoot her! How was it?"

"Fucking amazing." The words are out before Julia knows it, and Sana cackles. Julia joins in, and before long, she's taken out her camera and is showing the viewfinder photos to Sana, who oohs and aahs at the images. When Vera tells them that dinner is ready, the two women continue chatting as they make their way to the dining room, where another one of Vera's incredible feasts greets them.

Vera points at the various dumpling dishes. "Pork and chive dumplings, crab meat and pork fried dumplings, Szechuan chicken soup dumplings. And here we have sweet-and-sour fish, roast duck, and three-egg spinach." She beams at Emma, who is already seated in her high chair. "And my sous chef help with everything."

Emma nods proudly, and Julia bends down to kiss her forehead. "You are amazing," she tells Emma. As Julia slides into her seat, she pats her belly. "God, Vera, I've gained five pounds ever since you moved in."

"Yes, you are looking much healthier now. Sit, Sana," Vera orders.

Sana does so, and Vera starts heaping food onto her plate. "That's too much—" Sana protests, but Vera ignores her until Sana's plate is heaving with an obscene amount of food. Then Vera turns her attention to Emma, spearing pieces of fish and placing them on Emma's plate.

"You must eat lots of fish," Vera says. "Fish is good for your brain. You want to be smart like me, right?"

"I do!" Emma says, spooning the fish into her mouth.

By now, the sight of her daughter eating so many different kinds of foods no longer astounds Julia, but she still marvels at it. The way that Vera has somehow moved Emma so effortlessly away from her usual beige foods. As they eat, Julia gazes fondly at Vera and wonders just how in the world she got so lucky to have the old woman in her house.

Then, of course, she remembers that the only reason Vera is here is because Marshall is dead. Julia is devastated by Marshall's death, of course she is, but a teeny-tiny part of her is grateful that such a tragedy could lead to such a blessing. Sana told Julia that she, Riki, and Oliver spent the morning cleaning out Vera's teahouse. It's a reminder that Vera's stay here is temporary, which makes Julia sad. Hopefully, even after Vera moves back to her house, Julia's life won't fall apart again.

VERA'S NOTEBOOK

SUSPECT: ~~SANA~~

Sana promise she is not Marshall's killer. I think she is telling the truth. I have very good nose for sniffing out lies and Sana is terrible liar because she twitches whenever she lies. I must invite her to play mahjong one day. Easy win for me.

Well, that is one suspect out, so we are down to just three! I must say, living with one of my suspects is a bit of conflict of interest, because I start to like Julia very much. So I hope she is not killer, although I do think there is strong chance she is, because just imagine being married to Marshall. Terrible man. I think he is a very bad husband and very bad father. Just look how little Emma barely mention him. Julia says this because Marshall is rarely home, and when he is, he does not like to play with Emma. In fact, he will tell her go to bed, be quiet. Oh, if Marshall is alive I should like to give him a good scolding, that is exactly what he needs.

I get call from Officer Gray today. She is very angry about the break-in! She even call me "irresponsible citizen"! Can you imagine? I tell her that I even go to police station to chase up on the murder investigation, but it seems they don't want to investigate, so I decided not to bother them with small thing like burglary. Especially when nothing is taken. Hah! She has nothing to say to THAT. I wish she has come in person to see me so I can see the look on her face when I tell her off. She then say I must close up my shop while they look into it, and I say that's fine, it's already close up, they can come and go as they please. Maybe now they will finally do some DNA and fingerprint test, eh? I tell her that and she just sigh and tell me not to leave town. Like I will leave when so many exciting things are happening!

Anyway, I hope the killer is Riki or Oliver. Speaking of which, I am inviting Riki to the beach tomorrow, won't that be nice? He is a good boy. I will make many buns for him and Sana. They are both good boys, Riki and Oliver. I can tell. Well, aside from being a possible killer. But as they say, everyone is innocent until prove that they are guilty, so for now, there will be delicious buns for all.

TWENTY-SEVEN

RIKI

Riki has never liked Ocean Beach. He knows he's very biased, but having grown up spending his vacation days on the gorgeous beaches of Bali, Riki considers Ocean Beach a vastly inferior beach. For one thing, the water is always stunningly cold, even in the summer. For another, the . . . vibes just aren't right. He realizes this isn't a very cogent argument, but some places are beachy places. You know it once you arrive at the airport. Like Bali, for example. As soon as you land at the Ngurah Rai Airport, everything around you screams: *Beach vacation!* The air carries with it the smell of the ocean, clean and fresh, and there are plumerias everywhere and everyone is relaxed. But here in San Francisco, no one is relaxed. Everyone is erging (why can't they just freaking call it rowing?) and eating acai smoothies out of coconut-shell bowls, but they're also yelling into their smartphones and checking their Apple Watch every ninety seconds to make sure that they're getting in their ten thousand steps while negotiating multibillion-dollar deals. And on the border of this bustling city, there's Ocean Beach, the place where these techbros are supposed to go on their downtime. Riki went once, with his colleagues, and never again.

But what Vera wants, Vera gets, and that is why Riki is now at Ocean Beach at six in the morning. It's Sunday, he should be in bed, but nope, here he is, freezing his ass off and glaring bitterly at the sea as he struggles through the sand toward where Vera is standing.

"Riki!" Vera shouts, waving both arms. "Over here!"

It's obvious he's seen her, he's literally walking toward her, but still Vera calls out. The corner of Riki's mouth quirks into a smile. Vera is quite possibly the most vexing person he has ever met. But somehow, he can't not see her as an honorary mother figure in his life. Something about her makes him feel like everything will be okay. Nothing bad can happen with a Vera in your life.

"Ah, good, finally you are here," Vera says. "You don't see me waving back there? Why you don't wave back?"

"I did," Riki says.

"Hmm." Vera doesn't look convinced. "Well, anyway, I am glad you are here, because I have a question to ask you."

"You asked me to meet you at the beach at six in the morning to ask me a question? What's wrong with texting?"

"Ah," Vera says with a cunning smile. "If I text, then there will be permanent record of the texts, and this is sensitive question."

Riki's still too baffled to be nervous, but now he's growing uneasy. "Okay . . ."

"So I look in Marshall's computer—"

At this, Riki hears a keening sound in the center of his skull.

It's his brain shrieking, *Oh nooooo*. Somehow, he manages to not freak the hell out. "How did you get access to his computer?"

Vera tuts and flaps a hand at him dismissively. "Aiya, don't ask such irrelevant questions. As I was saying, I look in Marshall's computer and I find a folder with your name on it."

Oh god. He's going to have a heart attack. He knows it. This is how he perishes at the young age of twenty-five, being questioned by an old lady who must surely be an undercover CIA agent.

"I open the folder," Vera continues, unaware of or maybe choosing to ignore Riki's horrified expression, "and inside is something called 'Scalping Bot 2.' I open up the program, but of course I just a simple old woman, it doesn't mean anything to me."

A glimmer of hope appears in the screaming mess of Riki's head. Maybe Vera doesn't know after all. Like she said, she's just a simple old woman, she won't figure—

"So I search for it in the Google."

Oh shit.

"And it's very interesting result. It take a while for me to understand what a scalping bot is."

Why hadn't Riki thought to rename the bot to something else? But nooo, he had to name it "Scalping Bot" like a freaking idiot.

"It looks like there are many different kind of scalping bot, but they all want to do one thing: scam people." Vera looks at Riki sternly. "Are you scam artist, Riki?"

"No!" Riki cries. But then his conscience catches up with him and he chokes on it. He can't lie to Vera any more than he can lie to his mom. "Sort of?"

"Hmm." Vera narrows her eyes. "Well, you better tell me everything then."

....

This is how it began: with his little brother, Adi.

Adi was an oops; Riki was already thirteen by the time Adi was born. His parents had only wanted one kid because kids were expensive, but then came Adi, and that was that. For the first few years, Riki had largely ignored Adi. It wasn't that Riki didn't love Adi, or was jealous of him. No, it was that Riki was a teenage boy and wasn't very interested in a wriggly, squally baby, nor an energetic toddler who got into everything. But when Adi was four, he came home from nursery school with a tennis ball, and that evening, the two brothers went outside and threw the ball back and forth. Adi asked Riki questions about what it was like being seventeen, and there was such a sweet earnestness in the way Adi talked and the way that Adi looked up to him that Riki felt a sudden surge of fierce, protective, brotherly love. He looked at Adi and thought: *I would do anything for you.*

Their friendship blossomed. Adi was a rambunctious kid, and Riki was always a sweet-natured boy, and somehow, the combination worked. Whenever Riki came home from school, Adi would be looking out the window, waving madly when he spotted Riki down the street. But while Riki excelled in his studies and managed to get a visa to work at a tech startup in Silicon Valley, over the next few years, Adi continuously failed his classes. Riki finally told his parents that maybe Adi had a learning disability. They looked up the right therapists and scheduled an appointment for an assessment.

The results were both a blessing and a curse: Adi did not have a learning disability. In fact, Adi was gifted, and that was why he found his classes incredibly boring and hard to pay attention to.

This was only a blessing insofar as it made for a good story to tell all their friends and family, but in reality, it was more a curse, because there were so few programs in Jakarta for truly gifted kids. At nine years of age, Adi was placed in the grade above him; then when he found that too easy, he was moved up yet another grade. That was when the bullying started. He began coming home with bruises on his skinny little body. It was clear that simply advancing him ahead of his age-group wouldn't work. He needed a proper school for gifted kids. Riki looked up international schools and began the mind-breaking process of applying to various schools all over the world: Singapore, Australia, the States.

Slowly they received acceptance letters. Partial scholarships. It turned out there were many gifted children all over the world, so many schools were only giving out partial scholarships. Even with the scholarships and grants, Riki was going to have to find a way of making more money. His job at the tech startup paid enough for him to have savings if he stuck to instant ramen for all his meals. Every cent of his savings was sent home to Indonesia. He applied for loans, but being a foreigner from what was considered a third-world country, he was rejected.

Try as he might, Riki couldn't find a way to help finance Adi's education, and the more time went by, the more depressed Adi became. Their video calls showed Adi getting more and more sullen, his eyes going from bright and hopeful to losing their shine. It gnawed at Riki. In addition to his day job, Riki started taking on freelance programming jobs, working through to three a.m. before waking up at seven to commute to Mountain View. After three months of this, he was so exhausted that while making instant ramen, he mistakenly poured the scalding-hot water onto his left hand instead of into the bowl. The pain had been unimaginable. He'd shrieked so loud that his neighbor had banged on the wall and gone, "*Shut up!*" He ran to the kitchen and placed his hand under the cold tap and cried. After he bandaged up his hand, he logged back on to the freelance website.

And that was when he found Marshall's job ad.

Looking for programmer to make a bot. Pay: $25,000.

Twenty-five thousand dollars. The number seemed ridiculously huge. Coupled with the partial scholarship, it would easily cover Adi's education. With a trembling hand, Riki clicked on the job ad.

The truth was, Riki would absolutely do anything for Adi. And so when he met up with Marshall in person, and when Marshall told him more details about the sort of bot he needed, Riki knew it was a malicious bot. A scalping bot, designed to scam the NFT market by driving Marshall's NFT prices up artificially while driving down the prices of other NFTs. It went against every fiber in Riki's soul, but there was nothing he wouldn't have done for Adi. And so he shook Marshall's hand, feeling like he was giving a piece of himself to the devil, and he started working on building Marshall's bot.

When the bot was done, Riki sent it to Marshall and received a payment of one thousand dollars. One thousand dollars was a lot of money, but it sure as hell wasn't twenty-five thousand dollars. It wouldn't even pay for Adi's airfare to SFO. When Riki demanded the rest of the money he was owed, Marshall laughed and said, "You should count yourself lucky that I'm even paying you for such a simple job. This is the kind of thing that any shitty programmer on Fiverr would do for ten bucks. Now, stop harassing me or I'll inform the company you work for that you just created a scalping bot. Let's see if they'll want to renew your work visa then."

And that was that. Riki couldn't believe how stupid he'd been. There was no contract agreement between him and Marshall, of course there wasn't; neither one wanted to have such a thing on record. But why hadn't Riki insisted on a down payment, at least? He'd just been so desperate, so ready to grasp at absolutely anything. And now he'd not only been swindled, he'd been swindled over a completely unethical program that was going to scam many people out of money. Fury and anguish took over Riki. Why were their lives so goddamn hard? He'd worked himself to the bone at school, and now at his job, and still he was somehow failing his family. Meanwhile, men like Marshall did whatever the hell they wanted without any consequences.

Well, no more. Riki looked up Marshall's address and waited outside his house one evening. When he saw Marshall's car leave the driveway, he followed. Marshall stopped at a swanky restaurant and tossed his car key at the valet while Riki quickly found street parking. He hurried inside the restaurant and found Marshall talking to the hostess.

"Marshall."

Marshall turned, smiling, but his smile froze when he saw that it was Riki. Riki saw three lines of scratches down Marshall's cheek.

"What the—" The rest of his words were interrupted by Riki's fist crunching into Marshall's face. The hostess screamed. Glasses stopped clinking; conversations halted in mid-sentence. And it dawned on Riki what a horribly stupid thing he'd just done. Horror flooded him and he ran outside. Someone shouted at him to stop but he ran down the block, hopped into his car, and floored the gas.

He sped all the way home, his breath coming in and out in little gasps. Back at his apartment, he hid in bed like a little kid and waited for the cops to arrive. Because there was no way in hell someone like Marshall would let this go. Riki squeezed his eyes shut and willed himself to disappear.

But the night passed, and no cops came by to arrest him. In the morning, Riki went to work and nobody looked at him funny. They all went about their business normally. Riki wondered if he'd dreamt the whole thing up. But no, his knuckles were still bruised; working the keyboard was painful. Then the next day, he read about Marshall's death in the news. Marshall had died on the very same night that Riki had hit him. Had he damaged Marshall's brain, leading to his death? Had he murdered a man?

And that was why he had to go to Vera's teahouse. Because Riki thought that things had been bad before, but murder . . . he wouldn't be able to live with himself if he found out that he'd killed another human being, no matter how accidental it was.

Vera regards Riki for a long time after he's done talking. Riki's insides are churning crazily, but in a strange way, he feels better after spilling everything.

When she finally speaks, she says, "Well, now we know your punch is not as strong as you think."

Okay, Riki wasn't sure what Vera would say, but it was definitely not this. "Huh?"

"Your punch didn't kill him. It was pigeon, remember?"

"Oh, right." A shrill, nervous laugh escapes him. "Yeah. You have no idea how relieved I was when I heard that. This whole time, I was wondering if I was a murderer . . ." His voice cracks and he has to stop to blink away the tears.

"Oh, if I know earlier, I would have told you, you obviously don't have enough upper-body strength to kill a man with one punch." Vera reaches out and pinches Riki's bicep. "See? Too soft. You should do more muscle training."

Riki laughs through his tears. "You're right, Vera."

Vera pats his shoulder. "Yes, you will learn that I often am. Hmm, okay, so you are not killer." She seems somewhat disappointed by this. Riki wipes at his eyes as Vera takes out a notebook from her trolley bag and opens it up, licking her finger and flipping through the pages. "Ah, here is your suspect page." She takes out a pen and crosses out his name. "Oh no, that leaves Julia and Oliver. Oh, but I like Julia very much. And Oliver is so sad, he is like sad teddy bear. I would feel very bad if I have to send him to prison."

"But you would've been okay if it was me?" Riki says, finding this both horrifying and yet hilarious at the same time.

Vera snaps her notebook shut. "Aiya, asking such silly question. Of course not. I care about all four of you. It's too bad that one of you is Marshall killer, but oh well. We won't dwell on such inauspicious things. Now, since you are not killer, we shall have a picnic. Help me unload this."

Riki does as he's told, bending down to take out various Tupperwares from Vera's trolley. There is an astounding amount of food. "So you brought all this food here, but you would've let it all go to waste if it turns out I did kill Marshall?"

Vera sighs as she shakes out a picnic blanket. "Aiya, of course not. I invite Sana. She and I would have eaten all this food ourselves if it turn out you are killer. You would be in a police car, I expect."

"Sana?" Riki's heart starts hammering at the mention of her.

"Yes, oh, there she is!" Vera waves madly at a figure in the distance. Cupping her hands around her mouth, she hollers, "*Sanaaa!* Over heeeere!" The figure waves back, but Vera continues shouting.

"I think she's seen you," Riki says. "You can probably stop shouting now?"

Vera harrumphs and turns her attention back to unboxing the food. "Oh, now that we know you and Sana both not killers, you can date each other."

"What?" Riki hates the way his cheeks immediately burst into flames.

"Don't act so innocent, I see how you look at her. But I care about Sana, so I have to make sure that you are not killer before I give my blessing. Now you have my blessing, so you may pursue her. Tch, don't just stand there gaping like fish! Keep taking out the container, there are still so many left."

And as Riki resumes taking Tupperware containers out of the surprisingly large trolley, he realizes that for the first time in months, he feels lighter. The anvil that has been on his shoulders is still there, but it's as though Vera has taken up a position next to him and is helping him lift it, just a little. Just enough for him to take a full breath. He glances at Vera and feels, for the first time, immensely grateful for her unexpected presence in his life.

TWENTY-EIGHT

VERA

Vera is very excited. First of all, her investigation is going so well. Already she's crossed two suspects off her list. Anyone would be happy about that. She can't wait to see the look on Officer Gray's face when Vera finally identifies Marshall's killer. She will have to sit Officer Gray down and go through her method step by step, just so the officer understands every brilliant move that Vera has made. Of course, crossing off Riki now means she is down to Julia and Oliver. The thought of either of them possibly being the killer saddens Vera, but no matter. She cannot let her emotions get in the way of her fine detective work. Did Sherlock Holmes ever let his affections cloud his judgment? Oh no, of course not. And neither will Vera Wong Zhuzhu. Of course, Officer Gray might require some food to assuage her, since she was so annoyed the last time they talked, on account of Vera failing to report the break-in. But she'll get over it once Vera serves up the killer on a plate, Vera's sure of it. Vera wonders if Officer Gray has made any headway with the investigation into the break-in, but unfortunately, she is unlikely to get any more information out of the officer. Not without her cooking up a storm for the department.

The other reason why Vera is excited is she's finally getting to live out her dream as a Chinese mother: setting up two young people with each other. Okay, so neither of the two young people is her actual offspring, but since Tilly is so very disagreeable about any of her efforts to set him up with a nice girl, this is the next best thing. And maybe it'll train her for when she sets Tilly up on a date. Also, by now, Vera cares about Sana and Riki as though they were her niece and nephew. Such bright young people, and they both have something in common: Marshall. Maybe their respective experiences with the hoodlum will be a bonding exercise. Oh yes, this is a good, auspicious match. Vera can already see Sana and Riki walking down the aisle. She's going to make their kids call her Grandma, just like Emma does.

By the time Sana arrives at their spot, all the food is laid out beautifully on the picnic blanket. "Sit," Vera orders. "Eat."

She's made a veritable feast yet again. And she is very proud of this one. It's a bonanza of beach-friendly foods, none of them requiring cutlery. There are honey-glazed barbecued beef slices sandwiched in plump mantou buns with carrot and scallion relish. There are crispy fried egg rolls stuffed almost to bursting with shrimp and tofu. There are steamed dim sum: shao mai and salted egg custard buns and lap cheong rolls. One Tupperware is filled with neatly sliced watermelon and Korean pears to balance out all the meat. And to go along with all the food, there is a huge jug of iced poached pear tea with ginseng.

Nothing fills Vera with quite as much joy as watching loved ones eat her food. It's one of the many things she misses about Jinlong and Tilly. When it was the three of them at home, she'd cook up a storm every day and watch as Jinlong and Tilly ate, and food always tasted so much better that way. Living alone, Vera finds that much of the joy of cooking has leached out of her, to the point where she mostly eats plain rice and simple sauteed vegetables for dinner. Why bother cooking elaborate meals for just one person?

But now she has so many people to cook for. Her days are filled to bursting and she's constantly rushing here and there, and she can't possibly be happier than this.

"Oh my god, this is *so* good," Sana says, her mouth full with the beef bun. "God, Vera. You should open up a restaurant."

Vera flaps a hand at her. "Aiya, what rubbish." But she has to bite down really hard on her lower lip to keep from grinning. She looks pointedly at Riki, who's chewing on an egg roll. "How is it?"

Riki tears his eyes away from Sana. "Huh? Oh, yeah, this is really good. As always, your cooking is amazing."

Vera gives a satisfied grunt. Between the three of them, the food is soon demolished amid companionable chatter. When they're done eating, Vera gets up and takes a stick out of the trolley. It's a narrow bamboo pole about three feet high.

"What's this for?" Sana says when Vera hands her the stick.

"It's your new paintbrush."

"What?" Sana gapes at her.

"Get up," Vera says in her *do not even think about refusing* voice.

Sana does so, still looking confused.

Vera gestures at the beach. "The sand is your canvas. Nothing you draw will be permanent. So you don't have to feel scare about making the mistake or drawing something bad. The sea erase all of it."

Sana stares, wide-eyed, at the bamboo stick, then at Vera.

"You go and draw now," Vera orders. "Riki and I tidy up and chat some more. Oh yes, Riki, I forget to tell you, Sana does not have a pot catch, she is artist. One of the many artist that Marshall swindle, and ever since then she cannot draw." She turns to Sana, whose jaw is scraping the sand. "And, Sana, Riki is not a Buzzfeed reporter." Vera pauses long enough to glower at Riki. "You make me so excited about that. I think to myself: Wow, he is reporter, he can do article about my teahouse!"

"I'm really sorry," Riki says, not knowing whether he should be apologizing to Vera or to Sana.

"Anyway, Riki is programmer who is swindle by Marshall. So. There you go. Both of you are Marshall victim. Now, go draw. *Go*," Vera barks like an army general, and Sana jumps up, meerkat-like, and scampers away. Vera turns back to Riki, who's still looking stunned. "Why are you sitting there like a frog? Help me tidy."

Riki starts gathering up the Tupperware containers. "Sana's really an artist?"

"Yes, very talented too. Her paintings are very good." Vera is happy that this revelation has stunned Riki. He must be very pleasantly surprised by what a talent his future girlfriend is. But when she glances up at Riki, he doesn't look at all happy. In fact, he looks like he's about to cry. "What's wrong?"

"I wrote a bot that helped Marshall scam people into overpaying for his NFTs. His NFTs were stolen art from various artists. I knew about it and I never—I just—I stayed quiet. And now you're telling me that Sana is one of the artists he stole from, and because of him she hasn't been able to paint. I was part of his whole shitty business."

Vera isn't sure that she's following everything he's saying. All of this technological jargon is so hard to follow. She waves at him. "Aiya, is not as bad as you think. You are both victims, yes?"

"Well, sure, but I'm not exactly innocent either. Sana is, though." Riki sighs. "God, I'm a fucking asshole."

"Tch, don't be so drama!" Vera snaps. "Move past it. Put it behind you. Marshall is dead. You and Sana are healing after what he does to you. Maybe you do something slightly bad, so what? Now you learn from it. You have a better judgment now. Better morals, because you learn from your personal mistake. This what life is about, Riki. No one is perfect, making right decisions all the time. Only those who are so privileged can make right decision all the time. The rest of us, we have to struggle, keep afloat. Sometimes we do things we are not proud of. But now you know where your lines are. You are good boy, Riki. You have good heart. That is all that matters." She smacks him firmly in the middle of his chest. "Good heart! You remember that." Then she turns away and finishes putting away the containers in the trolley, satisfied that she has done her job very well indeed.

Sana ends up drawing for more than an hour, and by the time she's done, Vera has grilled Riki about everything from what his favorite food is (something called terong balado, she will have to look it up on the Google so she can make it for him), what his mom's favorite food is (grilled fish seasoned with sweet soy sauce, sensible woman), where he works (some startup doing something too complicated for their own good), what Adi wants to be when he grows up (a physicist), and so on. She wishes she could help ease some of Riki's financial burden, but she can't think of a way to do so, aside from maybe robbing Winifred's silly bakery. But Winifred probably doesn't have twenty-five thousand dollars lying around.

"That was amazing," Sana says. Her hair is wind-blown and her cheeks are red from all the effort of carving the stick through moist sand. Riki gazes up at her with a tortured look that makes Vera roll her eyes. These young boys. Always with the drama.

Vera stands and squints into the distance, where Sana has been drawing. From here, she can't tell what Sana has drawn, but she can see the whorls spread across the sand in fluid strokes. She smiles at Sana. "Good, you can draw. Tomorrow morning you will come here and draw some more. I will bring Emma. And more food, of course."

For a moment, she thinks Sana might protest; young people always like to protest for the sake of protesting. But then a slow smile takes over Sana's flushed face, and for the first time since Vera has met Sana, she looks young, the way she should at her age. It's hope, Vera realizes, shining out of Sana's eyes like two bright stars. The sight of it makes Vera's heart swell. Sana will be okay. Then she glances at Riki and frowns, because he's standing there looking sorry, no doubt still wallowing in his guilt. Well, no matter. Riki will be okay too. Vera will see to that.

TWENTY-NINE

OLIVER

It's a beautiful Sunday morning, and Oliver can't think of anything better to do than spend it at Vera's teahouse with Julia and Emma. Okay, well, maybe it would be better if the teahouse weren't gouged to within an inch of its life. But he's having the best time climbing up ladders to install new lighting fixtures and having Emma standing on tiptoes, reaching up to hand him a new lightbulb while Julia rips down the crumbling posters. Oliver is in his element, years of what he'd considered useless work finally coming in handy. He not only fixes up the ancient electrics in the shop, but also rejiggers the plumbing to ensure that everything works smoothly. By the time he's done, although not much is visible on the surface, beneath that, Vera's teahouse is basically a new, young thing, ready to get to work. Already, thanks to his newly installed lighting, the shop is looking brighter, more vibrant. He can't wait for Vera to see how different a simple change in lighting can make a space look.

"Well!" Julia says, stepping back to admire their handiwork.

She's ripped down all the posters, most of which had been mold-ing, and the walls are now a dirty off-white with scraps of leftover posters here and there. Objectively, it looks awful. But because they've worked so hard on it, to Oliver, it looks like a space that's slowly coming back to life. "Pretty good," Julia says, echoing his thoughts.

He smiles at her and gives Emma a fist bump. "Vera men-tioned that Sana's a painter, so I think the wall painting can be her responsibility? What do you think?"

Julia grins. "Awesome idea. Yeah, I saw some of Sana's work; she's pretty freaking amazing."

"Sana draws birds," Emma says with quiet confidence. Yes-terday afternoon, Sana had come over for teatime with Vera and had apparently doodled with Emma while Julia did another pho-tography shoot.

"She does," Julia says. "And flowers, and people, and it all looks magical, doesn't it?"

Emma nods. "I drew a bird of parrot ties."

"Bird of parrot ties?" Oliver imagines Emma drawing two par-rots tied together.

"Paradise," Julia says.

"Ah." Oliver grins down at Emma. "That makes more sense. I would love to see that. You'll have to show me the next time we see each other."

"We'll see," Emma says, and turns her attention back to her fingers.

Coming from Emma, that's a pretty hopeful note to end on. Oliver looks around the shop. "Okay, Riki said he'll work on the furniture, I've fixed up the electrics and the plumbing, so . . ." He shoves his hands in his pockets, feeling suddenly awkward. "I guess that's that. There's not much for you and me to do for now." Part of him is aching because he doesn't want to leave the teahouse just yet, because leaving probably means him going in one direction and Julia and Emma going in the other.

He has no idea how to feel about their renewed friendship. Not just because of their history, but also because Vera has told him that Sana and Riki are no longer suspects, which leaves, uh, well, him and Julia. And as much as Oliver hates to think about it, can barely bear to see Julia in this way, he can't deny how strong she is underneath the broken layers, that the core of her is made of steel. If he'd been the one married to Marshall, would he not snap as well? Would he not plot a way to escape the toxic marriage? Sometimes, the suspicion hits him like a wave and leaves him shivering in its wake, not knowing where to cast his eye.

The silence is broken by Julia asking, "How's your dad doing?"

That catches him off guard. "I don't know," he admits finally. "I haven't seen him for a while now. I text him most mornings, but he rarely replies." Just saying those words makes Oliver realize what a terrible son he is. So what if he regularly drops off groceries at his dad's door? It's such a laughably small act, just a token gesture, really, more to do with making himself feel better than actually helping out his dad.

"Wanna go visit him?" Julia says. "I mean, his place isn't far away, and it might be nice . . ."

"Sure." Inside, Oliver is quivering with a series of nos. But somehow, his limbs move to leave the safe cocoon of Vera's shop.

Julia suggests that they pick up some groceries, as well as pastries for his dad, so they walk to Stockton Street, where Julia picks out the best produce, before they stop by a bakery, where the three of them sit around a small table and Emma digs into a pineapple bun that's as big as her face.

"I like pineapple buns," Emma declares in her surprisingly deep voice.

Oliver breaks into a grin as he gazes fondly at his little niece. How the hell did someone like Marshall help create this wonderful creature? For a fleeting moment, Oliver allows himself to imagine that he's out with his family, that Julia is his wife and Emma is his daughter. The shame comes in a jagged stab. God, that was a terrible thought to have, fantasizing about his dead brother's wife and child. He clears his throat and asks Julia how the photo editing is going.

Julia's whole face brightens up at the mention of it. "I've finished editing all Cassie's photos, and they look amazing! Twenty-seven good ones in total, out of over four hundred. You have to tell me what you think." She digs out her phone from her back pocket, locates the photos, and hands the phone to him.

Even back in high school, Oliver always knew that Julia had real talent. It was one of the things he was furious at Marshall about; he'd watched as Marshall gently coaxed Julia away from photography, and he'd told Marshall to quit it one day, which led to the two of them not speaking to each other for more than a month. He knows she has the talent, but even so, seeing the pictures of Cassie takes his breath away. Behind the camera, Julia turns into something else. Something that is part camera, part human. Somehow, she instinctively knows how to position her subjects to get the most dramatic angles, and how to manipulate the lighting to bring out their souls.

Although Oliver has never met Cassie or seen any of her videos, just from the photos that Julia took, he feels like he knows Cassie. He can practically hear her laughter—it would be full of life and have the slightest tone of bashfulness behind it. He can see the fire in Cassie's eyes, the determined set of her jawline, so artistically touched by the late Californian sunset.

"Holy shit," he says. "These are crazy good, Lia."

Julia rolls her eyes, biting back the smile. "Oh, stahp."

"I'm being serious. Have you sent them to her yet?"

"No. I'll do it tonight. I was kind of worried about them, I guess. I was procrastinating a little."

Oliver hands her the phone. "I don't know what you're worried about; these are mind-blowing. I promise you she's going to be so happy with these."

Julia pockets her phone with a smile. "Okay, dork. Thank you."

There is so much that Oliver wants to say. He wants to tell her how happy he is that she's picked up photography again. He wants to tell her that he's missed her. How he's longed to have her by his side. As a lover, yes, but most of all, as a friend. He's missed being able to chat with her over lunch, or on their walks to and from school. He still remembers the way Julia carried her backpack, with her thumbs tucked into the straps. He wants to tell her all these things, but he knows that none of them is appropriate, not under the circumstances. And he's so grateful for her company that he doesn't want to risk annoying her. So he simply nods.

When they're done, they pick up everything they've bought for Oliver's dad and walk over to his place. Oliver rings the buzzer, and when his dad's voice rasps out of it, Oliver says, "Hi, Baba, it's me. With Julia and Emma."

There is a pause, then his dad says, "I can't. Not today."

"But we got food for you." Oliver glances at Julia and Emma, hating the plummeting feeling in his stomach. He can't believe that his dad is refusing to see his own granddaughter. What the fuck is wrong with him? Sure, Oliver has always known that Marshall was his dad's favorite, but surely this is crossing the line. Emma is his only grandkid. Most grandparents would be rushing down the stairs and picking Emma up in a flying hug. Emma, too young to understand what's happening, is waving her index fingers like a tiny conductor and going, "Da-dee-da-dum," under her breath. Oliver looks at Julia helplessly. She shrugs, then leans over to speak into the buzzer.

"Hi, Baba," she calls out. "We'll just leave the food by the door, okay? You can come and get it whenever you like. And if you ever want some company, just give me or Ollie a call."

There is a long silence, and they place the shopping bags on the ground. They're about to leave when the speaker crackles to life. Oliver turns back quickly, expecting the buzzer to go off and the gate to unlock, but all Baba says is, "Don't come here again."

THIRTY

SANA

If anyone had told Sana that at the age of twenty-two, she'd be not only a CalArts dropout, but a CalArts dropout who draws almost exclusively on sand, she'd have curled up and sobbed at what a failure she's become. But the truth is, Sana can't remember the last time she's felt this happy about drawing.

Every morning at sunrise, she goes to Ocean Beach with her bamboo pole and there, next to the slow rush of the Pacific Ocean, she guides her stick across the sand, relishing the way it feels as she pulls and pushes and swipes. Sand is a whole new medium to work on, requiring so much focus on muscle control that Sana doesn't have the headspace to hesitate. She loves the soft, scratchy feel of the sand parting beneath her stick, the reassuring shh sound that every stroke makes. Even the way that the sand feels under her feet, between her toes, is a comfort, rooting her to the earth, connecting her to nature, and grounding the anxiety that has for so long fluttered through her whole being. For an hour or two each day, the rest of the world melts away, leaving just Sana, the bamboo pole, and the sand.

Then Vera and Emma arrive with Vera's trusty trolley bag and Sana waves at them, and a feeling of overflowing joy fills her chest as she watches the old woman and the little girl make their way across the beach toward her. She knows that Vera's trolley bag contains way too much food, and that Vera will be constantly nagging her about having a healthy breakfast before coming out here, and that Emma will take out a pair of wooden chopsticks and hand one stick to Sana and say, "Let's draw, Sana." And Vera will shoo the two of them away to draw while she lays out the picnic blanket and food herself.

Drawing in the sand on her own is cathartic, but drawing in the sand with Emma is a whole different experience. Emma's into anything half-mermaid, so Sana draws the top half of a horse, for example, and then Emma, very carefully, with the tip of her tongue sticking out, adds a mermaid tail to it. Emma's chubby fist is still lacking the fine motor skills required to draw well, so more often than not, she makes a mistake. Before Emma can get upset, Sana says, "That's a great line, Emms. Look, if I extended it just so . . . it turns into a star! Yes, this mer-horse has a star on its tummy, isn't that cute?" And somehow, in teaching Emma that flaws can be turned into something unique and beautiful, Sana, too, begins to heal.

Then Vera calls out to them, and they retreat to the picnic blanket and eat Vera's food, which is, as always, too delicious to not finish. Sometimes, Julia joins them, but more often these days, Julia is busy shooting portraits. As Sana predicted, Cassie the TikTok influencer was blown away by her headshots and raved about Julia to her fans, which has resulted in Julia getting more and more bookings.

Once, as Sana is drawing in the sand with Emma, she looks up and notices a figure in the distance, just standing there. Is the stranger watching them? From this distance, Sana can't be sure, but from the way they stand, unmoving, Sana would bet money that their eyes are on Emma. It makes Sana feel uneasy, and when she raises her arm and waves, the figure hurries away. Her stomach tightens. "Vera," Sana calls out. "Did you see that person standing there watching us?"

Vera, of course, is way too busy unpacking her food. "What person?"

Sana hesitates, then says, "Probably just a beachgoer." She must have imagined it because of course she can't quite figure out how to exist without any drama in her life.

The truth is, Sana doesn't quite know how to feel about this newfound peace. It's ironic because Marshall is still very dead, and Vera is still openly suspecting Oliver and Julia, and yet they're all falling into a deep friendship with one another and it's very confusing. Sometimes, she finds herself wondering what kind of bizarre life she's stumbled into where there is an unsolved death that is maybe probably murder, plus a very mysterious break-in during which nothing was stolen. Speaking of the break-in, Vera has predicted that the cops will likely come to no conclusion simply because nothing was taken. And so far, she's been right. Part of Sana is still jumpy, awaiting the cops' arrival any day now, denouncing one of them as a killer/burglar, but the days pass and still there are no new developments.

Today, though, Sana has told Vera not to come to the beach in the morning because Sana is going for a hike in Muir Woods. What she fails to tell Vera is that she's going on said hike with Riki. Oh, Sana can just imagine the smug, gleeful look that Vera would no doubt have if she were to ever find out about this.

At around seven thirty in the morning, Riki picks up Sana and her sandy bamboo pole from Ocean Beach. She does her best to wipe down the pole before putting it in the trunk of his car, feeling strangely nervous for the first time, very much aware that they're not meeting up to discuss Marshall's case or Vera or anything. For the first time, they're getting together to simply spend time with each other, and what a strange and wonderful feeling that realization is. She can barely hold back the smile as she slides into the passenger seat.

"Hey," Riki says, grinning just as wide as she is. "Did you have a good drawing session?"

"Yeah, it was really good. Gets better by the day." Sana squeezes her lips together in an effort to keep herself from smiling idiotically, but nope, as soon as she lets go, her mouth springs back into a smile. *Damn it. Play it cool, please.* She can't help but notice the way that Riki drives—one hand on the wheel, other elbow resting on the open window of his door. Kind of really hot.

"How was your morning?" she says, trying to distract herself from admiring Riki.

"Well, it just started, honestly." He laughs a little. "I like to get my beauty sleep on the weekends, you know. So I basically got up, like, twenty minutes ago and came to get you."

God, even the way he says "came to get you" is somehow really hot.

This early on a Saturday morning, there isn't much traffic, and before long, they're on the Golden Gate Bridge. Sana gazes out the window as they go across the iconic bridge, taking in everything around her, trying to sear every detail into her memory. She used to look at things this way, seeing the artistry in everything, but Marshall's theft stole that joy from her for so long. And now, she is once again noticing the beauty of her surroundings, and she almost cries with the sheer, unending joy of it. How insanely gorgeous is this city? How has it taken her this long to notice it? She'd come here on a trip for vengeance and had completely failed to notice the colors around her. It's hard to describe the overwhelming hugeness of the Golden Gate Bridge. In photos where the whole bridge is visible, it looks almost like a toy. But in real life, each beam is impossibly tall and wide, spearing through the sky, and Sana feels that yearning again, the one she's lost for so long now, to create something beautiful and otherworldly.

By the time they get to Muir Woods, Sana's entire being is buzzing with possibility, with a newfound excitement for life. She gets out of the car and stretches, breathing in the clean, woody scent of the national park. Riki takes out a backpack from the back and then the two of them begin their trek. The conversation flows smoothly, effortlessly.

"I can't believe how huge redwoods get."

"Seriously. The cross section is bigger than my whole apartment," Riki says dryly.

Sana laughs. "Did you used to hike back in Indonesia?"

"Yeah, actually. There's a place, Bogor, which is about two hours away from Jakarta. I used to drive there with my little brother, and we'd hike up the hills to where they have those stepped rice fields, and then we'd swim in the river. Indonesia's hot and humid, so by the time we got to the river, we'd be so sweaty, and the cold water feels amazing."

"Wow, that sounds like an incredible hike."

"It is. Maybe one day I can take you." Riki seems to realize what he's just said entails Sana traveling internationally and his cheeks and the tips of his ears and the back of his neck turn bright red. "Um, you know, if you happen to be in the area."

Sana is not above delighting in his bashfulness. "Oh, you mean, if I just happen to be in Indonesia for some random reason?"

Riki shrugs, fighting back a smile. "Yeah, some random reason."

"I like how you've invited me to Indonesia on our first date."

Riki raises his eyebrows and looks at her innocently. "Wait, is this a date? I didn't know that, but okay."

Sana hits his shoulder, and the two of them laugh and walk deeper into the rich darkness of the woods. She can't remember the last time she made such a strong connection with a guy. Back at CalArts, all the other students had been so wrapped up in their art, each one secretly convinced that they were geniuses while at the same time fearful they might be found out as talentless frauds. She could never date another artist. No, what she needs is someone like Riki, uncomplicated and down-to-earth. Someone who calms her soul.

After a couple of hours or so, they pause to have some food. Riki's brought some cheese and bread and a nut mix. "I made it myself," he says as he pours the nuts into a bowl. "Almonds, cashews, peanuts, pumpkin seeds, roasted with some honey and sea salt."

"Lucky I don't have a nut allergy," Sana says, popping some in her mouth. The mention of "allergy" brings Marshall unexpectedly to her mind, and her mouth feels dry at the thought.

Riki must have thought the same thing, because his expression has turned somber.

Sana takes a gulp of water and sighs. "The whole thing with

Marshall . . . I still can't believe how everything went down. It's been a crazy few weeks, huh?"

"Yeah. And after all that, he died from a bird allergy. I mean, how weird is that, right?"

"For reals." Sana hesitates. "So do you think Vera's right? That somebody killed him?"

For a long moment, Riki doesn't say anything as he stares into the distance. "I really can't say."

"I mean, there was the break-in, which is too much of a coincidence, so it must be related to Marshall's death, which means he was definitely killed, right?"

"I guess, but nothing was taken. The police haven't found any evidence or anything, so I have no idea what to think."

Sana gnaws on her bottom lip. "Do you . . ." She hesitates, grimacing, then goes for it. "Do you think maybe Oliver did it? He was the only one who knew about the bird dander allergy."

"True, but maybe Julia knew too? She was married to Marshall, so she could've very well known. It's the kind of thing you'd tell your spouse, right?"

"Good point." Sana sighs. "I hate to think of either of them as the killer, though."

"Same here. You know, for a while there, I thought I—" His voice wobbles, but he takes a breath and continues. "I thought I'd done it. I punched him the night he died, and I thought that maybe . . ."

Sana's guts twist painfully. "That's a terrible burden to have to bear."

Riki nods, then he laughs. "Yeah, well, as Vera said, she could've told me that it wasn't possible because my arms are apparently too noodly to kill someone with a single punch."

"Oh my god, that is so Vera." Sana chuckles. Too easy to picture Vera saying that. "I also thought I might have had something to do with it too, for a while. That day he died, I'd gone to see him and I scratched him on the cheek. I've never attacked anyone like that before. I was so horrified—"

"Same here," Riki says, compassion thick in his voice. He reaches out and places his hand on top of Sana's, and the warmth of it calms her harried thoughts. "He had a way of bringing out the worst in people, didn't he?"

Sana nods. "I think that was what hurt so much. That it was the moment I realized that the world is cruel, and I felt so stupid for not realizing it sooner, because, duh, how obvious is that? And I felt like it was more my fault than anyone else's. That people like Marshall are always going to exist and always do what they do and it's my responsibility to protect myself, you know? I felt so ashamed to have fallen for his scam."

"I'm sorry," Riki murmurs, casting his eyes down.

Is it just Sana's imagination or does he look incredibly sad? Her chest tightens and she squeezes his hand. "Hey," she says, gently, "it's not your fault. He did the same thing to you."

"Yeah, but—" Riki bites his lip, like he's struggling for the right words, and something about this moment, when they are both being so sincere and exposing their wounds to each other, touches Sana's heart.

Without thinking twice, Sana leans over, closing the space between them, and pushes her lips against Riki's in a soft, sweet kiss. Whatever Riki was about to say is immediately forgotten as his hands go to Sana's back and he pulls her closer to him, both of them losing themselves in this single perfect moment.

THIRTY-ONE

JULIA

Julia still finds it hard to believe her eyes whenever she opens up her spreadsheet. Her spreadsheet. Yep, she's one of those people with a spreadsheet now, a spreadsheet filled with the names of clients. Julia hasn't been able to stop saying "spreadsheet." She says it at least seven times a day. "Oh, let me add that to my spreadsheet." and "Let me check my spreadsheet."

Julia's also got a calendar, oh yeah, she's real fancy now. A calendar that is shockingly filling up really fast, and not just with things like "Get Emma's favorite cereal," but with appointments like "April Woolson—maternity shoot," and "Heather + Rikuto—engagement shoot." Every time she gets a new booking, Julia skips to her computer and adds it to her calendar, and Vera breathes down her neck, squinting at the screen, and tells her, "You need to charge more. Rule of the thumb: Increase your price after every three appointment."

Julia stares at her in horror. "What? I can't do that; that's not ethical."

"Hah! Of course it is. Is not price gouging, is respecting your-self as photographer." Vera stabs a finger into Julia's chest. "Do you think you improve with every session?"

"Well, yes, of course, but—"

"So after three session, are you the same photographer as be-fore? You remain stagnant?"

"Well, no, but—"

"So then why your price remain stagnant?"

After a few moments of stunned silence, Julia admits to herself that Vera does make sense. And the real reason why she hasn't increased her prices isn't a business decision; it's more a decision made from a lack of self-confidence. And so she does what Vera says, increasing her fees by ten percent after every three bookings. And she's at eleven bookings right now, just mere weeks after she did Cassie's headshots! Some days, Julia still pinches herself, not daring to believe her good luck.

"Is not good luck," Vera snaps when Julia makes the mistake of mentioning it in passing. "No such thing as good luck in busi-ness. You make your own luck."

True, but Julia is grateful anyway for the opportunity to have worked with Cassie. Although Cassie's platform is far from viral, the TikToker is a hard worker, posting three to five videos every day. Each time Julia checks on Cassie's profile, the follower count continues to grow. And Cassie convinced Julia to create a TikTok account as well as an Instagram account before she posted her headshots and tagged Julia with a rave review. That post alone scored Julia three more customers, and the three customers had spread the word on their TikToks, which led to even more busi-ness. Sometimes, Julia wonders if she's accidentally stumbled into someone else's life.

Even Emma is different. She's still somber, but she's no longer as clingy. She doesn't even ask to nurse in the daytime anymore, only at night before she goes to bed, which Julia is absolutely fine with. In fact, Julia loves that she still gets to cradle her little girl at night and feel her warm little body smushed up against her own. But other than that, Emma has stopped wrapping her limbs around Julia and clinging to her like a little baby koala all the time, and it has been incredibly freeing for the two of them.

Julia's income from the shoots is still not enough to cover the mortgage payment; it's more than likely that Julia will have to downsize at some point. She doesn't mind. The house is nothing but a reminder of the life she had under Marshall's thumb. The thought of moving overwhelms her, though, and so she's still pro-crastinating over putting the house up for sale and looking for a smaller place to move to.

This afternoon, as Vera takes Emma to the park and Julia edits the photos from her last shoot at the dining table, she thinks she hears a noise from the back of the house.

Probably the wind, she thinks, and goes back to playing around with the exposure of the photo. But no, there's a clatter and a creak. The hairs on her arms stand on end, her ears pricking up. Someone's inside the house. Her throat goes painfully dry and her palms are somehow sweaty already, and she hasn't even gotten up from her seat yet. Julia stands slowly, careful not to push her chair back so it won't scrape against the wood floor. She casts about the dining room for anything that might serve as a weapon and picks up a decorative vase from a side table. Breathing unsteadily, Julia steps out of the dining room and down the hallway.

The hallway has never seemed so dark and so ominous before now. Julia feels light-headed, like she might faint, but somehow, she continues stepping forward, gripping the vase with her sweaty palms. One of the floorboards creaks and she freezes, her breath caught in her throat. From the master bedroom, she thinks she can hear the sound of someone freezing as well, if such a thing could make a sound. Or rather, the absence of sound, like a breath being held, and eyes opened wide with expectation and fear.

The tension builds until it overwhelms her and her instincts make a snap decision, propelling her forward. She charges down the rest of the hallway, the vase raised, ready for battle, and explodes into the master bedroom with ferocious strength.

There's nobody there. A shocked laugh coughs out of her mouth and she sags against the wall, her chest still thumping, the rest of her body shivery with adrenaline. Of course there's no one here. What is wrong with her? She releases her breath and plops down at the foot of the bed, focusing on restoring her breath. It will make for a very funny dinner story, at least.

Then she notices that the window is wide open, and her self-effacing laughter catches in her throat. Vera has taken over the master bedroom for weeks now, and Vera likes leaving the window open just a crack, enough to have some air circulation, but not so much that she can hear the neighbor's terrier yipping at squirrels. But now the window is fully open, the sheer curtains billowing from a breeze that chills Julia to her bones. Wrapping her arms around her body, Julia strides to the window and slams it shut. Vera must have opened it this morning, Julia tells herself. That's the likeliest explanation. She forces herself to take a deep breath and release it. Everything is fine. Everything is—

Her gaze falls on a stack of papers in the middle of the bed. Frowning, Julia walks to the bed and picks up the papers. On the first page are the words:

UNTITLED MANUSCRIPT
Oliver R. Chen

Whoa, okay. So she has in her hands Oliver's manuscript. She remembers now how, back in high school, Oliver was always scribbling in his notebook. On the weekends, they often took the tram around SF and got out at random stops. Oliver would find a bench to sit on and write while Julia roamed about taking photos, and then they'd hop on the tram again until the next stop. He never showed her what he was writing, promising that he'd show her when he was done. But then she started dating Marshall, and the idyllic weekends with Oliver stopped completely, and after a while, Julia forgot about Oliver's notebook.

She should probably respect Oliver's privacy and put this back on the bed. But even as Julia thinks this, curiosity overwhelms her. She's so happy to know that all these years later, Oliver is still writing. A peek wouldn't hurt, would it? She sits down in an armchair and flips to the first page.

David never asked to be Randall's younger brother. A twin, no less. Few things in life are as cursed as being the inferior twin. Even when they were little, it was obvious that David was the poor man's version, the knockoff of Randall. Where Randall was active and boisterous in that charming way that kids often are, David was so shy he found it hard to even say hi to people. Their parents were always apologizing on David's behalf. "Sorry, he's shy." "Sorry, he doesn't like strangers." Meanwhile, Randall would give his trademark gap-toothed grin and everyone would go, "Aww," and forget David's existence. Which was how he liked it, anyway.

Until he met Aurelia. He fell in love with her at first sight.
How could he not? Never before had he come across anyone
like her.

Julia feels the floor falling away from her. What the hell? What the—

Everything from her past comes flooding back to her mind. How close she'd been to Oliver, how he had been her best friend for so long. How she would often see him looking at her in a way that made her stomach feel funny. How the hell did she not realize that Oliver had feelings for her? In hindsight, she realizes nothing could've been more obvious.

Her mind goes forward, to how Oliver simply stopped being her friend when she started dating Marshall. Was it because he was mad at her? For not returning his feelings? Anger surges through her. How was she supposed to guess that he was in love with her? He never showed it, never tried making a move or anything. Over time she'd started seeing him as almost a brother, and to now find out that he'd been harboring these feelings for her all this time is a bit of a betrayal. And to abandon her as a friend just like that, no explanations given, like this whole time, their friendship was merely him trying to get into her pants and then giving up when he realized that his brother had gotten there first.

Marshall had always known, of course. He'd made all these snide remarks about how Oliver was her pathetic little servant. But she'd dismissed all these comments as harmless brotherly jokes. God, she was so stupid. By the time she realized that nothing about Marshall was harmless, it had been too late. She'd been broken by then, her internal compass whirring madly, unable to tell what was right and wrong. All of it, in the end, had been decided by Marshall. Who was stupid, who was worthless, who was worth their time.

She flips through the next few pages, skimming the words with increasing horror.

> *How much he loves her, everything about her . . .*
> *But of course, because David is cursed, because David is the lesser catch, all she has eyes for is Randall . . .*
> *Randall would often look over his shoulder as he walked with Aurelia, and, catching David's eye in the distance, Randall would then smirk and raise his hand in a small wave. Aurelia never noticed the way Randall would squeeze her waist, as if to remind David that she now belonged to Randall. Just like everything else . . .*

Julia wants to vomit. The way Oliver has written about her makes her feel so dirty and so small, like an inconsequential object. Is this really how he's seen her all this time? And why he's come back into her life now, after Marshall is gone? Does he see this as his chance to get a shot at having a life with her? And where does Emma fit in with his messed-up fantasy? She flips forward.

> *He sits in the dark and clicks through their photos, the perfect family. How painful that because he and Randall are twins, Randall and Aurelia's child looks like he could be David's. That same smile that goes ever so slightly higher on the right cheek, the way the eyebrows turn up like so . . .*

Oh god. So he's fantasized about Emma being his daughter. God, this is horrifying. Julia doesn't know what to do. She wants to stop reading, but she can't. Her fingers keep moving, keep flipping the pages, and she only realizes what she's looking for when she finds it.

"You're so fucking pathetic," Randall spits at David.

"Pathetic." The word that has haunted him his entire life. He looks at Randall without speaking, without doing anything, and as Randall laughs, David comes to a decision. He's going to end Randall. He doesn't know how yet, but he'll find a way.

The doorbell rings then, and a choked gasp claws out of Julia. She actually screams a little, jumping to her feet, blood rushing to her head. Her heart is pumping so hard and fast that it sounds like drums being beaten right inside her ears. The bell rings again. Shit, who is it? Oliver? Did she ask him to come by today? She's hurrying down the hallway when she realizes that she's still grasping the manuscript. She puts it on the sofa and places a cushion over it, then goes to the door, still breathing hard. She looks through the peephole, and oh god. It's not Oliver. It's Officer Gray. She can't actually decide whom she's more afraid of right now. Forcing herself to take a deep breath and plastering a smile on her face, Julia opens the door.

"Hi, Officer Gray," she says brightly. "What brings you here?"

"Can I come in?" Officer Gray says.

"Oh, um, sure." Julia ushers the officer into the living room, where she is painfully aware that Oliver's manuscript is hiding under the cushion. She gestures for Officer Gray to sit in a spot as far away from the manuscript as possible. "What can I do for you?"

"I won't take up too much of your time," Officer Gray says. "I was looking into your husband's death, you know, just crossing our t's and dotting our i's, when I noticed that you are due for a rather large insurance payout due to his passing."

"Wait, what?" The noise that has thus far been screaming in Julia's head grinds to a deafening halt. Life insurance? Then, belatedly, she recalls bits and pieces of it. "Oh," she says stupidly. That's right, when Emma was newly born, Julia had looked into her tiny sleeping face and was gripped in a fear so visceral that she'd marched straight to Marshall and told him that they had to take out life insurance. In case anything were to happen to them, she wanted assurance that their beautiful, perfect baby would be okay. It was the only time that Julia had put her foot down on something, and her fierce determination had taken Marshall so aback that he'd agreed to it without as much of a fight as she'd been expecting. They'd taken out a humble package, paying just thirty dollars a month for the two of them, and over time, because Marshall took care of all the bills, Julia had forgotten about it entirely.

And now here it is, come back to bite her in the ass.

"You're due to receive"—Officer Gray checks her notes and raises her eyebrows—"no less than seven hundred thousand dollars. That's quite the payout."

Seven hundred grand. That's life-changing money. She could pay off the house and still have enough left over to put into Emma's college fund, plus it would tide them over nicely until she gets her photography business set up.

Shit, she shouldn't already be planning how to spend the money now, with Officer Gray literally sitting right across from her, staring at her with that suspicious look. And who can blame Officer Gray? This is shady as shit! Her husband dies under strange circumstances and she gets seven hundred grand? No prizes for guessing who had motivation to kill him. Julia strives to come up with something appropriate to say, but what the hell is appropriate right now?

Officer Gray isn't done. "I spoke to your neighbors. They said they heard shouts on the evening that Marshall died. Angry shouts. They said they heard you crying and Marshall shouting?"

Her neighbors? Julia doesn't even know their names. Aside from Linda, that is. Marshall always told her to not get sucked into "housewife drama," and so she never bothered to show up at neighborhood gatherings. But apparently just because she's been unaware of their existence, that doesn't mean they've been unaware of hers. Bitterness sears her belly. What a sneaky thing to do, talking to the cops about her and Marshall. The logical side of her reminds her that if a cop had turned up at her house asking about her neighbor's death, she would probably try her best to be cooperative. But logic is trumped by the white-hot combination of fear and anger raging inside her.

"When we first came to your house," Officer Gray continues, "I noticed trash bags behind the door. Quite a few of them. What was in them?"

Julia has watched enough spy movies to fool herself into thinking that lying under duress is easy. But now, actually having a police officer asking her these things, she finds that she doesn't have what it takes to tell a convincing lie. Her mouth opens and she hears the truth flopping out of her like a dead fish. "Marshall's things."

Officer Gray raises her eyebrows, but it's obvious she's not surprised in the least bit by this answer. "Care to expand on that?"

Julia swallows. "He was leaving me." Her voice is soft to begin with, tinged with shame, but the more she talks, the stronger it gets, shame giving way to anger. "He said he was finally about to make it big and he didn't want to have to split the payoff with me because I had nothing to do with his success. Ten years we've been married and we have a beautiful daughter, but none of it meant anything to him. He walked out the door as I cried."

Officer Gray nods. "Then what did you do?"

Julia shakes her head, sighing. "I don't know, I . . . oh, Emma was crying too, so I comforted her and she fell asleep. Then I called his dad. I told him what had happened. I just had to tell someone, you know? I mean, I was a mess. Then I packed all of his things up. I was still bawling. I thought maybe I'd throw them in the trash or burn them, I don't know, but by the time I was done, I was too exhausted to do anything with them, and Emma had woken up from her nap, so I had to look after her. In the morning, what had happened seemed so surreal. I guess I was still hoping that he'd come back; that's why I didn't throw away his things. Then you came by and told me he'd died . . ."

"Hmm." Officer Gray is still watching Julia closely, and Julia can't tell what's going through the cop's mind. Does she believe what Julia just told her? It does sound ridiculous, even to Julia's own ears. "And where were you the night that Vera's teahouse was broken into?"

Julia is grasping at straws. "I—well, here! I have a toddler. I'm here every freaking night, okay?" Oh god, she hadn't meant to lose her temper like that. "I know how bad this looks—" Julia says, shifting uncomfortably, and her elbow knocks against the cushion next to her. The cushion covering Oliver's manuscript. Her eyes dart to the manuscript and quickly back to Officer Gray's face, and something in Julia's expression must have betrayed her, because Officer Gray practically pounces on the manuscript.

"What's this?"

"Oh, it's just—"

Officer Gray turns the manuscript pages with interest. "Huh. Oliver Chen. That's Marshall's twin brother, isn't it? He's a writer? He give this to you?"

"Ah—" Julia tries to think of something to say. But what? She doesn't even really know what she should say here. She's so incredibly furious at Oliver, yes, but she's not sure if she should be telling Officer Gray anything, not until she's fully figured out what the hell really happened. But now it's out of her hands, literally, and in Officer Gray's. "I found it here. He must've given it to Vera. Or maybe Vera took it herself, I don't know. I think it's just some made-up boring story." She gives the world's fakest laugh and reaches for the manuscript, but Officer Gray holds it out of reach.

"If you don't mind, I'd like to borrow this for a bit. I like to do a bit of reading now and again. Take a break from social media."

No, no!

But all Julia can do is sit there with her stupid fake smile. It's only after Officer Gray leaves that Julia speaks again. Just a single word, with a whole world of frustration behind it.

"Shit!"

THIRTY-TWO

VERA

Emma wakes up at five every morning, no matter how late she goes to bed, which suits Vera just fine. Finally, someone who shares her sensibilities of waking up early enough to seize the day! So, every morning, it is just her and Emma in a quiet, slumbering world. They move through the house slowly, their socked feet padding gently on the floors so as not to wake up Julia. Vera wipes the sleep away from Emma's face with a damp towel and hands her a toothbrush. While Emma brushes her teeth, Vera serves out the congee she's cooked earlier. The two of them have a quiet breakfast as they slowly wake up, then she takes Emma on her morning walk. Emma has adopted Vera's way of walking—elbows out, chin up, brisk tempo. Vera doesn't remember the last time she loved anyone the way she loves Emma.

Today, as on many days, they spend the morning drawing on the beach with Sana, whom Emma loves because Sana is always ready with tickles and kisses and fanciful doodles of mer-animals. Then Vera takes Emma to Chinatown, where they shop for groceries as usual. Emma asks Vera if they can stop by her teahouse, but Vera shakes her head; the last time she was there, the teahouse had been smashed beyond recognition, and she didn't want to ruin the lovely day by seeing the ghost of her past. A sense of dread gnaws at Vera; she knows that one day she will have to go back home. She is merely a guest at Julia's, nothing more. But she'd like to push that day back as much as she can—is that such a bad thing? She does, however, stop by Alex's house, but nobody answers the buzzer when she rings it and tells him it's her. Maybe he went out for a walk. Poor Alex. Vera hopes he's doing okay without their daily morning chats. She takes out a bag full of specially prepared tea mixes and hangs it at the gate. The bag has a note attached to it that says:

> *THIS FOR ALEX, APARTMENT THREE D.*
> *DO NOT TAKE IF YOU ARE NOT ALEX!!!*

Then off they go to the tram station and back to Laurel Heights. By the time they get off at their stop and begin the walk back to the house, Emma is visibly wilting, her steps meandering and her eyes fighting to stay open. Vera urges her on, feeling guilty that she didn't have the foresight to stop for a snack or a rest. Luckily, they make it back to the house before Emma reaches the point where she breaks down and demands to be carried. Vera unlocks the door with a sigh of relief, saying, "Come, we go inside and get you to bed. Oh, hi, Julia, we—"

She stops when she sees Julia's expression. The last time Vera saw that expression on Julia's face was the first time Vera laid eyes on her—looking frightened and lost outside Vera's teahouse. Instinct overtakes Vera and she gestures to Emma. "Here, you put

Emma down for her nap, and I will put away groceries; then we will talk."

Julia nods, bending over to pick up the already half-asleep toddler in her arms, kissing the top of Emma's head as she does so. "Oh, baby," she whispers to Emma. Emma's head droops on Julia's shoulder and Julia doesn't stop kissing it even as she walks down the hallway toward Emma's room.

Vera tidies away the groceries into the fridge, her mind racing. What could possibly have upset Julia like that? It must have something to do with Marshall. A million possibilities zip through her mind. Maybe Julia found out something about his murder. Maybe Julia is finally ready to confess to his murder! Oh, such an unlucky thought. Vera still hasn't removed Julia and Oliver from her suspects list, but she doesn't like to think of the possibility that either one might be responsible for Marshall's death. *Tch*, she tuts to herself. *And here you are, comparing yourself to the likes of Sherlock Holmes. What rubbish.*

She's in the midst of washing her hands when Julia creeps back to the kitchen.

"She went out like a light," Julia says with a weak smile. "You guys must've had quite the day."

"Oh yes, we are always having adventures." Vera wipes her hands dry and turns off the kettle, which is just about to boil. She takes out two of her specially made sachets from a canister and pours out two cups of tea. Hot tea in hand, the two women walk into the dining room. "So," Vera says, "it seems like maybe you also have an adventure?"

Julia closes her eyes and breathes out. "I don't even know where to begin. Officer Gray stopped by today. Apparently, Marshall's death is about to make me rich." She gives a laugh that has no humor in it. "Which of course makes me seem suspicious as hell."

"Oh? Why rich?" Vera takes a sip of the tea and sighs at it warms her up. It's one of her favorite combinations: candied winter melon peel with burnt rice—it tastes of caramel, rich and earthy.

"We both took out life insurance a few years ago. Anyway, while we were talking, Officer Gray noticed a manuscript." Julia shifts in her seat, her eyes drilling into Vera's. "Do you know anything about that? It's written by Oliver. I found it in your room. I wasn't snooping," she adds quickly. "I heard a noise from the bedroom, so I went to check, and that was when I found his manuscript."

"Oh yes, I have been reading it. But to be honest, I find it a bit slow, so it takes me a bit longer to read it."

Julia gnaws on her bottom lip. "And do you not find it suspicious? He wrote about two brothers who like the same girl and how one of them wants to 'take care of it'?"

Vera frowns. "Oh my, you read so fast! I think you overtake me already. You say you only find it today? How do you read so fast?"

"Vera," Julia says, sighing, "that doesn't matter. I skimmed it. Anyway—"

"Oh. You don't get much enjoyment if you do that. It will spoil the book for you."

"Oh my god, who cares about the book?" Julia says. "I'm telling you, there's something really wrong here. Oliver has been in love with me ever since we were teens!"

Vera's eyes widen, her mouth forming an O. *Oho! Now we're getting somewhere.* She claps. "Oh, that is very romantic."

"No!" Julia cries. "No, it's messed up is what it is. Like, he's been obsessed with me forever, and then he writes a whole book about it, and in the book his character snaps and decides to do something to Marshall. Vera, I think Oliver might have killed Marshall!"

Vera's mouth snaps shut. On the one hand, she's disappointed that it seems like a romance between Oliver and Julia might not be forthcoming after all. On the other hand, this is the first real lead she's had in a long while. And on the other, other hand, Vera is slightly annoyed that Julia has gone and skimmed through Oliver's book. That's taking a shortcut, and Vera does not believe in taking shortcuts because it's just another form of cheating. Harrumph. Also, Vera has been enjoying the gentle pace at which she is doing her investigation, and now Julia is forcing them to go in the fast lane. And another also, Julia has spoiled Oliver's book for Vera!

Still, Vera is nothing if not adaptable. She has been presented with new information, whether or not she likes it, and it does seem as though Oliver is the likeliest culprit. But then again, Julia herself has just admitted that she is about to become rich due to Marshall's death, so surely Vera can't take Julia off the suspects list yet? Although presumably if Julia had indeed killed Marshall to get the insurance money, then she wouldn't have told Vera about the windfall? Or maybe she did it to trick Vera into thinking that she wouldn't have told Vera if—oh, for god's sake. This is much too convoluted. Vera always lived by the belief that life would be much simpler if everyone simply said what they were thinking instead of beating about the bush.

What would Sherlock Holmes do? The answer to that is strikingly obvious. He would gather all the suspects in a single room, and he would share with them his theory, starting from the very top, crossing out suspects one by one until he came to the last remaining possibility. Upon which he would very dramatically ex-

plain why the murder could only have been carried out by . . .
drumroll *this person.*

Vera only has a vague theory for now, and that vague theory
may be jumbled and colored by her growing affection for everyone
involved, but she's not about to let it stop her. And anyway, isn't
this how young people are told to live their lives now? To fake it
until they make it? She's going to do just that. She will fake it even
better than a mediocre man interviewing for a job he's not quali-
fied for. Oh yes. And while she theorizes, she will be watching her
suspects very, very closely to see their reactions. By the time she's
done, she's sure she will have figured out who is the real killer.

Filled with renewed confidence, Vera lifts her chin. "I know
exactly what we need to do."

"You do?" Julia says, her eyes wide with hope.

"We will have a dinner party."

YOU ARE CORDIALLY INVITED TO:
An Evening with Vera Wong
World-Famous Tea Connoisseur
Novice Sleuth

THEME:
All Shall Be Revealed

DRESS CODE:
Black Tie

ENTERTAINMENT WILL BE PROVIDED.
This invitation is valid for one person only.
Do not bring a plus one.

THIRTY-THREE

OLIVER

Oliver stares with mild amusement at the invitation on his phone. He has no idea what to make of it, but over the past few weeks, Vera has wormed her way into his and everyone else's lives, and to be honest, he does not hate it. And a formal dinner at Julia's sounds far preferable to yet another evening spent alone in his apartment being harassed by 3B yet again for some other inane reason. Gosh, does his suit even still fit him? The last time Oliver wore it had been to—ugh—Marshall and Julia's wedding.

With a deep breath, he goes into his bedroom to root through his closet for his nice suit. He's still rooting around in the depths of his closet when someone knocks on his front door. Immediately, Oliver knows something is wrong. It's not the kind of knock that a neighbor asking for help with the plumbing or electricity might make. This knock is a demand to open up right this minute, before they decide to go from knocking to kicking down the door. Oliver hurries to the door, and the moment he opens it, his world falls apart.

A piece of paper is shoved in his face and Officer Gray says, "Oliver Chen, here's a warrant to search your premises. Please step aside."

Someone pushes Oliver gently but firmly to one side, and he watches, dazed, as police officers swarm into his tiny apartment. "Wha—" he hears himself mumble, but no other words come out. Within the cramped space of his living room, the cops seem enormous, their bulk overwhelming, their presence sucking the very air from the atmosphere until Oliver is struggling to catch his breath. Oh god, he's about to have a panic attack. Someone is speaking to him.

"Breathe. Count from ten to one."

He does so, focusing on his breath as the cops ransack his living space, turning over everything from the sofa to the ancient rug, picking up books and sifting through every cupboard. Every photo frame is picked up and inspected, even the ones hanging on the wall. "But—" Oliver gasps, but his breath runs out once more. He feels dizzy. He has to sit down. He stumbles out into the hallway and finds to his horror his neighbors peering out of their units. This is horrifying. It's humiliating. He stumbles back inside.

"While my colleagues are doing this, I suggest you come down to the station to chat with us, Mr. Chen," Officer Gray says.

"Wh-why?"

"We have a few questions we'd like to ask you about the death of your brother."

Oliver can barely process the words. "I don't understand. You said it was an accident."

"We're still reviewing evidence." She gestures at him to follow her, and he does, numbly, quietly, obediently. Because that's just what Oliver is, isn't it? Obedient. Pathetic.

He doesn't meet anyone's eyes as he shuffles down the hallway. He wishes he could be the type of person who'd bark, *The fuck you looking at?* But no. He's Oliver Chen, meek and mild, human doormat.

Officer Gray does him the courtesy of not taking him by the arm or pushing his head down as he gets into her car. Maybe they only do that in the movies. Or maybe she senses that there is no fight inside Oliver. They are silent as she drives to the station, and silent still when they arrive and walk through the lobby, where she signs into an interview room. After the chaos at his apartment and the bustle of the station, the silence in the interview room is deafening.

Officer Gray gestures for Oliver to take a seat before sitting across from him. She turns on a speaker and says, "This is Officer Selena Gray, conducting an interview with Oliver Chen. Mr. Chen has come here voluntarily. Are you okay for our interview to be recorded?"

Oliver nods.

"You have to say it so we have a record of it."

"Oh, right. Yes. I'm okay."

"And you have the right to have an attorney present."

Oliver gapes at her. "Do I . . . need one?"

"Well, we're not charging you with anything, but you can choose to have one."

Oliver's brains might as well be made of scrambled eggs. What does Officer Gray mean? Should he have one? Would that only make him look guilty? "Uh. I guess I'm okay for now." Is he okay for now?

"All right. So let's begin. Where were you on the night that Marshall Chen died?"

"Um, I was at home. Um. I was just watching Netflix."

Officer Gray makes a note in her notepad. "What show?"

"Uh." It's a struggle to remember. "*Narcos.*"

"Good choice. Tell me more about Marshall. He was your twin brother. You two close?"

Oliver shakes his head. "Not really. We only ever really see each other once or twice a year."

"That's rare, isn't it? Aren't twins usually pretty close to each other?"

"I . . ." Oliver shrugs. "I don't know, but we've never been close, even as kids."

"But you were close enough to know that he was very allergic to bird dander, though."

"Wh—" Oliver opens and closes his mouth. "Um, yeah? But." But what?

Officer Gray lets the moment stretch on and on until it becomes painful, then she launches into the next question, which turns out to be even worse somehow. "Would you say you disliked each other?"

Oliver opens his mouth, then hesitates. "Uh, I mean, that's a pretty strong statement." Can she tell that he's lying? Is his guilt written all over his face? Can she tell that he absolutely hated Marshall, hated everything that made Marshall who he was?

"I talked to a few of your mutuals, and they all said there was no love lost between you and Marshall."

Their mutuals? Who the hell are their mutuals? Oliver and Marshall have never run in the same circles. Oliver has always been too much of a loser to even come close to Marshall's circle. But maybe that's just it. Maybe Officer Gray has meticulously called up their old high school friends one by one and asked what

Marshall and Oliver's relationship was like. And if that's the case, then things are going to be bad for Oliver. He can just imagine what Marshall's buddies would say about him. Did say about him back in high school.

He's a creep.

A loser, always following Marshall around like a stalker.

He was so in love with Julia, anyone could see it, the way he watched her.

He's got serious American Psycho *vibes.*

As though she can read his thoughts, Officer Gray says, "Let's talk about Julia Chen. You were really close to her when you were teens."

It's not a question as much as it is a statement, and Oliver has no idea how to respond to that. Yes? No? I don't know? So he chooses to say nothing.

"In fact, you had really strong feelings for her, didn't you?"

His blood pressure is now so high that Oliver is somewhat surprised that he hasn't yet popped a vein. "Um, no?" he ventures. "I mean, we were just friends."

At that, Officer Gray's expression changes, morphing from neutral to a sharp grin that reminds him of a shark that's just caught the scent of blood in the water. "Funny you should say that, because according to this"—she pauses long enough to take something out of her bag; it falls onto the table with a loud thump—"you were madly in love with her."

The world opens up beneath him and he falls through an endless hole. From afar, he can hear Officer Gray saying, "This is your manuscript, is it not? David is you, Randall is Marshall, and Aurelia is Julia. Randall's a bit of a dick in here, and David's jealous of him and obsessed with Aurelia. His obsession remains even years after Randall marries her, because he believes Randall is mistreating Aurelia. One day, David decides it's time to punish his twin brother. You remember how David did it?"

Oliver is yanked back to reality. "Huh?"

Officer Gray leans across the table and says each syllable carefully. "What did your character do to Randall?"

The words feel thick and fuzzy coming out of his mouth. "I think it's time I consult with an attorney."

Officer Gray leans back, nodding like she expected this all along. "Okay."

"And, um, am I under arrest?"

She shakes her head.

"So I can . . . technically go?"

Officer Gray nods. "Yes, but trust me, it's much better talking to us voluntarily than the alternative."

"Right." Oliver considers this. "I think I'll go for now."

Officer Gray stands and opens the door. "Don't leave town."

Outside, Oliver strides quickly away, wanting to put some distance between him and the police station. Once he turns the corner, he leans over and vomits.

Oh god. Did that really just happen? Was he just questioned inside an actual police station? Over the murder of his brother? How the hell has it come to this?

He hadn't meant to do what he did to Marshall. He hadn't thought it would end up like this.

And how did Officer Gray get ahold of his manuscript?

The answer falls down on his shoulders like an anvil, crushing all the humanity out of him. Vera. He foolishly let her take it. God, why? Why had he? Because he didn't think she'd make anything out of it, because it had been so long since he'd read it himself, he'd forgotten about the important details. Like how David ended up strangling Randall in the story. How could he have been so fucking stupid? And how could Vera betray him like that? He looked at her as a mother figure, and she goes and does this.

Slowly, hot fury replaces the gnawing fear. Oliver has no idea what's going to happen to him now, but if he's about to go to prison, he's not going to go down without a fight.

First stop, Vera's dinner party.

THIRTY-FOUR

JULIA

Julia has never once thrown a dinner party, let alone a black-tie event. Well, back in high school, she'd thrown a few parties, but high school parties are guaranteed to be fun as long as you've got cheap beer and music so loud that it permanently scars your eardrums. What Vera has insisted on throwing is something else altogether.

The three of them spend the entire day preparing for the event, Julia and Emma putting up decorations while Vera cooks up a storm in the kitchen. Since Vera has told her that she is planning on uncovering the truth behind Marshall's death during the party, Julia isn't sure what kind of vibe she should go for. In the end, she settles on black and white streamers and a handful of gray and black balloons. The balloons are more for Emma to play with. Julia isn't sure about having balloons at a dinner party discussing the events of her husband's death. But then again, she is no longer sure of anything.

She's so nervous about seeing Oliver tonight. Vera tells her not to confront him about the manuscript, that Vera will bring it up when the time is right. But will Julia manage not to blurt it out the moment she sees him? She imagines herself flying at Oliver and hitting him, shouting, *How could you?* She's not even really sure, technically, what she's angry at him about. Surely there's nothing wrong with having a crush on someone, especially when they were in their teens. But then she thinks of the manuscript and how he's described the obsession with Aurelia and Randall, and she thinks again of how much time he's spent with her and Emma ever since Marshall died, and the newfound knowledge that he's been doing it with the hope of replacing Marshall makes her skin want to crawl right off her body.

Enough of that, Julia scolds herself as she dresses Emma in a black velvet dress. Emma beams at her reflection, turning this way and that to admire herself.

"Don't tie up my hair, Mommy," she says. "I'm too pretty already."

Julia's heart squeezes at Emma's self-love. It breaks Julia a bit to see how much little kids love themselves, how natural it is for them to accept their bodies. She thinks again of how Marshall broke her self-confidence down so insidiously that she hadn't known it was happening at all. *I would kill to protect you,* she thinks. *I would kill to make sure you are never in a relationship like Mommy and Daddy's.*

The thought surges through her so fiercely that it stuns her, but it's true, every bit of it. She would kill, and quite easily too, for Emma. She stands behind the little girl and puts her hands on her tiny shoulders and they both smile into the mirror. "Yeah, you're right, baby. You don't need anything else to make you pretty."

....

The dinner party is a huge success. Well, as huge a success as it can be with just five people in attendance. Oliver seems to be running late, something Julia can't decide whether to be relieved or disappointed about. She keeps glancing at the door, expecting him to show up, and going over her impassioned speech over and over. But aside from that, everything is going great.

As always, Vera's cooking exceeds all expectations. And everyone looks amazing. Vera has done something to her hair to make it three times the size it usually is, and it looks like a little cloud has floated down and decided to settle atop her head. She's wearing a jade pendant and a tweed jacket she has been telling everyone is a knockoff Chanel, though "you wouldn't know it, would you? Would you?"

"Riki, you look so dashing!" Julia says when Riki arrives, and he really does. His hair has been very carefully messed up in a way that makes you want to run your fingers through it, and he's wearing a suit that makes him look—there is no other word for it— dapper.

Sana arrives a minute later, looking very elegant and yet alluring in an LBD. "Sorry, my Uber ran late."

"I told you I could pick you up," Riki says, putting his arm around her waist and giving her a kiss.

"Nah, your office is in the opposite direction. But you can drive me home."

Julia's eyebrows have disappeared into her hairline. "Wait, are you two a thing?"

Sana giggles as she squeezes close to Riki. "Yes. Did Vera not tell you?"

"No! Vera!" Julia calls out. "You didn't tell me these two were a thing!"

"Hm?" Vera looks up from the dining table, where she's been busy the past five minutes rearranging the dishes to make sure the spread looks perfect. "Oh yes. Riki and Sana are things. Keep up, Julia. Emma knows, don't you, Emma?"

Emma nods solemnly, eyeing Riki and Sana. "Are you going to kiss again?"

"Um . . ." Sana says. "Do you want us to?"

Emma shakes her head.

"Okay, then we won't," Riki says with a wink at Emma. "Wow, Vera, this looks amazing. You've really outdone yourself."

"Oh, it's nothing," Vera says, grinning from ear to ear. "I just spend the whole day cooking, but is no big deal."

For the next fifteen minutes, they chatter easily, sipping champagne and updating one another. Julia is excited to update them about her growing business; it's been such a long time since she's had anything remotely interesting to say about her life that isn't about Emma. Sana and Riki seem genuinely happy for her until Vera says, "Oh, Julia, you can take Sana and Riki's engagement photos!" upon which both Sana and Riki choke on their drinks while Julia laughs, then the conversation moves on to how Riki is planning on refurbishing Vera's teahouse furniture.

Strangely, Vera doesn't seem too enthused about this. "Oh, you don't have to. It must be such a bother. Just take it slowly."

"Vera doesn't want to move back to her teahouse," Sana teases. "She's enjoying staying here too much."

"Such rubbish!" Vera snaps, without any bite to it. "Of course not! I hate being a bother. You know that, don't you?" she says to Julia.

"You're never a bother, Vera," Julia says, giving her a one-armed hug. "Emma and I love having you here. You can stay as long as you want. Right, Emma?"

Emma nods, then says, "I'm hungry."

"Ah, yes, let's eat, before food gets cold," Vera says.

Riki glances at the door. "Should we wait for Oliver?"

At the mention of Oliver, Julia's heart rate quickens.

"He is twenty minutes late already," Vera moans. "No, we should eat first, then when he comes he will feel guilty for being so late."

And so they retire to the dining room, where they dig into the food. Everyone agrees that Vera's cooking is out of this world and that meeting her has been very bad for their waistlines. It's right in the middle of eating that the doorbell rings. Before Julia can even get out of her seat, it rings again. And again. They all exchange curious glances as Julia gets up.

"Wow, sounds like Oliver really needs to come in," Sana says.

As Julia walks to the door, she rehearses what she will say to Oliver. She will be calm and cool, she decides. She will trust that Vera has a plan for tonight. That Vera will make sure that everything goes well. And if it doesn't, well, Julia is prepared to tell Oliver exactly what she thinks. She opens the door.

"Vera!" Oliver shouts, barging in and storming right past Julia.

"What the—" Okay, so she wasn't expecting that. And the unexpected rudeness triggers something inside her. She hurries after him. "You can't just—"

But Oliver stops at the dining room and points at Vera. "I can't believe you did that," he thunders.

Conversations stop in mid-sentence. Emma looks up from her high chair, startled, a piece of broccoli halfway to her mouth. Seeing how surprised Emma looks seems to shake Oliver. When he speaks again, his voice is lower, more level, though anger is still simmering beneath the words. "Vera, can I please talk to you?"

"This is not what I plan," Vera complains.

"I'm serious, Vera."

Julia's gut turns sour. She is angry and upset and everything else, but Vera only nods and leaves the table. The two of them go into the living room. Julia takes Emma out of her high chair and hugs her close as she, Sana, and Riki follow, stopping to listen from behind the door.

"I can't believe you handed my manuscript to the police," Oliver is saying.

"Why? Is there something you are hiding in it?"

"Wha— No! But I let you take it because I thought you were— I don't know, I didn't think you would betray me like that. I thought we were friends!"

"We are. But your story . . ."

Julia bites down on her lip so hard that she tastes blood. Vera is fishing, prodding for answers, pretending that she's finished reading Oliver's manuscript in the hope that he might reveal what the ending is. Sensing Emma stiffening in her arms, Julia whispers, "Hey, baby? Do you want to go into your room for a bit? Maybe spend some time in your relaxation corner?" The mention of the corner reminds Julia that it was Oliver who came up with it. Ugh. Everything is tainted now. But she'll have to deal with that later. For now, it's more important to make sure that Emma isn't being frightened. Emma nods and Julia lowers her to the floor, where she toddles off into her bedroom. Julia sighs with relief and turns her attention back to the argument.

"Is fictional!" Oliver is barking. "That's exactly what it is, a story. And thanks to you, the cops think I might have had some-thing to do with Marshall's death."

"Why?" Vera says. "What is inside your manuscript?"

"What? Did you not even read it before handing it to the po-lice? Jesus, I can't believe that, of all the fucked-up things—"

It's too much. His anger at Vera, a helpless old woman, his stupid, ongoing rant. Julia strides into the living room and says, "She didn't do it. I did."

Both Oliver and Vera turn and gape at her. There is a long si-lence, then Oliver says, "What?"

"To be fair, I didn't mean to. I wasn't planning on doing anything—well, I hadn't decided yet, I was still skimming through it when Officer Gray dropped by. She found the manuscript on the couch and took it with her."

While Oliver struggles to come up with a response to this reve-lation, Julia gathers her strength, sharpening her fury until it be-comes a single, sharp point. "And how dare you, Oliver?" Her voice is soft but steady. She is done with letting men's bullshit go.

"What?" Oliver says.

Can he not say anything else? she thinks. He's supposed to be a writer, and yet here he is, stuck with repeating the same word over and over again. "You've been in love with me since we were teens? And even after Marshall and I got married, you were still—what, pining for me? And fantasizing that Emma's your kid?" By now, Julia's voice is a poisonous hiss. Behind her, she can hear Sana's and Riki's soft gasps.

Color drains from Oliver's face. "No, Julia, it's not like that—"

"Really? Then tell me what it's like. You've hated Marshall your entire life. And okay, granted, that's understandable, because you know what? Marshall was a fucking asshole. Yeah," Julia says, nodding at everyone in the room. "I really did just say that about my dead husband. He was a total shit. And so I get it, Oliver. You hated him. I do too. But see, you actually wrote in your book that you're going to make sure that he no longer gets away with it. So tell me, what did you do? Because I didn't get to finish reading the book before Officer Gray showed up, but obviously, the ending was disturbing enough for her to question you about it."

"No, I didn't—"

"What," Julia says, enunciating every single word, "did you do to Marshall?"

"I planted drugs in his bag!" Oliver shouts.

The room falls silent except for the sound of Oliver breathing hard. "I was fixing up the plumbing at one of the apartment units and I found this little bag full of pills taped to the inside of the toilet tank. The unit had been recently vacated, so I had no idea what to do with them. I looked them up. They were ecstasy. I think? I don't know. I took them back to my place and I thought about throwing them away, or turning them in, but then I thought—hey, maybe this is a sign. Maybe these pills are a gift from the universe, a chance for me to finally get Marshall in trouble." Oliver rubs his hands down his face and groans. "I know how that sounds. I know it sounds completely stupid, but you don't understand, Marshall's been getting away with everything ever since we were kids. He'd do shit like shoplift or cheat during exams, and if he ever got caught he'd blame it on me, and no one—" His voice hitches with unshed tears, and despite herself, Julia wants to cry for him. "No one ever believed me."

The thing is, Julia understands completely. She's been there, after all. She's experienced firsthand the irresistible charm that Marshall had. The way you knew, deep down inside, that he was no good, but still you couldn't help but go along with it, you couldn't help but let him get away with it. And when she looks around the room, at Sana's and Riki's expressions, she knows that they get it too. That they'd seen for themselves what Marshall had been like. They were all, despite themselves, feeling horribly sorry for Oliver. Because sure, she'd been married to Marshall, but Oliver had shared a womb with him, had gone through all of his childhood and formative years as his twin brother, tethered to him. What would that have been like, to have to be so close to someone whose shine dazzled everyone and be the only person who knew that the shine came from a poisonous radiation?

"So I met up with him. The day before he died, and I slipped the drugs into his bag when he wasn't looking. I was going to call the cops on him, but then . . . I chickened out." Oliver snorts. "I guess that's what I do. I'm just a coward, after all. I thought of taking it back, but I couldn't figure out how to do that without making him suspicious, so I did nothing. The next night, he died. I was scared shitless. I had no idea what had happened. I thought maybe Marshall had found the drugs in his bag and took them. Maybe he had an overdose. Maybe the drugs had been cut with something toxic? I don't know! But then the autopsy report came out and, well, you all know the rest. Bird dander." Oliver snorts again. "After all that, it was fucking bird dander that got him."

Julia is staring at him, mouth agape, her mind on fire. The thing is, she believes him. She's known Oliver since they were practically kids. She knows when he's telling the truth. Slowly, she looks around the room. Everyone else is looking just as stunned as she feels.

"So you are not killer?" Vera muses, after the shocked silence becomes unbearable.

"No," Oliver says. He turns to look at Julia, and his face falls.

"Julia, I—I'm so sorry for writing about you like that. It wasn't about us, it—"

Julia shakes her head. "I don't wanna hear it. Just don't talk to me." He might not have killed Marshall, but it doesn't make everything he's done okay. And, in a way, she feels even worse now, because her emotions are all over the place. Does she get to be furious at Oliver still? Even though he didn't kill Marshall? And who the hell did kill Marshall? It's all too much, all of it boiling over. "I don't understand. So who killed Marshall? Vera, you said you'd figured it out! Who was it? Who killed him? Who broke into your shop?"

"I don't know who kill Marshall," Vera says quietly, "but I know who break into my shop."

"What?" they all say as one.

"I break into my shop," Vera says.

"*What?*" they all say again.

Vera sighs. "I come down one morning and I see that things have been move around. Some jars go missing."

"Which jars?" Riki asks. "I mean, are you sure?"

"Yes, of course I'm sure. I know how I arrange my shop, don't be silly. But I think to myself, would the police take me seriously? They don't take Marshall's death seriously, why would they take me seriously when I tell them that someone steal into my shop? They will ask, how much did the thief take? Well, no money is missing. What was taken? I don't know, I just know that my jars are moved. And I am sure it's the killer come back to look for the flash drive. So I decide, okay, I will take control of situation. The killer is too cunning to make it obvious, so I will make it obvious. Make it clear that someone break in, keep all of us working on a common goal: solving Marshall murder. So I do that."

"You smashed up your own shop to make it look more obvious that someone broke in?" Sana says, her eyes as round as dinner plates. "All those jars—"

"It hurt me to break them all like that," Vera says, "but I am willing to do anything to find killer."

"Wait," Julia says, "hold on. What do you mean, the killer would come back to look for the flash drive? What flash drive?"

At this, Vera looks strangely guilty.

"Vera," Julia says in a warning tone. "What flash drive?"

Vera releases a long, tired breath. "When I find Marshall's body, he holding a flash drive in his hand."

"What. The. Fuck?" Julia doesn't even know who said it. It could've been her, it could've been any of the others.

"And you just took it?" Oliver says.

"My god, Vera," Riki cries. "You—that's tampering with a crime scene! You could go to prison for that."

"I just know, you see, that police won't take case seriously." Vera looks so tiny and helpless, her cloud of hair waving this way and that as she shakes her head.

"Well, maybe they would've if you hadn't taken away evidence!" Oliver says. He rakes his fingers through his hair. "So what was on the drive?"

"Well, it turns out the drive is a key to unlock his computer. And the computer has these NFT and, oh yes, the bot that Riki make."

"Wait, what bot did you make?" Sana stares at Riki, who looks like he has half a mind to run away.

"Uh . . ." He glances guiltily at Sana. "Um. Marshall asked me to build a program. Um, and then he didn't pay me." For a moment, it seems like he's done talking, but then he takes a breath and blurts out, "It was a scalping bot. He wanted me to make a bot to scam people on the NFT marketplace." He turns to Sana, taking her hands. "I didn't want to—I felt so shitty the whole time I did it, and I didn't know he was stealing art at the time, I just thought—"

"You were part of his scam?" Sana says. Her words are hissed with such acidity that even Julia feels the sting.

"No!" Riki says. "No, I swear I didn't—it was the first time I had met Marshall, I didn't know—"

"You didn't know because you chose not to know," Sana says. "Did you ask him what his freaking NFTs were? No. Did you think about all the people being scammed by this bot you were building? No! People like you and Marshall are the reason I couldn't even stand to look at a canvas!" With that, Sana wrenches her hands out of Riki's and runs out, slamming the door behind her.

"Sana, wait!" Riki shouts, going after her.

Julia stares at the door, everything inside her a screaming mess. She makes an effort to sort through what she's just learned. "Where's the flash drive now? And the laptop? We should—ah, we should probably hand that over to the police—"

Vera shakes her head. "I been looking for it since yesterday and both of them are gone."

For a moment, Julia and Oliver are speechless. Then the enormity of the situation crashes down on Julia. This woman, this stranger, found her husband dead in her shop, and the first thing she did was to swipe the very piece of evidence that might have led the cops to his killer. And then this very same woman smashed up her own shop to make it look like a break-in has happened, all so that she could come and live with Julia and her small child.

It's a struggle for Julia to keep from screaming. She meets Vera's eye and points at the door. "Get out now."

For a moment, she thinks Vera is about to protest, but then Vera sees the look on Julia's face and simply nods. Lowering her head, Vera heads toward the door. She seems to have shrunk over the last few minutes, her shoulders drooping, her head wilted. The sight of it tugs at Julia's heartstrings, but her rage still burns over everything else. Vera stops long enough to take her purse, then she walks out and closes the door gently behind her, leaving behind a cavernous silence that Julia is sure will never be filled.

THIRTY-FIVE

VERA

Get out now.

Just like that, Vera's stay at Julia's place has come to an end. She has overstayed Julia's welcome. She has tried to solve Marshall's murder and she has failed miserably. It is clear, after tonight, that all of her instincts have been dreadfully, awfully wrong. None of her suspects have turned out to be the killer. Who is the killer? Did she just make it up in her desperation for some meaning, some purpose to her life? She was the one who smashed up her shop. Sure, it was because she had come downstairs one morning to find that things weren't where they should be. But is she one hundred percent sure that someone indeed stole into her shop?

Or is it possible that Vera wanted so badly for there to have been a killer who came back for the flash drive that she made it all up? Isn't that what the mind does as it ages? It starts conflating reality with imagination. Yes, Vera can see it now. Maybe herself had misplaced a jar here, a canister there, and then, having forgotten about it and with her imagination fired up by Marshall's death, she jumped to the conclusion that someone had been in her teahouse.

And then she'd taken that idea and run with it. And why? Because deep in her heart of hearts, Vera has been tired of the teahouse. Tired of opening it every morning and getting just one single customer, and even then, it's always been clear that the only reason Alex came by was because he pitied her. And the emptiness of her shop is merely a reminder of how she has failed. She hadn't expected Julia to offer to have her move in; that had been a surprise, and oh, what an incredibly wonderful time it had been, while it lasted.

For a few precious weeks, Vera experienced a renewed purpose in life. Received multiple hugs throughout the day, little arms around her neck, and a little sticky face kissing her cheeks. She had been brought back into the sunlight, and now, through her own doing, she has been cast back out into the darkness. And now that she has experienced the warmth of the sun, the darkness seems even more bleak than before.

Vera barely notices the long walk back to her house, but by the time she gets there, her feet are covered in blisters. She doesn't notice the blisters either. She does notice the sun-bleached sign that says: VERA WANG'S WORLD-FAMOUS TEAHOUSE, and the sight of it makes tears rush to her eyes. She chokes back her sobs and unlocks the door, letting it fall shut behind her.

The teahouse is empty. The walls have been stripped bare, the furniture taken out by Riki. It looks like an old abandoned shell, a house occupied only by ghosts. Her phone rings then, and Vera leaps back to life, scrambling to take it out of her bag.

"Julia!" she calls into the receiver.

There's a beat of silence, then someone says, "Ma?"

"Tilly!" Vera takes the phone away from her ear and stares at the screen. It does indeed say Tilbert Wong. "Oh, Tilly. You have called." She can taste tears at the back of her throat. Her son must have felt that something was wrong through their mother-son bond.

"Uh, yeah. You haven't texted or called for ages. Is everything okay?"

Vera nods, her face scrunching up into a silent sob. "Yes," she manages to say after a while. She looks around the dark, empty store. "Well, the shop is—well, is a long story, but the shop is a bit empty."

"Oh? Are you closing it down?"

Vera is about to say that no, of course she isn't, when Tilly says, "About time, Ma. Nobody even knows it's there. Thank god you're closing it down. You should sell. Prices in Chinatown are going up, you could get a really good price for it."

Thank god you're closing it down. So much relief in his voice. So much history in this little shop, Vera and Jinlong pouring their hearts and souls into it, and now her son is thanking god that she wants to close it down. And the thing is, he's not wrong. Vera knows this. The tiny flicker of hope that had sparked when her phone rang dies.

"Okay, Tilly. Thank you for calling. You're right. I go to bed now." She hangs up and trudges up the stairs, not bothering to turn on any of the lights. She goes straight to her cold bedroom and slides under the covers, where she curls up and makes herself as tiny as possible, wishing she could just simply disappear.

THIRTY-SIX

VERA

It seems it is daytime once again, the gray light streaming in weakly through the gaps in Vera's curtains, not enough to brighten the room, just enough to disturb her sleep. Vera turns, stares at the dribbly light for a bit. She has lost count of the number of times the room has turned dark, then light, then dark again. Now it is light, but it does not matter very much at all to Vera whether it is light or dark. She rolls over and closes her eyes once more.

THIRTY-SEVEN

RIKI

R iki, if you don't get rid of that trash in the parking lot, I will get rid of it," Mrs. Barrie says.

Riki bites back a groan of frustration and simply nods. After she leaves, he stands at the door for a while, grinding his teeth. The thing is, Mrs. Barrie isn't even being unreasonable. "That trash" is Vera's furniture, which he foolishly took back to his apartment building and begged for permission to stash in the parking lot while he works on refurbishing the lot. That had been almost two weeks ago, and he had indeed been working on them; about half is finished and looks pretty damn good, if he does say so. But then that horrible dinner had happened, and ever since then, just the sight of the furniture makes Riki feel nauseous.

But Mrs. Barrie is right. He can't just let the furniture sit there in the parking lot, taking up space and collecting dust. With a resigned sigh, Riki trudges downstairs to the parking lot to survey the mess. Once he's there, though, he gets a sense of satisfaction from seeing the pieces he refurbished. They still retain the same traditional shape, but he's sanded them down and painted them a matte black in color, and they look so sleek. He decides to load up the finished ones into his car and take them to Vera's; then at least she'll have some furniture in her shop while he continues working on the rest.

It takes quite a bit of maneuvering, but at last, all seven pieces of refurbished furniture are loaded into his car. Yes, there is a wooden chair resting on the passenger seat at a precarious angle, with one leg aimed at Riki's temple, and yes, if he were to get into an accident now he would most definitely end up with the wooden leg speared through an eye socket, but what is life without a few calculated risks? Still, Riki makes sure to drive very, very slowly to Chinatown, gulping when he gets to the ultra-hilly parts of the city.

Vera's neighborhood makes him think of Sana, which, three days after the awful dinner, still makes him misty-eyed. He texted her four times in the last couple of days before realizing that he needs to respect her space, and so had sent her one final message:

I'll be here when you're ready to talk. If you're ever ready. If you're not, I understand. I'm sorry. X.

He tries not to think of the last time he and Sana were here, laughing and chatting so easily as they cleaned up Vera's teahouse.

"Vera, Vera," Riki mutters to himself as he gets out and gazes at the teahouse. He still finds it hard to believe that Vera was the one who smashed up her own shop. The thought makes him shake his head, but he's also smiling. Despite everything, he still cares about Vera, even though she is obviously a bit batty. He goes up to the front door, carrying two of the chairs, and knocks. The door swings open, the little bell chiming dully. Huh. Maybe she's decided to reopen it already? But without any furniture?

But when Riki steps inside, it's clear that the teahouse is not, in fact, open for business. Although it's still bright outside, the inside of the teahouse is dark; none of the old lights or the new ones that Oliver installed are on. It feels empty. But then why is the front door open?

"Hello?" Riki calls out, placing the chairs down carefully. He looks around the shop and tries again. "Vera?"

"Are you looking for Vera Wong?" someone says behind him, making him jump. He turns around to see a short, plump lady around Vera's age.

"Um, yeah? Do you know where she is?"

"No, I have been wondering the same thing. I'm Winifred, from the French patisserie next door." Winifred says this with pride, as if Riki should be blown away by this fact.

He acquiesces, widening his eyes and saying, "Oh wow, hi, Winifred, it's nice to meet you. I love your pastries."

She beams, her pink cheeks shining, but the smile doesn't last long. "I have been worried about Vera. Weeks and weeks she is gone, and strangers coming in and out of the shop, making all sorts of noises—"

"Oh yeah, that would be me and my friends working on repairing the shop." As soon as Riki says "friends," sadness stabs through his gut. "And she was staying at someone else's house while we were doing that, but I think she should be back home by now." Julia filled Riki in on what happened that night after he and Sana left, and it sounded pretty bad. Now he's roiling with guilt at the realization that he should've checked on Vera sooner.

"I think I hear her coming back in the middle of the night

three days ago. But when I come by with some fresh *petit pain au taro*, nobody is in. Front door left open, so dangerous."

The bad feeling in Riki's stomach is getting worse. "Three days ago? And you haven't heard her leave or anything?"

"No. Well, not that I spend all my time watching, I am very bus— Hey, where you going?"

But Riki ignores her, hurrying to the back of the shop and rushing upstairs, taking the steps two at a time. "Vera!" he shouts as he goes. The living quarters are cold and dark. The fear grows stronger and stronger until it almost drives him away, screaming, back into the sunlight. But still he keeps going. Up another set of stairs, to where the bedrooms are. He looks inside the first one, but it's empty, and looks like it's been empty for years. In the second bedroom, there is a lump on the bed, so small that at first Riki can't believe that there might be a whole person underneath the duvet.

He creeps toward it slowly, clearing his throat. "Vera?" Oh god, she's dead, isn't she? He wants so badly to run out of here, but somehow, his feet keep going forward. He pats the figure gently and hears a soft moan. "Oh, thank god. Vera, it's Riki." He peels the duvet back and his heart catches in his throat. He has never seen Vera so tiny, so old, so defeated. "Oh, Vera." Sadness overwhelms him, guilt piercing his lungs. He yanks out his phone and dials 911. After giving the operator the address to Vera's place, he hangs up and takes Vera's hand. Her eyes open but don't focus, and Riki feels his entire being ripping apart at how broken she is.

"It's going to be okay," he tells her. "We'll take care of you. I promise."

THIRTY-EIGHT

SANA

Sana's shoes clack against the linoleum floors of the hospital as she hurries down the corridor. Ward 4, the receptionist said, and it feels like the hospital is so impossibly big, but finally she locates it and bursts into the room. There are four beds in there, but only one is occupied. At the sight of the person occupying the hospital bed, Sana's breath hitches into a sob.

"Oh, Vera," she whispers in a choked voice.

Riki gets to his feet. "Hey, thanks for coming."

She can only nod at him, her eyes still on the pale form on the bed. Vera has always been so full of life and fire and sparks, it's just so wrong seeing her like this, old and fragile and defeated, as though she's ready to leave altogether. Sana approaches slowly, her eyes swimming with tears. "Is she—"

"She's going to be okay," Riki says. "They said she's dehydrated, hence the IV drip, and she might have bronchitis, but they said she should make a full recovery."

Relief floods Sana's chest. She takes Vera's hand—the one

without a needle sticking out of it—and cradles it ever so softly. "Vera, it's Sana." She leans close to Vera and whispers, "I'm so sorry. But I'm here now. And you were right about everything." She longs so much for Vera to quirk a smile at that, but there is no movement, no flicker of facial expression.

"They say she's sleeping."

"Right, of course." Sana stands back, wiping at her eyes.

The door opens and Emma runs inside, followed by Julia, who's looking markedly more harried than she has been the past few weeks.

"Grandma!" Emma shouts, stopping short when she catches sight of Vera. She looks nervously at Julia, who looks at Riki and Sana.

"She'll be okay," Riki and Sana say at the same time. They startle, looking at each other, then Sana nods at Riki. He gives her a small smile, then tells Julia what he told Sana moments ago. The door opens again, and Oliver rushes in, stopping short when he sees Julia. Then he looks over at Vera and his face falls.

"Is she . . ."

"She's okay," Riki says, and repeats the information yet again.

They all crowd around Vera's bed, gazing down at her quietly. Then little Emma says, "I miss Grandma." And the tension breaks. They all look at one another with hesitant smiles.

"I miss my morning beach picnics with her," Sana says.

"I miss waking up to her cooking," Julia says. "And coming home to a house with her in it."

"I miss having her tell me that I'm doing okay," Riki says.

"I miss having her boss me around," Oliver says.

They all laugh at that, nodding in agreement. "She did cross a few lines," Julia says.

Oliver snorts. "Try breaking a few laws."

They laugh again. "But that's what makes her so . . ." Sana struggles to find the right words. "So very Vera." They all nod.

"I miss you," Riki blurts out.

It seems as though everyone stops breathing. "Sorry," Riki says, "I don't know why—uh, sorry, forget I—"

It spills out of Sana. "I miss you too." She goes around the bed and flings her arms around Riki. "You shitty asshole—oh, sorry, Emma. Don't ever say those words."

"Shitty asshole," Emma says, and Sana groans.

Julia gives Sana a mock glower. "You owe me at least a babysitting session for that."

"You got it." Sana turns her attention back to Riki, who's gazing at her like she's his salvation. "I've been thinking a lot about what you did, and—"

"It was inexcusable, I know, I—"

"Shush and let me talk."

Riki's mouth snaps shut.

"What you did was really wrong, but I'm not in a position to judge. I've always been comfortable. My mom may be hard in some ways, but she provides me with financial stability, and I never truly appreciated it. And if I'd been in your position, with all that pressure bearing down on me, who knows what I might've done? I'm not saying it's right, but . . . I can see why you did it." There. It's finally out, and once it's off her chest, Sana feels so much lighter. Color seeps back into her world. For the first time, she no longer feels that same bitterness toward other people. Even her mother. She's sure that her mom will manage to push her buttons soon enough, but for now, Sana thinks of her mom and sees that she is, in fact, lucky to have her as a mother.

The door opens again, and an Asian guy in his twenties walks in. He stops when he sees the crowd, and checks the number on the door. "Uh, is this where Vera Wong is?"

"Yeah," Oliver says.

The guy stares at them. "Who are you?"

"We're her family," Julia says. "Who're you?"

"Uh . . . I'm her son?"

Sana narrows her eyes. "The famous Tilly. We've got a lot to talk to you about how you treat your mother, young man." It strikes Sana that Tilly is probably older than she is, but she chooses to ignore that fact for now.

Tilly's mouth drops open. "It's Tilbert, actually."

"Hmm," Julia says in a way that reminds Sana very much of Vera. "We'll see about that, Tilly."

Much later, Sana stands in the middle of Vera Wang's World-Famous Teahouse with a massive paintbrush in her hand. Oliver has sanded down the walls to make them smooth and now it's down to her to paint it the way she wants. A blank canvas just for her, and while Sana can still feel the familiar terror lurking inside her, waiting to pounce and overwhelm her, weeks of drawing in the sand have taught her that there is nothing to be afraid of, that even if she ends up coming up with the worst painting that was ever painted, it will somehow still be okay. Because she's learned now that nothing is permanent. The waves will always be there to wash every mistake, every flaw, away. And like she's taught Emma, sometimes mistakes can be turned into something beautiful.

There is now something sparking inside her—hope, and excitement, and the knowledge that she is doing exactly what she has always been meant to do. To use her paintbrush to create something beautiful and true.

Smiling, Sana dips the brush in the pot of paint and begins to draw.

THIRTY-NINE

JULIA

For Julia, there is nothing quite like the joy of photographing Emma. The only thing better than that is photographing Emma when she is splashed with paint, working alongside Sana in her usual overly serious way. Sana has given Emma the very important task of painting teeny-tiny hearts here and there on the rich mural that she has drawn all over Vera's walls. Julia is still blown away by the fact that in just two days, Sana has transformed the walls of Vera's teahouse into something out of a Shanghainese dream—a river in the nighttime, its waters reflecting the tiny dotted stars up above, and on the riverbank, a huge Chinese teahouse, adorned with hundreds of red lanterns, patrons wearing colorful qipao and changshan spilling out of it. The sign above says: VERA WANG'S WORLD-FAMOUS TEAHORSE. Sana blames the spelling of "teahorse" on lack of sleep and says she will correct it if Vera complains.

Aside from the matter of the spelling error, the rest of the painting is incredible, larger than life, jaw-dropping. And combined with Riki's refurbished furniture and Oliver's new lighting, it has transformed Vera's shop into something that would have impressed even the pickiest customer. In theory, that is. Because despite the impressive changes, nobody knows about Vera's teahouse (or, indeed, her teahorse). Still, Julia would bet money that none of them regrets spending all this time and energy renovating Vera's teahouse. It's the least they can do, given how she has changed all of their lives in such a short period of time.

The tinkling of the doorbell catches Julia's attention. It's Oliver, carrying his toolkit. He's fixing the electrics up in Vera's living quarters since Riki told him how cold and dank her house is. He presses his lips into a thin line when he sees Julia, and gives her the barest of nods. Julia turns to Sana and says, "Sana, can you watch Emma for a bit?" Sana nods, and Julia reaches out, touching Oliver's arm as he passes by. "Can we talk?"

Oliver looks hesitant but nods and follows her outside.

"Uh, so . . ." God, why must these things be so difficult? "I just wanted to know how things are going with—you know—Officer Gray and all that?" Even though she still feels a bit squicky about how things went down between her and Oliver, she doesn't want him to get the blame for Marshall's death. She feels responsible for landing him in trouble in the first place.

"No, don't worry about that," Oliver says. "Tilbert was a huge help. You should've seen how he handled my case. He told Officer Gray that they didn't have enough evidence to charge me with anything and if they were to keep harassing me he'd file a complaint. It seems to have worked. I could definitely tell that he's Vera's kid."

Julia laughs. She was hard on Tilbert when they first met because of how neglectful he'd been toward Vera, but she can see that he's making a real effort, offering to represent Oliver pro bono after listening in complete shock and horror to the whole mess. "I'm glad to hear that," she says, and she truly means it.

"Thanks. Um, so I've been really wanting to apologize for . . . you know."

Julia's instinctive reaction is to wave his apology away and scuttle out of there, but then it hits her: She's always done that because she never thought herself worthy of an apology, and the thought of someone saying sorry to her makes her squirm. But she would like to hear what Oliver has to say, so she squashes her discomfort and makes herself stay.

"I—" Oliver takes a breath. "I had a huge crush on you back when we were kids, yeah. It lasted all throughout high school, but when high school ended, I moved on. I promise you, Lia. I went out with other girls and I had healthy relationships. But I sometimes thought of you, not in like an *I must have her* way, more like a concerned way because I've always known what Marshall was like, and I was worried. And I felt so guilty for not being friends with you anymore after you guys started dating. That was such a shitty move on my part."

"It was," Julia says. "I thought you were mad at me. Marshall told me it was because you were obsessed with me."

Oliver grimaces. "Honestly? I think I was more obsessed with Marshall than anything. The way he would mistreat everyone and get away with it. I couldn't let that go. Over time, I became more and more bitter. And the few times we saw each other over the next few years only made me realize how badly he was treating you. It killed me inside. I couldn't do anything about it. So I wrote that manuscript. It was—" He gives a long, pained sigh. "Yeah, most of it was based on my relationship with Marshall. The part with Aurelia . . ." He snorts. "I guess you could say it was bad fan fiction? I don't know, I did model Aurelia after you, but please trust me, Julia, these past couple of months, I wasn't spending time with you to—you know—I just wanted my best friend back. I've missed having you as a friend more than anything."

Julia looks into his eyes and knows, deep inside her, that Oliver is telling the truth. Just like the night he said he hadn't killed Marshall. She's always known when Oliver was being honest. The smile feels like it comes from the core of her, spreading slowly across her face like honey. She pulls her fist back and punches him in the shoulder.

"Ow!"

"I've missed you, nerd."

He grins at her. "I've missed you too, loser."

And together, they step back inside Vera's teahouse, each of them quietly grateful that they have the other one back in their life, exactly where they belong, as lifelong friends.

FORTY

VERA

It takes Vera an unreasonably long time to recover. "This is unacceptable!" she'd say to anyone who would listen—her doctor, the nurses, and . . . her family. The truth is, though Vera would never admit it, there is a thrilling feeling of happiness that comes from having your loved ones visit you at the hospital. It's so out of the way, and so completely not what anyone wants to be doing, that when they do it, you know that the only plausible reason is because they care about you. And so, despite the unacceptably long time that it takes those in charge to nurse her back to health, a not-so-small part of Vera enjoys lying in her hospital bed being fussed over.

And oh, what an eclectic crowd it is that rotates around her hospital bed! Everyone says so. Gladys from the bed across from her has remarked upon it—quite snidely, to Vera's delight—at least three times now. "Such a varied stream of visitors you have, Vera," Gladys said. "One might wonder what you got up to, to know so many different people."

"Wouldn't you like to know?" Vera said smugly, and that was that.

In the mornings, it is Julia and sweet Emma who come to her. Emma climbs into the bed and snuggles up against Vera and tells her that she smells bad and should think about brushing her teeth, to which Vera responds that Emma's breath doesn't smell that great either. Then Emma says, "You smell bad but I love you," and kisses her, and Vera says, "You smell of farmer's armpit but I love you," and kisses her forehead, and Emma smiles, and Julia groans and says, "Great, now she's going to spend the day telling everyone she smells like a farmer's armpit, thanks a lot, Vera."

After they go, Vera naps and only wakes up when Sana comes over for teatime. Sana usually brings with her something unhealthy but exciting, like samosas, at which Gladys squawks, "Do you know what those things do to your cholesterol?" Vera urges Sana to bring cocaine, not to snort, of course, just to see what Gladys will say, but thus far has been refused. Young people nowadays are so dreadfully boring.

Then, about an hour later, Riki joins them and he and Sana say, "Hey, you," to each other in such a tender way as to be utterly repulsive, and Vera throws them out soon after because there's only so much googly eyes a woman her age can take. "He seems a bit wet behind the ears, that one," Gladys says, and there, Vera has to agree with her. But he has Sana to keep him out of trouble, so Vera's not too worried about him.

In the evening, Oliver and Tilly come. Apparently they have become friends, bonding over sports and their complicated relationships with their parents, and Tilly is now representing Oliver. Tilly tells Vera that he's asked his colleague to represent her in case the cops come after her for tampering with evidence, but

Vera brushes him away, saying she would love to see them try. She shoots Gladys a glare as she says this, but the other woman has wisely decided to pretend to be asleep.

Finally comes the day that Vera's bronchitis clears and she is allowed to leave this godforsaken place. Everybody shows up to help her with the discharge process, which Vera says is ridiculous, but secretly she is rather smug about all the fuss. She hops off her bed and throws on her clothes, shooting Gladys meaningful side-eyes. "This is goodbye, Gladys."

"I will miss you, Vera."

The two old women narrow their eyes at each other, then Vera says, "Gladys, you are pain in my ass, but you should come visit my teahouse. These young people say they do something to make it nice. I think they destroy it, who knows?" She glares at the group of said young people, who grin uneasily at her.

Gladys gives a dramatic sigh. "Oh, would that I could. But I'm afraid that I can't take the risk of trying exotic herbs, who knows what they might do to my liv—"

"Oh, shut up, Gladys, and visit my teahouse when you get out." And with that, Vera strides out of the ward, with Emma, Julia, Sana, Oliver, Riki, and Tilly scurrying after her.

O h," Vera says, hours later. She barely recognizes her own teahouse. She stands in the middle of it, taking in the surroundings, which are somehow both foreign and yet familiar.

"Um, do you hate it?" Sana squeaks.

"Don't be silly," Vera snaps, and when she looks at them, her eyes are shining with tears. It takes a moment before she is able to speak without her voice wobbling. "This is . . ." Nope, not quite able to stop the wobble from taking over her voice. She takes a breath and tries again. "This is—it's good. Very good."

Tilly whistles. "Coming from her, I think it's akin to a standing ovation."

She shoots him a glare, and he grins and hugs her. "Come on, Ma. Just admit it. Sana's artwork blew your mind."

Vera releases her breath in a long sigh. "Okay, Sana's artwork is more good than anything I see before."

"Dang, that's quite the compliment," Julia says, nudging Sana, who's red in the face and grinning.

"You like it?" Sana says. "Really?"

"Yes, better than when I give birth to Tilly."

"Ooof," Tilly says. Oliver pats his shoulder.

"Nothing personal, Tilly," Vera says, "is just that you a very ugly baby."

"Yep, nothing personal about that, Ma."

The corners of Vera's mouth quirk up, then she turns her attention to the furniture, which looks almost brand-new to her, although she can still spot the little dents here and there from years of use. "Wah, these chairs . . ."

"Me, it was me," Riki says eagerly. Then he hesitates. "Uh, unless you hate it, in which case, uh, Oliver did it."

"Is very good."

"Okay then I shall take full credit," Riki says, grinning with pride, and the sight of his earnest, boyish face makes Vera go all teary-eyed again.

Vera isn't used to wallowing in such thick, heavy emotions, so she turns to the only thing she can think of. "Okay, now everyone sit down. I will make tea."

As everyone settles down, Vera bustles about behind the counter,

putting the kettle on and taking down various jars to put into a
special concoction. This is such a unique and wondrous occasion,
she simply must come up with the most groundbreaking tea. She
takes out some goji berries, then considers what might go well
with them. Ah yes, osmanthus, of course. She adds the osmanthus
to the mix, then stands back, thinking. It needs one more ingredient to move it from "good" to "out of this world." Ginseng? No,
that would clash with the osmanthus. She needs something milder.
Pea flower? No, the natural blue coloring from the pea flower
would stain the mix and turn it the most unappetizing brown. She
needs something sturdy, something to make a statement, something like . . .

Bird's nest.

Yes, that's it! Vera reaches up to the fourth row of shelves on
the right, but her hand grasps at empty air. She does a double take.
Her jar of bird's nest is missing. Vera thinks of that day she
smashed a few jars in her shop. She had cunningly picked the jars
with the cheapest ingredients to break. The low-quality wulong
teas and the stale chrysanthemum and that time she'd made the
mistake of ordering peony tea, which had ended up tasting like
gecko, not that she would know what gecko tasted of, but it just
tasted like geckoes would, Vera was sure of it. Anyway, she definitely would not have broken her jar of bird's nest. Bird's nest is one
of the most expensive ingredients in her shop. Maybe it got moved
when the others did up the place. Vera goes through each jar but
still can't find it, which is thoroughly vexing.

Her mind goes back again to that morning when she came
downstairs and felt so certain that someone had been inside her
shop and moved things around. Was she right after all? Did

someone come in and take her jar of bird's nest? Hundreds of dollars' worth of bird's nest there had been in that jar. She'd been so careful and so stingy with it, saving it only for her most special customers, like Alex—

Vera gasps. Everything clicks then. Marshall dying from an acute allergic reaction to bird dander. Her making Alex some bird's nest tea to take home. Alex looking so old and worn the days following Marshall's death.

"Vera, are you okay?" Julia says. The others stop talking and watch her warily. "Maybe you should sit do—"

Vera flaps with urgency at Julia to quiet down. Then she hurries from behind the counter and practically grabs Oliver by the collar of his shirt. "Oliver. What is your father's name?"

"Huh? It's Alex. Alex Chen."

It's as though the weight of the world has just been dropped on her shoulders, while at the same time the floor beneath her feet falls away. Vera doesn't know whether to feel vindicated or heartbroken about this. She's done it. She's proved everybody wrong and solved the unsolvable case. But all she wants to do right now is burst into tears. She needs to speak with Alex right this very minute.

The entire group runs to keep up with Vera as she storms down the street to Alex's apartment building, and they all keep asking inane questions like: "What's going on?" and "Maybe she's still not thinking clearly?" and "Vera, why won't you tell us where you're going?" Then, when she finally stops at the front of Alex's building, Oliver says, "Hey, this is my dad's apartment. Do you know him?"

Vera presses the buzzer. "Alex, this is Vera. You better let me in now." There is no answer. She leans into the speaker and says, "I know about bird's nest." The front gate unlocks, and Vera walks in with everyone scrambling to follow her.

"I don't understand what's going on," Oliver says. "Bird's nest?"

Upstairs, Vera is about to knock on Alex's door when it opens. At the sight of Alex, she sucks her breath in through her teeth. He looks awful, so thin and so hunched, his back curved like a banana, as though there is a great weight bearing down on him. It's the weight of having killed his own son, Vera thinks, her heart squeezing in sorrow for Alex. He barely registers any surprise at seeing her with the rest of the gang.

"I was wondering when you would figure it out," he says in Mandarin, shuffling back into the apartment. They all follow him inside the dark, dingy space.

"Ba, what's going on?" Oliver says.

Alex regards him silently with his watery eyes before his gaze moves to Julia. When he spots little Emma, his chin trembles and a sob escapes him. "You tell them," he whispers to Vera. "I can't."

"Tell us what?" Oliver says, his voice getting shrill.

"Before I tell them anything," Vera says, "what has confuse me this whole time is Oliver say his mother is dead. But your wife, Lily, she . . ."

Alex's gaze slides away toward the bedroom. "Lily is gone," he says in Mandarin. "All these years later, and I still haven't come to terms with it. I wanted to preserve your teahouse as a safe space, Vera. I wanted it to exist as a space I could go to where I was happy, where I could talk as if my wife were still alive. I made her healthy at first, because I wanted to remember her the way she was, so full of life. But then you kept asking to meet her, and asking why she never came by, and I had to make up a reason, so I said she's sick, and even that was better than not having her at all."

"I see." And she does see. She wishes she could have that space too, where she could chat with someone about Jinlong as though he were waiting for her to come home with some bread, or some tiny gossip she'd picked up at the market. "I have just one more question. Marshall's laptop and flash drive, did you take them?"

Alex nods. "I have a key to the house. I went in through the back door. I just wanted to—I missed him so much. I was in a fog of grief. I went inside his room, I wanted to take a shirt of his, or something. I don't know. I opened a drawer by the bed and saw the laptop and flash drive on top of it. I recognized the laptop, so I took it. I guess . . . I just had to know more about him, what he was doing."

"I see," Vera says. She'd thought that maybe Emma had moved the laptop and flash drive somehow, but no. "And why did you take the rest of my bird's nest? To remove evidence?"

Pain flickers across Alex's withered face. "No, Vera. It was to protect you. In case the police became suspicious . . ."

Vera can only nod. All this time, it had been him all along. She doesn't quite know what to say to Alex. She doesn't even know how to begin describing the storm that is raging inside her.

"Now you tell them," Alex says. "Tell these young people the truth."

Vera takes a heavy breath. This is it, then. Detective Vera Wong is finally getting the moment she's fantasized about for weeks, to tell everyone that she's finally figured out who Marshall's killer is, but unlike her fantasies, there is no joy in it. "Alex killed Marshall."

"*What?*" Everyone practically shouts it.

Oliver shakes his head. "No, that's not possible. Baba loved Marshall more than anything. He was always the favorite son. You always said if not for Marshall, you wouldn't have a reason to go on living after Ma died."

Alex utters a sob that is so wretched it sounds as though it might tear his frail body apart. "Marshall's whole life, I thought he was the sun. He was my world, my prodigal son. He shone so bright that you were left in the shadow, and I thought—" His voice breaks and tears stream down his withered face. "I see now that he blinded me. He made me think you were the bad one, that—"

Oliver is crying now, too. "Baba." He stops speaking then, because what can one say at this moment?

"I am so sorry, son. That day . . ." Alex wipes at his eyes and looks at Julia, switching to English. "You call me, in the morning. You say Marshall leaving you. He make it rich, you tell me, and he don't want to be married to you no more."

Julia nods.

"I think, 'This is impossible. How can? He love his wife and child. How can he just abandon? There must be mistake.' I call Marshall, I ask him what is going on, and he say, 'Ba, come out for dinner tonight, I've got something to celebrate.' So, okay, I go to fancy restaurant. When I arrive, I see Marshall at reception desk. I am about to say hi to him when someone—" He spots Riki in the crowd of people. His eyes widen. "Oh, it's you."

Like everyone else, Riki is gaping. "That night . . ." he gasps.

"Yes. I recognize you. You rush inside, you grab my son's shoulder, and you hit him." Alex shakes his head. "I am so surprise. I just stand there, I don't know what is going on. Then you run away, and Marshall is shouting all these things—I have never seen him like that. So many threats. I go to him, and he looks so surprise to see me. He immediately change, become the Marshall I know. It is so quick, the change. It disturb me, how easy he change his face."

Oliver nods. "He was always careful to show you only the good side of him."

"Then I look closer at him, and I notice that he not only have a bruise from the punch, he also has scratch mark on other cheek."

Vera glances over at Sana, who says, in a small voice, "That was me."

Alex's rheumy eyes slide toward her, and he nods. "I see. I ask him, why that boy punch you? And who scratch you? He say, don't worry about it, they are just asshole. But I am so shaken. I do not understand why so many people are so angry with my son. I ask him about Julia. Maybe he is shaken too, by the punch, but I see his mask slip. He is looser then, the bartender has give him double shot of whisky on the house because of fight. He say Julia just holding him back, he never love her."

This must be so painful for Julia, Vera thinks, but when she looks over, Julia looks more angry than sad.

"I am so shock," Alex continues. "I say, what about Emma?" He looks down at his granddaughter and fresh tears roll down his face. "You are so love, my dear. I am sorry. I don't want to say in front of her." His voice comes out in a whisper, and Vera's heart throbs with pain because it's obvious that what he's about to reveal would be a huge blow to little Emma, and all Vera wants to do right now is to whisk the toddler away and tell her that everything is going to be okay.

"Sana, can you—?" Julia says.

"Yeah, of course." Sana bends over so she is at eye level with

Emma and says, "You wanna go get a cookie?" Emma nods, and Sana picks up the little girl and leaves the apartment.

Once they're safely out of earshot, Julia turns back to Alex and, in a voice made of steel, says, "What did Marshall say about our daughter?"

"He say—" Alex lets out another sob. "He say, 'That little freak. I'll have a better one with someone else.'" He bursts into tears. "I have never see anyone talk about own child like that. I think, maybe he is just drunk, or angry because he just get punch. But then he tell me how he going to get rich, and that's why he leaving you, because he don't want to have to divide the money with you. I say, but you must provide for your wife and child, and he laugh. I say, just like the way you always look after me, I know you are good boy, you always buy me grocery, and he look so confuse. He say, what grocery?"

Now it's Vera's turn to be confused. Alex has been so proud of the way Marshall left groceries for him every week.

"I did that," Oliver says quietly.

Alex nods. "Yes, I figure that. All these years, I lose my relationship with you, and why? All this time, I think Marshall is only good one. When he go toilet, he leave his phone on table. I look through his messages, so many of them are from people demanding their money. And not just that, but one or two are saying thing like: 'Those stupid fucks, made some good money out of them.' I don't know what Marshall up to, but I know is nothing good, is all about cheating people.

"After dinner, I ask him back here for tea. I beg him not to do this to his wife and child. That is when he turn ugly to me. He say he is not going to be like me, living in this shithole apartment just because I can't let go of everyone who is pulling me back. He say he is glad when his mom die, because she always holding him back, always favoring Oliver. The things he say—" Alex weeps. "I feel like everything falling down. Everything is lie. I take out the tea from Vera and I think of how she is so kind to me, every day, and how I always tell her Marshall this, Marshall that. Marshall so good, Marshall so smart. I see that one of them has bird's nest. I know Marshall is allergic to bird dander. I don't know why—I don't know what I am thinking—but I choose that tea. I give to Marshall. I watch him drink."

For a few moments, the entire apartment is so silent that Vera can practically hear everybody's hearts beating.

"I kill him," Alex says quietly. "I kill my own son. His breathing get rough, he try to get his phone, but he can't type, his vision must be blurry, his hands all swollen. I watch him dying. He run out of here, stumble down street. Everything close by then. He cannot talk anymore. He see Vera's teahouse and he break inside. I think he want to give clue, that the bird dander is from tea."

Vera nods.

"But why was he holding a flash drive?" Riki says.

"Maybe to create more suspicion? Make it clear that this wasn't a simple death," Julia mutters. She stares at Alex with a mixture of pity and anger on her face. "Did you—" She shakes her head as though trying to clear it. "When I was taking photos of Cassie, I felt like someone was watching me . . ."

Alex nods, once. "It was me. I just want to make sure you are okay, even without Marshall. I follow Vera too, especially when she has Emma. I just—I can't believe I take away her baba." His voice cracks. "I have to make sure you are all okay."

One corner of Julia's mouth twitches into a half smile. "We're okay. We're better than okay. You don't have to worry about us."

She is still steely-eyed. Vera no longer recognizes the sniffly, frightened woman that Julia was when they first met. Julia now looks like nothing could possibly tear her down. Vera can't be any prouder of her.

Oliver, on the other hand, is sobbing like a child. "Baba," he moans. "I can't believe this."

"I am sorry, son." Alex walks to him slowly and puts his arms gingerly around Oliver. "I am so sorry for everything I've done to you. All those times I told you that you were worthless," he whispers in Mandarin. Oliver only nods, crying harder. "You are not worthless. You are not."

"I don't want to lose you, Baba."

"Me neither. Come and visit me, and we will talk." Alex grasps Oliver's hands so tight that his knuckles turn white. "We will talk."

Vera hopes that down the road, Oliver will look back on this moment and find a way of healing.

Later, they wait outside on the curb together, Oliver with an arm around his father's frail shoulders. As Alex is helped into the police cruiser, he meets Vera's eyes and says, "Thank you for everything, Vera. You are a true friend."

And Vera smiles through her tears and nods. She is already wondering what bento boxes she will be allowed to bring for Alex in prison.

EPILOGUE

Vera Wong Zhuzhu is a pig, but she really should have been born a rooster. At four thirty a.m. on the dot, her eyes shoot open and she levitates from the bed. She goes through her usual ritual of brushing her teeth with furious efficiency before heading to the kitchen to begin preparing breakfast. She has settled nicely into Julia's house. The youngsters are taking their sweet time clearing out all the junk from Vera's house, and Vera isn't hurrying them along. Julia has said multiple times over that she and Emma would like Vera to stay on at their house, and though Vera keeps waving them off and saying, "Oh, you'll want me out of your hair soon enough," in truth she is more than happy to stay. So for now, here Vera will remain.

Emma has requested a break from congee today. She wants an omelet. Vera has looked at a dozen different omelet recipes on the Google and hasn't figured out what the point of an omelet is, but for Emma's sake she is willing to try. Say anything about Vera, but she is extremely flexible.

At five in the morning, Emma, who is, in fact, a rooster, wakes up and shuffles down the hallway, rubbing her eyes with her knuckles. Vera hears her footsteps and calls to her in a soft whisper to go brush her teeth. By the time Emma gets into the dining room, there are four different omelets waiting for her—a cheese one, a mushroom and cheese one, a ham and cheese one, and a Chinese-style tomato and scrambled eggs. Vera narrows her eyes and meaningfully keeps her silence as Emma considers the four dishes. Then the little girl points to the tomato and egg dish and says, "That one," and Vera nods solemnly, though on the inside she is jumping with joy.

Surprisingly, this morning, as Vera and Emma have their breakfast, they are joined by Julia, who appears at the dining room with crazy hair. "Morning." She yawns.

"Oh, you are up early," Vera says. "No judgment, of course, but usually you let the whole morning pass by before you wake up."

"You do realize saying 'no judgment' before saying something very judgy doesn't make it less judgy?" Julia says, lowering herself onto one of the seats. "Ooh, omelets. They look good."

Vera and Emma share a secret smile.

"Anyway, I thought I'd go with you to the teahouse today," Julia says through a mouthful of mushroom and cheese omelet. "The photos I posted of it online have really good engagement, so I thought I'd take a few more."

"Hmm." Vera sniffs. "I should start charging you for modeling fee." Although she wouldn't, of course, because she loves being in front of Julia's camera way too much. Julia has already taken countless photos of Vera in the process of making various teas, and Vera has discovered that she is quite the peacock. But if Julia wanted to, she could easily pay Vera. She could easily pay anyone, now that the first installment check from Marshall's life insurance has been paid out. Julia has given a large chunk of it to Riki to pay him for the work he did for Marshall, which made Riki burst into tears. Apparently, Riki's little brother, Adi, will be joining them in the Bay Area any day now. Vera can't wait to spoil Adi rotten.

For a while, they were all worried that Riki might get in trouble over the scalping bot. But Tilbert assured them that there are very few laws in place when it comes to NFTs. It's a case of the law not quite catching up with the ever-changing world of tech, and since there's no actual signed contract between Riki and Marshall, it would be a real challenge for anyone to press charges against Riki for making a bot. Currently, he and Sana are working through Marshall's stash, contacting the other artists and returning their stolen art.

The rest of the money was put toward the mortgage, and without the weight of mortgage payments bearing down on Julia's shoulders, she's been able to blossom with her photography, taking more artistic risks and quickly creating a reputation for herself as the next photographer to watch.

Meanwhile, Alex's trial is still ongoing. Tilbert has managed to get one of the associates at his firm to represent Alex pro bono, and all Tilbert will say about it is that it's going "about as well as these things can go." Vera has visited Alex twice already, and each time, she brings food for the guards so they will be nicer to Alex. They keep telling her that they're not allowed to accept food from visitors, but Vera knows she will wear them down soon enough.

They make their way to the teahouse at a relaxed pace, chatting as they wait for the tram, taking in the beautiful, lazy sight of San Francisco as it slowly wakes up. When they turn the corner of Vera's teahouse, Vera frowns to see a small crowd. Ugh, they must be Winifred's customers.

But as they get closer, she sees that, in fact, the handful of people are waiting outside her shop. When they spot her, one of them nudges the others.

"It's Vera!"

"No soliciting," Vera says sternly.

"No," one of them, a young woman with purple hair, says. "We're customers."

Vera gapes at them. For once, words fail her.

"Surpriiise!" Julia says. "Oliver wrote this beautiful article about you and your teahouse and the rich history behind it, and the *Bay Area Times* actually bought it. They ran the story yesterday."

"Oh, I'm actually here because of your TikToks," the purple-haired woman says.

Julia blushes, smiling. "I told you, Vera, they got good engagement."

"I'm an art student," the woman next to her says. "I wanted to see the painting inside. Our art teacher showed it in our class."

Now it's Vera's turn to smile. She is so proud of what Sana has done with the space, how she's poured her incredible art out everywhere, even incorporating things like the light sockets. Every time Vera steps inside her shop, she is immediately transported to an otherworldly place, a space between real Shanghai and one that only exists in dreams, where she and Jinlong sit in a little boat and sip tea while letting the tips of their fingers trail in the cool, calm water. She is so pleased to hear that Sana's work is getting the recognition it deserves. Sana has been so busy; Winifred took one look at Vera's shop and immediately hired Sana to paint her bakery, that copycat. And before that's even done, Sana has already been hired to paint two more places—a dumpling shop down the street and a swanky restaurant opening at the Embarcadero. The latter has agreed to pay her mid-five figures, which pleased even Sana's mother.

"Well, I'm actually here for the tea," a bearded guy says. "Yeah, CassieRed was raving about it. She says your teas are W."

"My teas are . . . W?"

"It's short for 'win,'" Julia says.

"Why not just say 'win'? Is longer to say 'W.'"

"Just go with it, Vera." Julia sighs, gently turning Vera around to face her store. "Now, come on and unlock the place so we can all have some tea. The others will join us soon."

Even as she says this, Vera spots Tilly's fancy car parking up across the street. Oliver is riding shotgun, and Riki and Sana are waving at them from the back window. Happiness floods Vera's chest. She looks at the crowd—well, it is technically only three strangers, but as they say, three is a crowd—then at Julia and Emma, and Oliver, Sana, Riki, and of course, Tilly. She looks up at the sign that says: VERA WANG'S WORLD-FAMOUS TEAHOUSE. How funny that she used to long for her shop to be world-famous, when what she needed all along was a family like the one she now has. She slides the key into the lock and opens the door.

She turns to the crowd behind her and smiles. "Come in! What you all waiting for?"

Vera Wang's World-Famous Teahouse is open for business.

ACKNOWLEDGMENTS

Folks, when I say this book had the most incredible journey, I am not kidding. I got a vague, blobby idea for *Vera Wong's Unsolicited Advice for Murderers* one night. It was truly blobby. It was literally: A little old lady who owns a teahouse finds a dead body and decides to investigate. I told a friend, who encouraged me to expand it into a pitch, and so I did, crouched in the dark while my two little kids slept (yes, I sleep with my kids, please don't judge me). That pitch became what is now the back cover blurb.

I sent the pitch to Katelyn Detweiler, my agent, and asked her when we might be able to send it to Berkley. Due to my packed publishing schedule and contract clauses, we thought maybe the earliest that I could start writing *Vera* would be sometime in late 2023. Katelyn said we should share it with Cindy, my editor, anyway, just to give her an idea of what I might work on next. So we sent it to Cindy, and before Katelyn and I knew what was happening, Cindy said she and the entire team loved it, and could we push everything else back and publish *Vera* next?

The term "lolsob" has never been so appropriate. On one

hand, I was exhilarated to know that they loved my little idea. On the other hand, I did not have a plot. Who's the dead guy? Why is he dead inside some random teahouse? I don't know! I told Cindy I was unfortunately lacking that little thing called a plot, and I think she said she had faith in me—my memory of those days is hazy due to the fact that my brain cells were imploding and screaming, "WHAT HAVE I DONE?"

The next few days I spent in a panic, trying to cobble together a coherent plot. I went to a café, which serves suspiciously strong coffee, and after my latte jumpstarted my heart with the strength of a lightning strike, a plot began to appear. I grabbed at the ghost of the plot with my sweaty hands and choked it into submission. (I mentioned how strong the latte was, right?)

A week later, I told Cindy that yes, I can do this. Let's push *Dial A for Aunties* 3 and my upcoming adult suspense back one whole season so we can get *Vera* out ASAP. I mourned *Dial A for Aunties* 3 and the suspense, which I love dearly and can't wait to share with the world. Cindy got to work, and I did too. While I wrote *Vera*, Cindy paved its way. She took it to a sales meeting (and by "it" I mean the tiny pitch because *nervous laugh* there was no book then!) and arranged for cover art to be made. My friends joked that at the rate this was going, I was going to have a cover before I even wrote the book. This did end up happening, and once again, I lolsobbed because what a perfect cover it was, and also oh my god, now my book was not only going to have to be done on time, but it also had to live up to this beautiful cover.

Halfway through the first draft, I stayed at a hotel for three nights to see if I could speed up my process. It was my first ever writing retreat, and I completely, wholly plunged into Vera's world. I laughed at Vera's antics, I cried when Sana finally picked up her paintbrush, I cheered when Julia and Oliver repaired their friendship. It was the most magical three nights I've experienced (don't tell my husband this!) and typing the words "The end" was, once again, a lolsob moment.

So there you have it, *Vera*'s roller-coaster journey. There were so many instances where it could've—should've—been derailed, but the enthusiasm and dedication of everyone I work with saw it through to the end. I am so unbelievably lucky to be able to work with people who not only tolerate my whims, but actively encourage them and go out of their way to help make the magic happen.

Thank you to Tilly Latimer, who was the first one to push me into writing *Vera*'s pitch. Thank you to Katelyn Detweiler, my unicorn-wizard agent who makes my ridiculous dreams come true. Thank you to Cindy Hwang, who as you can see is an editor who is so enthusiastic, so kind, so generous, and so flexible that it seems almost impossible that she's real. If I were to see an editor as amazing as Cindy in a TV show, I would roll my eyes and say, "Editors are never that awesome!" But she is!

I'm so lucky to be working with my team at Berkley. Angela Kim, Jin Yu, Erin Galloway, Dache' Rogers, and Danielle Keir are the people who brought *Dial A for Aunties* to life, and I'm so fortunate to be able to work with them on *Vera Wong's Unsolicited Advice for Murderers*.

Thank you as always to the other people at Jill Grinberg Literary Management—Denise Page, Sam Farkas, and Sophia Seidner for handling all the tricky stuff in publishing.

As I write this, my film agents Mary Pender and Olivia Fanaro of UTA are about to send *Vera* out into the world. If you hear any exciting film-related news about *Vera* in the coming weeks, it'll all be down to Mary's and Olivia's hard work.

I wouldn't be able to do this without my writing friends. Laurie Elizabeth Flynn woke up super early to be able to do writing sprints with me while I was holed up in a hotel room. My menagerie friends—SL Huang, Elaine Aliment, Rob Livermore, Toria Hegedus, Emma Maree, Maddox Hahn, Mel Melcer, and Lani Frank are my chosen family. To my other incredibly sweet writing friends—Nicole Lesperance, Kate Dylan, Grace Shim, Sajni Patel, and May Cobb, thank you so much for listening to me whine nonstop throughout this entire process.

My husband, Mike, is the most encouraging, supportive husband one could hope for. He held down the fort while I stayed at a hotel and assured me repeatedly not to worry about anything, and to stay an extra night if the words were flowing. He's never once made me feel guilty for putting so much importance on my writing, and for that I will be eternally grateful.

And to my parents, of course, for giving me so much material to work with. Lol! I swear half of Vera's antics come from them. Hehe. Thank you so much for letting me draw inspiration from you, and especially to my mom, thank you for always being so ready to do videos to help me promote my books!

Thank you to my wonderful readers for coming with me on this wild journey. It goes without saying that none of this would be possible without you.

Jesse Q. Sutanto is the award-winning, bestselling author of adult, young adult, and children's middle-grade books. She has a master's degree in creative writing from Oxford University, though she hasn't found a way of saying that without sounding obnoxious. The film rights to her women's fiction title *Dial A for Aunties* was bought by Netflix in a competitive bidding war. Her adult books include *Dial A for Aunties, Four Aunties and a Wedding,* and *Vera Wong's Unsolicited Advice for Murderers.* Her young adult books include *Well, That Was Unexpected, The Obsession,* and *The New Girl.* Her middle-grade books include *Theo Tan and the Fox Spirit.*

CONNECT ONLINE

🐦 TheWritingHippo
📷 JesseQSutanto
♪ AuthorJesseQSutanto